MW00453821

Love on Main

a Romance Anthology

Patty Blount,
Melanie Hooyenga,
C. Vonzale Lewis,
Deborah Maroulis,
Jess Moore,
Shaila Patel,
Prerna Pickett,
Brandy Woods Snow,
Faydra Stratton,
Leanne Treese

Filles Vertes Publishing
Coeur d'Alene, ID

Copyright © 2020 by **Filles Vertes Publishing**

All rights reserved. No part of this publication may be reproduced, distributed or transmitted in any form or by any means, without prior written permission.

Filles Vertes Publishing
PO BOX 1075
Coeur d'Alene, ID 83814
www.fillesvertespublishing.com

Publisher's Note: This is a work of fiction. Names, characters, places, and incidents are a product of the author's imagination. Locales and public names are sometimes used for atmospheric purposes. Any resemblance to actual people, living or dead, or to businesses, companies, events, institutions, or locales is completely coincidental.

Book Layout © 2020 Filles Vertes Publishing
Cover Art and Design © 2020 JRC Designs/Jena R Collins
www.jenarcollins.com

Love on Main/ Filles Vertes Publishing Anthology -- 1st ed.
ISBN 978-1-946802-54-5
eBook ISBN 978-1-946802-55-2

Right before heartache,
left after first kiss,
and you'll find yourself in

Love
on
Main

FILLES VERTES
PUBLISHING

Contents

Intertextual Relations

The DJ's music bumps hard, the bass keeping perfect rhythm with my pounding heart. *Bah-domp-Bah-domp-Bah domp* in triple time. I inhale slowly, searching for calm somewhere in the wet-blanket humidity of the cloudless Southern night.

It isn't working.

I open my sequined purse and pull out the only provisions I could cram into the tiny space for tonight: a tube of Raucous Red gloss, much darker than I'd usually wear, but then again, special occasions call for a bit of risk-taking; my phone, abnormally silent; and two pristine prom tickets with the names on them.

Ryleigh Anne Royce and Plus One.

The warm glow of a gazillion strands of Edison lights criss-crossing the downtown Farmer's Market pavilion splash out like amber fingers to Main Street, barely reaching to the corner of Main and Trade where I stand alone under the dim glow of an antique streetlight, re-stuffing my purse and smoothing out the wrinkles from the jade-colored tulle of my dress.

And waiting.

He's supposed to be my Plus One, but where is he? His text said *meet me at 8:30 by the famous Main Street fountain.* Ironic since he's never even seen it. I guess I talk about the town too much in our conversations.

I press the button on my phone and the screen illuminates. 8:22.

Sweat droplets bead my hairline, and I try to pat them away from the loose blond wisps, keeping in mind the two inches of caked make-up on my face. Mom insisted on a full makeover at the department store beauty counter with more products than I'd seen before in my lifetime. More products than I ever hope to see again.

She's always been way more into the whole beauty thing than me. The curse of her growing up the high school beauty queen and homecoming queen. From Little Miss Fountain to Cotillion Queen, Dad always laughs and says if they made a tiara and sash for something, Mom had it. Except Drama Queen, of course, which went more by reputation than accessories.

Traveling the road she'd paved in our little town always left me feeling a bit DOA, like a slow possum straddling the center-line. How she ended up with an only daughter who lives for her GPA and volunteer work at the animal shelter, I'll never know. Some great universal force to restore balance, possibly.

Footsteps shuffle toward me from the sidewalk, and I crane my neck for a better view. My hopes deflate like a popped balloon when a boy I recognize from the baseball team and his date, a girl in a flowing baby pink dress, rush past me to the balloon-tunnel entrance. Immediately behind them, a short way down the sidewalk, a pair of guys amble toward me. One I recognize immediately; the other I don't.

His chocolate brown hair and broad shoulders I'd recognize anywhere. Even though I've been spending the last year trying to forget them.

My ex-boyfriend Caden steps out into the streetlight and I whirl around, half hiding my face with my sequined purse. Probably not a good idea with the light glinting off each sequin, and the bag itself hardly big enough to cover anything. I glance at the fountain for a moment and entertain the crazy thought of jumping in and holding my breath beneath the bubbling water.

Why is he here? He doesn't go to high school with us any-more—at least not since last year and all the trouble he stirred up. His frazzled parents sent him packing, straight to some mil-itary reform school down-state, where he has to wear uniforms and do things like KP duty and follow a bunch of strict rules.

"Ryleigh Anne? Is that you?"

No. Totally not me. Anyone but me.

Their footsteps thump louder behind me, and in one last act of self-preservation, I pull my purse to my chest and wrench my cell phone from it just as his fingers land on my bare shoulder. I shrug from his grip and turn around, mouth agape in all my efforts to seem surprised.

"Caden! What are you doing here?" I ask, my voice squeaking out an octave higher than usual.

"Last time I checked, I still live here, even if I've... been away. You're making me think you didn't miss me at all. But I'll be willing to bet that you *have* thought about me, haven't you?" He taps my forehead with his finger and laughs as I search for ways to break it in half. His arrogant smile twists my stomach. Caden's knack for making me want to hug him and then follow it up with a throat punch never fails to deliver.

Instead, I shift my attention to his tag-along friend who stands beside him, watching us saucer-eyed. His chestnut hair, the same shade as his eyes, is cropped short in a military-style like Caden's but with a few longer curls left poking out on top.

"Hey, I'm Alex," he says, stretching out his arm with a toothy grin. His voice is deep and gravelly with a Southern drawl so thick I could drown in it. I slide my hand in his, his skin warm and clammy against mine as he pumps it up and down a few times. "I'm Caden's roommate."

Bless his heart.

"All I can say to that is, I'm so sorry." I smile and side-eye Caden. "No one should be subjected to that."

"Obviously, I was very bad in a past life," Alex laughs and jabs Caden in the shoulder, but he only glares at the two of us before cocking an eyebrow.

"Say what you want, but y'all love me," he says, tugging at the lapel of his jacket with a smirk.

It dawns on me they're both wearing suits. Caden sports a traditional black one, but Alex's is a charcoal gray slimmer-fit variety. It hugs his toned body in all the right places, and I can't stop my eyes from wandering over all the hills and valleys.

Snap, snap.

Caden contorts his neck, obviously trying to track my stare, and repeatedly snaps his fingers in my face. I glance up as the rush of heat rockets up my neck to populate my cheeks.

"Sorry... preoccupied," I mumble, realigning my focus. Oh yeah, the suits. "Y'all are dressed up."

"And you're in a dress. It's prom, isn't it?"

"For me, yes. Not for you. You don't go here anymore."

"But I did. For three years, and I think it's kinda unfair I'd be kept away from what is rightfully my senior prom too."

"You sort of need a ticket to get in."

"It's an open-air venue, Ryleigh Anne, and the only thing standing between us and the prom is the same old security guard that's been walking the school grounds since our parents went to their proms. I've totally got this. I'm stealth."

I grimace. Caden's stealth all right. Except for that whole bout of public humiliation last year, of course.

"Not too stealth, or you wouldn't have been caught with that girl... or shoplifting from Peterson's. That's what got you sent to reform school." Not to mention the countless times he was caught cutting class and subjected to in-school suspension.

"First of all, I didn't get 'caught' with that girl. We were hanging out at the coffee shop—perfectly innocent—and the town gossip biddies started their usual tongue-wagging," he says, Pacman-ing his hand. "And it's not reform school. It's an elite military academy."

Potato, potahto. I roll my eyes. "Whatever you say."

Caden folds his arms and makes a dramatic production of looking around with a raised eyebrow. "So, where's your date? Or do you not have one?"

Alex shoots him a death stare but Caden doesn't notice. He just stands there with a wicked smirk pricking the corner of his lips.

I narrow my eyes and mirror his stance, folding my arms over my chest. "For your information, I do have a date. He's... on his way."

"He goes to school here? How'd you meet him?"

"None of your business."

"Oh, come on, Ryleigh Anne. We might be exes, but I still want the best for you. Just like you told me in that text you sent me."

I knew he'd find a way to hold that stupid text against me. After everything went down last year and his parents shipped his butt off to reform school, I had a moment of feeling bad for him. Caden's a pain, but it's still sad to have to leave everything you know just in time for senior year. I just wanted him to know I could be the bigger person and wish him well, so I sent that stupid text. And now he's throwing it in my face and prying into my new relationship. Mama was right. No good deed ever goes unpunished.

I bite my lip, grasping for a response that won't inspire further questioning. "I... I haven't really..."

A knowing glint shines in his eyes. "Wait. Is this a blind date?"

"No, it's *not* a blind date."

"So, you've seen this person?"

"Not exactly, but I know him."

"You know him? Based on what?"

"Our conversations."

"Like online?"

"No. Texting."

Our ping-pong match of retorts comes to a sudden stop when Caden crinkles his nose, shaking his head. "How do you meet via texts?"

I shrug. "He texted me by mistake, and we just sort of started talking."

"You've at least exchanged pics, right? Spoken on the phone?"

"Well, no. The camera on his phone is broken, and he's not allowed to actually make calls. He goes to a prep school not far from Charleston. Phone calls are against the rules, but he does get to sneak and text."

Sam gave perfectly logical explanations for everything, but somehow saying them out loud stirs an uneasiness in my belly. I know Sam's reasonings are legit—I know it—but seeing Caden's slack-jaw expression and Alex's sudden need to pick at his fingernails instead of making eye contact makes my heart skip a few beats. They think I'm stupid. Certifiable, even.

Caden's mouth drops into an "O" as he presses his fingers into his temples. "Oh my God, Ryleigh Anne. You're like the people on that TV show. I've seen it a million times but never thought I'd know someone who…" He blinks rapidly as if trying to process my relationship ineptitude and then wags a finger in my face. "This dude is gonna be like fifty or some pizza-face loser that crawls out of his mom's basement."

The fury swells inside. "Shut up! He is not. Sam is seventeen, brown hair, athletic build."

"You just gave a general description of half the damn school!" Caden yells so loud, a few people waiting to go into the prom look over at the commotion. He lowers his voice and grips my arm, his fingers pressing hard into the skin. "Do you want to be on one of those missing persons flyers? Do you want to be *that* girl?"

I wrench my arm from his clutches. "Why do you care?"

"I do, okay?"

My phone vibrates in my palm, and I pull it up close to my face. Finally. Now Sam can show up and prove them all wrong.

<Sam> *Something came up. It's going to be late when I get there. Go ahead and I'll text you when I arrive. Please forgive me.*

My stomach drops. This was supposed to be our night—the prom was going to be our first date—and now he's late? A sliver of Caden's cynicism edges into the thoughts swirling around my brain. Is this a hoax? Is Sam (if that's his real name) playing me?

I shake my head, squelching the voice of doubt. No way all those late-night conversations were a hoax. He told me things about himself—deep, personal things. And I spilled to him too. No way that was all fake.

He's just late. People are late. It happens.

"Is that Prince Charming now?" Caden squeezes beside me and cranes his neck to sneak a peek. I yank the phone to my chest, trying to block his view. Unsuccessfully.

"Surprise, surprise. Sam's running late," he says, framing Sam's name with air quotes. "*Of course* he is. I mean, he *could* be innocently lead-footing his way here as we speak, or he *could* be a weirdo, skeezing around, just waiting on you to be alone so he can kidnap you. Or worse."

I step sideways and turn away from them, wiping away a few tears puddling in my lower lashes. Of all people, Caden won't be the one to see me cry. To heap some sort of pity on me. The stupid too-trusting girl getting burned yet again. Maybe he's right. I had trusted him, and look how that turned out. I really thought Sam was different.

Not thought. I think. I *know* he's different. He has to be.

"Dude, stop. You're making her cry," Alex whispers not-so-quietly behind me.

Caden sighs and steps closer, bending around me to catch my gaze. "Go into the prom. Enjoy yourself. If he shows up, I'll come out first to verify who he is."

Alex walks beside Caden and elbows him in the gut. " *When* he shows up," he says and shoots me a thumbs up. The street-light glints off his eyes, making them sparkle. His little ray of optimism spurs a small smile.

One that quickly evaporates when I glance over my shoulder at the venue, now overflowing with all my classmates. My besties Tara and Kinley both know about my texting relationship with Sam and his plan to be my date for the night. That's why they helped me pull off the whole we're-going-stag ruse to my parents, who would've locked me in the basement before letting me come if they'd known the whole truth.

If I go waltzing in there alone now? I'll never live it down.

"It's just... I can't go in there alone. My friends know about him, and they'll never shut up about it if I go in solo."

Caden scratches his chin and lets out a long breath. "I'll take you in."

I snort. Yeah, that'd be a no. "That obviously won't work. For many reasons."

"Such as?"

Is he honestly asking me this question?

I tick each reason off on my fingers. "One, they'll know you're not Sam. Two, you're my ex. An ex who cheated on me, by the way, so why in the world would I go to prom with you after that humiliation? And three, if my dad gets wind of the fact you even talked to me tonight, you'll find yourself limping back to reform school."

Alex clears his throat and steps between us, a subtle whiff of his musky cologne spilling around us. "I'll walk inside with you if you want. I'm not from here, so it's not like anyone will recognize me. I can play Sam for the occasion." He sticks out his elbow, offering it to me.

My breath quickens as the idea stews. Walking into the prom with my ex-boyfriend's hot roommate would definitely be a coup—one that'd save me face and earn the envy of all my friends. And Sam *did* tell me to go ahead.

I lock eyes with Alex and slip my arm through his. "Okay, let's do this."

The open-air Farmer's Market pavilion is one of my favorite places in town. When the Saturday bustle with its rows and rows of fresh vegetables and baked goods isn't in full swing, the space rents out for lots of notable town events. Weddings, birthday parties, church socials. And now, my senior prom.

Red and black bunting drapes over each brick pillar and re-claimed wood post dotting the perimeter of the space, and a simple black chain spans the length behind them, a flimsy excuse for a security wall. Alex flicks it with his finger as we walk by, and it sways back and forth, clinking against the bricks.

"I don't think Caden's going to have a problem getting by this," he shouts over the noise.

After reluctantly agreeing to let his roommate be my im-promptu prom escort, Caden had darted toward the back of the market venue to find a way in as Alex and I had entered through the balloon tunnel, arm in arm. We push our way through the claustrophobic sea of bodies crowding the dance floor, Alex and I clinging to each other like life preservers on a wild tide. We ebb and flow with the movement of the bodies around us, ris-ing, falling, bending, and swaying with the rhythm.

Some guy doing The Sprinkler accidentally knocks me from behind, making me trip on my heels and launching me face-first into Alex. He grabs my elbows and steadies me on my feet, and then wraps a strong arm around my shoulders, guiding me through the maze of dresses, tuxes, and suits to a small wooden bench near the side of the dancefloor. I fit neatly in the crook of his arm, and my mind wanders to Sam. Will he be as tall as Alex? Will he be as strong, with muscles that ripple through his sleeves? Will he be this handsome?

Yes, yes, and yes. Sam will. He absolutely will.

Alex motions for me to take a seat on the bench and then sits beside me, close enough to show we're together but not too close to be weird. We take turns staring at everything else in the room—the tiered fountain of sweet tea, the silver Mylar balloons spelling out P-R-O-M, the fully-stocked dessert table. We look at everything except each other. Awkward.

Finally, he breaks the silence. "Would you like something to drink?"

"I'm good, thanks," I say. He nods and picks at a loose thread on the seam of his pants as a warm breeze wafts through the space. It's going to be a long night if I can't make simple small talk.

I take a deep breath and swivel on the bench to face him. "So, you never did tell me. Why are you here?"

He looks up with a smile, relief washing over his face. "Caden and I earned a weekend pass. He was coming home and asked if I wanted to tag along."

"You didn't have any family you wanted to visit?"

He balks, and I wonder if that question might be too forward. Some people aren't blessed with an easy life like mine. Like Sam, for instance. His family is one step away from a Dr. Phil talk show appearance.

"I don't have much family, and what I do have… we're not close. How about you?"

"Only child of two pretty cool parents. I sometimes wish I had a sibling, though." It was my single most requested item on each year's Santa list until I was ten and learned that Santa and the stork had no control over such things. After that, I started asking for a puppy. And after I met Sam and heard his family trouble, I began being grateful that it was just me after all. "Sam had a brother, but he died."

I'm not sure why I spill those details. It's not something I've talked about with anyone except Sam, but Alex does have one of those "you can trust me" faces that destroys my usual barriers. Like we're old friends instead of almost strangers.

His eyebrows jack up into his forehead with my abrupt declaration. "That's tough," he says. "What happened?"

"It's sort of personal, and even though you don't know him, I don't want to, you know, betray his trust. The whole thing just makes Sam really sad."

"Which makes you sad?" He cocks his head to the side, eyes narrowed as if he's trying to understand me.

"It does. Do you think I'm stupid for that, getting all emotionally involved with someone who, according to Caden, might not even be real?"

"I think he's real, if for no other reason than you believe in him so much." He stops and chews the inside of his cheek before saying, "And I also think he's one lucky SOB."

My heart flutters at the sudden softness in Alex's eyes. "Why do you say that?"

"Because he's obviously won you over, and you're a pretty awesome girl."

Heat flushes my face, and I massage my neck, trying to conceal the pinkish flourishes I know have invaded my skin. "Caden never thought so. He was always on the lookout for the next best thing."

"Better than you? Don't tell him this, but my roommate can be a total clueless jackass." He laughs and stares across the crowd to where Caden perches on one of the brick pillars, surrounded by a flock of adoring fans. "How does he do that? Come in and just rein everyone in?"

It's Caden's God-given talent. It's the reason I'd said yes to dating him. The reason I never saw all the signs that he was much more interested in playing the field than being with me—at least until the town pieced it all together and laid that on my doorstep. Yep, that's Caden. All façade and no depth.

Not like Alex, with his Southern manners and easy drawl, who voluntarily gave up his night to do me a favor for no other reason than to be nice. Alex, who ushered me to this bench and offered to get me a drink. Alex who thought I was a pretty awesome girl.

"All I can say is that Caden should send up prayers of gratitude to have you as a roommate. Hopefully, you'll rub off on him. He'd be so lucky."

He shoots me a quick grin and pulls his phone from his suit pocket, panning over a few screens. I reach for my own and open up Sam's text messages, thumbing back through the months and months of conversation, from the innocent "how was your day" with smiley-face emoticons to infinite lines of soul-bleeding inner thoughts.

"Oh my God! Is this Sam?" Kinley's soprano voice rings out above the crowd as she canters toward us on her stilettos, Tara hot on her heels. They both have that fat-kid-in-a-donut-shop smile, eyes gleaming as they rove over Alex, drinking him in.

We both put away our phones, and Alex turns to me, obviously waiting for me to take the lead. Go time.

"It's... it's him. He's here!" I say, adding too much pep to my voice and panning my hands in his direction like he's a winning showcase on a game show. Oh my gosh, this is not going to work. I can't even introduce him without sounding like a total idiot. Kinley, Tara, and I have been friends since elementary school. They know the tell-tale signs of my lies—giddy voice, fidgety hand movements, stuttering.

Mental note: calm down, shut up, and for heaven's sake, sit on your flailing hands.

Tara circles around the bench where we're sitting and positions herself behind Alex's shoulder, clearly in my line of sight. *He's hot,* she mouths to me over his shoulder, fanning herself with her hand and doing some weird twirly thing with her tongue.

Embarrassing, but nowhere near as much as Kinley, who parks herself in front of us, making no effort to hide the fact she's looking him over from head to toe. When I cough and issue her the stink eye, she smirks and unleashes a torrent of word vomit.

"We are so glad to see you. Ryleigh Anne's been talking about you forever. Sam this and Sam that, and honestly, when she said you were coming to the prom, we all were thinking that you wouldn't show up. I mean, how often would this sort of thing actually work out? We are so glad it didn't turn out to be some MTV special."

Take a breath much?

"Thank you, Kinley," I say, stop-signing my hand. "We get the point."

"No offense, Ry. You kept saying you knew he'd be hot, but wow. Sam, you do not disappoint."

Alex's cheeks blaze as he shuffles on the bench, obviously overwhelmed by the positive female attention, and I can't help thinking how I'd expect the real Sam to act in the exact same way. The honest-to-goodness hot guys—the ones who are both attractive and nice—never seem to know it.

As opposed to the hot guys who aren't so upstanding but still think they can walk on water.

From across the room, a loud giggle catches my attention, and I look up to see Caden hanging on the shoulders of a blond girl from the debate team as she snaps a selfie of the two of them. Mr. Celebrity back to ruling his roost.

Case in point.

"Earth to Ry."

My thoughts zip back to the present and the impatient eyes of my two friends staring down at me and Alex.

"What?"

"I said I wanted to get a good pic of y'all, but you have to scoot closer together." Kinley uses her hands to frame an invisible divide and then shrinks it to nothing. "He came all this way to see you, and you're sitting two feet away from each other," she says, her voice full of icicles. This from the girl whose puddling drool indicates she'd be sitting in his lap if given the chance.

And, like the true bloodhound she is when a juicy piece of gossip is afoot, Kinley has already narrowed in on a problem. I should've known this charade would never work. I should've never—

"She's not wrong." Alex turns to me with a wink and pats the bare wood beside him. "I *did* come all this way."

Touché. He flashes a thousand-watt smile, and for the first time, I notice a deep dimple on his right cheek. A fleeting desire to push my fingertip into its depths grips me and then recedes to the background. What was that?

Nothing. It's nothing.

I stand up, straighten my dress, and reposition myself closer to Alex. So close, our thighs touch, and his cologne blankets us. Musky with a distinct undertone—vanilla?—and very, *very* masculine. I swallow hard and lean in, my ear brushing against his as we pose and say *cheese* at Kinley's demand.

She flips through a couple of frames on her phone. "Cute. But we need some more spice. It's prom, and y'all are finally together after all these months." She stoops to our eye level with a devilish grin. "Kiss her!"

Tara hops up and down in her jeweled sandals. "Kiss, kiss, kiss!" she chants.

"No, no, no," I repeat back. Alex didn't sign up for all this, and I can't be waiting here for the real Sam to make an appearance while kissing another guy. That'd just be... wrong.

Beside me, Alex resorts to picking at his fingernails yet again, and I can practically feel the embarrassment rolling off him in waves as he stares at his shoes. The way a few of the longer curls trickle down over the top of his forehead when he drops his head is adorable, and there's this essence of vulnerability that makes me want to wrap my arms around him. I acknowledge the impulse and swallow it back down.

He turns ever-so-slightly so I can only make out half of his face, one eye trained on me and a side view of two pink and full lips.

"Should we humor them?" he asks, his voice low and husky.

Should we? A part of me screams that it would be some sort of an infidelity where Sam is concerned. Another part of me really wants to see if his lips feel as soft as they look. Why is this so hard? My gaze lands on Kinley and Tara, watching, waiting, scrutinizing. If the truth comes out about my Alex/Sam switcheroo, I'll be the town's gossip fodder again. A shiver runs through me as I remember the last time that happened. My stomach twists as the memory clamors forward. The looks and the whispers of all the people in town who knew before I did that Caden had been sneaking around behind my back. The pity. The judgment. Not again, thanks.

"Okay," I whisper, nodding my head. My breath comes out in heavy pants, and I close my eyes, licking my lips and bracing for impact.

He leans in, his breath hot across my face. His chest presses into the front of me, and my body jumps to attention, every part coming alive, every muscle rigid, every vein pumping hard. In that moment—that heady split second—I want him to kiss me. And I want to kiss him back. And then, his lips land soft and sweet... on my cheek.

My eyes snap open to his as they linger directly in my vision, close, our noses almost touching. A flicker of disappointment unfurls in my chest and fizzles out. It'd be so easy to lean the slightest bit forward and bridge the gap, give in to the temptation, but I don't move. I can't. There's Sam to think about, not just my racing hormones. I have something to lose. Something real, no matter what Caden thinks.

My hand springs up to the lingering warm spot on my cheek. "Why'd you do that?" I whisper. "Kiss my cheek, I mean."

"You have to feed the beast, if you know what I mean. Give them what they want." He side-eyes my oohing and aahing friends who are pouring over the pictures on their phones, and then leans in further, his lips brushing against my ear. "I also thought your *real* kiss of the night should come from Sam. It would only be right."

What a sweet guy. I could kiss him…except for…yeah.

"Thank you for being such a good sport," I whisper, grabbing his hand and squeezing it. "I know this isn't what you had in mind for tonight."

"No, it's better than I could've imagined. I'd much rather hang out with you than Caden." He laughs, a puff of hot air washing down my neck and leaving chills in its wake. "But right now, I think your girlfriends want to chat, so I'm going to go get us some sustenance. Make sure to talk me… I mean, Sam… up."

Alex stands up and excuses himself, heading toward the dessert table. Kinley and Tara waste no time flocking to my side, sandwiching me on the bench. They unleash a barrage of questions: Was it love at first sight (as opposed to love at first text)? What did we say? What did we do? Was he what I expected? I do my best to answer something believable, but once again, my overexaggerated hand motions and squeaky voice teeter on the verge of giving me away.

"You're embarrassing her," Tara laughs, poking at my cheeks. "Look at those red splotches."

"Speaking of red," Kinley starts, "you'll be seeing red when I tell you that Caden's here. Can you believe he had the audacity to show up? And he's flirted with every girl here and not even bothered to talk to you, the one he humiliated in front of the whole town! He's on a mission to rub it in or something."

Once again, thanks for the reminder, Kinley.

"Oh, I don't know about that," Tara says, ticking her head toward Caden, who's now alone and standing near the food stations, staring at his phone. "He's looked over here about a hundred times in the last five minutes. And when Sam kissed you? I thought Caden's head was going to explode. Somebody's jealous."

In the midst of their giggles, my phone vibrates under the sequins. I open my purse and retrieve it. Sam's name is on the screen, and a swarm of butterflies rises in my chest. Is he here? I click on the message, and the butterflies burst into flames.

<Sam> *I'm scared. What will you think when we come face to face? What happens when you know the real me, not just the virtual one? I never want to disappoint you.*

I try to swallow the boulder in my throat and tap out a quick reply.

<Me> *You could never disappoint me.*

Buzz.

<Sam> *We'll see.*

Kinley pokes my arm, nearly knocking the phone from my hand. I slip it back into the safety of my purse and glance up as she once again nudges my arm and then points toward the dessert table. In unison, the three of us watch as Caden nods a curt hello to Alex and chats with him over the cheesecake bites. Tara and Kinley begin speculating about a brewing fight, and I play into it, though I'm more concerned their casual conversation will end up blowing my cover than lead to some fake fight for my attention. This is a fragile operation for goodness sake.

"I better go handle this." I spring to my feet, smoothing my dress. When the girls follow suit, I glance over my shoulder and say, "Alone."

I saunter across the tiled floor, head held high, broad grin plastered across my face despite the whispers and stares lining my path. The boys turn and watch me approach. If they're smart, they'll see my smile for what it is—a warning sign.

"What's going on here?" I ask through gritted teeth. "Everyone's wondering why my ex and my new boyfriend are chatting? I believe a betting pool has started on who will win the fight."

"Ooh, a fight. Interesting idea. Shall we, Alex?" Caden smirks, grinding one fist in the other palm, only stopping when he catches my glare. "I mean, Sam."

I thread my arm through Alex's and lean my head on his shoulder. That should appease the masses. "Don't be so eager.

The straw polls have my boyfriend kicking your ass in the first round."

"Boyfriend, huh? You seem to be enjoying this charade. I wonder what Sam will think about that?"

His innuendo hits me like a bucket of ice water. I yank my arm from Alex's and physically put a foot of space between us, but he reaches out and grabs my hand. Our fingers intertwine, and my knees become instant Jello-O. I can't seem to thwart his effect on me.

With a firm grip, Alex throws Caden's overstep back in his face. "Wow, dude, that's a low blow. We agreed to help out Ryleigh Anne with her problem, and now you're what... trying to sabotage it?"

Caden jerks back like Alex just landed the first punch. His eyes never leave our joined hands, the muscle in his jaw clenching. In and out, in and out. "Nice loyalty."

Alex snorts. "Says the resident expert?"

Caden crushes the plastic punch cup in his hand and tosses it in the trash bin. "Enjoy pretending, Alex, but remember your place. When Sam shows up—the *real* Sam—you're over." With that, Caden turns on his heel and storms across the room to a mixed group of seniors and juniors talking loudly in the corner.

"What the hell is his problem?" I ask.

"He's jealous." Jealous. It's the same thing Tara said. But why would Caden be jealous? We're exes. He didn't even want me when he had me. He was too busy looking elsewhere. "It's not hard to see what he lost when he lost you. Some people just don't realize what they have until it's gone... or until someone else wants it."

Too little, too late. I want good things for Caden, but not at my expense. That ship has sailed. Like, to China.

"Here. Nothing makes you feel better than your favorite dessert," he says, handing me a salted caramel brownie.

I take it and sink my teeth into the salty-sweet goodness, taking a minute to savor the flavor on my tongue. That's when it dawns on me. "How did you know it was my favorite?" I mumble between bites.

"Oh... um... Caden mentioned it once. I just happened to remember."

I stuff in another bite, covering my mouth with my hand as I simultaneously chew and talk. "A nice guy who actually listens? You're going to make some girl very happy one day."

"Can I get that in writing, like a reference letter?"

I laugh, popping the last morsel of brownie in my mouth, and then use my tongue to scrape away any remnants from my teeth.

"You have a crumb in your lipstick." He reaches out, tilting up my chin with his hand, and brushes his thumb lightly over my bottom lip. The airy touch leaves a phantom wake of tingles that filter down to my toes. I don't pull away, and he makes no effort to remove his fingers from my chin. We stare at each other, lost in an insulated bubble, the sounds of the prom muted to a low background hum.

That is until Tara appears in my line of vision, sporting kissy-lips and two thumbs up. And beyond her, in the midst of a raucous group of senior guys, Caden stands in the middle, talking to no one and glaring at me and Alex. I glance around, finding numerous other eyes on us in that moment.

"I think people are gossiping again," I whisper.

"Maybe we should play into that... for effect." He holds out his hand, open palm up. "Would you like to dance?"

I bite my lip, holding back the truth I shouldn't say out loud, and only nod instead. Translation: *Yes, Alex, I'd love nothing more than to dance with you.* As my fingers slide into his, he tightens his grip around them and smiles, walking toward an open spot on the dance floor. When he turns and pulls me to him, front to front, hip to hip, my breath catches in my throat. The urge to run, to retreat outside and reclaim my waiting spot by the fountain, claws inside. I should go. This fake date has morphed into playing with fire, and the guilt drops on me like a heavy blanket. But the magnetism is stronger. It locks me into him, the embers glowing at every point of contact. A kinetic force reverberates in the friction between our bodies.

I shut out the back-and-forth in my brain and wrap my arms around his neck as he circles his around my waist. We sway in soft rhythm with the music but don't look at each other. We completely avoid the other's eyes, as if any accidental connection with us being this close would somehow set off a combustion of our energies. I explore the skin of his neck, teasing the edges of his hairline, looping a few longer curls around my fingers. He sighs and tugs my hips closer, eliminating all space between us.

I sink my head to his chest, the hollow *bump-bump-bump* of his heart teasing my cheek. The smell of his cologne wafts around us, stronger now, and I wonder whether he's the type of guy who sprays it straight on or spritzes it in the air and walks through. I breathe in a deep pull of the vanilla musk. Not too overpowering, but subtle, with just a hint of spiciness. The perfect scent for Alex.

His hands migrate up my back, rubbing circles along the edge of my dress where the tulle meets the bare skin, and the crackle of electricity spirals out under each touch. I shiver and burrow closer to his chest, and he rests his chin on the top of my head. No guy has ever inspired such an immediate physical reaction in me; no one has ever stoked that chemical heat in such a way that my skin becomes flame.

Song after song we dance, never budging from our positions, never even talking. Just holding and feeling and clinging to each other. Each knowing the truth: tonight will last for just a moment, and that's all it can ever really be.

"Can I cut in?"

His razor-edged tone shatters the peace. My eyes snap open, heart pounding against my ribs as if awakening from a dream. Somehow the dancing—the easy sway in Alex's insulating embrace—had lulled me into oblivion, where the rest of the world melted away. I push away from him but don't relinquish my grip on his arm.

Caden stands in front of us, lips flat-lined, with arms crossed. His accusing stare switches from me to Alex and then back again. When neither of us responds, he heaves out a heavy sigh and licks his tongue across his teeth, the universal sign of an impending Caden Temper Tantrum.

"What?" I ask.

"Could you spare some time for your ex-boyfriend to have a dance? Not ten in a row like this guy." He motions toward Alex. "Just one. I wouldn't want to monopolize your time."

Always the gentleman, Alex gives me a nod and says, "I'll just take a quick restroom break and be back... shortly."

As he steps away, Caden slips into his vacated spot and grabs my waist. "No rush," he mumbles after Alex.

I am not in the mood for one of Caden's meltdowns and his sudden creepy fixation on me. "What now, Caden?"

He narrows his eyes to slits and picks up the pace as he moves me in a circle on the dancefloor. "Did you forget about Sam, or are you using Alex in some ploy to humiliate me?"

"Humiliate you?" I laugh out loud as the words leave my mouth. Spoken like a true narcissist. A completely deluded one.

He comes to an abrupt standstill, stooping so we're face to face and lowering his voice to a low angry whisper. "Everyone's watching tonight, and you're smashing your body into Alex with no regard about how that affects me, how it makes me look."

The absurdity of his accusations hit me like a brick, and the fury rides up my esophagus like a torrent of lava and spews out. "If people are looking at you in any particular way, that's your doing, not mine. You're my ex, and for good reason I might add."

The hard edge dissipates from his face, leaving behind something softer, some more kid-like. Regret? "I apologized. I thought we were past that."

I wiggle out of his grasp and take a few steps back. "Oh, I'm over it. I'm *so* over it."

Caden opens his mouth like he's going to say something but then closes it, almost as if he's weighing the next words. "Are you going to hate me forever, Ryleigh Anne?"

There it is. The question I've asked myself a million times since last year. Did I hate him? Or was I just hurt? I'd struggled with my true feelings until one person had helped me sort through everything. Sam.

The mere mention of his name in my thoughts softens the steel in my muscles, and everything relaxes.

I lay my hand on Caden's arm. "I don't hate you, and you can thank Sam for that. He's been my sounding board for so much over the last year. He's helped me discover who I really am and let go of the rest. He helped me forgive you a long time ago."

Caden's chest rises and falls, and he drops his arms to his sides like a statue. "If he's so great, why can't you seem to keep your hands off Alex? You two have been playing this ruse pretty well tonight. Almost convinced even me."

Caden shakes his head and trudges off, disappearing into the balloon tunnel and taking all my confidence with him. I backpedal off the dance floor and crash into Alex, who's making his way back from the restroom. He grips both shoulders and pivots me to facing him.

"Are you okay?"

I shake my head no, and Alex places a strong hand on the small of my back and leads me toward the back hallway of the venue, out of sight and earshot of the rest of the crowd.

"What did Caden say to you?"

"He said I'm embarrassing him in front of everyone. He said…" My breath escapes me, the guilt burning in my gut. "He insinuated that Sam would be disappointed in me."

"Why?"

"Because of you. Because of… us." I whirl away from Alex, covering my face with my hands, and smash myself into the brick wall, mumbling through my fingers, "That sounds stupid just saying it out loud. Of course you don't—"

"It doesn't sound stupid. It sounds… accurate."

"What?" A chill rockets down my body, and I lower my hands just enough to get a full view of his stormy eyes, the brown so dark they're almost black.

Alex takes both of my hands. They shake against his warm skin. "If I had texted you first, would you have talked to me?"

Buzz.

My phone vibrates in my purse, and a wave of panic crashes over me as Alex's question lingers in the air above us like a gray cloud. I yank my hands from his and fumble through my purse. My fingers locate my phone, and as I press the side button, the screen illuminates.

One New Text Message.

<Sam>*I'm ready for our big reveal. Are you? Meet me by the fountain.*

"He's here." Is it possible to feel everything at once? As if the heart is an overfilled balloon just waiting to pop.

Alex circles my waist, tugging me close. "If you get out there and you're disappointed, can you remember the fun we've had tonight? Can you remember me?"

"I… I mean…" My mouth dries up like desert sand. Tonight with Alex was unexpectedly wonderful, but Sam is the reason I'm here in the first place. It's been Sam on all those late-night texts, bearing our souls and secrets. It's Sam who's come all this way—for me. I swallow down the lump in my throat. Physical attraction is one thing, but Sam… he's a soul thing.

Alex steps away, letting his hand slip from the small of my back, the warmth replaced by chill bumps. "Wow. You have real feelings for him, don't you?" Before I can answer, he shakes his head. "Don't answer that, just…"—he takes a deep inhale and blows it out—"I hope he deserves you, and I hope he keeps deserving you."

Heat swirls into my cheeks, and I stare down at my shoes, composing myself and internally cursing fate, who in spite of nearly 18 years' worth of giving me the finger in the dating department, has now planted two viable love interests on my doorstep simultaneously. But what my heart was floundering on, my brain has decided. Alex would be here for tonight, but Sam had been here all along.

I grab Alex's hand, giving it a squeeze. "Thank you for everything. And just so you know, I won't forget you. A girl doesn't forget her senior prom date."

He laughs, a small smile barely parting his lips and creating a sparkle in his chestnut eyes. "Good luck. And what is it that they always say in the movies at moments like these?" He clears his throat and slides his other hand over the top of our joined ones, encapsulating mine in the middle. "I hope you find what you're looking for."

I wink and pull my hand away, clenching my fingers into the sequins of my purse and holding it up in front of my chest like a shield. Against what, I don't know. My nerves? Alex's soft eyes? My own wishy-washy feelings?

"I've already found it. I just have to go get it."

He ticks his head toward the entrance, and I offer one last smile before turning and jogging toward the balloon tunnel, as fast as my three-inch heels and the swirliness of my green tulle layers let me. I don't look back.

I can't.

As I emerge from the tunnel, Caden catches my arm. "Where are you going at 90 mph?"

"He's here. Sam's here. At the fountain," I say, tugging my arm, struggling to break his grip.

"You're not going alone. We haven't checked this guy out yet. I'm coming with."

I wiggle loose and shove him away. "Get lost."

"Is that any way to talk to an 'amicable' ex-boyfriend?" I love how he air quotes the amicable part. That's definitely an up-in-the-air descriptor, especially based on his current attitude.

"You've done quite a bit of talking yourself tonight, Caden. Right now is not about you. It's about Sam. Me and Sam."

Across the plaza, the shape of a guy takes shape in the dim streetlight. He's wearing a dark suit, hair gelled into place. My pace quickens, the short jaunt to the fountain morphing into a mile-long trek. The drumming of my heart in my neck leaves me breathless, the oxygen deprivation spurring one of those lightheaded, euphoric waves. Behind me, Caden's steps thump against the concrete pavers.

"Sam!" I yell out, but he doesn't turn around. Of course he'd let the suspense build. My chest feels like Mt. Vesuvius in the moment before it blew.

I stop running when I get to the front edge of the fountain, slowing down just enough to straighten my dress. The humid night air folds around me like a heavy curtain, a weight that becomes a two-ton boulder when he looks up, lipstick smeared across his face and neck and a leggy brunette practically glued to the front of him.

Wait. Logan from the football team? "Logan? What are you doing here?"

"Trying to make out with my girlfriend, if you don't mind." He rolls his eyes and waves his hand, motioning me away.

Whatever. "I'm supposed to be meeting someone here. I'm not leaving."

He snarls in my direction, but his date grabs the lapel on his coat, redirecting his attention to her pouty lips. "Why don't we go back to the prom? I'd love to dance some more," she coos in his ear.

"Fine," he grumbles, shooting one last death glare at me over her shoulder before they leave. Wah-wah, I cramped his game. Big deal. I have bigger problems, like where in the hell is Sam?

I walk toward the street and look left and then right. No one in sight. No one headed toward the fountain, and in a moment, the anticipation turns sour. I stumble backward, feeling behind me for the rock ledge around the fountain's edge. "He's not here." The words barely make it out before the first tears streak my cheeks. What's even happening right now? I don't understand. How can someone who's always been there for me do this now? No possible scenarios make sense.

"There's a reason for that," Caden says, stepping in front of me. "I have a confession. It's me. I'm Sam."

My body goes limp, only the rock ledge supporting my weight. Like gravity's force has been removed. My brain may have exploded because suddenly, the words aren't making sense.

"You what?" My voice finds a deeper echo in the dark. Over Caden's shoulder, Alex stands there, mouth agape and eyes of stone.

Caden puts up both hands like stop signs. "I didn't mean for anyone to get hurt."

A sudden numbness works its way up from my toes. I can't even muster any anger. There isn't enough room inside me with the ginormous cavern that's opened up in my chest. Sam is Caden? I mean, Sam did know a lot of stuff about me, but I'd always assumed he just really paid attention to the things I said. And the fountain. He wanted to meet at the fountain. A place someone who'd grown up here would know all about.

Oh my God. My stomach lurches and the urge to vomit grips me.

Caden steps closer. "Ryleigh Anne, are you okay?"

Alex lunges in from the side, giving Caden a rough shove. "Of course she's not okay, you dumbass. You're so full of shit, dude. Don't be a jerk."

Caden steadies himself on his feet but doesn't bow his chest at Alex. Instead, he shrugs, looking like a scolded child. "I'm not a jerk. I just... I felt bad about the way things went down between us last year, and then you sent me that text... and I finally realized how special you are. How stupid I'd been."

I'm special? "I can't believe it was all a lie. All those conversations—your parents, your brother, your dreams—that was all fantasy? And then tonight you show up here and... you have the nerve to accuse me and Alex?"

They said he was jealous. Everyone thought so, and I shrugged it off.

I am so naïve.

"I mean, I just wanted to... and then tonight..." Caden's eyes lock with mine for a whole three seconds before he drops his head. "Yeah."

Alex steps forward again, fisting Caden's shirt at the neck. "Yeah? You just drop that load of bullshit on her and all you can say is 'yeah'?"

Caden shoves him off and Alex stumbles backward, catching himself on the ledge. "Why do you even care? You've known her like a whole two hours!"

"That's enough time to know she doesn't deserve this! I can't believe you'd..."

Their voices fade behind me as I trudge toward the iron park bench up the block. The one hidden in the shadow of the buildings. The one where I can escape.

I stare down the deserted Main Street, counting the lightning bugs as they twinkle in the distance and actively trying not to think about tonight's revelations. I loosen the bobby pins from my updo, allowing my wavy blond hair to spill down over my shoulders. At least I can use it as a curtain to mask my tears.

"Ryleigh Anne? Can we talk?"

I look up at Alex, who stands a few feet away as if he's afraid to get too close without my consent. His jacket is slung over one arm, his shirt unbuttoned at the neck and sleeves rolled to his elbows.

"What's there to talk about? You must think I'm so stupid."

He steps closer, his shoes scratching along the pavement. "Never. I think you're smart and caring and... beautiful. And no matter who sent those text messages, it's evident he sees how special you are."

There's that word again. Special. A special kind of stupid, all right.

"He told me, and I didn't listen." I slap my forehead. "The first thing he said tonight was that I was like one of those naïve people from that television show, believing someone—any-one—truly wanted to know me. Hell, athletic build, brown hair and eyes—that's him. Or half the football team. Or…"

"Me?" Alex walks closer still and sits down beside me on the bench, his knee touching mine.

I snort. "I don't have that sort of luck."

"What's that supposed to mean?"

"Nothing."

"I'm so sorry, for everything. You don't deserve any of this."

"Maybe you should go catch up with Caden. You'll need a ride back to your school."

"I'll wait. I'm sort of pissed at him right now for ruining tonight."

"He ruined mine, not yours. There's no reason for you to be mad at him."

"Maybe what you need is closure. I saw a therapist once— family stuff—who was all about closure helping you move on."

"Suggestions?"

"I think you should go back to where all this started. Send 'Sam' one last message, and then you can start fresh."

I bite my lip, holding back another barrage of tears. This has to end, but I knew I'd miss it. Even if it had all been an illusion. "Okay," I whisper, and pull my phone from my bag, taking a few deep breaths before opening up the message.

<Me> *One positive thing I got from all this is realizing I'm strong. Sam gave me that. So, in a strange way, thank you.*

I stop, staring at the message on the screen. This is good-bye, and my heart relocates to my throat, a pulsing brick stifling my voice. I have to let go.

"Send it," he says, nodding toward the phone. With trembling fingers, I press the arrow, my eyes clamping shut with the wave of finalization.

Bing.

The sound stomps my lungs, forcing out all the air, and I slit my eyes, training them on the phone in his hand. The one lit up with a new text message with my name on it.

Our eyes lock, and his bottom lip trembles. "I'm Sam."

Everything stops. No heart beating, no lungs expanding, no buzz from the streetlight, no laughing from the distant prom crowd. Silence wraps around me. A weird, loud silence that completely consumes me as I try to merge the imagined face of Sam with the very real, very close face of Alex.

The small whimper that eeks out from between my own lips breaks the vacuum we're standing in, the mish-mash image of two faces dissolving into two chestnut eyes.

"That's why I was so mad at Caden. It was me who's been texting you. It was me who texted you and told you I was at the fountain, because I intended to follow you out there, but then... then Caden butted in and concocted that stupid story about it being him."

My fingers wrap around the iron spindle of the bench in an attempt to anchor myself. "This doesn't make any sense. Why would he do that?"

"Apparently, he lied because he really did think you were being stood up, and after seeing us dancing tonight, feeling jealous, he thought he'd take the opportunity to try and win you back." Alex runs his hand through his hair, curls splaying out everywhere. "He didn't know he was crashing my big reveal. I never told him about Sam."

My emotions explode like a fireworks finale. I kick off my heels and get up, pacing back and forth in front of the bench. None of this makes sense.

"How did it just happen to be you who 'mistakenly' texted me? That's too much of a coincidence for me to believe."

"That's because it wasn't a coincidence." Alex stands up, half-blocking my path. His voice wavers, his eyes pleading his case. There's a part of me that thinks I should leave him standing here with his stories, but another part, a much deeper one, wants to hear what he has to say. Because the Alex I met tonight does sync with the wonderful months I've spent talking with Sam. And more than anything, that truth brings me relief.

I clench my teeth and stare him down. "Explain."

"Caden told me about you. He showed me that message you sent him, and I... I just had to know you. Someone so good and genuine, especially after everything I've lost in my life. I needed something to care about again. Some*one* to care about." He cups my chin, tilting my head so that our eyes lock. There's truth there. And something else. Something deep and authentic. "Nothing I ever told you was a lie. None of it. And yes, I shouldn't have misled you. I know that, but I was afraid. I thought if you knew who I was, you wouldn't give me a chance. Why would a girl like you want a loser like me, fresh out of reform school?"

I manage a small grin. "It's an elite military academy. And you're not a loser."

"No," he says, pointing at me. "Don't be nice to me. Put me out of my misery, read me the riot act, whatever. I know I'm worse than Caden." Alex slumps onto the bench, head in his hands.

"You know, there's still one thing I can't figure out. How could you have sent me those texts? You were with me almost every time I received one tonight."

"Easy," he says, pulling up our text messages on his phone and pointing to the three dots in the top corner. "I put them on a delay. You can set them for whatever time you want them to go out."

"No freaking way."

"I just needed to see you first, spend time with you in 'real life.' My biggest fear is that you wouldn't want me. But then, when we started to dance… I had hope."

I sit beside him, my fingers itching to run through his curls. "All of those months. All of those texts."

He catches my hand and pulls it to his lips, planting a kiss against my palm. "Those were honest. Those were me—Alexander Samuel Calhoun—falling for you."

Alexander Samuel Calhoun. Alex. Sam. One person. Falling for me.

I swallow hard. "Did you say you're falling for me?"

"Ryleigh Anne, how could I not? You've meant more to me over this last year than… well, more than I could ever text."

A few happy tears gather in my lashes, and I brush them away. "I fell for you, too, Alex, and I want to start over—as me and you."

He bites his bottom lip and then picks up his phone to tap out a quick message. My phone buzzes against my palm, and I open it to see Sam's name on the screen. Mental note to correct that. One simple line pops up.

<Sam> *Hi, I'm Alex. It's nice to meet you.*

I send a quick response:

<Me> *Hi, Alex.*

He reads my reply and smiles. "This might be harder than I thought. That damn Sam left some really big shoes to fill. What can I, Alex, possibly do or say that he never did?"

I have at least one idea.

<Me> *You can give me our first real kiss*

Bing.

He reads my text and then licks his lips, scooting toward me on the bench. When he slides his arms around me, I let my guard down, feeling his strength and the ripples of his body without shame. He folds around me and I snuggle in close, lifting my lips to meet his in a connection that's everything I hoped it would be—soft, strong, and exciting.

Because now he is mine. And he had been all along.

Other Published Works

READ MORE BY BRANDY WOODS SNOW

Meant to be Broken – Filles Vertes Publishing – 2018

As Much as I Ever Could – Filles Vertes Publishing – 2020

FOR MORE, VISIT

www.brandywsnow.com

Chasing the Story

The Adventures of Victoria Miller

Bass thumped, the pulse vibrated through me, and I swayed my hips to the rhythm. I would have loved to get out on the dance floor and let loose, but I wasn't here for that. Maybe, if the interview went well, I could come back. Bring Marcus with me. He loved to dance. And I loved to secretly watch him from my bedroom window.

Who was I kidding? Neither of those things were going to happen. One, I was here to expose the owner—Antonio Vargas, aka Eugene Fredrick as a fraud and a cheat. And two, Marcus and I were just friends.

I wiped the sweat from my neck and fanned myself, in a fruitless effort to cool off. Despite my hair being pulled up off my neck, I was still a little overheated. A group of women passed by my spot at the bar, giving me a once-over. I smiled, hiding the unease brewing inside me. Seventeen, with a fake ID in my bag, I shouldn't be here.

I sipped my third watered-down ginger ale and scanned Club Vargas again. Two hours and forty bucks later, and still Antonio was a no-show. My phone vibrated, and I pulled it from my purse. *Crap.* My Uber would be here in forty minutes to get me home before curfew. Making this yet another wasted night.

This was the third night this week I'd been here, and I really didn't want to spend another night watching the same idiots try and dance, or waste another dollar on overpriced soda. But sadly, it was looking as if I might just have to. I wasn't giving up on my story.

"Can I buy you a drink?" a man said, easing up close.

I also didn't want to have to fight off unwanted attention anymore, either. The first two nights, I actually tried being nice. Turning them down with a polite, "No, thank you," or, "I'm waiting for someone." Tonight, I'd reached my limit.

"Go away," I said.

The guy shifted closer, his strong cologne making my eyes water. I sighed heavily and continued to scan the crowd. It was the third guy who had approached me since I'd gotten here two hours ago. Couldn't they read my body language or the "leave me the hell alone" look in my eyes?

"I said, can I buy you a drink?" he asked.

I took another sip of the watered-down ginger ale and shifted away. Speaking of, just why were they watering down the soda? Might be a good story. I mulled it over, then quickly dismissed it. No, I'd stick to the original one.

The man reached out and touched my arm.

I pushed off the bar. "Don't touch me, dumbass!"

He moved closer. "Don't be like that, pretty girl."

Was he serious? I stuck my hand in my purse, wrapping it around my can of Mace. Since words weren't working, I'd give him a face full of civilian-grade tear gas. He'd definitely get the point then.

"I don't think she's interested," a familiar deep voice said.

I turned toward the speaker and gasped. Marcus Killian. My next door neighbor. He smiled his knee-weakening smile and winked. My heart fluttered. It was almost as if my thoughts had conjured him out of the blue. Okay, maybe that was a bit too much wishful thinking on my part. He had to be here with someone. Most likely the captain of his fan club at school.

The man shuffled away and Marcus took his place, sidling up to me.

"How'd you get in here?" I asked.

"Same way you did."

I got in here by buying a fifty-dollar fake ID from Dorian Randle who, I believe, has decided to remain a senior for the rest of his life. Or until Baxter High kicked him out.

"Are you following me?" There was a thin note of hopefulness in my voice and it pissed me off.

"Maybe." He smiled. "I saw you get out of Jason's car down the street and climb into another one." He shrugged. "I thought I'd follow and see what you were up to." He looked over at me, took a brief perusal down my body, and made eye contact again. "Nice outfit."

I glanced down at my tight black, shimmering jeans and white dressy halter top. Not my usual choice in clothing. But I could admit it was nice. Even made me feel a little sexy. And judging from the hooded look in Marcus's eyes and the small smile on his face as he continued to stare at me, he thought so too.

"Thank you." I checked him out. "Didn't you wear those jeans to school today?"

"You keep track of what I wear every day?"

Heat bloomed on my cheeks, and I turned away.

He leaned forward, pulling my gaze back toward him. "So, what story are you chasing now, Vicki?"

"Who said I was chasing a story?"

"You're always chasing a story."

"Oh, you know me so well." I took another sip of the ginger ale.

He moved closer and whispered in my ear. "Yes I do. Are you dating Jason now?"

Was that jealousy I detected in his voice? "No, of course not." Why was I squeaking? I cleared my throat. "He was a decoy for my mom. I told her I was going to a party with him. So,"—I waved my hands in the air in a circling motion—"he agreed to help me."

"Why are you so nervous?"

I snatched the napkin off the bar and started ripping it to pieces. I needed to keep my hands busy. Otherwise, I'd start waving them around like an idiot again. He did this to me. Driving to school together was fine. He mostly focused on the road and let me prattle on about whatever story I was working on at the time. But this level of focus from him turned me into a nervous girly-girl. I hated it. And secretly loved it too.

"I'm not nervous!" Even I didn't believe my protest.

"You always squeak and use way too many hand gestures when you're nervous."

I turned to him. He reached out and took the shredded napkin from me. "You don't have to be nervous around me, Vicki."

"I... I know," I sighed. "I just..."

He moved closer. The heat from his body sent a shiver down my spine. My stomach quivered. "You just what?"

No matter how hard I tried, I couldn't take my eyes off him. "You really like my outfit?"

He laughed, breaking the spell. I sucked in a breath and let it out slowly. "Don't laugh." I picked up my glass and took another sip of ginger ale. I really needed to stop drinking this crap.

"I can't help it. You asking about clothes? Laughable."

"Whatever, Marcus." I smiled and turned back toward the club.

Just then, Antonio Vargas strode across the dance floor with a dark-haired woman, wearing a white suit.

I set my glass on the bar top. "Well, I have to go. Don't drink the ginger ale. It's horrible."

I started off in Antonio's direction, only to be stopped by Marcus's warm, strong hand on my arm.

"We need to talk, Vicki."

I looked back. The seriousness in his eyes made me pause. "About what?"

He moved close, his hand sliding down my arm, leaving a slew of goosebumps on my flesh. I suppressed a shudder. Well, I tried to suppress a shudder. My eyes fluttered and his dark green eyes pierced mine.

"About us," he said, finally.

I opened my mouth to say something. No sound came out. I tried again. Still nothing. He smiled and my knees went weak. And suddenly, I was twelve years old all over again, fawning over the cute boy who just moved in next door. Writing his name in cut-out hearts and taping them to my wall. Staring out my bedroom window hoping to get a peek at him. I had it bad.

Worse still, when he found out, he dismissed me in front of his friends. Two long, agonizing hours after that horrific event, he'd come to my door and apologized. My mother had thought it was cute. I just wanted to crawl under my bed and hide.

We'd never talked about it again. But old insecurities had reared their ugly little heads.

"Can it wait?"

"How about I wait right here for you?"

Butterflies swarmed in my belly. What could he possibly want to talk to me about? I briefly entertained the thought of just giving up on my story and staying here with Marcus. My heart loved the idea, but my brain had other plans. If I didn't act now, chances were I would never get this story. After all, I had stolen the information off my aunt's desk. She was bound to find out sooner rather than later.

"Umm… okay. I'll be right back."

Once I made it across the dance floor, I glanced back at the bar. Marcus leaned against it, forearms propped up on the polished wood, watching me.

The swarm of butterflies in my stomach turned into a full-on kaleidoscope.

Antonio stood next to the black, steel door leading to the back. "No Entrance" was written in bright, yellow, blocky script. The woman in white stood next to him, scanning the club. When he put his hand on the knob, I called out. He turned, eyes narrowing.

I stretched my mouth into a friendly, welcoming smile and rushed the last few feet. "Hi," I said, sticking out my hand. "My name's Victoria Miller." I pulled a counterfeit press badge for *El Alma Tribune* from my little clutch and showed it to him. My Aunt Caroline would kill me if she found out I'd made one. "I wanted to ask a few follow-up questions on the story we did for you last week."

It was a lie. The note I'd found on my aunt's desk a week ago alluded to Antonio getting a coveted spot on our Historic Main Street by illegal means. The building his club currently occupied was supposed to have become a family restaurant. My classmate, Jesse Smith, said his father, Robert, had gone through all the necessary paperwork. Had the old building rezoned so he could add a kitchen and even saved enough money to cover expenses for an entire year. Yet, last month, his application had been suddenly denied and the club moved in.

That was the story I was after. And that was the story I was going to get.

Did I feel bad about scooping my aunt? Not really; I come from a long line of ruthless reporters. Besides, after it was all said and done, she would be proud if I actually got the story.

Antonio scowled. The woman placed her hand on his arm. "More publicity for the club is good, Antonio," she said, in a subtle French accent.

He nodded and signaled across the room to the man behind the bar. "We can talk in my office."

Antonio opened the door and walked in ahead of me. Rude bastard. I followed behind him; the woman took up the rear. The steel door slammed behind us, enclosing us in a dimly lit hallway, muting the music. All except for the base still vibrating through the concrete floor. A heavy smoke smell lingered in the air.

Antonio glanced over his shoulder, his eyes hard with a small sneer on his face. I placed my hand on my bag, feeling the outline of my canister of Mace. My having it was illegal, but its effectiveness far outweighed my concern for that. And if all else failed, I wasn't above kicking Antonio in the nuts.

We stepped into Antonio's office—red and leather everywhere as if he'd got all his furniture from the set of some B-rated mob movie. He even had a desk made of glass. I shook my head slightly at the display. Part of my prep for this interview had been to dig a little further into Antonio's past. Turned out, before he moved to El Alma, CA, he owned a frou-frou coffee shop in Miami that sold not only tea and coffee but also baked goods he made himself. Back then he went by the name Eugene Fredericks.

So why was he trying to be a mobster now? Or was he hiding from something... or someone?

The woman sat in a chair next to the desk and laid her arm across the glass, displaying an expensive-looking silver watch. My first impression of her, when she strode across the club, was that of an expensive piece of arm candy. Now, looking into her calculating grey eyes, I wondered why such an attractive, obvious intelligent woman was associating with the likes of Antonio.

A commotion by the door had me turning. I had to fight hard to keep the surprise off my face when Marcus followed the bartender in.

"Sir, this gentleman says he's with her." The bartender walked over carrying a tray with three glasses. One was a ginger ale. Mental note: Don't stay in one place too long when you're trying to be inconspicuous.

When the bartender handed me the glass, the woman said, "Did you want something stronger?"

I smiled. "No, this is fine."

The bartender left, and one of the bouncers came in and took up a position by the door. Did he think I was going to hurt his boss?

Antonio took in Marcus, assessing, and then turned to me. "And who is this?"

"My photographer." I turned to Marcus. "Were you able to get the camera out of the car?" I asked with only mild irritation in my voice.

"No. I'm..."

I waved off his reply and pulled my cell phone out of my clutch. "Use this." I handed him the phone—warning him with a look—and turned back to Antonio. "I would like to get some additional pictures of you before we begin."

Antonio stood, a grin on his face, and sauntered over to his black leather couch. After situating himself in the middle, he spread his arms out over the back of the couch, drink dangling from his right hand, and smiled.

Marcus, *God bless him*, fell in line, moved in front of Antonio, and took a few pictures.

I nearly threw up in my mouth at the sleazy display. The woman took a sip of her drink, watching the whole exchange over the rim of her glass. Her eyes narrowed. Looked like she wasn't too happy with the outrageous performance either. *Who was she?*

When she focused on me, I glanced away, put a ridiculous smile on my face, and said, "Well, thank you, Mr. Vargas, for that." I turned to Marcus. "Why don't you go on out. I should be just a minute."

"Would a good photographer leave his reporter in the middle of an interview?" He winked at me. "I don't think so."

My mouth dropped open. No, the hell he didn't!

He turned away. "I like your office, Mr. Vargas."

Antonio got up. "Please, call me Antonio." He extended his hand, and Marcus shook it.

"Marcus Killian. Nice to meet you."

"You work at *El Alma Tribune* as well?" Antonio walked over to his desk and sat.

The woman stared at us. Waiting.

Marcus nodded and shifted from one foot to the other. I could tell he was having trouble with all this. Too bad. He should have left when I gave him an out.

"Both of you are so young," the woman said. "You must have started working for the paper right out of high school."

"Umm…yes."

"Do you miss it?"

"What?"

She smiled. "High school?"

I shook my head. "Not really?" Again, who was this woman? And why was she asking me about high school?

She cut her eyes in Antonio's direction. "You didn't introduce us."

"Oh, forgive me. I forget myself sometimes. This is my associate Bunny," Antonio said. Bunny, No-last-name. I wasn't buying it.

Bunny smiled. "I hope you don't mind if I stay while you interview Antonio, Ms. Miller." It really wasn't a question.

"No, of course not."

Antonio snapped his fingers. "Yes, the woman who interviewed me last week was named Miller."

"Yes, she's my aunt."

He smiled, displaying a mouth desperately in need of dental hygiene. "Nepotism. Yes, the American way, right! No need to work for anything when you have family to help."

My family owned the paper. So, it was understood that I would not only work there after I graduated high school next month but also, eventually, take over as editor-in-chief. So, this wasn't the first time I'd been accused of nepotism. I ground my teeth and fought the urge to respond.

He leaned back. Bunny watched me with a condescending smile on her face. Sweat broke out on my upper lip. Something in the way she scrutinized me felt as if she could see right past the farce. Why else would she ask me about high school? Yes, we both looked young. But not that young. Was I being paranoid?

I pushed a little more steel into my spine and opened my notebook. "Yes, well as I indicated, I wanted to ask a few follow-up questions. I understand you used to own a coffee shop in Miami." I consulted my notebook and continued, "Eugene's Coffee, Tea, and Cookies?"

"Where did you get this information?" Antonio (aka Eugene Fredrick) asked.

I furrowed my brow and looked down at my notes again. "From the Miami Herald. They did a piece on you a few months ago."

"The press loves him," Bunny said.

I nodded. "Yes, I can see why." No, I couldn't. "I was just curious as to why you changed your name? And why open a nightclub instead of another coffee shop."

"Coffee shops are a thing of the past. And I wanted to reinvent myself," he said.

He did *not* just say that. If anything, coffee shops were taking over.

Bunny turned a glared at him. Maybe Antonio wasn't the one I should be interviewing. He clearly wasn't playing with a full deck.

"What I mean is—" He cleared his throat. "A big city like this, you don't open a coffee shop. You open a nightclub."

El Alma was not that big. And a coffee shop at this location would have made a lot of money.

I sighed and turned the page in my notebook. "I understand Robert Smith was going to open a restaurant at this location. Did Mayor Bradburn tell you why he decided to give the space to you instead?"

Antonio slammed his glass down. "This again!"

Again? *Oh, crap!* Had someone already tried to get the story from him?

Marcus grabbed my arm. I couldn't settle on how I felt about that. On one hand, he was obviously trying to protect me. My heart loved the idea. But the place where my grit and determination dwelled didn't appreciate the assumption that I couldn't take care of myself.

Antonio jumped to his feet. His chair slid backward, slamming into the wall. "I think that is all the questions I will answer, Ms. Miller," he grunted.

Bunny crossed her legs and watched me with a mild curiosity in her eyes.

I started to say something, but Marcus stepped in front of me with a warning look in his eyes. He didn't know the real Antonio. Or, should I say, Eugene. It was confusing. But in all honesty, neither did I. How far had Antonio taken this charade? He obviously wanted people to believe he was some sort of gangster. Had he gone the extra mile and hired real thugs?

"I will get an answer," I gritted out as I put my notebook back in my purse. "Maybe not today, but one day real soon. *Eugene.*"

"Is that a threat, Ms. Miller?" He looked behind us.

"No, it's a promise." If not for my need to maintain the illusion of having no fear, I would have cringed at my cliché response. Seriously, a promise?

His bouncer stepped in front of me, his beefy arms crossed over his mighty chest, and glared down at me.

Not wanting to push it further, but still wanting to leave with my dignity, I simply smiled and left. Marcus (again, on the fence about his protectiveness) walked out a few beats after me.

Well, on to Plan B.

The cool air hit me when we made it outside. I bit back a scream of frustration as I snatched my phone from my purse. My Uber driver had texted me while I was in Antonio's office. *Damn.*

"Well, faithful photographer. Looks like you're taking me home," I said.

He smiled, shaking his head, and started toward the parking lot.

"Vicki," he said after a brief silence. "Just what the hell where you thinking?"

We got in his silver Subaru WRX STI.

"What do you mean?" I asked, fastening my seatbelt.

I knew exactly what he meant. I blamed my temper. I just couldn't stand there and let the mobster wannabe talk to me like that. My aunt had repeatedly warned me about my temper when I'd tried working for her last summer. It was one of the reasons I had to make a duplicate press badge; she took back the last one when I called Doris Michels—the owner of Lace and Frills—an uptight biddy. Hell, even her store name screamed uptight.

I blew it in there. But, if I was honest, I didn't expect to really get the answers from Antonio. I was more interested in gauging what his reactions to my questions would be. Now, having learned that others were asking him questions about his past and his current relationship with the Mayor, I had to act fast. Like, tonight. Only, Marcus couldn't come along. Things were going to get illegal and dirty.

"Vicki?" Marcus glanced at me. "Are you going insane? You just insulted and threatened a mobster and could have gotten us both killed."

He was being dramatic. I gave him the backstory on Antonio.

Marcus drummed his fingers on the steering wheel while we sat at the light. After a short while, he started laughing. "Eugene the baker wants to be a mobster." He shook his head. "He should have moved to LA."

"What did you think of Bunny?"

"Fake name and obviously in charge."

I nodded and looked out the window. "My thoughts exactly."

By the time we pulled up to my house, I was rethinking my assumptions about Antonio. I knew I had to dig deeper and find out the connection between him and Bunny.

Marcus parked and turned off the engine.

"Why didn't you park in your driveway?" I asked.

He looked out at our quiet, boring street as he drummed his fingers on the steering wheel. "Remember when I first moved in, and you and your dad came over to say hi?"

Yes, I remembered my inability to string two sentences together when I got my first look at him. It had been mortifying. "Yes," I said hesitantly. Where was he going with this?

He shifted around and faced me. "Why haven't we ever dated?"

My eyes threatened to pop out of my head. "Are you serious?" I tapped his head. "Did you forget about making fun of my flat chest with your new friend, David, when we were twelve?"

He winced. "Yeah, and I apologized for it, too."

"Okay, but…" I had to physically stop myself from making any anxiety-induced erratic hand movements. Since apparently Marcus knew all my telling signs.

He looked behind me at my house. It was past my curfew, and I was willing to bet my mother was standing on the porch. *Please don't let her be wearing that ratty blue bathrobe.*

"Can we talk about it tomorrow? Maybe go to lunch at Delia's?" he asked.

Delia's was a local sandwich shop on Main Street where all the high school kids hung out. I opened my mouth to respond. When no words came out, I opened the car door and climbed out.

"Vicki?"

"Sure," I said, slamming his door. I rushed up the walkway, hiding the blush that had bloomed on my cheeks. Marcus started his car and backed it into his driveway.

"I thought you went to the party with Jason?" my mother asked as she watched Marcus get out of the car. I refused to look.

"Yeah, well Marcus did too, and offered to give me a ride home."

My mother looked at me. "Why are you blushing?"

"He asked me out?"

She smiled. "I'm tempted to ground you for being ten minutes late."

I cringed. "That bathrobe is punishment enough. Please stop wearing it outside."

She laughed and pulled me into a hug. "I'll forgive you this one time." We walked into the house. "Tell me about your date? Oh, and your Aunt Caroline called."

Busted.

Everything suddenly became more important than returning my aunt's phone call. It started with my moment of suspended dis-belief at the realization that Marcus suddenly wanted to date me and ended with me standing in front of my full-length mirror.

Supposedly, most girls my age had an unhealthy relationship with their body image. This lovely opinion came from an article Jeanne Pannier had written six months ago for the paper. In it, she claimed that all girls went through a phase of not liking themselves. At the time, I had believed it to be complete crap. I'd never been insecure about my body. That is until this very moment. Standing here. Staring in the mirror, wishing for my body to suddenly morph into something more. More what? I honestly didn't know. But the desire to be different was there.

Please tell me I wasn't turning into a girly-girl because Marcus had finally noticed me!

I looked at my cell phone and sighed. I couldn't avoid calling my aunt any longer. Yes, it would have been better if I had been able to get the story out of Antonio. Why was I still referring to him as Antonio? Anyway. If he had somehow decided to spill his guts, I could have called her with an apology, yes, but also a success story that would have quelled all of her ire.

But the famous Miller temper had reared its ugly head and derailed all my careful plans.

I'd replaced the club gear for breaking and entering gear: black turtleneck, black pants, black shoes, and a black beanie. Was it overkill? Probably. But it also telegraphed power and intrigue and mystery. At least, that's what I was telling myself.

Laid out on my desk were the items I would need to help me with plan B: newly acquired lock picks since I'd lost my old ones; a heavy-duty flashlight, for illumination and defense; a digital recorder, it was illegal to record someone without their consent, but I didn't care; military-grade binoculars, belonging to my Uncle Frank; and a pair of gloves, to match my ensemble. Tied to my bedpost and hidden underneath an area rug was a length of rope that allowed me to climb in and out of my window without waking up my mother.

My phone vibrated and I glanced down at the display. Aunt Caroline was persistent. Better get it over with.

"Hello," I said in a sleepy voice.

"Cut the crap, Vicki. Do you have something you want to tell me?"

"I'm doing fine, Auntie. How are you?"

"Well, Vicki, not too good. I seem to have misplaced some vital information for a story I was working on. Have you seen it?"

"Can you tell me a little more about it?"

My aunt didn't respond. Silence stretched on as I held the phone to my ear, contemplating what I should do. There wasn't any anger in her voice—of that I was sure. But there was something there. I just couldn't put my finger on it.

"Please be careful, Vicki," she said, finally. "I'd hate to have to pick you up at the police station again."

I sat down heavily on my bed. "I'm being careful." I smiled into the phone. "Just like you taught me."

"Now I'm really worried." She chuckled and hung up.

My father once told me that my Aunt Caroline and I shared the same reckless tendencies. He had died two years ago and I wondered, if he saw me now, would he be proud or fearful that he had been right.

After cramming my phone in my back pocket, I opened my room door an inch. My mother's snores filled the hallway in short bursts. Satisfied that she was asleep, I went to my window, opened it, lowered the rope out the window, and tossed my backpack onto the bushes.

After removing all the items off my nightstand, I eased my body into position, wrapped my hands around the rope, and started my descent down the side of the house. When my foot slipped, I had a moment to think about this continued avenue of sneaking out. My thoughts went from, "This was bound to happen sooner or later," to, "Oh shit!"

I landed with a thud, my body in between the hedges and my ego still straddling the windowsill. A sharp, intense, throb raced down my back like a freight train. My vision doubled as I swallowed the scream lodged in my throat. I worried I'd broken something. Moving slowly, I cursed under my breath as I eased myself off the ground. My turtleneck was torn; a large piece of the cotton fabric hung loose around my shoulder.

"Oh, this is just lovely!" I said as I grabbed my backpack and pushed my way out of the bushes. Thankfully, no one was around to see my complete and utter failure.

"Why didn't you just use the front door?" someone whispered behind me.

I jumped, let out a deranged battle cry, and threw my backpack at the person behind me. Marcus caught it and smiled.

My chest heaved up and down as if I'd just run a marathon.

"What the hell are you doing out here?" I growled through clenched teeth as I snatched the backpack from him, my cheeks flushing once again.

"I've been waiting on you for an hour."

"Why?"

He tilted his head to the side. "Vicki? Seriously? This has been your MO since we were fifteen." He thumbed toward his house. "I used to watch you sneak out all the time. I even watched when the patrol car brought you home." He laughed. "This time"—he stepped in close—"I figured you were going back to that club and wanted to come with you. So I can keep you safe."

"You watch me all the time? That is so creepy." My heart and the sudden kaleidoscope of butterflies in my stomach didn't agree.

My phone buzzed. I pulled it from my back pocket—surprised it was still in one piece—and looked at the display. "Well, it's been nice chatting with you." I stepped around him. "My Uber is here, and I have to go."

He reached out and grabbed my arm. "I'm serious, Vicki. I'm coming with you."

It took a little longer than necessary for me to remove my arm from his warm, strong hand. A real long time. So long, I received another text from the Uber driver.

"No," I said with absolutely no conviction in my voice. "I am going by myself."

"You don't sound too sure of that."

I swerved around him and made my way to the curb. His footfalls sounded behind me.

A white Lexus sat at the end of the block. It was the same driver that had picked me up earlier. Pradeep. I broke into a jog as I made my way to him. Unfortunately, Marcus did too.

Pradeep got out and opened the back door for me. "Hello, again, Vicki." He looked at Marcus. "Is your boyfriend coming with us?"

"No, he's not." Maybe I should have corrected the assumed relationship status too.

Marcus pulled his wallet out and extended a twenty to Pradeep. "I'll give Vicki a ride."

Pradeep stared at the money for a brief second. Shrugged. Took the money. Got back in the car and drove off.

"I can't believe you just did that!"

"Look, we can stand here and argue all night." He pushed into my space. "But in the end, I am coming with you. I know that you're going back to the club. I don't care if the guy is a poser. He could be dangerous."

"First of all, how do you know I'm going back to the club? I could be heading out to meet someone."

He took in my outfit. "In your stealth gear? And besides, you had that look on your face when we left earlier."

"What look?"

He moved even closer, and suddenly, I couldn't breathe. His eyes locked on mine, almost rooting me in place. "The determined one." He ran a finger down the side of my face. "The one that I've been mesmerized by since the first time I saw it. You get that look when you're after something. I only hope one day that something is me."

His words and their meaning punched a hole in my defenses and my common sense.

Like a puppet on a string, I rose on my toes, moving into his space. My mission? To finally feel those sexy lips on mine. Only it seemed, as Marcus stepped to the side, I was the only one on that current mission.

"Let's go," he said, taking my hand and pulling me back down the street. "We don't want to linger outside for too long."

Was he serious? How could he lay that heavy revelation on me and not act on it? I snatched my hand away and pushed past him. "You know what? I think it's best if you stay here. I don't need your help."

He grabbed my arm and turned me around. Before I could protest, or kick him in the nuts, his mouth came down on mine. My mind went blank. Those lips I'd been dreaming about for what felt like forever were finally touching mine. No more pretending my arm was his lips, I finally had the real thing.

Too soon, he pulled away. I might have whined a little, but I wasn't going to acknowledge it.

"Nice to know the feeling is mutual. Now, let's go."

I opened my eyes, bringing my surroundings into focus.

Marcus stood by the open passenger door of his car, waiting—his mouth stretched into a wide grin.

"You… you…" What did I want to say? Old insecurities reared their ugly little heads, and I couldn't get enough air in my lungs.

"Are you coming?" he asked, his smile suddenly dropping.

I licked my lips, tasting the remnants of him there.

"Why did you kiss me?" Oh, that's perfect. Why did you kiss me? I sounded pathetic.

He ran a hand through his hair. "Truth?"

I tossed my backpack inside the car and turned to him. Even though the door was between us, I could still feel the sensual pull toward him. It was making me want to do something irrational. I had to pull myself together.

"I wanted to see how you felt about me. And I really wanted to know if you'd kiss me back."

Again, he had rendered me speechless. We stood there, staring at each other for a long while. Finally, I managed to say, "Why not ask?" Not much squeak in my voice that time.

He stared at me, shifting from one foot to the next.

"We should get going," I said, giving him a temporary out. Besides, I could corner him in the car. Less chances for him to run from my question.

I got in the car and waited. After a brief hesitation, he got in too.

For the past week, I'd been chatting up the cleaning man at the club. Turns out, he didn't like his employer all too much and had volunteered to help me get inside and get some dirt if I needed it. I'd wanted to go the legal route first, but I also knew that eventually I'd have to do something illegal. I just hadn't counted on Marcus coming along for the ride.

Neither one of us talked on the ride over. I was still trying to wrap my mind around the kiss we'd shared that was supposed to determine how I felt about him. I had him park around the corner of Dunlap and Main Street.

"What now?" Marcus asked.

I paused. "Umm… well, now we wait." I ran my finger across my lips. Maybe we could…

"For what?"

"Oh, yeah. We wait for Jesse. He's going to text me when Antonio leaves."

"Who is Jesse?" Was that jealousy I detected in his voice?

"The night janitor. I'd texted him earlier and told him I needed to get into the club tonight."

Marcus shifted in his seat and faced me. "Vicki." He took my hand. "How do you feel about me?"

"Can we roll down the window? It's getting a little warm in here." I said. And here I thought I'd be cornering him.

He chuckled. "The window *is* down."

"Oh, okay."

"Stop stalling, Vicki."

I have always been uncomfortable around boys. Ever since my one and only attempt at having a relationship (maybe that is too strong a word for a preteen crush), I'd remained on guard, never allowing anyone close enough to hurt me. And honestly, most of the boys at Baxter High just didn't do it for me. Sure, there were some good-looking ones roaming the halls that all the girls fawned over. And yes, I had been asked out on a few dates. Even went on one. It didn't work out. He wasn't Marcus. Now, sitting in his car, having him hold my hand, finally, should have filled me with infinite joy. But it only made me suspicious.

I turned to him, removing my hand from his grip. "You first."

He drummed his fingers on his steering wheel. Oh, this was interesting. Marcus, scared? I'd never seen him act like this. The curiosity was killing me. A slew of questions kept running through my head. But the one I really wanted an answer for was, why now? After all this time?

Finally, he cleared his throat and said, "You know that columnist at the *El Alma Tribune* that's always giving out advice about relationships?"

"Jeanne Pannier." Of course I did. She was the one that had written that self-reflection shit-piece that had me all of a sudden questioning everything about the way I looked.

"Yeah, that's the one. Well, she did this column last month about the three signs you have found your true love."

I swallowed hard. Was he trying to say I was his true love? Hope wormed its way into my soul. Then I thought about what he said. Jeanne Pannier wrote many "how-to" lists. But I didn't readily recall one about finding true love.

"The first sign…"

My phone vibrated. "Oh, fuck me!" I yelled as I snatched it out of my back pocket. Just when things were getting good.

Jesse: All clear! You have thirty minutes.

I texted back that I was on my way and paused. I turned to Marcus. He watched me, his eyes filling with… something.

"Let's get this over with so you can finish telling me about true love," I said, infusing levity into my voice.

He nodded and climbed out of the car.

We made our way around to the alley between the buildings. Muted light spilled out on the black concrete creating shadows along the fence. Jesse stood at the back door smoking a cigarette. Most likely his fifth one since he started cleaning a few hours ago.

"Vicki," he called.

I pasted a smile on my face as I walked up to him. "Hello, Jesse. How are things?"

He shook his head, blowing out a stream of smoke. "Very good." He nodded. "Very good." He smiled at me. "I heard some buzz that Antonio was insulted by a young reporter." His eyes danced with laughter. "It made my night."

I rolled my eyes. "I hardly insulted him." I turned to Marcus. "This is my friend. He's helping me tonight."

Jesse nodded again, closing his eyes as he inhaled more smoke. "Well, be quick. The night guard will be here soon."

I slipped him a twenty. "Thank you."

He pocketed it and continued his love affair with nicotine and the night.

The club reeked of stale beer and sweat. We made our way toward Antonio's office, our shoes squeaking on the concrete floor.

"What exactly are you looking for?" Marcus asked as we entered Antonio's office.

I placed my backpack on the floor and opened the first drawer on the roll away cabinet under his desk. While I searched, I told Marcus about the note my aunt had on her desk referring to Antonio bribing the mayor.

"And you expect him to have this information laying around?"

"Maybe?" I shook my head and closed the first drawer— piles of useless paperwork on shipments. "He strikes me as someone who likes to brag. So, do I think he might have something here? Yes. However, I won't know until I search." I looked up at him. "You want to help me?"

He looked at my hands. "You have another pair of gloves? I'm not leaving my fingerprints on anything in this office."

I laughed. "No, just the one set." Mental note: always pack an extra pair of gloves.

I searched the next two drawers. Nothing.

I moved over to the file cabinet. "So," I started. "Why don't you tell me about the three signs you know you've found the one?" I was proud I managed to say that without squeaking. Not having to face him might have had something to do with it.

I felt him behind me but didn't turn around. "Okay, well, the first sign is that you truly enjoy their company."

I closed the first drawer and moved on to the next. "Outside of you giving me a ride to school every day and freeloading dinner every once and a while, we don't spend that much time together." Now that I said it out loud, it did seem like a lot of time. I mean, he came to dinner at least three times a week. His father never learned how to cook when his mother left them six years ago.

"Who said I was referring to us?"

I paused, my eyes blinking rapidly. My heart plummeted. He had to be talking about us. Didn't he?

Marcus laughed. "Just kidding. I'm definitely talking about us."

"Oh." I should slap him. "Okay, well, I stand by my original statement." My heart thumped in my chest.

"Vicki, I'm sitting here helping you search this man's office. Illegally. And I can't think of a time I've been happier."

"So." I shut the file cabinet and turned to him. "You're saying you know I'm your true love based on us spending time together? Come on."

He got up off the desk and moved toward me. My hands shook and my eyes went wide. *Please kiss me again. Please.*

"Why do you think I always wait after school for you to get out of your journalism class? Or sit out in my car in the morning even though you always make us late for school?"

"Um," I squeaked. He smiled and looked at the stack of pictures I had clutched in my hands.

"What did you find?"

I blinked a few times, trying to recall why I was holding pictures. I handed them to him. "I found..." I cleared my throat. "I think..." Humiliation clawed at me. Why was I acting like some lovesick teenager? Okay, maybe I was a lovesick teenager. It didn't mean I had to act like one. He was doing this on purpose. Had to be. I let that thought penetrate the fog he'd created and pointed to the picture of a man and woman on a yacht. "Doesn't that look like Bunny?" That was so not her name.

He studied the picture. "Yeah, it does. Only with blonde hair."

"Look who she's standing next to."

"Oh my God!" He looked up at me, eyes wide. "That's the deputy mayor."

I took the picture from him. So, maybe it wasn't the mayor Antonio made a deal with, but the deputy mayor. Yet, the deputy mayor didn't have the authority to approve, or rush, Antonio's business application. Or did he?

"I knew something was off about Bunny." I turned the picture over. Written on the back was, "Margaret Bisset and Daniel Long." "So now the question is, who is using who? It's clear Bunny, or shall I say Margaret is in charge."

"I have to agree with you on that."

I looked at the picture again. "So, why does he have this picture of her and the deputy mayor?"

"Confusing?"

I nodded. "Very confusing." I shoved the picture, along with the more risqué, ones in my backpack, as well as a copy of the business application for the club. The dates were off, and I needed to review my notes to figure out why.

"Maybe you should just photograph the evidence and leave the originals."

I smiled. "Normally, I would have. But I want Antonio to sweat a little. So when I'm done making copies, I will mail them to him."

"Pretty dirty of you, Vicki." He smiled. "And very sexy."

Heat spread throughout my entire body. Marcus moved toward me. "Reason two?" He asked.

"Yes." My voice sounded small.

He tipped my chin up. "You can't stop thinking about them."

"You… you think about me?"

"All. The. Time." His lips touched mine and a loud bang sounded.

We both jerked apart and stared at the open doorway.

"I didn't know you were coming back, Mr. Vargas. I still have more to clean."

"Fine. I will be in my office. Come get me when you're done."

Oh crap! We were literally trapped. We couldn't shut the door and couldn't walk out. There wasn't a closet in the room. That left the small space behind the couch. We both must have come to the same conclusion at the same time. We dove behind the couch, and I landed on top of Marcus just as Antonio walked in the room.

It was then that I realized my backpack was on the floor next to his desk. My eyes rounded as I stared down at Marcus, willing him to understand my fear. He mouthed, "What?" and I mouthed, "Backpack."

My heart rammed in my chest, and the blood rushing in my ears rendered me momentarily deaf. I didn't have a plan. I closed my eyes, and Marcus wrapped his strong arms around me.

Antonio's chair squeaked, and my stomach plummeted. Was he getting up? Did he notice the backpack? Marcus tapped my cheek and I opened my eyes. "Are you okay?" he mouthed. I shook my head no.

I'd been in some scary situations before, but never anything like this. Yes, I believed Antonio was full of hot air, but I had no way of knowing if my assumption was correct or not.

And to top it all off, Marcus was in this mess with me. I leaned down and whispered in his ear, "I'm sorry."

He smiled and shook his head. "First sign," he whispered back, and my heart skipped a beat.

A phone started ringing. I had a brief panic attack before I realized it was Antonio's.

"Yes," he answered.

There was a long pause. The sound of a zipper being pulled down froze the blood in my veins. *Oh God, no!* Marcus cupped the back of my head and pulled me to him. I buried my face in the crook of his neck while I tried to stop my heart from escaping my chest. It wasn't a matter of *if* Antonio was looking through my backpack, more of which compartment was he searching. I'd shoved the evidence in the back.

"I will be there in twenty." His chair squeaked again.

"Mr. Vargas. I'm ready to clean in here now."

"Is this your backpack?"

"Yes, yes."

"What do you need a flashlight for?"

I let out a silent breath of relief. As long as he didn't search any further, I'd be okay.

"The lights went out last night. I thought I'd make sure I was prepared."

Good! Jesse was quick on his feet.

"Here. Next time, let me know about it."

"Yes sir, Mr. Vargas sir."

"Sir. Yes, I like that." Antonio chuckled.

After a short pause, Jesse said, "Vicki?"

I reluctantly stood up, Marcus following me. "Thank you," I said as I made my way around the couch. "You handled that well." The flight-or-fight mode was still coursing through my body, making my hands shake.

Jesse handed me the backpack. "That was too close. Did you get what you needed?"

"Yes, I did. And again, thank you."

He smiled. "If you bring that slimy bastard down, I will buy you dinner." He looked at Marcus. "Both of you."

Even though we had enough incriminating evidence for a story, it wasn't enough for me. I had to figure out what the connection was. How the key players all fit together. Marcus and I sat in his car, staring at the municipal building where the mayor's offices were.

"Are you sure about this, Vicki?"

I looked at the darkened building. *Was* I sure about this? This story had taken a turn in a direction I wasn't ready for. And I doubted it was as simple as I'd first believed. Not only that, but the mayor didn't seem to be the one involved. I needed more information. More than what I'd found tonight. Especially about Margaret. Maybe she was the real story, playing both men.

I turned to Marcus. "Tell me what number three is."

His eyebrows drew together and he studied me for a minute. It made me smile.

"Now?"

I shifted so that my body was completely facing his. "Yes, now."

He ran his hands through his hair. "Okay." He nodded as if reassuring himself. "Well, number three is you can't keep your hands off them." I watched his throat work as he swallowed.

"Interesting."

He looked at me, eyes wide, and I erupted in laughter. He pulled back as if I'd slapped him. I leaned over, cupped the back of his head, and pulled him into a brief kiss.

"Oh, Marcus," I said, staring into those warm eyes. "That is such bullshit. Did you forget my family owned *El Alma Tribune*? Did you think I didn't read the paper? I've read every single column Jeanne ever wrote." I sat back. "She has never published a list like that."

He chuckled. "You caught me."

We both grew silent, staring at one another.

"What made you come up with that?" More importantly, why? Despite my laughing at his ridiculous list, I was still filled with nervous jitters.

"I was having a hard time figuring out how to talk to you. And when I saw you with Jason, I knew that if I didn't say something, I'd lose my opportunity. We graduate in a month."

"We live right next to each other."

"Yeah, but I remember you saying you were going to school out of state."

"So, you thought we'd have some summer fling," I squeaked.

He smiled. "Yes and no." He shook his head. "I don't know, Vicki. I just wasted so much time being scared to talk to you, I couldn't waste any more. If that meant we only had the summer…" He shrugged. "Then I would have to settle for that."

I glanced over at the municipal building. "Yeah, well, I think my plans have changed. El Alma Junior College has a perfectly good journalism program." I turned back to him. "Going there would give me the opportunity to dig deeper into all these connections."

"So you don't have enough for your story?"

"Oh, I plan on writing a story about Antonio, or shall I say, Eugene and his connection with the deputy mayor. But the bigger story is Margaret. And for that, I'm going to have to do some digging. But first, I have to copy what I have and return the originals to Antonio's office without him knowing. He might get suspicious of Jesse. And if I have to continue digging, I don't want to lose my inside man." I should have thought of that before, but I was way too preoccupied with Marcus and his list.

Yes, the more I thought about it, the more I realized I could be looking at the biggest scoop El Alma had ever seen. I didn't want to rush it. And, it could mean a trip to Miami during the summer. Now *that* would be an adventure.

"So, what now?" Marcus asked.

"Now." I climbed on his lap. "We spend a little time on reason number three."

He gave me a crooked grin. "Here?"

"I thought you knew me so well." I leaned down and kissed him. The kaleidoscope of butterflies could be a problem, but the way Marcus oh-so-casually cupped my butt was nice.

I leaned back and studied him. "Are you up to exploring reason number one?"

He laughed. "What did you have in mind?"

"How about a trip to Miami when we get out of school?"

"So, we're chasing the story?"

I kissed him lightly on the lips. "Oh, yeah, we are so chasing the story."

To be continued...

Other Published Works

READ MORE BY C. VONZALE LEWIS

Monsters – *Flicker; Stories of Inner Flame*
– Filles Vertes Publishing – 2018

Lineage – The Parliament House – 2019

The Sin Exchange - *Masks; a Mardi Gras Anthology*
– Filles Vertes Publishing – 2020

FOR MORE, VISIT
www.cvonzalelewis.com

Culture Clash on Main

Michael

I rushed into the used bookstore a half hour late for Momma's fundraiser. She and her cadre of volunteers and donors always held the Friends of the Library event a week before school started. I navigated my way through the well-dressed crowd, only stopping when the mayor of Rock Hill intercepted me.

"Michael! Great to see you."

"You too, sir."

He laid an arm around my shoulders and turned me from the group he'd been chatting up. "How have things been since the funeral? You and your momma okay?"

I tried not to stiffen. "We are, thank you. Grandpa's been checking in on us every day."

"Good. Good. As it should be." He nodded toward the back of the room and winked. "Saw him over there stuffing his face. You know how that old coot is."

I gave him the expected laugh, promised we'd get to the state championships, and made my way to Momma. I found her entertaining a group of ladies.

"There you are, Michael." Elise Bradford paired a huff of motherly frustration with a phony grin—for the benefit of her friends, no doubt.

"Sorry, Momma." Leaning in, I gave her a peck on the cheek and whispered an explanation. "I was at his grave."

Momma's breath hitched, but her face remained as passive as ever in front of her friends. I squeezed her shoulder. In keeping up with appearances, I greeted her team and offered to refill their drinks. My parents brought me up to be a gentleman, and nothing calmed Momma's "frayed sensibilities" more than seeing me perform as her star son.

After an hour of fake chuckles and several dozen handshakes, Amy Whitten and her mother walked in. I cursed under my breath. Momma heard and discreetly pinched my arm as she laughed at something Mrs. Barnes had said. After the woman moved on, Momma spun toward me, her back to the room, and frowned.

"Now listen to me." If her tone could wag its finger, it would have. "You will reconcile with Amy and invite her to dinner this weekend."

"You seem to have forgotten." I forced a smile. "We broke up again this summer." I'd lost count of how many times I'd called it off in the last three years.

"She's your high school sweetheart—"

"Momma? Can we not do this here?"

Her eyes flashed, but she didn't say more. She turned and waved at Amy and her mother.

Amy knew we weren't couple material, but like Momma, she refused to accept that I didn't want a happily *never* after with her just to please our parents. Our dads had grown up together, become lawyers, and then opened up their law firm. Along with the Bradford family legacy hanging over my head, a future with Amy wasn't just set in stone; it was as sacred as Pastor Thomas quoting biblical prophecy.

Dressed in a white summer dress and spotless white shoes— the color deliberate, no doubt—Amy sidled up to me. She stopped short of linking her arm around mine. *Smart girl.*

Mrs. Whitten's smile flashed brighter than the pearls around her neck. "Michael, how lovely to see you. It's been a while."

"Same to you." I didn't know what Amy's mother thought of me after I'd broken up with her daughter again. It had been right after Dad's funeral, and I'd had it. But according to

Momma, not a one of them truly believed this would be the actual end of our relationship.

The polite drivel went on for another ten minutes. I clenched and unclenched my hands, the urge to flee overwhelming. When Gramps thumped my shoulder and snagged my attention, I nearly choked on my relief.

"So, son, how's the team shaping up?" he asked. Our circle widened to include him and Grandma.

Before I could reply, Amy did what I was dreading. She linked her arm through mine— because of our audience—and looked at me with heart eyes that churned my stomach. I knew she was pretending, but I wasn't a jerk. I dragged on a smile, finished the conversation, and peeled her arm off me as soon as I could.

"Sorry, Momma. I gotta go. I'll swing back and pick you up."

She masked her annoyance quickly. "What's so important you have to leave your darling date stranded?"

If I'd been on the football field, I'd have whipped off my helmet and hurled it a good twenty yards. I balled my hands instead.

Amy and her mother had sense enough to move away. Momma inhaled and dropped all pretense of civility then. "Nothing would've made your daddy prouder than for you to marry his best friend's daughter. Every relationship has ups and downs, Michael. Ours did, too." She blinked back tears. I had no doubt they were genuine. I cleared my throat and studied my shined shoes. "But in the end," she continued, "we honored the family legacy and got married. You're right for each other, just like your grandparents, your great-grandparents, and your daddy and I were."

All Bradford men who married their high school sweethearts and became successful lawyers.

What a legacy.

Since Dad had died, Momma had clung to the idea that everything could be normal again. Indulging her felt like the least I could do.

I sighed.

"I know, Momma. I need time." I forced myself to kiss her cheek and left, ignoring her protest.

Pushing through the exit, I loosened my tie and guzzled in the August air. Even with the sun dipping below the horizon, the mugginess stuck to my skin. The bookstore sat on Main Street in Old Town Rock Hill where Great-Grandpa Robert had proposed to his high school sweetheart at the 1952 centennial celebration. They'd probably strolled along the very street I was stomping down.

I needed a place to lay low. Sure as I could throw a football, Momma would be sending Amy after me.

Shreya

"Shreya?" Mom stepped out from the café's kitchen. She scanned the dining area, as if there were customers, and then faced me, pulling out several sheets of paper from her apron pocket. "These are for you."

"A new recipe?" I asked.

We'd opened our restaurant on Main Street two days ago, and other than a sign proclaiming us to be Nita's Indian Café, no one really knew *what* to expect. People had peered through the front windows enough times that I had to keep the Windex handy, but only one woman had entered. She'd marveled at our fusion menu and eight different chai selections but ended up buying a latte.

When Mom had talked about opening the café, I'd told her a small town in South Carolina might not be the place to experiment with Indian food and chai. She'd disagreed.

I unfolded the papers and held in a groan.

Mom's eyes gleamed. "Janviben emailed me her son's Harvard essays from last year. Now you can draft your own as practice."

Yay. I exhaled slowly and nodded.

Nineteen countries in seventeen years. Going away for college was *so* not on my radar.

Diplomats didn't usually relocate that often, but Mom was a "special bean," as my stepdad, Tim, described her. She spoke eleven languages and had enough experience to make her invaluable to the State Department. And now that we'd finally settled down, I'd be moving *again* next summer—to Harvard, if Mom had her way. She'd been a student there before she'd gotten pregnant with me and dropped out. Sure, she'd gone on to get several degrees from local colleges and online universities, but apparently, she wanted to live out her fantasy of being a Harvard grad through me. With applications due in a couple of months, I had to find the courage to shatter her dreams.

"Shreya? Are you listening?" Mom poked my arm.

"Hm? Oh. No, um..."

She huffed. "Clean up out here and then close. I'll be upstairs if you need me."

When Mom and Tim had finally decided to give up the nomadic life, he'd accepted a prestigious teaching position in economics at Winthrop University. We lived in an apartment above the café, and even though we'd only moved here two months ago from Moscow, it already felt like home. It might only be because Tim's job and the café anchored us here like roots, but that was enough. It was a start.

I crouched behind the display case and wiped down the inside until the jingling bell above our door caught my attention. A tall man walked in. I stood and watched him glance back outside as if making sure no one had followed him. He wasn't peeking *inside*, so that was new.

Once he turned to check out the place, I realized he wasn't an older man but someone younger, closer to my age. The suit had thrown me. And he wasn't hard on the eyes, if you liked that boring blond, blue-eyed, and built sort of thing.

Glued to the front entry, he seemed unsure of what to do.

I cleared my throat. "If you're hiding from someone, it's probably best not to stand by the windows."

He did a double take when he found me beside the register and then smiled. With a loose stride, he navigated around the tables with an agility and power that screamed *athlete*.

"Was I that obvious?" The rich sound of his drawl pegged him as a local.

I shrugged. "I've been running from the law all my life. Takes one to know one, right?"

He laughed, and *that* was in no way boring. When he stepped up to the counter, I swallowed. This guy appeared totally different up close... better. How could a laugh possibly increase anyone's hotness factor?

His gaze roamed over the place, lingering on the pops of jewel-toned colors and etched brass fixtures. The décor was a bit gimmicky for my taste, but this had been Mom's dream. He surveyed the bright floor pillows and low tables. Mom thought adding some alternate seating would give patrons an *experience*.

"Great hideout you got here," he said, grinning. "There's a lot to see. You're almost camouflaged by default."

I tapped my temple. "By design." I motioned to the board hanging from the ceiling. "Want something to drink?"

He contemplated his options for a few moments, his forehead wrinkling several times, as if unsure about a particular flavor combination. It gave me the opportunity to examine him—marvel at how his solid jawline and sharp cheekbones could support such soft eyes—eyes that caught me ogling.

I turned and wiped up some imaginary crumbs on the counter.

"I didn't know there were so many chai choices." His voice carried a hint of amusement.

Damn. He knew I'd been checking him out. I faced him in time to catch the flush on his cheeks. *Ok.* That was unexpected. An answering heat climbed my neck.

"Like there are coffee combinations?" I let my slightly breathless words carry a playful edge.

"Ah, touché. Sorry. I don't know much about Indian food."

"Well, lesson number one, chai is a beverage, not a food." A technicality, yes, but it was the best I could do considering he was muddling my senses. If Mom was here, she would've dismissed his apology and jumped into an oral dissertation about Indian tea and flavor profiles and likely offered a recommendation after thoroughly quizzing him on his beverage tastes. *Yeah… not my style.*

"Oh, I'm—"

Before he could apologize again, I waved it off. "Don't worry about it. Do you like sweet or spicy?" I channeled my mom despite myself.

"I can handle spicy."

I smashed my lips together at the cheesy line, hoping not to laugh.

He scrunched closed his eyes. "Uh… I mean, never mind." His features soured. "That came out wrong… again. Sorry?"

"How about I make the ginger chai?" A chuckle escaped anyway.

He scratched the back of his head, his cheeks reddening again, and agreed.

When I finally brought his cup and saucer to the pickup counter, he stayed there, watching me clean up.

"It smells amazing," he said.

"Thanks. Sweeteners are over to your left."

Out of the corner of my eye, I peeked as he sipped hesitantly. Then he blew on it and took a larger gulp. He smiled, and when he lifted his head, I looked away, not wanting him to catch me.

"This reminds me of fall and my grandma's ginger snap cookies."

I beamed at the image. "Thanks."

"I'm Michael Bradford, by the way."

"Shreya Sanghani. My mom's Nita." I motioned to the window sign. "We just opened."

"Awesome. Do you go to school here in Rock Hill? I don't remember seeing you around."

Was he implying he would've remembered me? Or would I have stood out because I was Indian? A ribbon of apprehension threaded through me. Would he end up being like all the rest? "Probably because we only moved here two months ago. I'll be at Prep next week when school starts."

His face lit up. "Hey, I'll be a senior there."

I returned his expression. I couldn't help it. "Me too."

He told me about the school and how their football team was poised to win another state championship—not that I understood the game. *That* had him choking on his chai. I found myself standing opposite him, my arms folded on the counter, laughing and soaking up his *Wiki*-like explanation of the sport.

"Anyway," he said. "Our school loves football, but they're also fanatical about prepping us for college essays."

I made a face. "My mom could work there then. She wants me to go to Harvard, but…" I shook my head, stopping myself from oversharing. I'd been here way too many times. *Make a new friend and open up too quickly. Check. They introduce me to their friends. Check. Bite my tongue when the group makes me feel like an outsider. Check.*

Because if I didn't, my new friend would call me "too sensitive."

"I can understand an overbearing mother," he said, his tone soft as he stared into his now empty cup. His shift in mood unsettled me.

When the bell above the door jingled, we both turned. He spun back toward me, grimacing. The girl who charged in was obviously the person Michael had been hiding from. *Lover's spat? Obsessed stalker?*

"Sorry," I whispered to him. "I left my invisibility cloak at home."

Michael barked out a laugh and grinned, his spirits lightening like I'd hoped. If eyes *were* the windows to our soul, he gifted me with an awe-inspiring view of his—so carefree and inviting. My heart reacted as if I were strapped into a parachute and standing at the lip of an open plane.

Who would willingly jump? Not me. Not anymore.

"There you are," the doll-like girl said to Michael. She inspected the colorful interior like she would a spider web to avoid and glided into place beside him. "Your mom wants us to—"

"Jesus." Michael sidestepped her. "For once, can you drop it?"

I hightailed it back to the display case to give them privacy, tamping down my inconvenient curiosity about who she was. Their hushed argument finally ended, and they came to the register.

He took out his wallet. "How much do I owe you?" he asked.

Before I could answer, his friend stomped her foot. "Aren't you going to buy me anything?"

He froze, scowling at the ten he'd pulled out. After a quick glance at me, he bit out a "Sure."

She tapped a manicured fingernail against her chin as she contemplated her chai options. "Isn't there anything normal to drink?"

Normal? I rolled my lips between my teeth then pointed to the other board with all the coffee drinks. Michael glared at her but said nothing.

"I'll have a mocha latte."

I asked her which size, then got to work. While I packed the coffee, she rambled on about a library fundraiser and then suggested they go somewhere "normal" to eat. My face burned.

"I'm Momma's ride," Michael snapped.

The fact he didn't call her out said it all. But why would he? He'd just met me. I was nothing to him.

Regardless, the disappointment choked me. He *would* be like every other new friend.

Before I'd moved here, I'd promised myself I'd speak up— even if I lost friends. I wouldn't be a doormat in order to fit in.

As usual, Mom's words echoed in my mind. *Compromise is essential in a healthy, balanced relationship.* But every time I'd tried to compromise, I'd ended up sacrificing my feelings instead.

The girl stepped closer to him. "Your momma would be happy to ride with mine if she knew we were going out."

"Not happening."

"You can't escape forever, you know."

The sound of the steamer drowned out his response. Once I capped the to-go cup—hoping they'd grasp the hint and leave— I slammed it down by the register a little harder than I'd intended.

"Sweeteners are to your left," I said.

I could feel Michael staring at me, but I didn't dare meet his eyes. He held out some cash and cleared his throat as if to get my attention. I accepted the money and ignored him.

"Uh… Shreya, this is Amy. Amy, Shreya. She just moved here. She'll be at Prep too."

I gave her a small wave, closed the register, and handed him his change.

"Oh?" She wrinkled her brow, as if she realized his introduction meant he'd been talking to another girl. She scrutinized me like I was the spider on the web she'd passed through. "What country did you come from?"

I froze, and Michael cursed. Technically, I *did* just move from outside the U.S., but considering I didn't have an accent, she'd only asked because of the color of my skin.

Bite my tongue when the "group" makes me feel like an outsider. Big red check.

How many times would I have to hear what the question implied—that I didn't belong? *She's a customer. Be nice.* More of Mom's diplomatic words came to me. *She could simply be making conversation.*

"Russia," I answered. Trying to take the high road only earned me a case of road rash though.

"Oh," Amy said. "I performed in Tchaikovsky's *Swan Lake* last year. Remember, Michael?"

He had his head bowed and was pinching the bridge of his nose. "She's joking, Amy."

His words slapped me as though *I* was being the cruel one.

"No, I'm not," I said. "Just because I'm Indian-*American*"—I gave Amy a pointed look—"doesn't mean I didn't live in Moscow."

His face fell. "Crap, I-I didn't mean…"

My resolve wobbled, but I couldn't invest in another friendship only to have the inevitable happen. I crossed my arms to hide trembling fingers. I would not regret speaking up.

"Forget it. Is that all? I need to close."

"Uh…" Amy peered at Michael then me. "Well, see you around, Shera."

"Shreya," I said, pronouncing it slowly, my eyes narrowed.

With a curt smile, Amy sauntered out, but Michael didn't budge.

"Sorry," he whispered. "We—I didn't mean…"

I shrugged. A jumbled mess of emotions whirled through me. He'd eventually defend his friends because it would be easier, and then I'd be the troublemaker by being "too sensitive" or "not playing nice."

Michael rubbed the back of his neck. "Intent versus impact," he muttered.

My eyes widened.

Blue irises locked onto me. "What I intended isn't important if I hurt your feelings. I am sorry." He stuffed his hands in his pockets and walked out.

His insight surprised me—and confused me even more.

Michael

The first-day-of-school mob seemed larger than last year. I reached Mr. Osborne's first period history and carefully peeked inside. Amy would be here, and sure enough, she sat up front. *Damn.*

Before I could decide how I'd play this, someone brushed past me, knocking my backpack off my shoulder. "Hey—"

"Sorry—"

We both froze on either side of the door. *Shreya.*

Expressive brown eyes blinked up at me. If the smile on my face stretched any wider, I'd look like some lovelorn sap. I shut that down real fast though because she wasn't smiling at all.

Ever since the night at the café, I'd replayed what had happened a hundred times. It embarrassed me how things had ended, but it was more than that. We'd hurt her—*I'd* hurt her. Dad used to say that being a true southern gentleman wasn't only about respect and manners but also humility.

And I'd been wrong not to call Amy out for her insults, and to assume Shreya would belittle her by lying about Moscow.

"I didn't mean to…" Shreya pointed at my bag.

"No worries. I was blocking the door, so…"

She bit her lip and glanced inside the classroom. "You're in here too?"

Waves of her dark hair fell around her shoulders, and strands of it had caught under the strap of her bag. At the café, I'd wondered how long it was. She'd worn it in a messy pile on top of her head, and she'd kept tucking locks of it behind her ear while listening to me. I'd wanted to order another five chais and talk to her all night—before Amy had come and ruined everything.

"Michael?" Shreya lifted her eyebrows.

"Um—oh, yeah. I'm in here too." I waved her in, trailing after her like a puppy. At least I didn't offend her this time.

Without meaning to, I followed Shreya past Amy—ignoring her glower—and toward the only remaining cluster of seats in the back. Empty desks dotted the front, but if I changed course now, Shreya would think I was avoiding her—which I'd rather not have her believe. *Geez.* When the heck did I start obsessing about crap like this?

When she settled into her chair, I slid into the seat beside her. Shreya's brow furrowed, but she said nothing. She faced the teacher and drank from her travel mug as Mr. Osborne started class.

At the end of the period, Mr. O described a multi-media presentation we'd have to do in pairs, and my insides knotted. Amy would guilt me into being her partner if I let her. *Please assign us someone.* When it was clear he wouldn't, I scrambled to my feet at the sound of the bell and asked David sitting on the other side of me to be my partner. His girlfriend stepped closer to him and put an end to that. I spun to the guy who'd sat in front of me, but he'd already left.

Amy marched up my aisle. Being sacked by two three-hundred-pound defensive ends would've been better than watching her make a scene.

"Michael—"

"Sorry, not gonna pair up with you."

Amy scowled. "Our families expect us—"

I didn't wait to hear the rest and sprinted down the other aisle instead. No doubt, I was a coward.

As several people cleared the path, I moved forward and almost tripped over someone crouched on the ground. Shreya was wiping coffee off the floor. Her other hand held her open mug. I couldn't have been happier.

"Let me help." I knelt beside her, grabbed the almost empty travel pack of tissues she had, and leaned close. "Please tell me you'll be my partner," I whispered.

Amy rounded the aisle behind us.

Shreya gaped at me. "Uh, I don't know if that's a smart idea."

"Hey, Shera." Amy's snide voice could annoy the devil.

Shreya rolled her eyes. "Hey, Amy—and it's Shreya." She exaggerated each syllable. "You know, like Tchaikovsky, but shorter." Snatching the tissues from me, she leaped to her feet. I did too.

"Sure, Michael, I'll be your partner." She said it loud enough for Amy to hear, and I couldn't help but smile. Shreya muttered something that sounded like "doormat" and stormed off. Maybe now I'd have my chance to make amends.

"See ya, Amy." Thankfully, we had no more classes together.

I stood outside the classroom and scanned the hallway for Shreya. Call it pride, but I had to convince her working with me wouldn't be terrible. Craning my neck and maneuvering through the crowd, I spotted her and jogged past Andrew and the guys to catch up to her.

"Shreya!"

She jerked to a stop, causing a pileup of grumbling students, and moved to the side by a bank of lockers.

"Hey," I said, coming up beside her. "Thank you. I'll be a great partner. Promise. I figured we should decide on when to meet. My practice and game schedules are pretty tight, so I…" My words died off as I noticed her stiff posture. One hand had a white-knuckled grip on her backpack strap while her other arm wrapped across her waist.

She was *uncomfortable*… with me.

The thought bruised like a tackle to the gut—and not because of my pride. I'd hurt her bad enough to make her uneasy. Even though we stood a foot apart, I stepped away to give her more space but not without a pang of disappointment. "Listen, if you really don't think this is a good idea, I'd totally understand if you wanna switch partners. No hard feelings."

Shreya's mouth dropped into an "O" and her cheeks flushed. A second later, she pushed off the wall and relaxed her shoulders. "I, uh… No, I'm fine. It's just that…" Her gaze darted around us before settling on the ground, and then, as if deciding something, she straightened her posture and lifted her eyes. "We moved around a lot, like nineteen-countries-in-seventeen-years *a lot*. It isn't always easy fitting in, trusting new people—"

"Michael, my man, let's roll." Andrew and the guys invaded our space. "Can't be late. Coach's rules."

If Shreya worried about fitting in, I had the power to fix that. "Hold up. Lemme introduce you all. Shreya, this is my best friend and wide receiver on the team, Andrew." I named off the rest of them as she gave a cautious smile and a little wave. "Guys, this is Shreya. She's new to Rock Hill. Her momma's got a café on Main."

They all welcomed her, and a rush of pride spread through me.

"Just moved, huh? Where from?" Andrew asked.

"Moscow, actually," she said.

Jake, one of my linemen, hefted his eyebrows. "No, shit. So where are you from?"

Shreya's jaw popped, and my proud buzz fizzled. Jake's question was as rude as Amy's had been.

"Is my accent not American enough?" she asked, her tone clipped. "I should go. See ya guys." She bolted down the hall.

Crap. I glared at Jake.

"What?" he asked. Andrew whacked the back of his head, and I dashed after Shreya.

"Hey," I said when I caught up. "I'm sorry. Jake's really a nice guy. He's nothing like Amy—"

"Of course, he's not." Shreya stopped and rounded on me, her eyes blazing. "But how would you like it if everyone constantly reminded you that you didn't belong? That you looked different? That you spoke with a weird accent? And then imagine if they did those things in your own country."

"People can be cruel—"

"That's just it. Did *you* think Jake was cruel? You just defended him, so I guess not, but I'm supposed to grin and bear it, right? Otherwise *I'm* the bitch, the one who's too sensitive, the one causing problems." She heaved a breath and closed her eyes for a beat. "I know he was trying to make conversation, but pointing out I'm not from around here because of the color of my skin isn't being any sort of *nice*. He could've asked a million other questions. When you hear that stuff once or twice, it's no big deal. One mosquito isn't so bad, right? But a swarm of them? It gets old real fast."

Jesus. "You're right. I'm sorry." The crowd thinned as everyone found their classrooms.

Her gaze met mine and softened. "Thanks for introducing me, but I really don't need to fit in that badly." She twisted her hands around her bag's strap. "Let's just work on the project and leave it at that, okay?"

I nodded, bowled over by my helplessness, my anger on her behalf, and an urge to make it right.

She gave me a half-smile and disappeared down the hall.

Shreya

Over the next two weeks, Michael hadn't avoided me like I'd expected. If anything, he ran into me regularly. He'd check up on me but would never stick around for long. I couldn't blame him. In case he'd regretted being my partner, I'd offered to switch, but he'd refused.

We'd worked on our project for the first time last night. The awkwardness of being alone with him irked me because I couldn't stop wondering if his kindness was a sort of penance. It had me on edge, like watching a paper cut about to happen in slow motion.

I sat by myself at lunch since the girl I usually joined wasn't in fourth period. The wild ruckus of the cafeteria soon became white noise as I scrolled through my phone. I'd barely finished chewing a bite of my sandwich before two jean-clad legs straddled the bench beside me.

"Holy crap," I said, grasping my chest and nearly dropping my phone.

"Sorry." Michael grinned. He wore a blue Darius Rucker T-shirt that caused the color of his irises to pop. I might have gawked at him for longer than appropriate.

"You gonna eat that? It smells incredible." He pointed to the second half of the sandwich Mom had made. I nudged it toward him, eyeing the nearby students sneaking peeks our way.

"Where's your lunch?"

"Already ate it. What is this?" he asked with his mouth full.

"An Indian butter chicken sub. Mom's version of a meatball sub."

He hummed. "Damn. This is amazing."

I let out a laugh. "It's just a sandwich." He'd also enjoyed Mom's version of a shrimp po' boy yesterday with its tandoori spices.

"Not really." He absently picked at the bread before swallowing. "You've lived in all these cool places and eaten things I can't even imagine. I wish I could visit half the countries you have. Instead, I'm stuck here, expected to live the same life the last three generations of Bradfords have."

I scoffed. "Seriously? I've never celebrated my birthday in the same city twice, and I don't even have a best friend because it's too hard to keep in touch once I move. Do you know what I'd do to have *your* life? A stable home, extended family I could see regularly, a true circle of friends... *roots*?" My chest rose and fell with my outburst, and the shame of how ungrateful I sounded pricked at my eyes. I stared at my lap and curled my fingers into a ball.

Michael wiped his hands and reached out, gently prying open my fist. Frozen, I watched him brush his thumb along the top of my palm, leaving me speechless at how he both cooled and warmed my skin.

I glanced around the cafeteria, but no one seemed to notice our clasped hands under the table.

His lips quirked. "The only time I'm lucky enough to learn something about you is when you're yelling at me."

"I wasn't yelling at you." Hearing him laugh, I *tsked*, hiding my smile. "Sorry. So why do you feel stuck?"

Michael exhaled. "Because of my family's legacy." He told me how he was expected to become a lawyer and marry *his* high school sweetheart—Amy. My stomach lurched, and I yanked my hand from his grip.

"No, wait," he said. "It's complicated with our families, especially since my dad died. Momma's having a hard time letting go, but it is over between us. She and my mom just haven't accepted it."

After a moment of studying him, I nodded. "Sorry about your dad." I almost covered his hand with mine but decided against it. "I totally get 'complicated.' I don't know how I'm gonna tell my mom I'd rather stay here in Rock Hill and go to a university like Winthrop, instead of moving *again* to go to Harvard."

"You don't seem to have a problem telling *me* anything." His blue eyes twinkled as he took another bite.

If only my issues were as simple as that.

Michael

By the time October rolled around, the sugar maples had mostly changed colors and the city had planted mums in hanging baskets along Main Street. Mrs. Sanghani's chai blends had become popular too, judging by how many people had come in today while Shreya and I worked on our project.

We sat on floor cushions in front of a short table piled high with library books. We were trying to decide on the final look of our presentation, but nothing Shreya suggested sunk in. Instead, I'd catch a whiff of her floral scent and my mind would wander.

I had it bad. I wanted to ask her to the Fall Frolic at the Greenway, but I didn't think she trusted me yet.

And it ate at me.

After what had happened with Jake, I'd been Googling what I could about racism and microaggressions. Despite having disregarded Shreya's feelings that day, I hoped I could earn back her trust. At least she wasn't indifferent to me like she was to Jake.

An hour after the café closed, we happened to be sitting smack up against each other so I could see her laptop over her shoulder. I kept wondering how to ask her out, but the press of her body against mine shot my concentration to hell.

Shreya shifted, as if trying to put space between us.

"Sorry," I said, jerking away. "Is it rude for me to sit that close?" I glanced toward the kitchen where her mom was.

"Rude?" She gaped at me. "What does that even mean?"

Not again. "I feel like I'm gonna cross some cultural line I don't know about."

"By sitting next to me?"

"I don't know!" I ran my fingers through my hair. "I read South Asians were strict about dating, but that their views depended on where they lived in the world, and since you never stayed in one place for long, I didn't know how I should act." I gulped a huge breath.

"Dating?" Her eyes widened. "Me?"

"I mean, just... you know... I-I wanted to learn not to offend you. Jesus. I'm walking on eggshells."

Shreya's expression warmed. "Please don't compare yourself to Amy or Jake."

I snorted. "But I've hurt you too."

"Well, yeah, hearing you defend Jake did upset me." She averted her attention. "But honestly? I was more disappointed than hurt because... I *liked* you."

My pulse whooshed through my ears. "Past tense?"

She scooted closer and shook her head. "I didn't move away because you did something wrong, but because you're distracting in a... can't-catch-my-breath sort of way."

I smiled and reached for her hand. "Thank God, because I really want us to be more than friends." If my heart had been racing a second ago, it was breaking the sound barrier now. "Come to the Fall Frolic with me tomorrow?" *Smooth.*

Her brow wrinkled. "Oh... um... I mean..."

And just like that, my pass into the end zone was intercepted. "Or not, you don't—"

"It's not that I don't want to, but... if it's still complicated between you and Amy and your mom, maybe we shouldn't do this right now?"

I didn't want to admit it, but she was right. To be fair to Shreya, I needed to finally confront Momma about letting go of the legacy.

Shreya

All night I'd replayed how I'd basically rejected Michael yesterday. Was it so wrong to want *un*complicated? What if he chose Amy because his grieving mother pressured him? I couldn't even blame him if he did. I hadn't had the courage to tell Mom about Harvard.

Until this morning.

And it hadn't been so bad. Tim had actually been thrilled I wanted to become a Winthrop Eagle.

Now I needed to have faith in Michael, which was why I was sitting on a bale of itchy hay outside the corn maze at the Greenway.

The scent of pine trees and pumpkin spice filled the air, and even a bit of tractor exhaust when one rumbled past pulling a kids' ride. It was cool enough for jeans and a light sweater—the sleeves of which I'd been fidgeting with while I waited.

What if he comes with Amy?

I was about to stand and pace off my nervous energy when my gaze collided with his. He jogged toward me with a huge grin, and I hopped off the bale in time to be engulfed in his arms.

"Damn," he said, his lips grazing my ear. "You smell better than the funnel cakes."

I laughed. He smelled nice too—like the barest hint of cologne mixed with the outdoors. Michael's heart thumped against my chest, but it could've been my own echoing back. Coming here had definitely been worth it.

Michael pressed his forehead to mine, and I barely registered the ground beneath my feet.

"What does this mean?" he asked. "Please tell me I didn't make a fool of myself."

I loved that he felt comfortable enough in my presence to be a fragile mix of confidence and insecurity, kind of like me. The urge to kiss him overwhelmed me, so I popped up on my toes and pecked him on the lips.

"I wish I had my invisibility cloak," I said.

The skin around his eyes crinkled, and his laugh boomed. With his fingers threaded through mine, he led me toward Lake Haigler. Orange, red, and yellow leaves seemed to glow above the trail, bathing us in a dappled light.

During our short walk, he asked why I'd changed my mind about coming. I told him how I'd broken the news to my parents about Harvard and thought if I had found the courage, maybe he could too. He stopped abruptly, cupped my face, and told me he'd been planning to talk to his mom tonight—that I'd deserved as much. I smiled, and when he leaned in for a kiss, a passing biker called out for us to step to the side. Michael groaned and kept us moving until we reached a bench facing the lake. Sunlight glinted off the ripples in the water, and his grin matched the intensity of my emotions.

A breeze blew a lock of hair in front of my eyes, and he brushed it back. "It'll be the first time I won't have some grand plan for my life. I don't know how Dad would've reacted, but I imagine he would've come around."

I held my palm to his heart. "Are you nervous?"

He shook his head. "Restless and excited, maybe. Like I'm about to run in a touchdown."

"Ugh. A football analogy?" I giggled, and he scoffed.

"You may be a woman of the world, but you've got a lot to learn."

The flash of humor in Michael's eyes reminded me of the first night we'd met, when they seemed like windows into his soul. He wasn't walking on eggshells with me now. Maybe it was like how I knew the top step to our apartment was a smidge taller than the rest. Once I'd made a point to remember it, I'd stopped tripping.

And once he relaxed, he could be himself.

My pause must have freaked him out. "Oh, crap, did I—?"

"No!" I cupped his cheeks this time. Even the curl of his eyelashes seemed familiar to me now. "I like you like this. You're being... *you*. Don't stop, okay?"

He kissed me then. Slow enough to feel the line of stubble above and below his mouth. Slow enough for me to relish his soft lips and how firmly he pressed them against mine. Slow enough for me to smile against him and revel in the sensation of both floating and being anchored for the first time in my life.

Michael

The insistent buzzing in my back pocket finally registered. *Crap. Andrew.* I pulled away and watched reality seep into Shreya's eyes. Her lips were puffy and her gaze soft. She untangled her fingers from my hair and brought them down to my stomach. The warmth of them there felt new and private and had me leaning in for another kiss.

My phone buzzed again.

"Sorry. That's gotta be Andrew." Sure enough, he'd texted several times and called twice. I gave Shreya an apologetic look and dialed him.

"Dude, we're at the wagon ride. Where you at?" Andrew asked as soon as he picked up.

"Hold up a sec." I punched mute and asked Shreya if she wanted to go. "Totally up to you."

A small wrinkle creased her forehead before she gave me a tight smile and nodded. I paused, unsure of how to read her expression. Was she nervous about seeing my friends again? Or something else? She motioned for me to return to Andrew, so I told him we'd be there in fifteen.

I slipped my arm around her and led us to where the tractor-pulled wagon rides began. As we neared, the crowds thickened, festival scents filled the air again, and squealing kids drowned out any noise.

When I saw Amy in the group gathered by Andrew, I almost cursed. Shreya must have sensed my apprehension and put space between us.

I reached out for her. "No, wait—"

"Michael, there you are." Momma came out of nowhere and grabbed my arm. "Amy's here, and I expect you to be attentive. She's devastated you haven't asked her to Homecoming—"

"Momma!" She started at my harsh tone, but I couldn't let her go on. Our talk might not hold till tonight.

Shreya bit her lip, and I nudged her forward. "Momma, I'd like you to meet Shreya. Shreya, this is my mother, Elise Bradford." I couldn't help but smile at the warm greeting Shreya gave her. Momma's awkwardness scared off any good vibes though. I sighed and rubbed my neck.

"Michael," Andrew called. "Over here." The tractor hadn't arrived with the wagon yet, so I held up a finger for him to wait. When I turned back, Momma was waving at Amy, trying to draw her attention. I blocked her view. "Momma! Will you quit?" I whisper-yelled. I didn't want to argue in front of Shreya. Everything was still so... new.

Momma's eyes brimmed with disapproval. "Amy won't be too happy about this." She had the decency to lower her voice, but no doubt Shreya had heard because she inched away and studied her boots.

"Amy and I are *over*," I whispered. "We'll talk tonight, but for now, can you at least be polite to Shreya?"

The steely set of Momma's features didn't bode well. "So, Shreya, tell me about yourself."

"Well, uh…" She licked her lips. "I'm a senior like Michael, and my mom has an Indian Café on Main Street. My stepdad is a professor at Winthrop."

"Oh, how nice." Momma's voice was flat. "Have you been to their café, Michael?"

"Yes, I have. It's—"

"I have too," Amy said, striding up to us. *What the hell?* "It's nothing like Amelie's though."

Shreya raised her chin. "It's not supposed to be. We're not a French bakery."

Amy waved her hand. "Oh, I know. I mean your place doesn't have the normal stuff we're used to."

Not again. Pure rage tensed every one of my muscles. "Who asked you to—?"

Shreya tugged on my forearm as if to stop me. Not wanting to upset her more, I dropped it and laced our fingers together. The move didn't go unnoticed. I glared at Momma.

She smiled and focused on Shreya. "So, where are you and your family from?"

I stiffened, and Shreya rubbed her thumb against my skin to soothe me—*me*—while they flung crap at her. My helplessness gutted me. I didn't want her to think she couldn't handle herself, but I couldn't stand by and do nothing.

"From Russia," Amy said, stepping beside Momma and crossing her arms.

Shreya ignored her. "My mom was a Foreign Service Officer for the State Department, so yes, we just moved from Moscow."

"She's lived in nineteen different countries," I said, oddly proud.

"But Shera's Indian," Amy said.

That's it. We were getting out of here.

"It's *Shreya*," Shreya and I snapped in unison.

"Close enough." Momma waved her hand dismissively.

Shit. Shreya opened her mouth, closed it, and then blinked rapidly. "You know what? I should just go." She tore her hand from mine, and when I made to join her, she held up her palm. "No, don't bother. Nice to meet you, Mrs. Bradford." Shreya turned and bolted.

Momma seized my wrist, but I wrenched it away. She scanned our surroundings, noticing the curious glances.

"How could you?" I asked, resisting the urge to yell. "Did you think insulting her was gonna make me want Amy? That's never going to happen." Amy had been smart enough to wander off.

A flash of desperation crossed Momma's face. "But your father—"

"Wouldn't have wanted me to be miserable my whole life, but apparently you do!" I left a shocked Momma and ran after Shreya, dodging families strolling toward the wagon ride.

Would Shreya really call it quits because of this? Could I blame her if she did?

She jogged toward the exit, but I chased her down, jumping in front of her to block her way.

"Please stop," I said.

She did but then stepped out of reach. The distance killed me.

"I'm so sorry," I said. "I can't believe... I-I don't even..."

Her eyes glistened. "At first, it was your friends. I was scared you'd pick them over me if I spoke my mind, but you didn't, and I'm grateful." She shook her head. "But your *mother*? How can I expect you to choose?"

"I'm not asking you to—"

"You don't have to!" She rubbed her temple. "Look, what Amy and your mother said wasn't your fault, but I'm sorry, I can't be around you and constantly worry about that happening. It'll keep putting you on the spot and eventually you'll feel trapped, and I'll lose out. I-I can't..."

Shreya darted around me and rushed off.

Trapped? My hands grew clammy. Was she right?

"Michael?" Momma's breathless voice came from behind me. When I turned, she had tears in her eyes. My chest tightened.

"I'm so sorry," she said. "I don't want you to be miserable. Ever since your dad..." Her lip quivered. "I want you to be as happy as we were."

Her shoulders slumped, and she wiped her face. Concerned people glanced our way, so I did the gentlemanly thing and gathered Momma against me. I led her down a ways, where several pumpkins and a scarecrow flanked a bale of hay. With our backs to the main path, I cleared off the potted mums for her to sit. She hadn't even broken down like this at the funeral.

I tried to catch a glimpse of Shreya by the exit, but I'd lost her—probably in more ways than one.

And that felt like its own kind of trap.

Shreya

After closing the café, I was cleaning the outside of the espresso machine for the third time when Mom put down the kettle of chai she held and crossed her arms.

"What's wrong?" she asked.

"Nothing."

"Try again."

I hadn't realized how tense my shoulders were because when they slumped, an achy soreness settled in.

I fiddled with a damp rag. "I kinda sorta got my heart bruised today."

"By Michael?" she asked, a mama-bear edge to her voice. "What happened?"

I gave her a rundown of today's mortifying events and how I'd left him.

Mom sighed and enveloped me in a hug. "Some people," she muttered against my hair. She lifted my chin to meet her gaze. "I'm sorry you were hurt. Unfortunately, there will always be someone who'll treat you differently because of the color of your skin. But if there's one thing I've learned—"

"Not another Diplomacy 101 lecture. Please?"

She pursed her lips. "Well, moping around here isn't solving anything, is it? I didn't raise a quitter."

"I'm not quitting," I grumbled. "I'm... I don't know! Re-grouping?" *Liar.*

Guiding me by the shoulders, Mom directed me toward the tables. "Sit." She joined me a minute later with two mugs of hot chai. The fragrant aroma of lemongrass and spices relaxed me.

"Have you talked to Michael yet?" she asked.

I shook my head, watching the milk form a skin on top of the cooling liquid.

Mom blew on her drink and sipped, humming quietly like she always did. "So here's the plan. If you want things to work out, you have to come up with a list of what you want from this relationship. Like, do you want his mother's blessing or not? What do you expect Michael to do about her? Do you want to take it slow? Or merely be friends?" She tipped her mug toward me. "And once you're done, you'll have a sort of blueprint. Something you can share with him to begin negotiating."

"Oh my god, Mom. We're not countries."

"No, but the process of conflict resolution isn't very different."

I worried she'd segue into one of her tirades about the state of the world, but she didn't, thankfully. I blew aside the skin on top of my chai and drank.

Mom set her mug down. "There's nothing wrong with stepping back and regrouping, but don't use that as an excuse to avoid facing problems head-on."

"But how do I deal with his mother? And why should I even have to?" I choked on the sentence. With two words, "*Close enough*," Mrs. Bradford had erased my identity by dismissing my *foreign* name. I hadn't wanted to rail against her because she was Michael's *mother*. I couldn't ask him to take sides. I wouldn't.

Call it a silver lining—tarnished though it might be—but I'd *chosen* not to speak up against her, and it had nothing to do with wanting to gain her acceptance.

That felt huge.

Mom's nostrils flared—a sign she was reining in her anger with a deep breath. If Mom ever met Mrs. Bradford, I doubted diplomacy training would be enough to keep their conversation civil.

Mom placed her palms together and rested her fingertips against her lips. "I know I've told you this before, but you have to communicate your concerns—to Michael and eventually his mother."

"It's not my job to teach her why she was wrong."

"No, it's not." She folded my hands in hers. "But his mother is part of the package. If she's willing to change and learn, then you can decide if you want to play a role in her growth or not. And if she's not, then you have a decision to make about him."

Michael and I had had problems at first, but he'd genuinely tried to learn—and he did. It made it easier to value his intent more than how his words and actions impacted me, but he didn't *expect* me to do that. Could I give his mom the same chance?

After another sleepless night, I trudged alongside Mom the next morning while helping her. Sundays didn't get all that busy at the café, but we usually had a steady stream of Winthrop students coming here to study. And now, with Mom and Tim's blessing, I could be one of them next fall. I smiled to myself.

While Mom was grinding spices to use for the week and the café was empty, I lounged on the floor cushions and worked on my list of what I wanted out of a relationship with Michael.

Acceptance topped the list, along with having the freedom to call out his mom if I needed to—politely, of course. I wasn't going to hide my hurt so she wouldn't feel bad about insulting me. I also wanted Michael to openly support and acknowledge me—especially if she caused us problems. At the same time, I didn't want him to sacrifice his relationship with his only remaining parent.

And finally, I wanted a commitment. His feelings for me had to match my feelings for him. It would totally suck if he thought I was simply a vacation from Amy.

It was a lot to ask when we hadn't officially started dating, but was it really? I had a right to know I could count on him and a right to expect an equal say in things.

I snuggled into the cushions and inspected the ceiling, tapping a pen against my chin. A shadow drew my attention to the front door.

I froze. Michael stood outside, watching me with a travel mug in hand. A hesitant smile played on his face. The tinkling of the bells above the door jarred me out of my trance.

"Hey," he said.

"Hey."

Mom came from the kitchen, ready to greet a customer, but stopped her usual welcome spiel. She gave me an assessing glance before addressing him. "Hello, Michael. Let me know if you'd like anything to eat."

He smiled at her. "Yes, ma'am." Instead of his typical athletic getup, he wore khaki shorts and a denim-colored button-down.

I smoothed my hair and straightened my rumpled T-shirt.

Michael cleared his throat, and I snapped my head up. He'd moved closer and now hovered over me. I scrambled to extract myself from the mound of pillows, but only managed to knock my knee into the table. *Ow.*

"No, don't get up." He put down the travel mug and crawled in beside me, crossing his legs like I had.

"Did you want a chai to go?" I asked, pointing to the container.

He grinned. "No, it's for you."

"Thanks?" Why would he bring me coffee?

He laughed, moved my notebook aside, and slid the mug toward me. I snatched the list and flipped it over so he couldn't read it.

"I, um… made chai for you," he said. "What do you think?"

"Oh." I took a sip and let the flavors coat my tongue. The familiar hit of ginger and pepper lingered, and its warmth settled in my chest. "It's delicious." I gave him a tight smile, returning the drink to the table. "I guess you don't need to come here now." He'd become quite a fan of Mom's chai.

His face fell, and he cursed. "No, Shreya, that's not why. It was supposed to be… I-I was trying…" His face reddened, and he combed his fingers through his hair.

Oh. "Is this a peace offering?"

Michael slumped into the cushions and pressed the heels of his palms into his eyes. "Apparently, not an impressive one."

I bit back a smile and pulled at his arm. His muscles bunched under my touch. "No, it is. I swear."

He linked our fingers and tugged me closer. I looked at our joined hands, not knowing how to start the conversation we needed to have.

"You know," he said. "I drove to Charlotte last night to a Patel Brothers and bought all the ingredients to make chai."

I let out a laugh at the thought of him roaming around an Indian grocery store. "No way."

He gave me a sheepish grin. "When you left yesterday, I worried you were right about me feeling trapped. But then I had my talk with Momma and realized you and I would never have to go through that if we were open and honest with each other."

I leaned in and kissed his cheek. "I like that idea."

He wrapped his free arm around me. "Momma's agreed to stop pushing Amy on me and let me date you in peace. It's not an excuse, but after Dad's death, she wanted everything to be the same, wanted me to be as happy as they were. She realizes it was wrong, and she's sorry she treated you badly."

My eyes widened.

"Believe it or not, Momma and I talked some more over chai this morning."

"Really? Did she like it?"

Michael smiled. "She actually loved it. Had two cups before church. By the way, she wants to make amends with you at dinner tonight."

Oh. This was it. I swallowed. "As long as I can speak freely."

He kissed my palm and held it against his heart. "Always."

I nodded, inhaled deeply, and glanced at the notebook.

His lips brushed my ear. "Is there a reason I saw my name at the top of that page?"

My gaze flew to his. "Uh… no it wasn't?" *Crud.* Why did that come out like a question?

Michael grabbed the list, and when I dove for it, he lifted it out of reach, causing me to tackle him against the pillows. Between shrieks of laughter, he somehow pinned me beneath him.

"No fair. You're used to tackling people." I sounded embarrassingly breathy.

He pressed our mouths together in a lingering kiss. "But no one as gorgeous as you." Goosebumps erupted everywhere. He motioned to his breast pocket. "Can you get that?" The ripped edge of a folded piece of paper stuck out. I pulled it free, and with a nod, he gave me permission to read it.

It was a list like mine.

Michael

Having Shreya in my arms felt like winning a championship game. Sappy, sure, but I didn't think she'd even taste the chai

I'd spent hours tweaking this morning. I'd gone through a whole gallon of milk before I'd found a recipe I actually liked nearly as much as her mom's.

Shreya didn't push me away to read my list, and while I loved the feel of her, I doubted her mom would approve. I sat us up and tucked my arm around her.

She cleared her throat and read aloud. "Number one, I want to have an open and honest relationship with Shreya. Two, I don't want to hurt her with any more ignorant or insensitive comments made by me or anyone in my family. I want her to feel comfortable and welcome around us. And three, I want the freedom to fall in love with her." Her voice cracked at the end, and she met my eyes with tears on her lashes. I kissed her forehead.

After church, I'd visited Dad's grave. He'd always told me the best way to represent his clients was to figure out what they wanted. Only then could he "work his magic." And since I needed some today, I'd sat beside his tombstone and drafted my list with him.

And when I'd seen Shreya's notebook on the table, I couldn't help but believe he'd brought me to this moment.

Shreya reached for her list and handed it to me. *What I Want in a Relationship with Michael.* My heart thundered as I read the rest out loud.

I met her eyes when I finished. "I want this too. I never want you to be anyone but yourself."

She wound her arms around me and squeezed. I tossed the notebook aside, scooped her onto my lap, and buried my face against the crook of her neck. Her faint floral scent relaxed me.

I peppered her soft skin with kisses until I reached her ear. "So what d'ya say?"

Shreya pulled back. "About?"

"Will you be my girlfriend?"

She beamed. "Duh."

"Good, 'cause you know what Momma realized by the end of breakfast?"

"I'm afraid to ask."

"She mentioned the Bradford family legacy might yet come true if you became my high school sweetheart."

"Your high school swee—?" Shreya's eyes narrowed and then widened. "Oh my god. Talk about pressure!" She play-punched me.

I threw my head back and laughed.

Nope. Not a bad legacy to have after all.

THE END

Other Published Works

READ MORE BY SHAILA PATEL

Soulmated (Joining of Souls #1) - Month9Books – 2017

Fighting Fate (Joining of Souls #2) –
East Girl Publishing – 2018

Enduring Destiny (Joining of Souls #3) –
East Girl Publishing – 2019

FOR MORE, VISIT
www.shailapatelauthor.com

The Storm of the Decade

Snow drifts in a slow dance, swirling to the ground.

"They say it's going to be a big one," Carey says. He shivers and shakes his head. "Biggest storm of this decade."

I turn my attention to the coffee machine and brew another batch. "Biggest storm *so far* this decade," I correct him. "Besides, they always say that, and they're always wrong."

I grab a cup and pour Carey another one. The smell of the coffee grounds settles into my limbs, the warmth of the cup shooting up my arms. The feeling is almost euphoric, but mostly it feels familiar, like home.

Carey nods. "You got that right, Priya." He takes the cup from my hand, his own gloved one cupping it like it's the Holy Grail. "But I think they might be right this time. You ready for it? Got chains on your tires? You didn't drive that little prissy car today, did you?" Carey takes a sip of his drink, his hat sitting low over the white hair that frizzes out the sides of it. His ruddy face pinches when he swallows.

I roll my eyes. The "prissy car" he's referring to is a Toyota Camry. Carey thinks that anything other than a pick-up is a prissy car.

"Don't worry about me. I have my dad's SUV today." No way would Dad let me drive the Camry when there's a threatening storm brewing. He watches the weather channel obsessively, paranoid that somehow I'll end up dead like my mom if he doesn't. It's shocking that he even lets me drive. I even had to wait until I was seventeen to get my license, and it wasn't until this winter that he allowed me to drive to work. We actually had a fight about it last night, and he finally relented when I agreed to drive his beast of a car.

"Your pops is a good one."

I smile and turn back to the wall lined with cups and bags of coffee beans. The café is quiet today. Main Street is almost dead, which is surprising given it's the middle of a Saturday afternoon. People must be huddling in their homes, avoiding any chance of getting stuck in the oncoming storm.

Even though I have to close up tonight, I'm not worried. I really don't think the storm is going to be as epic as they say. Besides, Dad's car is pretty reliable. Walking to the side counter where all the containers sit, I check to make sure they're all full. Turns out the creamer is almost out. I bend down to grab some more from the minifridge when the doorbell chimes.

"Hi, welcome to Caffeinated Heaven." I stand up, then freeze when I see who it is. "Hey, Ollie." I swallow and ignore the flutter in my belly.

Ollie pulls off his beanie, letting his mass of soft curls loose. His hair is longer than he kept it in school, touching his ears, falling over his eyes.

"Priya." He gives me a lopsided smile. The same one he wore prom night.

I step behind the register, wiping my suddenly sweaty hands on the back of my apron. "The usual?"

Ollie takes out his wallet and hands me some cash. "Yes, please." He doesn't look at me again, and there's a slight flush to his cheeks, but I'm not sure if it's because of the cold or because of me.

I give him his change and he walks to the counter, pulling out a barstool and taking a seat, and doesn't speak again. Which is how Ollie usually operates with me. Which is annoying given our shared history.

Oliver Hollis graduated from high school last year and has the most beautiful green eyes. Last year at prom, I went solo with my friend, Katelynn, after dumping my idiotic ex, Liam, the week before because I couldn't deal with his inability to remain monogamous. Ollie didn't go with anyone either, so I finally worked up the courage to ask him to dance with me. He said yes. For three glorious minutes, he held me in his arms and I finally got a really good look at those dark green eyes. Three minutes which ended up being a bit longer than three, but neither of us talks about any of that.

"You ready for tonight, kid?" Carey asks Ollie.

Ollie taps the counter and wears that silently contemplative look I recognize from Physics class. The one where he seems far away, but in reality, he's taking all of it in. "I'm hoping it won't be too bad. Maybe people will actually listen and not drive in this weather."

"Well, we got the tow truck all ready to go just in case." Carey finishes his drink and sighs before smacking the counter. "I'll see you both later. Priya, just give us a holler if you need anything, got it?"

I finish mixing up a cup of hot chocolate, Ollie's usual, and make sure to add extra whipped cream before handing it to him. "I'll keep that in mind. Be safe out there, Carey."

Carey gives Ollie a pat on the back. "Same to you."

The bell chimes when Carey opens the door and the cold wind seeps into the cafe, settling for a brief moment before dispersing. The silence drops heavy as soon as the door closes. Ollie sips his drink while I try to figure out what I should do next. Ollie and I haven't been alone together like this in months.

He keeps his head bent and chews on his lips, a nervous habit. He did that during tests, or whenever, Talon, his best friend, made him go to a party. He was chewing his lips a lot while we danced at prom.

"Your uncle always this nervous about snowstorms?" I ask Ollie, breaking the silence. This is ridiculous. Ollie and I sat at the same lunch table for almost two years. It shouldn't be this hard to talk to him. Carey should be used to the winter storms up here in Maine. He owns the local mechanic shop and is always pulling people's cars out of ditches during the winter.

Ollie finally looks up at me, his mouth shaped like an "O" as if he's just as surprised by me talking to him as I am doing it. Usually, Ollie's in here with Carey so neither of us really has to make an effort to talk.

Ollie leans forward in his seat, both hands wrapped around his cup. "Only during the first big one. He's superstitious about it." Ollie's voice is gruff and he stares at the counter when he talks to me. He does that a lot. The not-looking-me-in-the-eye when he talks.

I guess that's what happens when you kiss someone and never mention it again. I stare down at Ollie's mouth. I think about that kiss entirely too much given how it ended. With Ollie telling me, "We should have done that a long time ago," and then not returning my calls or speaking to me for weeks afterward. And then us both ignoring the giant elephant in the room. Which wasn't that surprising given what happened during homecoming sophomore year, but I had hoped Ollie and I were finally moving forward and getting somewhere. I was wrong.

It shattered my heart a little.

"I'm sure it'll be fine," I say, swallowing.

I turn away from Ollie and clean up Carey's empty cup. When I'm done with that, I check the milk containers. Again. Anything to keep away from Ollie and the memory of that fateful kiss. But I can't keep my eyes away from where he sits by the counter, hunched over, curls hectic and messy, but also perfect.

"You all set for the storm?" he asks when I make it back behind the register. The question is almost shy, like he has a hard time asking it in the first place.

I fiddle with the napkin dispenser. "I think so. Carey already grilled me about it," I say with a soft laugh.

Ollie moves his arm and his cup tips a little, splashing chocolate on the counter. "Sorry," he mumbles, fumbling to grab napkins, soaking up the mess.

I turn to the sink and grab a rag. "Don't worry about it." I lean across the counter and wipe down the rest of the spill Ollie's breath hits my neck and goosebumps line my arms. I startle and our eyes crash. I didn't realize how close we are to each other. Close enough for me to smell the chocolate on his breath. Close enough that if I tilted my head a couple of inches our lips would touch.

My heart thumps so hard I can't hear anything else. Ollie's eyes flick to my mouth. I wait. It's like I'm always waiting. For Ollie.

Ollie breaks the spell by moving back and reaching for another handful of napkins to wipe his hands. I notice the grease stains underneath his chewed-up nails. Ollie is also a mechanic at Carey's shop. Or training to be one. While all of his friends went off to college, he stayed behind. I asked him once if it was his dream.

He'd looked over at me with that contemplative expression, his eyes staring into mine, back when he actually met them, and the side of his mouth tipped up. "Would you judge me if it was?"

I had shaken my head. "No. Dreams come in every form imaginable. You should be proud if it's yours."

His ears had turned red at that. "Thanks." And then he went back to ignoring me.

I take a stuttered breath and move back.

"I need to get going." Ollie stands up suddenly, frowning. "Be careful tonight, okay?" He pulls his beanie back on and hurries out the door before I can respond. I swear sometimes Ollie can sense my memories, my thoughts, like he's in tune with all of them.

I squeeze my eyes shut when he's gone. Will myself to forget. I wonder if Ollie thinks about that kiss the way I do. How right after we finished our dance I asked him if we could step outside for a minute because I needed air. I had promised myself that I would finally tell Ollie that I had feelings for him.

I figured he would say no, but he surprised me, and we ended up outside of the school gymnasium, the beginning of the summer breathing all around. I found the courage I didn't even know I had to reach up and touch his face. I pulled his lips to mine, ran my hands through his hair. He'd responded. Kissed me back. It felt like we were out there with our hands all over each other forever. Then he said those words and we went back into the dance and acted like none of it had happened.

I went to hang out with my friends, and he went to his. We acted like nothing had happened when in reality so much had changed. Then when I called him the next day so we could talk about that kiss, he didn't answer. He disappeared.

Another customer makes their way into the café, jolting me out of my memories. I push them away, bury them deep, because I really don't think Ollie thinks about that kiss the way I do. More customers trickle in over the course of the next few hours, while the storm brewing outside finally lets loose and snowflakes that appear to be the size of my hand start dropping. It helps me forget about Ollie.

I bite down on my lower lip and tap my foot. Maybe Carey was right. The snow is starting to pile. Fast. The customers don't stick around and I'm grateful for it. I need the quiet after the weird exchange with Ollie. I wipe down the counter and tables. My phone vibrates, and I see Dad's face flash across the screen.

"Has your boss called you?" Dad asks as soon as I pick up.

I hold the phone up between my ear and shoulder while hauling a few dirty ceramic cups to the sink. "No, Dad. I get off at ten tonight."

"I think you should call her and let her know that the storm is getting worse. There is no way you can drive home in this." There's a slight hint of hysteria in his tone, and I force myself to breathe evenly instead of telling my dad to stop being so overprotective.

"Dad, I told you already that Bella said I could crash at her place."

Bella, my best friend, lives a few blocks away from Main Street, whereas my dad and I live on a small farm on the outskirts of town about a thirty-minute drive away.

"Okay, okay," he releases a breath on the other side, satisfied with my answer. "Keep me updated."

"I will. Love you."

"Love you, too. Bye."

As soon as I hang up, I lean against the counter, touching my chin to my chest. Dad doesn't know that Bella is out of town visiting Talon at college this weekend. I'm sure her parents wouldn't mind if I called them and told them my situation, if I were to get stuck in town that is. I tuck a piece of my thick, dark hair behind my ear and turn my attention to the window. The snow hasn't stopped falling down in rapid heaves in almost two hours. It's only four in the afternoon, but the clouds cover the sun and it's dark and gloomy outside.

I haven't seen a car drive by in some time. Walking to the window, I peer closer. I can barely see anything out there because of the flakes of snow being dumped around. The world has turned pure white.

Maybe I should leave. Before it's too late. As if the heavens hear my plea, the store phone rings. I run to the back wall where it sits. "Hello?"

"Priya! It's Sandra. Everyone is closing up shop because of the storm. I think it would be best if you do, too. Before it gets worse."

"Okay. I can do that."

"Stay safe, okay?"

"Will do!"

Placing my hands on my hips, I take a look around the shop. We didn't have many customers today because of the storm, so the cafe isn't a disaster. I could go now and avoid any more snowfall. Except that I hate the idea of leaving any sort of mess behind. With a deep breath in and out, I decide that I won't be able to sleep tonight if I don't clean up before I head out. First, I take all of the dirty cups to the back and put them in the dishwasher. Then I dump out the remaining coffee and wash out the containers. By the time I'm done with everything, it's almost five and even darker outside.

The snow is piling so high I can't tell where cars begin and end. Oh no. How am I supposed to dig myself out? I don't have a shovel, and the roads are covered. How could I be so dumb? I panic and think about calling my dad, but he'll lose his cool. I don't want him driving in this weather either. I could walk to Bella's, but I don't have snowshoes. I start pacing the floor. I could wait here until the storm ends. I mean, there's a couch. If I get hungry, I can warm up one of the sandwiches in the freezer. I would totally pay back Sandra, of course.

The more I think about it, the more the plan starts to make sense.

I decide to make myself some hot cocoa and start for the back room when the lights flicker. I fumble my steps. The lights flicker again. Until there's only darkness, and the lights don't come back on.

Well, there went that plan. But they could come back on any minute. I won't freak out. Not yet anyway.

Two hours later, I'm huddled inside my jacket, teeth chattering. The lights haven't come back on, and I don't think they're going to any time soon. It's cold and only getting colder. If only this place had a fireplace.

My fingers are starting to numb even though I have on my gloves and hat. I should have left when Dad told me to. Actually, I should have called Sandra right when Carey said it was going to be bad. I should have known Sandra would wait until the last minute to call me. She's ridiculously busy these days, what with opening another coffee shop near Logan Falls College.

I don't know what to do. I never expected to be in this situation, ever. My phone rings. It's Dad again. I suck in a breath and put on a fake smile.

"Hey, Dad!" I sound cheery. Too cheery. I need to tone it down. "What's up?"

"Are you still at the store? I heard there's a power outage in town."

I grimace. "No. I'm at Bella's. Don't worry about me. I left right after we talked."

"Why didn't you call me?"

Because I knew you would get in my little Camry and drive out here to get me, risking your own life while you were at it. I think this, but I don't say it. I'm tired. Of having to explain where I am at all times, of trying to settle Dad's paranoia. I squeeze my eyes shut and open once I've calmed my heart "I-I just got caught up watching reruns of *I Love Lucy*." Bella has thing for shows from the fifties. Actually, we both do.

"Okay. Just making sure. I'll call in the morning. And tell Bella's family thank you."

"I will!"

He hangs up, and I stare at the phone. It's for the best that I didn't say anything. I don't need to deal with a Dad freak-out on top over everything else. The cold infiltrates my space, and I huddle up again.

An hour later, I think I might have hypothermia. Actually, I don't think I would be able to hold a coherent thought if I was hypothermic.

I can't last in here all night. The storm is whistling outside, and it hasn't stopped snowing. Maybe this is how it ends for me.

Surrounded by coffee beans and baked goods. Honestly, it's not a bad way to go.

I close my eyes, exhaustion slowly slipping into my limbs, when bright lights sweep in front of me. I notice a giant truck outside of the shop, the headlights pointed right inside the cafe. Help. There's help!

I jump up and run to the door just as a knock resounds. Someone in a giant fluffy jacket stands on the other side.

"Anyone in there?"

"Yeah. It's me. Priya Sharma?" I unlock the door and open it. The wind blows through, almost knocking me to the side.

The giant coated figure enters and throws back his hood after closing the door behind him. And I know this exact *him*.

"Ollie?" I whisper. "You came back."

His green eyes turn to mine.

"Of course. Glad you're alive." An uncertain smile curtains his mouth.

"Yeah. Me too. What are you doing here?"

He clears his throat. "Um. So. I—Uh. Uncle Carey," he finally stops fumbling. "He said you're not the type to ask for help even if you needed it, and I should check in to make sure you actually made it out of town." He scratches his ear, which I know to be an Ollie tell. Why is he lying to me?

"I'm glad *he* did." I lean against the closed door, going along with the lie.

"What are you still doing here, Priya? You trying to freeze to death?" I can see his breath in the dark; it's a white fog that rises in small puffs.

"I tried to leave too late. I couldn't dig my car out, so I decided to hunker down here, but then the lights went out. Can you take me home?"

He shakes his head. "It's still coming down too hard for anyone to be driving. I'll take you to my place until the roads are cleared." His place. I open my mouth to protest, but nothing comes out. "Unless you're uncomfortable with that, then I can take you somewhere else," he says.

I think he's blushing because his face darkens a bit. "You can take me to Bella's." I don't know if I'm ready to be alone with him at his place. My heart hammers and my stomach twists at the thought.

"Isn't she visiting Talon at college?"

Crap. Talon is Ollie's best friend, but I'd assumed now that Talon's away, they weren't keeping in touch that much. "Yeah?"

"I know for a fact that her parents are in Greenville, so they're not home either."

Greenville is a town over, and I completely forgot Bella's parents were spending the weekend there for their anniversary.

"Is there anywhere else?" he asks, shaking off the last bits of snow clinging to his jacket.

I stare up at his face. His mouth is set, jaw sharp. His dark hair, the way the curls jostle with his movements. My body suddenly feels warmer than it has in hours. I clench my fingers because I am very tempted to reach up and cup Ollie's face. Just like I did the night we kissed. "No. Your place is fine."

"Try not to sound so disappointed," he says with little tilt to his mouth.

"Sorry. I just don't want to put you out." I don't mention the fact that we haven't been alone for more than a few minutes since prom and the fateful kiss.

"I wouldn't be here if that were the case. Come on."

I grab my purse and lock up behind me before following him to his giant truck. It's warm when I get in and I relax in my seat. "I forgot how good it feels to be warm," I say between chattering breaths.

Ollie laughs. It's a quiet rumble that makes my blood pump fast. "How long were you without power?"

"I don't know? A few hours?"

Ollie shakes his head. "You should have called someone." As he starts driving down Main Street the truck bumps up and down over the snow-covered road. He flips on the wipers, but the snow is falling so fast they can barely keep up.

"I didn't want my dad to freak out. He's super paranoid about this kind of stuff because of my mom."

He nods like he gets it. And maybe he does. Ollie's dad died serving in Afghanistan.

"Still should have called. You could have gotten hypothermia if you stayed there all night."

"I kept thinking that the lights would come back on."

He gets quiet, and I fidget. He probably thinks I'm an idiot.

"You hate being an inconvenience," he says so quietly I almost don't hear him.

"Excuse me? What's that supposed to mean?" I frown at his words.

He shoots me a look before turning back to the road. "When we were in school, you did everything in your power to make everyone else comfortable."

"How's that?"

"We used to eat lunch together, Pree." I like the way he says my nickname. "Whenever you got the last of the chicken nuggets, which are Bella's favorite, you always gave them to her. Or, if you wanted to go ice skating but Katelynn wasn't in the mood, you would go along with other people's plans. In Physics, there was an odd number of kids, and instead of making one group a threesome, you volunteered to work alone. You never want to inconvenience people."

I found myself without words. "I didn't think you noticed anything about me," I whisper.

Ollie pulls up in front of a tall, red brick building. "Why wouldn't I?"

"Because we didn't eat lunch together. Not really. We ate at the same table, but you kept to Talon's side and I kept to Bella's." At times, it felt like there was this wall between us.

"You're kind of hard to ignore, Priya." He turns off the truck and jumps out before I can respond.

I follow him out of the truck and into the building. Ollie lives above Shelly's Sweet Bakes bakery on Main. Only a couple of blocks away from the coffee shop.

He unlocks the side door to a staircase. I follow him up, the cold making me shiver again. He unlocks the door at the top of the staircase and pushes it open, stepping aside to let me in first. I duck past him into the warmth.

Ollie shuts the door behind us, and I step aside while taking off my coat and unwrapping my scarf. I'd been curious about Ollie's place ever since I found out he moved out on his own. I've tried to stop wondering about him all the time, but it's hard when he's constantly at the coffee shop, reminding me of the way his lips tasted like cherry lip balm and his tongue like peppermint.

The apartment is one large room with a bathroom straight across from the entrance and a kitchen to the right. There's a small living room with an old, worn-out grey couch and re-cliner, and beyond that, a full-sized bed that hasn't been made.

"Sorry about the mess," Ollie says, pulling down his snow pants to reveal a pair of dark jeans underneath. He takes off his beanie, gloves, and jacket, tossing them to the side. He's wear-ing a dark blue thermal underneath. The kind of shirt that's snug against his muscles. I stare at him for a beat too long and force myself to look away. He brushes past me, picking up socks and tossing them into the basket. He quickly makes his bed and grabs the bowl and cup that sit on the coffee table in the living room.

"It's fine. Actually, it's cleaner than I expected." In fact, it's fairly neat. Ollie has a TV sitting on a stand in front of the win-dow along with a video game system. There's a bookshelf filled with worn spines, and all of his game cases are lined up in a neat row on a shelf on the TV stand.

"Thanks?" he says like he's not sure if that's compliment or not. I'm not even sure if I meant it as one, so I don't remark on it.

"How do you have power?" I walk over to the window and peek out of the blinds. Main Street is still dark and empty. Well, except for the snow that is.

"Backup generator," he says. He's suddenly standing next to me, his body radiating heat. I force myself to remain still, staring up at his profile. "It's beautiful, isn't it? All that snow makes the Earth appear untouched, brand new. Like we're the only ones here."

His words make me lose my breath for a moment and I have to remind myself to breathe. I turn back to the window, my chest feeling heavier.

"You hungry?" Ollie asks, moving away from me, ending the quiet moment of reflection. He enters the kitchen and opens the fridge.

I take a step forward, then stop. I'm not sure what I'm sup-posed to do here. Or how to act. Do we keep pretending like nothing happened between us?

"I'm okay." I shake out my hair. The snow has melted on the exposed parts of it, making it wet. I pull off my hair tie and put it in a braid before it frizzes.

Ollie faces me, placing a couple of containers on the kitchen counter. "You sure? I have Uncle Carey's famous chicken casserole." He holds up one of the plastic containers, wearing a shy smile.

I bite down on my lip. "I didn't know Carey cooked."

He shrugs. "He does all right. Kind of had to learn when he took me in after my dad died and my mom ran off." He says it so casually, but I can sense the undercurrent of tension. He drops his gaze and yanks off a lid, the muscles on his arms flexing. "He's a good cook. I'm not bad either, but he still brings me meals a few times a week. Says he doesn't know how to not cook for me now." Ollie grabs a plate from the cupboard and dishes himself up some food before putting it in the microwave.

Carey took Ollie in when he was thirteen. Ollie lost his dad at twelve and then, not even a year later, his mom disappeared.

Two years later, my mom died. A drunk driver didn't stop at a stop sign, and she was gone. I was fourteen at the time and completely devastated. People came and went; they left messages, brought meals, sent flowers. But then eventually, they all stopped. Life went on. I put on a happy face because I didn't want to bring down my friends. I kept it all in. I smiled, I laughed, I pretended to move on. Meanwhile, beneath it all, I was crumbling.

About six months later, I went back to school. It felt almost normal. I was used to it. But when I opened my locker, there was a note. The scribbled writing wasn't familiar when I read it. The words appeared rushed, loping sideways. All it said was, "It's okay to be sad."

I kept that note in my backpack for the rest of the school year. It wasn't until junior year, when Ollie and I were in Physics, that I realized he was the one who wrote me the note. I missed class one day and needed notes. Ollie lent me his to copy during lunch. I remember sitting there for way too long, staring at his handwriting, how familiar it was, and it suddenly dawning on me that he was the one.

The microwave beeps, wrenching me out of the memory.

I remember where I am. In Ollie's place. Alone. His head dips while he mixes up the casserole on his plate. He seems to sense my eyes on him because he looks up. My face burns and

I clear my throat. I decide to sit on the couch with my back to him to keep myself distracted.

Of course, as soon as I sit down, Ollie walks up to the recliner next to the couch.

He hands me a cup. I take it and stare at it for a minute.

"It's ginger beer," he says before I can ask.

A soft smile curves on my lips. "Thanks."

I always brought ginger beer with me to lunch. Talon thought the stuff was vile, and Bella didn't care one way or the other, but always backed up Talon because that's the kind of girlfriend she is. On one particular day, Talon wouldn't let go of his disgust for the stuff, and Ollie spoke up in that soft yet thundering sort of way he holds around himself.

"Can I have sip?" he'd asked.

It took me a few seconds to realize he was talking to me. Ollie and I didn't really interact much. We kept to our sides of the table.

"Sure?" I slid the drink over to him.

He picked it up, took a sip, and nodded. "Not bad," he'd said before sliding it back to me.

Ollie started bringing his own ginger beer with him to lunch. Talon shut up about it after that.

"You sure you don't want any food?" Ollie asks before taking a bite.

I pull my legs up to my chest, curling into a smaller version of myself. I shake my head. "I ate at the store." Plus, my stomach is tied up in too many knots for me to have an appetite.

I think about saying something, anything really, to Ollie about the kiss. I wait for him to start. For him to talk. Even though I know he won't. There's a solemn quietness to Ollie. He never says anything unless he means it. He's not one for idle chit-chat. So often, he's in his own head.

I think that's why he got along so well with Talon, who never shut up. I always thought Talon hogged all of the conversations and felt bad for Ollie, but after a while, I realized that Ollie didn't seem to mind at all. I tried to get him to talk on more than one occasion and all Ollie would do was give me a half-smile and a one-worded answer. That seemed to satisfy him. Ollie wasn't a man of many words. And I'm tired of it. Of him not talking to me. Of ignoring what happened.

"Why didn't you call me?" I finally address the elephant in the room. The one we've avoided for six months. "After prom?"

Ollie finishes his bite and puts his plate on the coffee table. He takes a sip of his drink and places it next to the plate. Then he rubs his palms over his jeans. All the while, that one little curl that refuses to be tamed wobbles back and forth over his left eyebrow.

"Because you scare me."

I stare at him, a bit bewildered, mostly surprised, and burst out laughing. "*I* scare *you*?" I point to myself.

Ollie leans back and scrutinizes me under his gaze. It's that intense look that makes my heart race faster and my mouth go dry.

"You're freaking terrifying, Priya," he states matter-of-factly.

I frown at his words and grab my cup to take a sip of the ginger beer. The carbonation tickles my nose. I take a breath. "I don't understand. What exactly is so scary about me?" I shake my head, disbelieving.

"You scare me because you're exactly the kind of girl I could fall in love with, and I'm exactly the wrong guy for you."

His words smack me right in the chest. I force myself to take even breaths, to stay calm, even though right now, that's so far from what I am. My whole body is flushed. "Oh."

"Is that all you have to say after all this time?" he questions me under his long lashes. "I know you've been meaning to all these months. I see it in your eyes, on your face, every time I come into the store."

At first, I'm startled by his revelations. Then I'm angry, turning his words over and getting more upset. How dare he? How dare he notice anything about me? After all this time. Months of ignoring me, years of never knowing what was going on in his head.

I take a breath through my nose. "Why exactly do you come in if it bothers you so much? When you know I work there?"

"I never said it bothers me. And it's because I can't stay away. No matter how hard I try."

I look away from him, clenching my jaw. "Why do you try? If you know how I feel? You have to know. Don't you, Ollie?"

I stare down at my socks. There are little yellow rubber duckies on them, and it feels highly inappropriate to be wearing such ridiculous socks when I'm confessing my feelings to a boy who just told me he could fall in love with me.

"I know. I mean, I didn't, not at first. But after prom, I knew." His words are hushed, reverent, uncertain. Every sentence Ollie speaks carries so many emotions, it's hard for me to decipher each.

"I don't understand why you're the wrong guy for me." My throat is tight and there's a lump when I swallow. I stare at the abandoned plate of food on the coffee table. Ollie doesn't seem to want to eat it anymore.

Ollie stands up and walks out of the room. I stare at empty space, confusion settling along my body. I turn to see where he went and find him standing in the bedroom area next to his dresser. He pulls open the top drawer and takes something out of it. I can't tell what because his back blocks the view.

I resist the urge to put on my coat and shoes and leave. It's heavy in my bones, the need to escape. Except I don't, because despite my embarrassment and anger, I want to know what he has to say. I need to know.

Ollie's steps are quiet; he barely makes a sound when he walks back to the couch. He stops in front of me. I crane my head to look up at him. The soft glow of the lamp presses around him, highlighting the firmness of his mouth and the uncertainty lifting along his eyes and face.

"Here." He reaches out his hand and opens his palm. There sits an object wrapped in faded blue tissue paper. I stare at it and then up at him, sending him a questioning glance. "It's for you. Take it."

I lift it out, my fingers brushing Ollie's palm, sending shockwaves up my arm. Ollie drops his arm once I have it, and I see him clench and unclench his hand before he drops back down on the recliner.

He leans forward, elbows on his thighs, head hanging.

Biting down on my lip, I begin to unwrap the crinkling tissue paper. Bit by bit. The object, whatever it is, is heavy, and I'm curious to see what it could be. I pause when I find out. It glints beneath the shadowed lights of the apartment. Silver and blue. It's a hummingbird brooch.

I pick up it with my other hand and the rhinestones shine. "Why?" is all I can ask.

Ollie finally looks up at me. "You said they were your mom's favorite. When we danced."

My hands are trembling. In fact, my whole body trembles. I close a fist around the hummingbird and squeeze my eyes shut. I don't remember much of what we talked about that night. It was only three minutes for crying out loud, but I do remember mentioning the fact that Mom had a hummingbird brooch she loved. We buried her with it, and I've missed it every day.

"I don't understand. Why did you disappear for days afterward, Ollie?"

I went to his place the next morning, after our kiss, after tossing and turning all night, unable to forget the memory of his warm mouth on mine. He wasn't there. He didn't answer my calls, either.

"I didn't disappear. I was on a mission," he says, his face almost a grimace as he says so. He readjusts in his seat, almost like he's uncomfortable. "I went everywhere to find that brooch for you. I wanted to give you something that showed that..." his voice drifts off and he rubs his forehead.

"Showed what?" I urge him, shifting in my own seat to get a better look at him.

His eyes flick to mine and there's a pained expression there. "That showed how much I liked you. I was trying to be thoughtful."

I curl my fingers and stare at the brooch. "Why didn't you give it to me?"

"I tried," his voice is husky. "I came back into town and wrapped it up for you. I was headed to your place when Uncle Carey asked me to come in because he was short-staffed at the shop. When I got there, Liam Denson was bragging about how the two of you had hooked up at some party."

My racing heart almost drops out of my belly. I cannot believe I actually dated that scumbag for so long. I could seriously throttle Liam right now. I can't believe he went around telling people that we hooked up when that wasn't the truth at all.

Feeling down about how things between Ollie and I hadn't worked out, I went to Bella. She told me to stop moping around and have fun. We ended up going to a party and Liam happened to be there. He was a little drunk and wouldn't stop begging me to take him back. I told him no, but he wouldn't listen. He kissed me, even though that was the last thing I wanted. Thankfully Bella was able to help me get away from him. I spent the rest of the night huddled outside in a dark corner of the backyard where the party was being held. Bella told me we could leave, but she and Talon were having too much fun and I didn't want them to feel obligated to go because of my idiot ex.

"I figured the kiss we shared didn't mean anything to you, so I tried to move past it. Except I haven't exactly been able to do that."

The anger is hot in my veins again. "If you had bothered to talk to me about any of that I could have cleared things up for you, Oliver Hollis." I stand up because I can't sit anymore. I need to move with all this energy building up inside of me. "I would have explained that Liam kissed me even though I didn't want him to. I would have told you that I liked you, too, and that I couldn't stop thinking about that kiss either."

I release a long breath and shake my head. "And even if Liam and I had hooked up, what business would it have been of yours? You never told me about your feelings. You never called or texted. I tried reaching out to you and you didn't respond. What was I supposed to think? I can't read your mind. My voice rises higher and higher, and my breathing grows more erratic. "You say that I always try to please everyone else, but you? You run away, Ollie."

Ollie's face falls. The tension between us tightens and I'm afraid it will snap at any moment. "What does that mean?"

"Every time Bella and Talon got into a pissing match during lunch, you'd suddenly have to be somewhere else, and I was left to referee the two of them. Then there's homecoming." Sophomore year Bella and Talon started dating, and we started having lunch together with him and Ollie. Bella knew I had a crush on Ollie, and she told me that Talon had said something to her about Ollie liking me. She said he planned on asking me to do the dance. But he never did, and I ended up going with Liam.

"You never asked me even though you'd told Talon you would. I know you're the one who wrote that note after my mom died and you never said anything So yeah, you run away."

Ollie lets out a breath. Ollie stares up at me, a look of wonder taking hold of him. "You're right. I do that. I didn't ask you to homecoming because I got scared. I never told you I liked you for the same reason. But then we kissed, and I thought that did a pretty good job of explaining how I felt about you." He lifts a brow.

That is definitely the wrong thing for him to say. "First of all, I kissed you. Second of all, you didn't say anything afterward. I thought you hated it and I was embarrassed."

Ollie runs a hand through his hair, tousling his curls, and stands up. "I remember being an active participant in that kiss. I wouldn't have reciprocated if I didn't like it." Ollie steps closer, looming over me. Not in a menacing way, because he stares down at me with this little tilt to his mouth I can't decipher, but in a way that makes the anger puff away into nothing.

"Why are you smiling?" I ask, trying desperately to hold onto the last tendrils of anger. It doesn't work though. I find myself staring at that mouth and wondering if he's still as good a kisser he was last summer.

"Because." He shrugs and stuffs his hands into his pockets. "I think this is the first time you've actually stood up for yourself, and I kind of like it."

I freeze. I am so frozen that I can't even make my brain work correctly. It's short-circuited. Ollie takes a hand out of his pocket and touches the side of my face, jolting me out of the shock.

"You kind of like it?" I frown up at him.

He steps closer. Both of his hands are on me now. The one on my face and the other on my waist. "No. Not kind of. I definitely like it. A lot."

My body grows warmer. The familiar scent of lemons and lavender fills my senses. Ollie always smells nice, like warm summer nights filled with fireflies. He leans forward, and I stand on my tiptoes. His mouth brushes against mine, hesitant like he's testing my reaction.

I place my hands on his chest and wait. I was the one who initiated the kiss last time and now it's his turn. He doesn't wait long, thankfully, putting me out of my misery. His lips crash into mine and I fall against him. He's sturdy though, and barely budges when my knees go weak and I lean into him for support.

His lips are soft and taste like lip balm. The same cherry flavor he used every day at school. Ollie has always been meticulous with his lip care. Probably because of all that lip chewing.

My arms wrap around his neck, our chests press against each other, and I feel him breathing against me. His thumb traces down my neck, and I shiver. All too soon, the kiss is over, and he presses his forehead against mine.

My calves ache, and I put my heels back down on the ground, my hands running down to land on his chest again. We don't say anything for a while. I feel his chest move beneath my hands, feel his fingers press into my hips. It's just the two of us, alone, while the outside world continues to fall under layers upon layers of snow.

Ollie takes my hand in his and squeezes it. "I'm not running away anymore," he whispers.

I press my ear against his chest and close my eyes. I think I must be dreaming, but the pounding of his heart echoes around me, and I know I'm not.

"Where did you find it?" I ask Ollie, holding the hummingbird brooch up against the light. We're laying on his bed, his arm tucked under my head, one of my legs thrown over his. He fiddles with the bottom of my shirt. It's almost midnight and we've spent the last few hours talking and kissing.

"In Richmond," he says. "At this little thrift store. I want to take you there some time. I think you'll like it."

My heart jumps a little. He's planning things for us. I drop my hand and place the brooch on his nightstand before turning back to him.

"Everything okay?" he asks, running a hand down my neck.

"Why did you say that you're the wrong guy for me?" He never explained when I asked him earlier.

Ollie's hand stills on my belly. "Because you're leaving."

I stare up at his throat. "What do you mean?"

"You've always talked about leaving for college. You have plans for the future and I don't want you do forget them because of me, because of us. It's why I didn't say anything to you for so long, even though it was pretty obvious you and Liam weren't together anymore."

I suck in a breath. He's right. I do want to leave. Have been desperate to for years. And that's not going to change because Ollie and I are together. Ollie presses a kiss to my forehead.

"What does that mean? That after tonight we forget any of this happened? That we have feelings for each other? Again?"

"No," Ollie's warm breath brushes against my hair. "It means that we still have time. Graduation is months away."

He's right. There's time.

"Good." I run a thumb along the fluttering heartbeat on his neck. "Because I like kissing you a lot and would like to do so for as long as I can."

Ollie's hands resume their touch, moving up my belly. "Then let's not waste any more time."

"Why did you leave me that note in my locker?" I ask after we take another break. Ollie got me a glass of water earlier and I'm nice and toasty beneath his blanket with his arms wrapped around my waist.

Ollie's mouth presses into a thin line. "Because I saw how much pain you were in and how you built a wall around yourself to make it seem like you weren't. You don't need to pretend around me, Priya. You'll never inconvenience me with your truth."

He pulls me to his chest and I snuggle into him. He's warm and soft. He feels like home. "I didn't know what else to do. I felt like I had to be strong for my dad. Or that my friends would abandon me if I allowed myself to be weak."

"They wouldn't be real friends if they did."

"Do you miss your mom?" I ask. I wait for a heartbeat. "I'm sorry. I shouldn't have asked that."

His laugh rumbles in my ear. "No. It's okay." He's quiet again. I'm sure he's wearing that contemplative expression. "Yeah. I do. But I guess it's the idea of a mom that I miss more than anything."

"What do you mean?" I move back to look up at him.

"I mean, my mom was never a typical mom. She wasn't a great cook, she barely remembered to feed me. Uncle Carey took care of me long before I moved in with him. Then when Dad died and it became too much for her. I used to be angry about her leaving, but I honestly think it's the best thing she could have done for me."

I take Ollie's hand in mine and squeeze. "Do you ever think about finding her?"

"I did."

I sit up. "You did? When?"

Ollie scoots up and leans back against his headboard. "After graduation. She sent me a letter with a return address, and I decided to see if she was there."

"And?"

He picks at his nails. "And she was." I wait for him to continue. I can tell he's gathering his thoughts, plucking the perfect words from the air. "It was terrifying seeing her. I thought she would be a mess, but she's doing all right. She has a stable job and a decent place. She doesn't have a second family like I thought she would." He hangs his head.

"How do you feel about that?"

"I'm relieved. I worried about her for years. Now I don't have to feel guilty about being glad she left."

I scoot closer to Ollie and lay my head on his shoulder. "I can't wait to graduate. Because I want to get away from my dad." I've never said those words out loud before. I wait for him to say something. Lecture me for wanting to get away.

"Is it because he's so over-protective?"

"His reputation is pretty well known here."

Ollie puts his arms around my shoulder. "The man texted you constantly while you were in school. You always had to call him when you got to your destination and when you left. He didn't let you drive into town by yourself until recently. I'm surprised he even let you out today."

"Yeah, he only let me leave because I drove his car and told him I would stay at Bella's if things got bad. I think both of us figured the weather report would end up being wrong." Like it usually is, but I'm so glad it was right. This storm might be the best thing that's ever happened to me.

"Do you think I'm awful for wanting to leave?" I scoot away to look at him.

He shakes his head. "No. Not at all. I think you need to get away. Spread your wings. Figure out what else is out there for you. It used to scare me, knowing that you were going to leave, but now? I'm happy for you, Priya. I'll always be happy to see you pursue the things that you want."

"I'm scared," I confess. "Of what happens next. Between you and me, with college, and my dad."

"You can't let fear rule your life, Priya."

I bite down on the inside of my cheek. "I know. Doesn't mean I don't worry."

Ollie grabs me around the waist and pulls me forward. I let out a yelp when he rolls me to my back. His face hangs above me, his arms caging me in.

His lips land on mine. I sigh against them and pull him closer so his weight is heavy on me. We kiss until we're out of breath, until my lips are swollen, until we're both breathing hard.

Ollie moves to lay down next to me. He lifts my hand to his mouth and places a kiss on it. "If you decide to leave... *When* you decide to leave," he clarifies. "It'll be fine. It'll work out, Priya. I promise. You don't need to worry about me. You do what you want to do. For once in your life."

"You won't hate me?"

"For living your life? Never. I couldn't hate you even if I tried. But I will definitely be upset if you put your life on hold because of me."

His words settle my fears. This is just the beginning of Ollie and me, I remind myself. I hate the idea of leaving him behind. But I also know I can't stay here after graduation.

But that's months away. I still have time. Time with this boy with the greenest eyes, the kind that remind me of hot summer nights and cool mornings at the lake. Tomorrow, we'll have to go back to reality. Life will begin anew. The snow will stop and the shops will open. My dad will call and ask when I'm getting home. But it can wait. Right now, I'm going to enjoy being wrapped up in the warmth of a boy whose heart I stole. And who stole mine.

"What next?" I ask.

"Next, I take you out on a real date."

"A real date, huh?" I chuckle.

"A real date. No running away. Remember?"

I move closer to him, nose to nose. "No more running away, Ollie." I kiss him, deeply, and relish the feel of him all around me. And I thank the stars for the storm of the decade.

Other Published Works

READ MORE BY PRERNA PICKETT

If You Only Knew – Swoon Reads – February 11th, 2020

FOR MORE, VISIT

www. prernapickett.com

Silver for Gold

Speech is silver, silence is golden. — Thomas Carlyle

To sin by silence when they should protest makes cowards of men. — Ella Wheeler Wilcox

Ethan

Gulls circled the dock and music played softly from the restaurant behind me. Smiling couples holding hands walked along the water's edge, but all I could think about was Malala, the girl shot in the head half a world away just for wanting to go to school. With a sigh, I powered down the e-book I was reading during my break and headed back inside the restaurant to finish my shift.

My parents had this stupid rule that, until I was sure about what I wanted to do with my life, I'd be heading to community college this fall, so I'd been reading everything I could get my hands on to help decide on a major. So far, I had it narrowed down to law, journalism, or business. Malala had earned a Nobel prize by the time she was seventeen. Me? I was eighteen and still waiting tables. I blew out a sigh. How did anybody figure this out?

"Ethan." Angelo, my boss, tapped the Rolex on his wrist and thrust a basket of bread into my hands when I stepped through the door. "Table 32 asked for warm bread five damn minutes ago."

I stifled a groan. I'd been on break for the last fifteen minutes, so if they'd asked for warm bread, they hadn't asked me, but there was no sense even reminding Angelo of that.

He wouldn't hear me. He'd already decided it was my fault.

That was the whole problem with talking, if you asked me.

People heard only what they wanted to hear, spoke when they should listen, or talked more when they should take action. Say the wrong thing and you could get kicked to the curb. Humans learned to talk in the first year or two of life, but when I saw all the books available in stores on things like subtext, body language, or rhetoric, I figured none of us had ever actually mastered it. Honestly, it was exhausting, so I did as little talking as I could get away with.

Stayed out of a lot of trouble that way, and it sure seemed to make my family happy.

I took the basket of warm bread to the table, astounded by how Malala could get shot for fighting for education, while here in the U.S., hard dinner rolls apparently caused civil unrest. #Firstworldproblems, am I right?

Angelo was a tough boss. He paid great, but he had a bunch of stupid rules that all ended up with the customer always being right...even when they were wrong. *Saluti, Italian for Greetings*, was popular with our town's country club and tourist set, people used to getting what they wanted when they wanted it. One of my customers once demanded Pepsi instead of Coke (we only carried Coke products) and Angelo said no problem. He sent me to the grocery store for a two-liter bottle of Pepsi just for her.

I delivered the breadbasket to the table, ignored the disapproving looks and sarcastic remarks from the guests sitting there, and worked the rest of my tables. *Saluti* was a beautiful spot on the east end of Long Island with panoramic views of the ocean, soft music, and four-star dining. I lived in nearby Amagansett, in a modest house with a not-so-modest tax bill Dad stressed out about all the time. Customers routinely dropped two- or three-hundred dollars on dinner here, so my tips alone could end up paying my first semester's tuition.

My plan was to keep working even after school started. Dad claimed the service industry built character and provided insight into the human condition. If the condition was spoiled rich people acting badly, then yeah. I had insight.

The restaurant was packed. I worked my section, taking orders, refilling drinks, delivering trays of food. At about 7 p.m., Angelo flagged me over to a pay station. "What's up?" I asked.

"Ethan, this is Alli Santana, new server. I want her to shadow you tonight."

I turned to the girl standing beside my boss and didn't hear another word he said. She was a tall, brown beauty with dark hair that hung in a glossy curtain down to her waist, bright hazel eyes that crinkled when she smiled at me, and a cluster of freckles across her nose that made her damn near adorable. I didn't remember much about that moment, other than Alli Santana was the most beautiful girl I'd ever seen.

"Hi, Ethan. Nice to meet you," she said. Her voice was soft, and I grinned.

"Come on. I'll show you where you can put your stuff and change."

"Change? I don't have a uniform."

"I'll get you something." I led her to the rear of the restaurant to the staff locker rooms. Five minutes later, she was wearing our usual white shirt with one of my black ties.

I spent the next fifteen minutes showing her around, introducing her to people like Tina, another server, and Dominic, one of the bartenders.

"How old are you?" I asked Alli.

"Um, eighteen." A blush tinted her skin. "Why?"

"Same as me. Okay, since we're underage, we're not allowed to handle alcohol. When your customers order drinks, do this." I doodled a quick sketch of a four-top table with the table's number in the center. At each place at the table, I wrote drink orders. "Got it?"

"Sure. Easy enough."

"Then come to the bar here, by the register. Don't just leave it here and walk away. Make sure Dominic or one of the other bartenders takes it, understands it, because he'll deliver the drinks for you, okay?"

"Yep, got it."

I showed her where the trays were kept for bussing tables, where the pay stations were, how to deliver checks, process credit cards, and where to find stock for her apron, like napkins, straws, extra pens. Lastly, I had her write today's specials on a slip of paper taped to her tray.

"Okay, ready to try one yourself?"

"Um, yeah?" She phrased it as a question and I laughed.

"You got this. Come on. I'll be right there with you."

I led her to a table for two where a couple sat studying menus. They were older, and I hoped that would go well for Alli. More patience.

"*Saluti*," I said. "I'm Ethan and this is Alli. We'll be your servers this evening. Can we get you something from the bar?"

"Um, yes, please. Two white wines?"

I glanced at Alli's pad, indicating she should write that down like I showed her. She'd already written Table 14 in the center and printed WW at each place. I grinned.

"Would you like to hear the specials?" I asked.

"Oh, yes," the woman said with a smile.

"Alli?"

"Oh. Right." Alli cleared her throat. "Tonight, the chef has *osso buco*, slow-braised in red wine and served with baby pota-toes..." she recited.

I took that opportunity to deliver the drink order to Angelo and hurried back to Alli.

"...and our soup of the day is *pasta e fagioli*." She pro-nounced it like an Italian native and I wanted to high-five her.

"We'll give you a few minutes with the menu. Can we get you an appetizer while you wait?"

"Uh, yes, please," the man said. "Hot antipasto, please."

"Right away."

I led Alli to the kitchen, stopping at a pay station first. "Okay, let's start Table 14's check." I tapped at the touch screen, showed her how to enter the two white wines and the appetizer our customers had ordered so far. "It'll take about five minutes or so for the appetizer. Meanwhile, let's get them their bread-basket."

I showed her where the baskets were, lined one with a cloth napkin, took a pair of tongs and filled it with an assortment of breads, rolls, breadsticks from the warmer, as well as a few packets of wrapped crackers. From a chiller, I took a small dish and scooped a ball of butter into it. I put both on her tray.

"Okay, head back to 14 and smile. Put this in the center of the table and say, 'Some fresh bread for you.'"

"Is it fresh?"

"Yeah. We don't recycle the bread. If they don't touch it, it's tossed here." I showed her the bin.

In the dining room, I watched her deliver the breadbasket appropriately.

"Good. Now let's check in with my other tables."

We walked through the section, refilling beverages, taking dessert orders, and replacing dropped silverware.

"Okay. What should we do next?" I asked her.

She frowned and cast an anxious glance around my section. "Um. I don't know. Everybody has what they need."

"Table 14?"

She glanced at the older couple. They'd put their menus down and were sipping their white wines. "I think they're ready to order."

"Good answer. Let's go."

Once again, I let Alli take the lead. The man ordered the *osso buco* special and the woman ordered *chicken francese*. Alli remembered that both entreés come with salad and pasta and took those orders too.

"Very good," Alli said and headed for the pay station to add the meals to the check.

"You're a natural," I told her. "It's been more than five minutes now."

"Oh! The appetizer. I forgot!"

"It's okay. Look here." I showed her an indicator on the screen. "This means that Table 14 has an order up."

"Oh, that's handy."

We headed for the kitchen's prep counter, found our hot antipasto order, and slipped it on Alli's tray. I showed her where to find small plates for the appetizer and added those to her tray too.

"Ready?"

"I am." She grinned, and I was breathless for a minute.

We delivered the appetizer to Table 14 and took two soft drink orders for our couple. *Saluti* stayed busy, but Alli held her own all night. At the end of shift, she was tired but happy.

"That was pretty awesome. Thanks for being so patient with me, Ethan."

I shrugged. "No problem. You're pretty good at this. Is this your first service job?"

She shook her head. "No. I've waitressed in a few diners and a chain restaurant before."

I nodded. "Yeah, you seemed pretty sure of yourself."

She looked at me sharply and guilt twinged inside me. I didn't mean to insult her. But she didn't say anything. I sighed. Talking always got me in trouble.

"Do you have a ride home?" I asked after a minute.

"Oh, well, I was gonna call my mom when the shift was over."

"I can take you home if you want."

She smiled and nodded. "Okay. Yeah. That sounds great."

My heart thudded behind my ribs. "Cool. Um. Okay. Let's finish up."

Alli

I walked beside Ethan to a Hyundai parked at the rear of the lot. He unlocked the doors with the button on his key, but still opened the passenger door for me.

"What's your address?" he said with his eyes on his phone.

I recited it and he tapped it into his phone's GPS app, tucked the phone into a dashboard holder, and put the car in gear. Riverhead, the town where I lived, was about a forty-minute drive from the restaurant, which would give us plenty of time to talk. I'd been hoping to talk to Ethan all night. He was really nice to look at, with light brown hair, a bit of scruff on his jaw, pretty green eyes, and a smile that maybe revealed a dimple just to the right of his mouth. It could have been a trick of the light and I really wanted to see it again to be sure.

"Thank you for all that you did tonight."

"You thanked me already."

Oh. Okay, then. "I hope I didn't slow you down."

"You didn't."

"Will we work together again tomorrow?"

"No. I'm off tomorrow."

I shot him a worried look, but he never took his eyes off the road.

"When's your next shift?" I asked.

"Saturday."

"Awesome! I'm working Saturday too, so hopefully we'll get to partner again."

This time, he did look at me for a second. "Yeah. Hopefully."

A mile went by in complete silence, and I slid a little lower in my seat. Ethan Lewis was a great guy, but maybe he was just polite. I really liked him, but maybe all the courtesy and patience he showed me tonight didn't mean he liked me back.

The thought made me sad.

Thirty-five minutes later, he stopped in front of my house and put the car into park.

"Well," I said, sliding my hands down the front of my pants. "Thanks for—oh. Right. Already thanked you for that. Um.... oh! Thanks for the ride home."

"No problem." He shoved a hand in his pocket, took out some cash and handed it to me.

"What's this?"

"Your share of our tips tonight."

I glanced down, fanned the bills. "Are you kidding me? This is great!" There was over a hundred dollars there.

"You did great work."

Smile. Dimple. It did exist! "Um. Well. Okay. Good night."

"Night."

He didn't open the door this time. But he did wait for me to get inside.

I smiled as I shut the door. I couldn't wait for Saturday.

"Alli, how did you get home? I waited for you to call."

"Hey, Mom. One of the other servers drove me home. I'm sorry. I should have texted you so you could go to sleep."

"I'd have waited up anyway. How was your first shift?"

In response, I showed Mom the cash Ethan had handed me. "My tips."

Mom's eyes went wide. "Good work! This will really help, Alli."

My smile faded. It was a drop in the bucket and we both knew it. "Yeah."

Mom and I were all we had in this world. My dad was long gone—took off after I was born. My grandparents threw Mom out of the house when she got pregnant with me at seventeen. She'd held a series of crappy jobs over the years to support us. Now that college was on my horizon, she'd surprised me with a tiny college fund. It was just enough for community college, and I knew exactly what I wanted to study.

Women's Studies.

With a degree in my hand, I wanted to go into politics and smash the patriarchy. But first, I needed to save enough money for a decent car that would get me to school while Mom was at work. It was her suggestion to look for work in the Hamptons on Long Island's South Fork. The Hamptons were tourist attractions for the rich, the bored, and the famous, and if tonight's shift was average, I'd net a decent sum by the end of the summer.

"I was looking at the college website. Did you know they have a Harry Potter class?"

I smiled at the wistful note in her voice. We'd read Harry Potter together, seen every movie, and planned to drive all the way to Florida one day so we could hit the theme park. Mom was more of a Potter Head than I was. But our shared love of all things Hogwarts wasn't what put the wistfulness into her voice.

She'd really wanted to go to college too. She'd never had the chance. We ate a lot of noodles, but I always had clean clothes and school supplies. She was my best friend, and I wanted so badly to give her a chance at her dream too.

That's why I'd applied for a grant. I figured if I won the grant, she could use the money she'd saved all these years for *her* tuition.

I curled up on the threadbare sofa in our living room and tried to imagine going to college with Mom. She'd be Miss School Spirit. I smiled, picturing her wearing school apparel, attending every game, memorizing the words to the school song. She'd volunteer for all the events, giving tours to incoming freshmen.

I had to make this happen for her.

She'd given me everything.

It was time I gave back.

"Alli, come with me," Angelo, the restaurant's manager, said.

He was an older man, balding on top, with blue eyes that crinkled at the corners. He always wore a suit and when he nodded, he really put his back into it, practically bowing.

Angelo led me to a locker room at the rear of the restaurant and handed me a key.

"This is your locker. You can store your belongings in here, and change into your uniform over there." He waved a hand toward a restroom. "Speaking of, here's a uniform you can wear today." He angled his head and studied me. "Do you have something to put your hair up with?"

"Yes, I have bands and clips. Do you need me to wear a net?"

He shook his head. "No, that's not necessary. I would like you to wash your hands every time you leave this room. Oh, and please stash your cell phone in the locker. I don't want to see you texting or scrolling through your phone when you're out on the floor."

"Yes. Okay."

"You'll be working with Tina Laurelli today."

After Angelo left the room, I took the uniform into a restroom stall and got changed, then spent a few minutes braiding my hair and pinning it up.

I met Tina outside in the dining room. She was working a different section than Ethan and I had last night.

"Hey, Alli. Welcome to *Saluti*. It's nice to meet you."

"You too. So what's first today?"

"Ethan showed you around last night, right? Did he show you where the bus trays are, how to work the pay stations and all that?"

"Yes."

"Really?" She gave me a look of disbelief that I didn't understand. Would I lie about this? Then she shook her head. "Okay. Come on."

Tina explained how to bus tables, replace the linens, flatware, and water glasses. There were no condiments on the tables, only salt and pepper shakers. As for decór, a single white candle in a glass sat in the center of each two- and four-top table. Larger tables had more than one candle. She handed me a long slim lighter and ordered me to light the candle when I greeted customers.

"Hey, Tina. Can I ask you something about Ethan?"

"Sure, but if you're looking in that direction, don't bother. He's, like, painfully shy."

Shy? Hmm. Ethan didn't strike me as shy. Just introverted. He was entirely comfortable being by himself. "What's his story?"

She shrugged. "I honestly don't think he has one, you know? He lives in the next town. Only child. Keeps to himself. Seems nice enough. Respectful, you know?"

Yes! That was exactly the right word for Ethan Lewis.

It was early, barely four o'clock, but we had a few diners to serve. Like yesterday, everything went well and my shift flew by. Late that night, I left the restaurant and waited for the Uber I'd ordered to arrive. Instead, a familiar Hyundai pulled up beside me.

"Hi, Alli."

"Ethan? What are you doing here?"

"Had an errand. Saw you sitting here. Figured you might need a ride?"

I thought about it for less than a minute and grinned. "I do. Thanks." I walked around to the passenger side, climbed in and used my phone to cancel the Uber. "This is great. Thanks a lot."

"No problem."

Silence for a mile.

"How'd your shift go today?" he eventually asked.

"Really good. Tina was today's teacher. She's almost as good as you," I said with a laugh. I wasn't sure since it was so dark, but I think he blushed.

"Tina's nice. When do you work again?"

"I've got tomorrow night and Sunday afternoon shifts."

He nodded. "I can pick you up and drop you off if you want."

Did I want? Definitely. "That would be awesome. I can give you some gas money."

He shook his head. "Don't need it."

Several more miles went by in silence and guilt began to prick at my conscience. Tina said Ethan lived in the next town, and he was willing to go all the way to Riverhead just for me?

It *had* to be a good sign. I had to know. Did he like me as much as I liked him?

"Ethan, I have a question for you."

He glanced at me for a second before returning his gaze to the road. He was a good driver. He signaled when he changed lanes, allowed people to merge in front of him, kept both hands on the wheel, and didn't take chances.

"What?"

I couldn't do it. I couldn't bring myself to ask the question. "The tips! The tips you shared with me last night. Is that a typical night's work here?" Tonight's tips had been less.

He shrugged. "It depends."

"On what?"

"Lots of things. How busy we are. What the specials are. How big each party is. How many turnovers we can manage."

Okay, that all made sense. Tina and I had not served as many tables as Ethan and I had.

We lapsed back into silence all the way home.

"Pick you up at three?"

"My shift starts at four so yeah, that's perfect. What time do you start?"

He shrugged. "Doesn't matter. See you at three."

Once again, he waited for me to get safely inside my front door. When I did, I just leaned against it for a minute.

It was official. I liked Ethan Lewis. Really liked him.

Two weeks passed much the same. Ethan picked me up, we worked, he drove me home. On nights when our schedules did not overlap, he was driving by, had an errand or other reason to be outside the restaurant, ready to drive me home.

One afternoon, on our way to work, I asked him a personal question.

"So what do you like to do when you're not working?"

"Uh, read. I read a lot."

My heart went splat. I adored guys who read. "Tell me about the last book you read."

"I just finished *I Am Malala*."

I thought about that for a minute. "Oh! That was the girl the Taliban shot?"

"Uh huh."

Silence.

"Was it any good?"

He looked confused by my question. "Well, yeah. I wouldn't have finished reading it otherwise."

"Great. Now tell me why."

"Why?" he echoed.

"Yeah. That's when you tell me what you thought was so good about it," I explained with a teasing smile.

He sighed. "There's... a lot."

"Uh huh," I prodded. "That's good. I want to know all of it."

He shifted in the driver's seat, and it suddenly hit me that he was miserably uncomfortable.

"You don't like to talk, do you?"

His face turned to mine so fast I was shocked I didn't hear a snap. "Not really, no."

"How come?"

He lifted a shoulder, let it fall, and didn't say anything until we stopped for a red light. "Talking always gets me into trouble," he said cryptically. I couldn't imagine him saying anything that would upset anybody.

"Okay, first, this is a book discussion, Ethan, not a negotiation for world peace. Just give me one reason why the book was good."

"Malala."

I laughed. "That's cheating. The whole book is about Malala. It's an autobiography, after all."

The light turned green and again, he was silent for about half a mile.

"She's courageous, but I think that was forced on her," he admitted. "She's... persistent," he finally said. "There were threats, but she didn't waver away from her convictions. She wanted an education. Deserved it. She spoke out for that. Even after they shot her, she kept speaking out."

"You admire her for that."

"I admire her for talking about the things she feels so strongly about."

I glanced at the truck driving beside us in the right lane and then turned back to Ethan. "You don't feel strongly about things?"

Another shrug. "Not enough to talk about."

That made me laugh. "Fair enough."

After a few seconds, he smiled too.

It was the best ride to work yet.

Ethan

Driving Alli to and from work became the favorite part of my day.

Until she'd asked me about the last book I read. Now I was rethinking my entire plan.

A trickle of sweat slid down my back. I couldn't think of a single thing to say and finally remembered how persistent Malala was. Alli liked hearing that part.

"Fierce."

Her head turned away from the passenger window. "Malala?"

I nodded. "She believes education is good for girls."

"It is."

"We know that *here*. But in her country, girls don't have the same rights, so she fights for them."

"You think they—I mean, we—should have rights?"

"Definitely."

She smiled. "I agree. I plan to major in Women's and Gender Studies."

I took my eyes off the road long enough to glance at her. "Cool. Where are you going?"

"Suffolk Community."

My stomach did a long slow roll at this news. "Me too."

"Really? That's awesome! I already have one friend in college and haven't started yet."

Friend?

Pride spread at that word, but with it, a strong sense of disappointment. I wanted to be more than friends with Alli. Alli was bright—a star in a dark sky, and I couldn't help but fall into her orbit. She made me want more, more for me and for us. But for there to be an us, I had to *talk* to her, and I wasn't sure I could do that.

Memories of all the times my parents had me tested played in my head. Mom was convinced I was on the spectrum.

"Do you see how you're upsetting your mother? Just speak, damn it. It's not difficult!"

"What do you plan to study?"

I jerked. "What?"

"I asked what you plan to study?"

"Don't know yet." I shrugged and then braced for the sigh of frustration that always came in conversations like this.

"That's okay. You'll figure it out. You're smart."

Shocked delight nearly had me stopping the car right there on Montauk Highway. Smart? I didn't know about that. I mean, sure, I got good grades on tests, because it was easy to take tests when you didn't have much else to do except study.

"If you could have anything in the entire world just by making a wish, what would you want?" Alli asked as I reached the edge of town.

You, I thought. I want you. Wishes were pointless. What I wanted, no one could give me. I wanted my parents to be proud of me whether I talked or didn't talk. I wanted words to come easy and not get stuck in my throat, choking me with guilt and anxiety.

Alli nodded. "I totally get that."

I almost plowed through a stop sign. I'd said that out loud? How? How was that possible? I turned to look at Alli.

It was her.

She was magic.

"I never met my dad. It's just me and my mom, and I really want her to have a life. She had me when she was seventeen. I want so badly for her to be able to do the things she didn't get the chance to do when she was my age. That's why I'm working all the way out here. Better tips in the Hamptons. I need enough to buy a car. Then, I'll go to school even through summers. The sooner I finish, the sooner I can get a job that will take care of her. How about you? Got any siblings?"

"Two brothers, both older." My parents were in their thirties when I was born. I wasn't sure they'd ever really wanted *me*.

"That's cool. I always wanted brothers."

Bitter memories rushed through me and I shook my head. "Trust me, you don't."

She laughed and the sound made me smile. I'd made a joke and she'd laughed.

"So how come you think your parents aren't proud of you?"

My hand jerked on the steering wheel. "I didn't say that."

"You didn't have to. I could just tell."

"My brothers are heroes. One's Navy. The other's FDNY. Then, there's me."

"How old are they?"

"Twenty-eight and twenty-four." I pulled into the parking lot, found a spot, and shut off the car.

A brilliant idea hit me. I tugged my phone out of my pocket, handed it to her, and said, "Put in your number so I can text you about the books I've read."

"Sure." She tapped at the screen and handed the phone back to me. "Here you go. Have a good shift!"

I sat in the car alone for a minute longer, staring after her. It wasn't until I caught sight of my reflection in the mirror that I realized I was grinning. With a laugh, I started a text message on the phone still in my hand.

Alli

My phone pinged when I reached the staff locker room. It was Ethan.

Puzzled, I opened the message.

Malala fascinates me because she's just a few years older than me and has fought for so much. Not just her right to an education. She fought for her life! She continues to fight for things she cares about even though she was shot for speaking up. Someone told me to shut up once and it stuck with me I guess. I can't imagine feeling so certain, so outraged over something, that I'd be willing to speak up about it like she did. I hope I will one day. My mom says I have a nice voice.

I read the message twice and finally tapped back one of my own.

You have a great voice. Deep and rumbly. I like it. Can I borrow your Malala book? I think I'd like to learn more about her.

A moment later, my phone pinged again and I grinned. It was an alert from Amazon informing me that Ethan Lewis shared a book with me. I kept that smile while I finished changing.

The door squeaked and Tina strode in. "Hey, new girl. How's it going?"

"Good," I said with a grin.

"Must be. You got Ethan Lewis to speak in complete sentences. I'd thought he was, you know..." she circled a finger near her head.

I shook my head. Ethan was cool. Yeah, he was quiet, but that didn't mean he was slow. "So, you're saying Ethan's a quiet guy?"

"Quiet? Sweetie, that boy is practically mute."

I shrugged. "I think he's nice."

"Oh, he is, totally, but I swear to you that boy is silent as a statue on most days. Getting him to talk practically needs a Congressional order and even then, he'd probably just plead the Fifth."

Maybe so. But that didn't change how I felt about him. The butterflies that took flight in my belly whenever I heard his deep voice, the skip in my heartbeat when he looked at me. "I want to ask him out."

"Wait, what?" She stared at me, brown eyes wide. "You can't do that."

"Oh, God. He's seeing someone?"

"No." Tina waved a hand impatiently. "You just can't give a guy that much power. Ever."

I laughed. "Okay, then what's your suggestion? If I wait much longer, we'll both be off to college and never see each other again."

She blinked. "Okay, that may be a small point, but still. Asking a guy out just reveals your whole hand, you know?"

Maybe that was true, but I didn't care. I wanted to go out with Ethan, and I was running out of time. "Talk later? I have to hit the floor."

"Me too. Have a good shift."

Ethan

"Whoa, is that a smile, Ethan?" Dominic taunted me from behind the bar. "Better watch it or Angelo will make you take a drug test."

I rolled my eyes. "Hey, I smile."

"Yeah, about as often as you speak in complete sentences. So what put that smile on your face? Anything to do with a certain new server you keep arriving with?"

The smile dripped off my face.

"Yeah. I had a feeling." Dominic glanced toward section two, which was now Alli's section. "She's gorgeous. And nice too."

"Smart," I replied.

Dominic's eyebrows arched. "You like smart, huh? Me? I'm a giggle kind of guy. When a girl has a great laugh, I'm all in."

I grinned. Alli had a great laugh too.

Dominic shielded his eyes. "Whoa, dude. Dial it down a notch, okay?"

Laughing, I turned when I heard my name.

"Ethan." Angelo motioned me over to the hostess stand. "Party of twelve. Push together tables 12, 13, and 14. You and Alli will both serve."

Alli? My day just got brighter.

I made my way across the busy floor and began assembling the table.

"Hey, Ethan!" Alli joined me. "We've got a twelve-header. How do you want to tackle this?"

I smiled. "How about if I take the back six, you take the front?"

"Works for me," she said.

Alli's glossy curtain of hair was currently tied back in a braid, and she looked amazing in her server's uniform. It had been about two weeks since she started, and there was no doubt in my mind she could handle this large party.

Angelo led the group to the table and seated them with menus and the wine list. Alli murmured, "I'll fetch the bread. How many?"

"Four," I replied, and signaled one of the busboys to fill the water glasses. "But hold off a minute." I led her to the head of the table where an older man sat, clearly the host of this party.

"*Saluti* and welcome," I began. "My name is Ethan and this is Alli. We'll be your servers this evening. Would you like anything from the bar while you decide?"

"Yeah!" one of the guests called out, a young guy in his twenties. "I'll have a Bud and a shot and her phone number." He ran his eyes up and down Alli's body, licking his lips, and my smile evaporated.

"Matt," the older man said. "Maybe you could wait until your mother and sister have ordered?"

"Honestly, Matt." The woman identified as Matt's mother gave him a smile.

I waited a beat, but nobody scolded Matt for what he'd said to Alli.

The guy called Matt rolled blue eyes to heaven and waved a hand in an overly magnanimous gesture for the ladies to go first.

I turned to his mother and took her drink order, followed by the order from a younger woman I had to card. Twenty-one on the nose. Today's date matched the birthday on her ID, and I wondered if that was the reason for their visit.

When it was finally the obnoxious guy's turn, I asked, "Still want that boilermaker?"

He shot me a look that clearly said I was a moron. "Uh, I asked for a beer and a shot."

I suppressed an eye roll of my own because that's what a boilermaker was. I carded him too. Twenty-five.

"Also, I still want your partner's phone number."

"Not on the menu."

He held out a twenty-dollar bill between two fingers. "Make an exception."

"No."

The bill disappeared and Matt shrugged.

I asked Alli to recite today's specials while I delivered the drink orders to Dominic at the bar, then hurried back to help take orders.

"Uh, hey. Could you repeat that one with the steak?" Matt asked Alli.

"Yes, sir. It's a certified Angus Beef sirloin, sliced and sautéed with a Cabernet mushroom sauce, served with garlic mashed potatoes, and a choice of house or Caesar salad."

"Done. I'll have that."

"Matthew." Again, his father snapped at him for forgetting proper etiquette.

"Jeez, Dad. Relax. It's okay. Alli here's got me covered. Right, Alli?" Matt snaked an arm around Alli's waist and tugged her to his side. She stiffened, and I came dangerously close to grabbing a butter knife and throwing it ninja-style at his throat. But she was cool under pressure. She smiled politely, the grabbed his thumb and peeled it away so she could neatly side-step out of his grip.

Dominic arrived with the drinks, served Matt's mother and sister first before making his way around the table.

"Boilermaker for you, sir."

I swallowed a grin at Matt's flash of annoyance.

At the opposite end of the long table, another man motioned me closer with a wave of two fingers. He was older than Matt, but not by much. "Dude. Extra tip for you if you water down my brother's drinks. He's an obnoxious drunk, and this is a big day for our sister." He jerked his chin toward Matt.

I nodded, not bothering to add that Matt was obnoxious sober too.

Alli and I took the group's dinner orders and headed for the kitchen to fetch the bread.

"That Matt guy is gonna be a problem, Ethan," Alli warned.

Yeah. I had the same feeling. "Want to talk to Angelo?"

Alli's eyes went wide. "What? No! I don't want to give them a reason to leave no tip."

"He touched you. That's not okay."

"Yeah. I was there. And you're right. It's not okay. But I can't afford to make a big deal out of this, Ethan. I've been putting up with crap like this since I was eleven."

I spread my hands. "What do you want to do, then?"

"Swap sides with me?"

"Done."

"Really? You don't think I'm being too dramatic or something?"

"No."

Her shoulders fell an inch and she put a hand to her chest. "Thanks. There's something else I want to talk to you about."

"Now?"

"Sure." She grabbed four baskets and I lined them with cloth napkins, adding fresh rolls from the warmer. Alli was deliberately not looking at me. "Would you, maybe, um, like to go out with me sometime? Dinner or a movie?"

The roll I was just about to drop into the last basket squirted out from between the blades of the tongs and landed on the floor. I dove for it before someone slipped on it, tossed it into the waste bin. Still holding the tongs, I turned to face her. "You want to go out... with *me*?"

Huge hazel eyes melted when the anxious smile on her face broadened into a full grin. "I do. The question is, do you?"

"Yeah."

She blew out a breath and dropped her shoulders. "Thank God. I was afraid maybe I'd misunderstood the signals."

Wait, what? "Signals?"

"Yes, Ethan. Signals. You're pretty good at the whole nonverbal communication thing, you know." She angled closer to me, dropped her voice a little. "Picking me up when I know you don't live anywhere near Riverhead, the way you study my face when you talk to me, especially my mouth. I figure you must really want to kiss me."

Oh, I really did.

"I'd really like to kiss you too. I thought you should know."

With two of the four bread baskets in her hands, she disappeared through the kitchen door, leaving me with a big goofy grin on my face—and half the kitchen staff staring at me like I'd just hatched from a free-range egg.

I took the other two baskets and quickly followed.

Alli

That went well.

Ethan seemed happy—a little stunned—but happy, and I thought I might have a boyfriend.

The thought put a little hum in my heart. There was something special about Ethan. Ethan Lewis was tall, hot, and possessed a devastatingly sexy voice. He had sandy brown hair worn a bit messy, a light beard, and the most amazing green eyes I'd ever seen. They changed colors. When he was wearing wait-staff black and white, they were green. But in street clothes, they often looked yellow, depending on the color he wore. And his voice was like *whoa*. Deep. Slow, almost a drawl. It was *compelling*. He didn't use that voice often, but when he *did* talk, it seemed like the entire restaurant went quiet just to hear him. Every time I looked at him, I had this feeling that his quiet demeanor hid a deep and interesting mind—ripples on water that was fathoms deep.

"Fresh bread for you," I murmured and put the first basket down at the head of the table near Matt and his father. I moved down the table to place the second basket. Ethan was right there, delivering the third and fourth baskets.

We shared a smile across the table.

"Oh, so that's why he wouldn't give me your phone number," said Matt. "He's doing you."

My jaw dropped at the crude term, but I managed to maintain professionalism and ignore the little jerk. I stepped around the table to Ethan's side and cleared my throat. "Are you ready to order or would you prefer a few more minutes?"

"I know what I'd prefer."

Ethan's head snapped to Matt, but I gently stepped on his toes.

"We're ready to order," Matt's father said.

As agreed, Ethan and I split and began taking orders at opposite ends of the long table, meeting in the center.

"Oh, and I'd like hot and cold antipasto platters for the table."

I nodded, added that to the order and returned to the kitchen. At *Saluti*, we delivered our own food. Runners were used mostly for bar orders. Ethan had shown me how the kitchen was organized. Cold appetizers were made in batches, so I retrieved a platter from the walk-in, put it on a tray. The hot platter had to be made.

"Let's do a section check," Ethan reminded me.

I left the tray on the counter and followed him. We stopped at each of our tables, refilled drink orders, supplied extra silverware and napkins, and took dessert orders. Ethan headed for the bar and I'd just dropped the check on a table for two when The Jerk stepped in front of me.

"There you are, sweet thing," he said, aiming a grin at my chest. "Thought you forgot about me."

Forgot? Frantically, I searched my memory. Had he ordered something I'd forgotten to serve? I'd done the drinks, delivered the bread baskets. Their appetizers, salads, and entreés were in prep right now.

"No, sir, just busy serving my customers. Did you need something?"

He laughed a low, kind of smarmy laugh. "I do need something, but I keep hearing it's not on the menu." He leaned closer and whispered a crude comment in my ear.

Check, please! We're done here.

"Alli, can you give me a hand?" Tina called out from the pay station.

I spun around and joined Tina with a nod of thanks for her handy escape route. I gave myself a pat on the back for not smacking that smarmy grin off the jerk's face.

"I don't really need help. I just thought you needed an escape. That creep looked like he wanted to throw you up against a wall."

"Yeah. Thanks. He is a jerk." I told her what he'd whispered in my ear and her jaw dropped. "Thanks again." I headed for the kitchen to check on the appetizers.

At that moment, Angelo caught up to me. "Hey, Alli, what's the issue with your large party? One of the customers just informed me that you ignored him when he requested a birthday cake for his sister."

"No one asked for a birthday cake, Angelo."

Angelo shut his eyes and cracked his neck to one side. "Alli. I know you're still new, but I don't like when my staff lies to me. I just saw him talk to you and you spun around without so much as a nod. That is *not* how I want customers treated in my restaurant."

"That's because he was ordering *me*, not cake, on my knees, Angelo. I thought it was best that I simply ignore him. Do you understand?"

"Alli," Angelo said, hands lifted in a conciliatory gesture. "Sometimes the customers get a little fresh and you have to learn how to handle that politely and without embarrassing them. It's part of the job. If you can't handle that—"

"Angelo, I think I handled the situation extraordinarily well given that your customer is not currently sporting a fat lip for what he just said to me."

Ethan stepped through the kitchen door at that moment, eyes darting from me to Angelo and back again.

"Problem?" he asked.

Angelo turned to me. "Alli needed to be reminded to be more pleasant and courteous to our customers. Make sure that she is." He strode out of the kitchen before either of us could reply.

"Ethan, I'm sorry." I let out a loud sigh.

He shook his head. "Don't apologize. I heard what that guy said to you."

"You did? How?"

"A customer at another table told me. I never should have left you alone."

I shot out a hand, waved it around the restaurant. "It's not your fault some guy with entitlement issues thinks because he's spending some money he can get whatever he wants. I just wish I wasn't the one in trouble because of him."

"Oh. Well, I—um."

I grabbed the platter of appetizers and delivered them to their table. The Jerk wasn't in his seat, so I relaxed a bit. I was just about to place a heavy platter of hot antipasto on the table when I felt fingers squeeze my bottom. I spun around, finding Matt sitting beside me, and forgot all about the hot platter in my hands, sending peppers, mushrooms, and mussels marinara flying. Gasps, shouts, and scrapes of chair legs on the tile floor filled the dining room, but the only thing I heard was the indignant insult lobbed from the head of the table.

"You clumsy idiot! Look what you did to my daughter's dress."

I lifted my eyes, saw the birthday girl's designer duds splashed with sauce and olive oil, and my heart sank. That dress was ruined now.

"I'm sorry," I told her, but that seemed to be the wrong thing to say. She leaped up and ran from the table, crying loudly. Her mother ran after her, spearing me with a glare as she ran.

And Angelo was suddenly right there. "Alli? What happened?"

"Angelo. This customer grabbed me inappropriately while I was serving a hot dish."

A curse sounded from the other end of the table. "Matt, what the hell did you do now?"

"Me? I'm just sitting here, Luke. Not my fault Angelo employs clumsy people."

"Listen up, you little jerk," I slammed back, but Angelo shot me a warning look. Yeah, yeah, the customer's always right. I needed this damn job, so I shut my mouth.

"The girl says someone grabbed her, and that's your M.O.," said the man at the far end of the table.

"Luke, that's enough," the older man at the head of the table said.

"Ethan, there you are," Angelo said.

I whipped around, saw Ethan standing beside the table.

"Did you witness any of this bad behavior Alli is accusing our customer of demonstrating?"

"Bad behavior?" he echoed.

I waited for him to say something, but Mr. Strong and Silent was mute. I scanned the rest of the dining room and no one would meet my eyes. That was perfect, just perfect.

"Yes, Ethan," Angelo snapped. "Bad behavior. Try to keep up."

"Yes. I did. He put an arm around her waist earlier," he said with a scowl. "And said a few inappropriate things."

"And? What's wrong with a friendly arm around you?" the father demanded.

Ethan's eyebrows met and his scowl deepened. "He didn't ask first."

"That's ridiculous!" the older man said. "It was a harmless friendly gesture." To Angelo he said, "I demand an apology from that server. Her incompetence ruined my daughter's twenty-first birthday."

"Dad, jeez, it's spilled food. It's not a big deal," the one the man had called Luke said.

The man stood. "It *is* a big deal," he insisted.

Luke stood too.

"Where the hell are you going?" his father demanded.

"I'm not going to stand here and watch you berate the server for Matt's rudeness."

"Me? How was I rude?" Matt asked. "I've been nothing but charming."

Charming? Seriously? I rolled my eyes.

"Did you see that look?" Matt's father waved a hand toward me.

When Angelo turned to me with fire in his eyes, I knew it was over. If I didn't apologize, I'd be out, and I really needed this job. I'd really needed the tip from this service tonight too. But if I *did* apologize, it would be admitting I'd done something wrong. That I was clumsy, stupid, incompetent, or whatever else they called me.

I was *none* of those things.

I blinked, trying like mad to stop the tears that burned in the back of my eyes. It wasn't fair. I was the *victim* here, not the perpetrator. I'd dropped a hot dish of food because someone touched me inappropriately.

I shot beseeching looks to Ethan, to Tina, to Dominic at the bar, to the rest of the staff, but no one, not one person spoke up for me.

I was completely alone in this.

I turned and left the dining room.

Ethan

Rage ignited in me—a match thrown on gasoline. "This is his fault," I said, glaring at Matt.

"Ethan. Quiet," Angelo snapped. "Mr. Reilly, I assure you my servers are carefully trained—"

"Carefully trained? That's a joke. Any girl who doesn't know when to expect a friendly touch or an appreciative hug isn't cut out to serve. My son—"

"Is out of line, Dad, and you know it. Stop defending him for once and apologize for the damage you permitted to occur." The man at the other end of the table flung his napkin down. "Matt is a spoiled brat, and all of this drama is due directly to his behavior from the minute we sat down." He waved a hand at me. "If *he'd* given Tiffany that same *friendly touch*, you'd have had a lot to say then and you know it."

"That's ridiculous." The father turned to Angelo. "I expect you to handle this to my satisfaction."

Angelo's hands came up, surrender style, and he wore his customer service smile, the one designed to soothe and pacify.

Throughout the drama, Matt continued to sit, the stupid little smirk never faltering. I wanted to knock that smirk off his face for what he'd done to Alli. One by one, the other guests at the table stood and murmured their apologies as they walked out, leaving only Matt, his father, and his brother staring each other down.

Slowly, I scanned the entire dining room. Servers all looked away, pretended to be busy. Other customers stared in disbelief or disgust at Matt and his family. Dominic stood with his arms crossed behind the bar, jaw clenched.

But not one person said a word.

No one stood up and told Angelo that Alli wasn't the one at fault here. My chest ached and I breathed through the pain, but the ache became a flame, burning through my bones, my muscles, my skin, until I had no choice but to let it out.

I opened my mouth, chest heaving, and pointed a finger directly at Matt, still sitting, still smirking, still enjoying the hell out of this play he directed. "You."

I waited until those bland blue eyes shifted, focused on me, until the words, all the words, lined up on the tip of my tongue, ready to rush out.

"What you did here today was completely classless. You have no honor. No respectability. You do all men a disservice and you," I turned on his father. "You enabled him instead of corrected him, you scolded him only when he failed to consider his sister or his mother, but my colleague was insulted and molested and then got the blame for spilling food that your son made her spill, and yet you said absolutely nothing. No wonder he has no idea what it means to be a good man. That girl," I stabbed a finger in the direction Alli had run, "is trying to save enough money to get herself to college this fall, but nobody at this table saw her as a human being."

My voice, rusty from so many years of silence, grew stronger with every word until I was practically shouting.

"I saw you, *Matthew.*"

His name on my lips tasted bitter.

"I saw you lick your lips as soon as you noticed Alli. I saw you track her movements across the restaurant. You waited, deliberately, until she'd approached another table so you could get away with a disgusting suggestion. You exploited her role as your server, not once but many times, physically communicating your sexual interest in her even though you were told clearly and more than once that she is not on our menu."

"I have heard all I'm going to take—" His father stepped toward me.

I spun toward him so fast, he jolted and froze where he stood. "What kind of man teaches his son to tell a woman he does not know to get on her knees for him? What kind of man can stand here while his son gloats and demand that a young woman be fired when she is the victim of a crime?"

"Oh, give it a rest. There was no crime here. I was having a little fun. Big deal."

I jabbed a finger toward him. "That, right there, is your problem, Matthew. You don't see the crime here. Women are here for no other reason than to pleasure you. Deliver you some food, deliver you some sex."

His smirk split into a grin. "Still not seeing the problem, chief."

"The problem, *dimwit,*" I shot back, "is that you put your hands on someone without consent. That's illegal."

He shrugged. "My bad. I'll pay a fine, say I'm sorry. Can I get my meal now? I'm hungry."

I turned back to his father, eyebrows raised. A muscle in Mr. Reilly's jaw twitched. "Still nothing to say? I'm done with you."

I spun, faced Angelo. "These… people," I said with a sneer, "are not up to *Saluti* standards and should not be permitted back. Alli deserves an apology. Fire her, and I will quit."

Angelo's jaw dropped.

"So will I," Tina Laurelli called out.

"Me too," Dominic said.

The door to the kitchen opened. Chef stood there. "Me too."

Angelo adjusted his tie, shifted his weight. Then he took out his phone and snapped a picture of Matt Reilly. "Dom, would you print this out and hang it near the bar? Instruct all staff to refuse service to Matthew Reilly."

"With pleasure." Dom came around the bar, took Angelo's phone, and headed for the locker room in the back.

"I will have your license for this," Matt's father shouted. His face was as red as our pasta sauce.

"The exit is straight ahead and to your left."

Two uniformed police officers stepped inside at that moment and walked directly toward us.

"Who's in charge here?"

"Uh, me." Angelo raised a hand.

"Someone molested one of your servers?"

"Molested! Oh, come on!" Matt's father objected.

"He did, officer." I pointed to Matt.

The second officer walked around the table, took handcuffs from his belt, and ordered Matt to stand up.

"You witnessed this?"

"I did. Twice. He wrapped an arm around our server's waist, said something inappropriate to her, and then squeezed her rear end, causing her to drop a platter of hot food."

"It was harmless flirting!" Matt's father protested. He rounded on Angelo again. "Do you know who I am? I can shut this place down for good."

"Can you arrest him too, for threats and harassment?" I asked one of the cops.

"Who called the police?" Matt's father spun on the spectators. "Which one of you with your little cell phones and social media accounts decided to call the police?"

"I did, Dad."

All eyes snapped to Matt's brother, Luke.

"I called them because even though you think Matt's adorable, the truth is, this was entirely his fault."

"Lucas. Your own brother! How could you?"

"How couldn't you?" Luke shot back. "How come you didn't stop him the second he asked for that young girl's phone number? How come you don't see what's right in front of you? Matt's a twenty-five-year-old infant who does not understand the meaning of the word NO."

The snap of the handcuffs around Matt's wrists was loud enough to hear across the dining room. The officers perp-walked him out of the restaurant, his father already on his phone, calling a lawyer no doubt.

Luke, Matt's brother, tugged a wallet from his pocket. He dropped several bills on the table and turned to me.

"I apologize for my entire family today, Ethan. I wish I could tell you this was out of character for them, but sadly, it's typical. This is for you and for Alli." To Angelo, he said, "Please don't fire that young lady."

He walked out of the restaurant too, leaving us staring after him.

"Okay. Back to work, all." Angelo waved his hands and then moved from table to table, assuring the rest of our diners that the trouble was over.

"Ethan." Tina jerked her chin toward the rear of the restaurant. I followed her gaze and found Alli staring at me with tears in her eyes, both hands pressed to her mouth.

My stomach dropped. A wave of panic surged through me, freezing me where I stood. Oh, God. *My words.* I'd made Alli cry. The first time in my entire life I cared about something enough to speak up, speak out, and—

I'd hurt her.

Alli

My hands shook as I stood in the corridor at the rear of the restaurant that led to our locker room.

I'd heard every word Ethan said.

Ethan.

The boy who hated to talk just delivered a silver-tongued speech and told off a room full of people—including our boss.

My eyes blurred and my throat burned, but I made my way back to the dining room and watched him take command of that room.

I liked Ethan Lewis. Really liked him. I liked him when he patiently trained me on my first shift. I liked him when he drove me home. I liked him when he was quiet. I liked him when he told me he hated to talk. But seeing him stare down that fool and his family, hearing the words, those beautiful, perfect words he spit at them? I wanted to run to him, fling my arms around him, and never let him go.

I pulled in a deep breath and stepped back into the dining room. Tina saw me first and told Ethan. My face heated as I walked toward him with everybody watching, including the rest of our customers still at their tables. Ethan dropped his head, and it hit me that he must think my tears meant I was angry.

I wasn't angry one bit.

I walked toward him, trying to put into words just how deeply his actions today affected me. But for Ethan, actions always spoke louder than words, so I walked straight toward him and wrapped my arms around him. He gasped and then sighed, and a second later, he was hugging me back.

A second after that, applause filled the restaurant.

"I thought I upset you."

I pulled away, just far enough to look him directly in the eye. "No. Ethan, I am so incredibly grateful for everything you said."

"You... you heard everything?"

I nodded. "You were amazing." I flashed him a wide smile. "My favorite part was when you called him a dimwit."

Ethan smiled and that dimple teased me. "I made you cry. I didn't mean to."

"Good tears," I assured him.

A throat cleared. We split apart, found Angelo standing behind us. "You two might, ah, want to take a short break right now."

Right. Of course. I took Ethan's hand and headed for the rear door, diners still applauding as we went.

Outside, I led Ethan to a bench near the water and sank down to it, happy to be off my feet for a few minutes. Ethan sat beside me. It was hot and a little humid outside but neither of us complained.

"So," I began. "For a guy who hates talking, you brought the house down with that speech."

A snort of laughter burst out of him. "Yeah. I guess I did."

"How did it feel?"

He rubbed the back of his neck and made a face. "I'm not entirely sure. I think maybe I was possessed or something."

"Were you scared?"

Ethan's expression turned serious and he looked away. "To the bone."

Tenderness filled my heart. "But you said all those things anyway."

"Well, yeah. Someone had to. Angelo almost fired you."

I nodded. I'd heard. "Thank you."

We sat in silence for a few minutes, looking at the water.

"I used to talk too much back when I was little. Made my parents crazy."

His words were rushed, like they'd just broken through a dam, and they held so much pain it took my breath away.

"I was four or five years old. I had an early bedtime and sneaked down the stairs because I heard everybody laughing. Mom, Dad. My brothers. They were laughing at me. How I never shut up. Made their ears bleed. Exhausted them. They put me to bed early just to get some peace."

My throat burned while I tried to stifle a sob, but I stayed quiet so he could finish, get it all out.

"My brothers, they're both older than me. Wanted. Loved. I was...an accident. It started as a punishment. You know," he explained with a tight smile. "Like, 'I'll never talk again and then they'll be sorry.' Only it worked even better than I'd expected." He shrugged like it was no big deal, but a storm swirled in his eyes and my heart cracked down the center. "They kept saying what a good boy I was, how much I'd grown up, how proud they were so I just... kept it up."

And I was telling him the same things for doing exactly the opposite. The crack in my heart widened. I took his hand, waited until he looked at me. When he did, there was no trace of the pain I'd heard.

He'd gotten good at hiding it over the years.

I swallowed hard. "Ethan, how do you feel right now?"

A frown line creased his forehead. He didn't answer for a minute.

I took my phone out and opened the text message he'd sent me earlier. "You told me before, '*I can't imagine feeling so certain, so outraged over something, that I'd be willing to speak up about it like she did. I hope I will one day. My mom says I have a nice voice.*' Well, you did it. You spoke up over something that outraged you. You saved a job I need pretty badly. And for the record, your mom is right. You have an amazing voice."

Slowly, the line on his forehead smoothed and his lips twitched. "I... guess I feel proud of myself," he finally answered.

"For the record," I began, taking his hand in mine, "I like you when you make incredible speeches *and* when you're quiet. I like you when you're training me, when you're driving miles out of your way just for me, *and* when you're sitting by yourself reading books on your phone. You never have to earn that, Ethan. You never have to fake it with me. It just *is*."

His smile was so wide it made his eyes crinkle. He lifted a hand, touched my cheek, making me shiver in the hot, humid air. My heart sped up, and I might have stopped breathing until the moment when his lips touched mine—warm and soft and perfect, like I imagined they would be. Better, even. I closed my eyes and sank into the kiss I'd wanted since my first shift. Ethan's hands shifted to my hair and I melted into him, deepening the kiss. It went on and on and on, speaking the words Ethan hadn't been able to say.

Until now.

Other Published Works

READ MORE BY PATTY BLOUNT

Send – Sourcebooks Fire – 2012

TMI – Sourcebooks Fire – 2013

Some Boys – Sourcebooks Fire – 2014

A Match Made at Christmas (Christmas in New York #4) –
Tule Publishing Group – 2014

Nothing Left to Burn – Sourcebooks Fire – 2015

His Touch (Heroes of New York #1)
– Tule Publishing Group – 2015

The Paramedic's Rescue (Heroes of New York Book 1)
– 2015

The Way It Hurts – Sourcebooks Fire – 2017

Nobody Said It'd Be Easy – Tule Publishing Group – 2018

Someone I Used to Know – Sourcebooks Fire – 2018

FOR MORE, VISIT
www.pattyblount.com

Star-Crossed Lovers and Other Strangers

I slam on my brakes as soon as I see her. Blonde hair flying everywhere as she springs from the curb. I crank the wheel hard and my tires almost follow her up the sidewalk. Pounding my '73 Chevy into park, I leap from the driver's seat. She paces between my truck and the town's one and only pizza place, mumbling something I can't hear. Like sitting on a curb isn't risky and I'm the one at fault just because I took a second too long to decide where to park.

"What kind of person sits in the street? I could've hit you!" My voice is an octave higher than normal thanks to the mass amounts of adrenaline pumping through my body. I clear my throat and point to the spot where my tire is jammed against the curb. "Do you know how dangerous that is?"

She balances on one very shapely leg while bending and straightening the other. "Maybe if you paid attention to where you were going, I wouldn't have pulled every muscle in my leg trying to *not* become roadkill."

"Maybe if you paid attention to, you know, cars. In the street. Where they belong? You wouldn't have to worry about *becoming* roadkill." My words are as punchy as her expression, but I don't look away. Normally, I'm the first one to give in, but this is a new place. Might as well try a new attitude. She stares right back, too, her chin high, huffing like a bull about to charge. I've only been here a few weeks, and I've already made a potential enemy.

Awesome.

I have no idea who this girl is. She's pretty enough: button nose and large brown eyes. She could be town royalty—the new Miss Fish Derby Queen, or whatever they call those girls competing for the privilege of posing for the paper, wearing waders standing next to a bass. Even if she's not Miss Derby Queen— which I'll apparently be covering in a month or so—my boss at the paper told me there's a mere 347 students at the high school, which means I'm bound to see her all the time. If I want any shot at a hassle-free senior year in this one-stoplight, blink-and-you-miss-it place, I should try to make peace.

I miss San Francisco.

Taking a deep breath, I run my hand through my hair and shake away the dark brown pieces that fall into my eyes.

"Obviously, neither of us was paying all that much attention. I'm Tristan. I'm fairly new around here, so I didn't realize I should've been scouring the curbs for seated innocents. We sit on benches in the City." I flash a smile, hoping she'll do the same.

"Is that your attempt at an apology? Are you curb shaming me right now? Seriously?" She shakes her hands like she's flicking water. "Maybe if you had a vehicle from this century, you'd be able to see properly. It's 2002. Get with the times. They have electric locks and power steering now, *Tristan*." She spits out my name like she's Malfoy and I'm Potter.

"Are you truck shaming me? Seriously?" I match her tone, more than a little surprised I've kept up this long. She rolls her eyes. Trying to calm down, I take a deep breath. "Look. No one got hurt." I open the passenger door and hoist my camera bag over my shoulder. "I just came here to do my job."

"What's that? Committing vehicular homicide?" Her hands stop flicking and rest on her hips. I drag my hands down my face. *So much for a peaceful senior year.* Pretty or not, this girl is a lot.

"Yes. My job is to commit vehicular homicide. Right after I take pictures for *The Vine Press.*" I motion to the paper offices across the street. "And I need to make my appointment, so if you don't mind…"

"You aren't the only one with things to do." She pivots to the door of Pizza Magic. Exactly where I'm headed.

Great.

I jog ahead of her, open the door with one hand, and motion for her to go through with the other. But she stands there, arms crossed and a death glare aimed right at me. Damn, her forehead makes a cute little crinkle when she stares, all stubborn and angry.

"I'm trying to be nice," I say through gritted teeth. *Manning up,* as my dad says.

"I don't need anyone to hold a door for me. You were here first. You go."

"Fine." I walk into the restaurant, letting the door swing shut behind me. I literally bite my tongue so she can have the last word.

I scan the room searching for someone in charge. Most of the tables are empty. A few people lurk by the bar in the back corner and no one's taking orders at the counter. There's a few girls hanging around the video games against the right wall, but I can't find anyone in an apron or Pizza Magic T-shirt.

Curb Girl slams into the far corner booth next to the stage, which is—you guessed it—right where I need to set up. I shake my head, sending the universe an ironic message for Thoughts and Prayers that I can quickly take enough pics of Karaoke Night for tomorrow's copy and get out of here before she explodes. She faces the kitchen and glares, shooting death rays to some poor unfortunate. I follow her angry gaze to a couple of aproned, well-muscled guys coming out of the storeroom. I can't help but wonder which one is the lucky recipient of Curb Girl's hate stare.

Getting back to work, I kneel and set my bag on the ground in front of the stage, then loop my camera strap around my arm. Curb Girl sighs so hard I'm scared all the napkins have flown off the table. Ignoring her, I fumble with the lens, making sure the focus is correct. She sighs again. This time, it's more voice than breath.

I am not turning around.

I take a few practice shots of the stage, studying how I want to frame people when they're at the mic. Now she's mumbling something unintelligible but loud enough to be distracting.

Lowering my camera, I face her. "Are you all right?"

"Mind your own business." She bolts from the booth toward the kitchen and drags one of the guys tossing balls of dough into circles into the storeroom. The group of girls who'd been hovering by the Ms. Pac-Man descend on her abandoned booth, claiming the seats for themselves.

Raised but unintelligible voices thunder from behind the kitchen, and a hush falls over the quickly filling seats. It's obvious everyone in town knows what's going on. Pretty much a small-town requirement. The girls in the booth smirk at each other—they look way too happy about the argument to be her friends. Maybe she's not the Miss Fish Derby type after all.

I snap a few pictures of the karaoke equipment and playlist to fill the time.

An older man wearing an Oakland A's baseball cap and a sauce-stained apron tucked under his belly barrels onto the stage waving frantically and clearing his throat. Something metal crashes onto the floor in the kitchen. The man nods to a mustached skinny guy behind the bar, who plods toward the noise.

The man on stage does his best *Dazed and Confused* impression. "All right, all right, all right!" Ignoring the action in the back of the building, I take a few pics of him while the audience is forced to switch their attention from the back of the restaurant to the beginning of karaoke night. Some other guy in a cleaner apron flips on the monitor as a few people line up to choose songs. I back up to the order line for some wider shots of all the activity.

Behind the counter, one of the guys pushes pizzas around the inside of the oven with a huge spatula while another sprinkles cheese over sauce and dough. I stall by shooting a couple frames of them working on the off chance I might see Curb Girl. Not that I want to see *her*, I only want to make sure she's okay. For potential post near-death injury claims.

I cringe at my logic. Even I know that's lame.

Loud, angry voices bellow from the storeroom behind the oven. I should go back there. See if she's all right. Mustache Guy hasn't come out yet, and based on the size of the guy she dragged with her, she might need help.

But she told me to mind my own business. And I should. I don't even know her except for the tiny mishap of almost running her over. Plus, she's not the nicest person I've ever met. Of course, said tiny mishap might have something to do with her not so pleasant disposition toward me. I drop my camera to my side and let out a resigned breath. I guess I owe her at least a small check-in.

I lean over the counter as much as I can, craning my neck for a view into the back room. An arm flails the doorway, and bits of sentences become clear. "Yours... Can't..."

"Need something?" The cheese sprinkler cocks his chin toward me.

"Checking out some angles. For the paper." I hold up my camera and hope he buys my story. He half shrugs and goes back to his toppings.

A loud crash bangs from the back room, and several large cans roll into the kitchen. Curb Girl storms out after them, pushing her way past the people bottlenecking at the bar and wiping her tear-stained face. She weaves through the tables and stops next to the Ms. Pac-Man machine. Arms folded, she leans against it and meets my eyes. I nod an, "Are You Okay?" to her, but she looks away.

The man on stage taps the mic and announces the first singer of the evening. The overhead fluorescents dim and the stage lights up in blue and red spots, and some overly lipsticked woman with way too many hair clips takes the stage. I snap a few pics and record her name and song choice—"Stand by Your Man"—in my notebook.

Then, Curb Girl's blonde hair flies everywhere again as she pushes to the front of the sign-up area, sending grumbles through the rest of the line. She whispers something to the emcee, and he recoils with a disapproving look. I move opposite the bar to capture a different angle of the stage, not to mention the reactions of the crowd and kitchen staff. When Lipstick finishes her last off-key note, the emcee eagerly takes back the microphone.

"Thank you, Brenda, for that lovely anthem. Now up, Leda will sing 'Special' by Garbage." He scowls in her direction and clips the mic onto the stand as she clomps to center stage.

Leda. Of course. Even her name is pretty.

The booth girls giggle and toss furtive glances toward the kitchen. The rest of the crowd shifts uncomfortably and can't seem to decide to watch Leda or the muscular boy she dragged into the storeroom scowling at her from behind the counter.

She smooths her hair and exhales, then grabs the mic with both hands. She screams more than sings the lyrics into the stunned-silent crowd, her fiery glare boring holes into the back of the room. The boy runs his hands over his cropped brown hair and pinches the bridge of his nose.

Halfway into the Leda's chorus, the boy hops over the counter and storms through the restaurant. He pauses long enough to throw his apron onto the bar, the muscles in his arm working so hard, the swan tattooed on the lower half of his forearm appears to be swimming. He slams through the double doors to the parking lot. Leda stops singing and shoves the mic into the emcee's chest, then follows the boy outside.

One of the girls in the booth leans over the table and whisper-yells how she saw Leda in *that* section of the drug store, and Swan Boy isn't taking the news too well.

That's why she's so mad. For some reason, my chest pulls inward.

I scan the sidewalks and parking lot through the windows for signs Leda is all right, but both she and the boy are long gone.

A new singer belts out another song, jolting me back into the moment—the weight of my camera in my hand reminding me why I'm here. And I realize I have zero pictures of the most interesting event of the evening.

"Well, shit," I say. Though I'm not sure if it's because I don't have the pictures, or because all I want to do is chase after the girl.

After I snap enough pics of karaoke-rockers and ballad-belters, I foot it to the newspaper office across the street. It's on the second floor of the corner building, just above The Windmill, the town's bar. Somehow, the owner managed to prop an actual windmill—the Holland kind, not the energy ones—on the oversized ledge above the door. It totally blocks the view of Main Street from the newsroom, but when it's rotating, we get a partial view through the slats. Not that I care much. When I'm there, I'm usually in the darkroom.

After my parents and I moved from San Francisco to this small, East Bay town, Dad told me I had two jobs. One: Unpack my room. Two: Get a job ASAP. Like, how is getting a job an actual job?

Parents.

The first place I tried was *The Vine Press,* the last independent small paper around. Lucky for me, the full-time photographer decided eighty-five was the perfect age to slow down a bit, so he relinquished some of his duties to me. I cover local color and sports. He covers everything else, although I'm not entirely sure what else there is in a town where the bait shop doubles as the Post Office.

This place may not have late-night taco stands or a decent music venue, but at least I found a paying gig that gives me experience in the field I want to study. Back home, I'd be lucky to land an unpaid internship with one of the papers before my senior year in college. Plus, driving around helps me get to know the town faster—not that it takes all that long to see everything anyway.

I tread around the building to the back, fumbling with my keys. Leda's planted in the middle of the staircase leading to the office, full-on sobbing. Not wanting another scene, I stop in my tracks and debate how important it is to have actual pictures of karaoke night next to the print story. Her "mind your own business" see-saws with "vehicular homicide" in my head as I decide what to do. Yeah, she's rude. But also, she needs a friend after everything that went down at the pizza place. And Swan Boy isn't exactly here doing the comfort thing. I blow out a huge breath and hang my head.

I must be a glutton for punishment.

Rummaging through my bag, I dig out the emergency handkerchief I keep for outer lens cleaning and trudge to where she sits on the stairs.

"Here." I hold out the cloth.

For a second, she looks at it like it's on fire or a giant bug or something equally as repugnant. When she realizes I'm the one holding it, she straightens her posture and wipes her face with the bottom of her Cranberries T-shirt, then rubs her hands on the thighs of her faded jeans.

"Are you following me?" She looks me up and down. "You don't look like a stalker."

"I am not, in fact, following you." I glance at the top of the stairs. "You are, in fact, sitting in the middle of my commute to work." *Again.* But I don't say that. She follows my glance and a shadow of realization dusts her high cheekbones. But as she faces me, she raises her chin and practically looks right through me.

"Well, if you are a stalker, you can stop. We're good. I accepted your apology, lame as it was." A tear betrays her and slides down her cheek. I hold out the handkerchief again. This time she takes it.

I rub the back of my neck and curse the timing gods for this entire scenario. How can I want to keep talking to her when it's the last thing I should do? She certainly has other priorities.

I should go upstairs. Just forget about her. Do the work. Get the paycheck. She doesn't want to talk. She certainly doesn't want my friendship. Or maybe any friendships. The whole restaurant watched her blow up, and not one person offered to help or acted like they were on her side. She came to the back of this building to be alone. Or maybe it's the only place she could choose to be alone. And I should let her.

"You want to talk? Come upstairs and wash your face?"

I must hate myself.

"You work here, right?" She wipes her nose with my—now her—handkerchief. Maybe she wants to talk after all. The tiniest ray of hope fractures the clouds looming over my mood.

"Yeah, tried getting hired at the bar, but they saw right through my fake ID." I crack a smile.

"I heard there was a new kid."

"Cue the Eagles song."

She props her head to the side and squints.

"'New Kid in Town'? *Hotel California*? The greatest album to ever come out of 1976? Heck, the best album to come out of the entire decade."

"Nothing good came from that decade." She stands and shakes the cold from her legs. Deciding to have a little fun, I step back, gasping, and bring my hand to my chest.

"Excuse me? Pink Floyd? The Ramones? The Rolling fucking Stones?" My voice gets louder with every syllable. "You're probably into Britney and boy bands." I shudder for effect. She gestures to her shirt.

"Pretty sure there is evidence to the contrary." She purses her lips, but her eyes are lighter. "First your truck, and now your music. Do you own anything from this decade?" she asks. The fractures between the clouds burst into full-on streaks. There is nothing more beautiful than a witty girl.

"Well, let's see. I bought this shirt in 1999. New Year's Eve shopping spree at Gadzooks. Close enough?" I knit my eyebrows together in a lame attempt to keep a straight face, but the corner of my mouth disobeys and slides into a half-grin. Hers follows suit, but quickly dies.

Damn, I'm a sucker for a good smile.

She crumples the hanky into a ball and extends her arm. "You want this back?" Her voice cracks a little and she coughs. I shake my head, surprised to be more than a little disappointed the banter is done. "I can get it back to you when it's cleaner."

She moves down the steps and I press myself into the railing to make room.

"You don't have to. I have plenty." I inwardly cringe. Super smooth. Every girl swoons when they hear a guy has plenty of snot rags. "I use them for the camera."

She turns at the bottom of the steps and looks at me. I mean, really looks. The kind of look where you know the person looking sees You. A spark shoots up my spine.

"Sure you do." She ambles down the sidewalk into the evening air.

With a sigh, I drag myself up the rest of the stairs and into the darkroom. Switching on the red light, I remember the smug looks on those girls' faces as Leda stormed out of the pizza parlor. If they're right about her, they can suck an egg. Because that girl has more gumption than the lot of them put together.

As I hang the photos to dry, I'm still thinking about the way Leda's lips turned up ever so slightly before she left. My heart crashes against my ribs, and I nearly stop breathing as I realize something. I won't be able to rest until I get to see her whole, beautiful smile.

"Well, shit."

A freak storm pelts the windows of the newsroom. I'm sitting alone except for Phil, the copy editor dozing in the corner, while I wait for my photos of the washed-out Lion's Club annual pancake breakfast. As raindrops race each other to the windowsill, I notice a familiar shape slosh down the sidewalk in front of Pizza Magic. It's Leda, hunkered down and without a coat, hair matted to her face as she lugs a duffle bag over her shoulder. It's been three days since I gave her my handkerchief, and I haven't seen her since. She stops in front of my truck and looks up, right through the rotating windmill and rain-fogged windows, straight into my soul.

And I duck.

I lunge under my desk, then curse myself for being stupid. She can't possibly see me. And it's not like I'm stalking her. If anything, she's creeping on me. But my truck is right there, parked on Main Street for all the world to see. She obviously knows I'm here.

Climbing onto my knees, I risk a peek at the street, but she's nowhere to be found. The only person still out in this weather is Mr. Lancaster on his daily stumble from the bar to his house. From this view, the town is eerily still for a Saturday afternoon.

The door crashes open and I nearly plant my face into the window as I jump to my feet. Leda's huffing in the doorway, dripping pools of water onto the newsroom floor.

"I need you to take me somewhere. Like, ASAP." She hunches her shoulder and adjusts the bag hanging over it.

"What? Why me?" I glance at the darkroom. "I have pictures."

"Well, I carried a watermelon. Can you just get your keys? Please?" She nods to my camera bag, and it's like my brain can't process what's happening.

I stand there, mouth half-open. "Did you just quote *Dirty Dancing* to get me to take you somewhere?"

With a glance to the now-awake Phil, she makes a beeline to where I'm glued to the floor. She leans close and whispers,

"I need to go, now. Today. And you're the only person in this stupid town who won't say anything because you don't know anyone."

"You did quote *Dirty Dancing* to get me to take you somewhere."

"Can we just go?"

All that's left for the pancake breakfast pictures is to give them to layout, but they still have to finish drying. Maybe Phil will do it. I turn to ask, but his chin is back resting on his chest. With a sigh, I look back at Leda. Her eyes are amber pools of pleading and anger, like the storm somehow shifted from outside into her. And she's asking me to be her umbrella. How can I say no?

"Give me a minute." I scribble a quick note and slide it onto Phil's desk. Grabbing my bag, I stuff a box of tissues into it and shut the door behind us.

The truck's windows immediately fog over as we settle in. Rain pelts the roof so hard, all other noise is muted, like we're the only people on the planet. Taking the box out of my bag, I offer her a glob of the stolen tissues. I crank the engine and then the defroster.

"It'll take a minute to warm up," I say.

"Thank you for this. I owe you one. Really." She pulls one of the tissues from the clump and pats her face and the bare parts of her arms. Little pieces stick to her cheeks and neck. I almost pick one off, but right now I'm driving the getaway car. And I'm pretty sure invading personal space isn't part of the job description.

"Call it even for almost running you over." I smile, hoping she'll return the favor. "So... where are we going?"

"Couple towns over. I need to go... somewhere. A place." She streaks her tissue wad across the passenger window, but it fogs up as quickly as she wipes. She slumps in the seat and stares at the roof.

"I'm probably going to need the name. Of the place. Easier to find and all."

Nothing.

I mouth "okay" and pull onto the road when the windshield defrosts. As luck would have it, the one stoplight in town turns red for no other reason than it's supposed to. As I roll the truck to a stop, I sneak a glance in her direction. She's a thousand miles away, probably lost in some memory or future scenario. Maybe this isn't such a good idea. It's not like I know her that well. And she certainly doesn't know me. I try again.

"Also, how far is 'two towns over,' because I might need gas."

She half sighs, half grunts.

"Hey, I didn't know I was playing Clyde to your Bonnie today, so forgive me for all the questions." I roll my eyes. "I mean, I assume this is the right way?"

She shoots a daggered look in my direction, opens her mouth and then deflates. "I have to go to the clinic there, okay?" Tears form in the corners of her eyes and slide down her cheeks, taking some of the tissue bits with them.

"Wait, what? Why?" If she thinks I'm taking her to get her prescription so she can be with Swan Tattoo when I have actual work... Then, what that girl said after Leda stormed out of karaoke flashes in my mind and everything fits together. My cheeks heat and I have no idea where to look or what to do with my body.

"Kind of private?"

"So private the whole pizza place knows?" My voice is louder than I want it to be. She must think the same thing, because she bolts upright and unbuckles her seatbelt.

"Never mind, then. Pull over."

Now it's my turn to wither. "Hang on a sec. That was a jerk thing to say. I'm just trying to get my bearings."

"Let me out."

I steer the truck from the middle of the street and park in front of Burger Villa, the one restaurant where I've eaten so far with decent fries. Flinging open the door, she jumps out, dragging along her bag.

I raise my arms in question, then drop them onto the steering wheel. This girl. My neck is starting to hurt from all this whiplash. First, she demands to be left alone. Then she's invading my work like some crazed Viking, and my ability to give her a ride is some treasure hidden under the altar. Now she's gone. Again.

Dammit, why does she have to be the one I can't get away from? The one I don't want to get away from? With a sigh, I shut off the engine and jump out after her.

"Hey!" I yell over the rain. She speeds up, so I have to jog to catch her. "Wait!"

She doesn't, and my confusion converts to frustration.

"You don't get to storm off. Not when you force me out of the newsroom on some mysterious errand you have to do right this second. Then, when I ask where we're going, so I can, you know, get you there, you jump out of my truck and bolt the opposite way." I swipe raindrops off my face. "At least I think it was the opposite way. I don't exactly know because you never told me which direction!"

She flips around so fast I almost knock into her. And her expression is so twisted, I can't tell which storm is causing the water streaming down her face. Underneath the pain and defiance, she looks so tired. Maybe it's the rain seeping into my clothes and rushing down my sopped neck, but whatever frustration is left in my body runs into the gutter with the rest of the water the street can't hold. I pivot so we're facing the same direction and nod to the burger place.

"Come on, let's go inside. Get a milkshake or something. We can talk. And, if we're lucky, dry off a little." I extend my hand, stopping just short of her bag, and raise my eyebrows. "Can I carry that?"

She lets me take the bag, and I chuck it over my shoulder.

"Who gets a milkshake in the middle of a storm?" Raindrops hit the bit of tissue still stuck to her cheek. I can't resist pulling it off. She lets me too.

"We do. Come on, my treat."

She softens, but only a little.

"Fine."

"Fine indeed."

We collapse into a corner booth. The place is empty except for two employees in the back. The storm must've closed down the town. I slide her bag under the table as she pulls paper napkins from the dispenser and repeats her pat-down from the truck. The waitress, a stocky older woman wearing an old-fashioned uniform and granny hose, delivers two glasses of water and two dry towels.

"Thought ya could use these," she says. "How ya two doin'?"

"Good, Miss Bonnie," Leda says.

"Yes, apparently we are fine," I add. Miss Bonnie sharpens her gaze on me.

"You the new kid?"

"Until the next one comes to town."

"Eagles, huh?" She chuckles. I shoot an incredulous look to Leda, who rolls her eyes. "What can I get you kids?"

"Vanilla milkshake for me, please," I say.

"One straw or two?" Miss Bonnie asks. I nearly choke on my saliva. She winks.

"I'll have chocolate, one straw," Leda adds.

"You got it." Miss Bonnie pivots on her thick soles and bellows our order to the bored-looking guy at the grill. I let out a low whistle.

"Well, Miss Bonnie is a spunky one, isn't she?" I use the towel to wipe my forehead.

Leda nods. "She's worked here since it opened. I don't think I'd recognize her out of that uniform." She squeezes water from her hair.

I stick out my tongue and fake a gag. "Well, here's hoping you never have to."

She smacks me with her wet towel. "I meant in street clothes. Not naked." She flattens her mouth into a straight line. "Boys."

"Hey, I don't judge." I raise my hands in surrender. She makes a face and snorts.

"Okay." Condescension drips from her tone.

The whir of the milkshake machine echoes off the walls. "What? I don't."

"Okay, you don't judge." She shrugs and looks out the window. The rain is lighter now, and bits of sun streak through the heavy patches of clouds.

"When did I judge?" I ask over the whirring.

"You didn't. You just told me you don't judge. I'm obviously way off about the judging."

I roll my eyes but say nothing. The whirring stops.

"In the truck. Just now. I saw your face when I told you where I have to go." Her voice is small, and I have to lean over the table to hear her.

"You want cherries, kids?" Miss Bonnie yells over the counter. I nod a quick smile in her direction. The blender stops.

"I wasn't... I didn't." I press against the high-backed bench and sigh. "I was surprised is all. Can't blame me for being surprised."

She stares at the table. I rest my hands on the red Formica and lean in.

"Some girl I barely know barges into my work and charms me with *Dirty Dancing* quotes to get me to drive her to an undisclosed location in the middle of a storm. Next thing I know, said girl is flying out of my truck before I've barely parked, carrying the heaviest gym bag known to man. You've got to let me catch up. That's all."

"That's all?"

"Yep. I am the quintessential lack of judging anyone. We're talking a Sandra Day O'Connor-free zone. Robert Blake level of acquittal." I nod for effect. Miss Bonnie drops off our shakes.

"There you go. One straw, two cherries each." With a wink, she goes back to her spot behind the counter.

"Maybe a little judgment for Miss Bonnie's joke," I say. A slight smile forms at the corners of Leda's mouth.

"Okay, I believe you. I guess I did come on a little strong." She sips her shake. I almost spit mine out.

"A little?"

"Fine, a lot." She takes a deep breath and wrings her hands. A few people trickle in as the sun breaks up the clouds. "It's not a gym bag."

"I wondered. I don't think I've even seen a gym in this town. You carrying around all your belongings?" I swallow. "But no judgment! Carry your stuff in a duffel bag. Suitcase. Whatever. I don't give a damn whose suitcases are better."

"Okay, *Holden*." She sips so it hides her smile.

My stomach flutters, and I press my fingers into my gut as if that could stop the feelings making my body react this way. Neither of us need that kind of complication right now. I press a little harder for maximum effect.

"My dad told me not to bother coming home if I didn't, you know, do something about it." She plays with her straw, drawing it out of her shake and letting the melting liquid drip into her glass.

"Wow." My eyebrow twitches as I draw in a breath.

"That's one word for it."

"What about...?"

"The dad?" she finishes my sentence. "You were there. You saw how well that went over. I'm surprised it wasn't on the front page." She puts her hands up like she's sky-writing the headline. "Local tart tackles motherhood but can't even take out the garbage."

"That's a terrible headline. No one would use that headline." I force a laugh. "Besides, I heard the photographer that covered the event didn't take any useable pictures to contribute to the story."

She huffs—more breath than laugh.

I stare at the chocolatey cream dripping off her straw. We sit in silence as a few more people come in. Some pick up to-go orders. Others settle onto counter stools or in booths. Miss Bonnie checks to see if we have everything we want and slides our tab onto the table.

"Whenever you're ready, hon. No rush."

"What do you want to do?" I ask Leda after Miss Bonnie leaves.

"What do you mean?" She rests her hands on her lap. I shrug.

"What is it you want? Not your parents or Swan Tattoo Guy. You."

She smirks at the nickname, but her skin pales. "His name is Chad. Chad Swanson. Hence the—" She points to her forearm. I nod but don't say anything, since what I want to say isn't very nice. "I don't know what I want. Today, when I showed up at the paper, I was in meltdown mode." She stares at her lap. "I don't have anywhere to go, so I don't think I have a choice."

"Can I offer a small suggestion? Completely judgment-free, promise." I draw an X over my heart.

Still staring at her lap, she shrugs.

"Maybe take a day or two and think about it. Figure out how *you* feel." I pay the tab, leaving an extra couple dollars for

Miss Bonnie, while Leda gets lost in thought. "Come on, let's take a walk. I have a hankering for some Red Vines. And I hear the best place to get them is at Elvis Katz's Bus Stop and Candy Emporium." I stand and hold out my arm like they do in old movies. She reaches for her bag. Remembering my gentlemanly responsibilities, I lunge for it, hitting my head on the corner of the table. "Oof." I suck in a breath and return to standing.

"That'll teach you. I can get my own bag. You okay?" Her eyes aren't laughing exactly, but they're not *not* laughing either.

"Five by five." I rub the spot on my scalp that knocked against the table. I take her bag, and we head for the door. "We can drop off your stuff in my truck if you want."

She squints against the sun breaking through the clouds then nods.

"Can I ask you a question?"

"Sure."

"Seriously, what is the deal with combining businesses around here? Are there not enough buildings? Or do we like our bait mixing with the mail? Bus exhaust all over our candy? And why does he call it an emporium? The whole store is about as big as a closet."

"I don't know. It's pretty convenient to be able to buy your nightcrawlers while also picking up some stamps."

"How terrified am I that you know nightcrawlers right now? What even are nightcrawlers?" I unlock the passenger side of my truck and set her bag on the floor.

"That's because you're from 'the City.'" She air quotes the last part. Her tone says she's at least seventy-five percent done with my jokes and twenty-five percent charmed. "We small-town folk don't have fancy shows or gourmet restaurants. We have to occupy ourselves somehow."

Despite the percentages, she joins me when I laugh. As the day gets warmer, so does her mood. Consequently, so does mine.

"How can you eat Red Vines after drinking an entire milkshake anyway? Aren't you afraid you'll go into a sugar coma?" She peels off her damp sweater and hangs it over her arm.

I don't want to tell her that it's not about craving candy. It's that I don't want to have to say goodbye to her. Not yet, anyway. I shrug and offer my arm once again. She looks at it, scoffs, and crosses her own. I poke at her with my elbow.

"My gentleman arm is out of control! Better take it before it gets worse."

"Some gentleman, if it's forcing itself on a lady."

I put it down. "You have a point." I smack my elbow. "Bad gentleman arm. Behave."

And she smiles. Like, really smiles. Her whole face is starlight and sweetness and freedom and everything I thought it would be.

I press super hard on my stomach and, thankfully, she doesn't seem to notice.

When we come out of the candy store with our Red Vines and a few candy necklaces and bracelets—Katz is running a sale and wouldn't take no for an answer—Chad Swanson is standing on the corner. I'd think he's a statue except for all the huffing and foaming at the mouth.

"Shit." Leda stops in her tracks and stares, pulling the half-bitten licorice out of her mouth.

"That's one word for it." I look at her. "Am I in danger of being punched? I mean, is it cool to say 'not in the face'?" Maybe a good one in the stomach would be just what I need.

"Stay here."

"You sure?" Without responding, she crosses to the corner where he's standing. He jerks his head in the other direction and tries taking her hand, but she shrinks back and leans against the wall instead.

She folds her arms and lifts her chin. The same thing she did to me the first day we nearly collided. And it's cute, even when it's not aimed at me. I massage my forehead.

"I was looking for you. Your dad said you were gone, then someone said you came this way. I'm thinking you're on your way to… and now I find you with some random guy?" Chad Swanson points at me. I swallow hard, my heart pounding more from fight or flight than milkshakes and Red Vines with a girl I have no business falling for.

The guy is an oak tree.

"You broke up with me, remember? Told me to figure it out? Well, I'm figuring it out."

"Dammit, Leda!" He's shaking his head and biting his thumb nail, his gaze shifting from me to her. "This isn't what's supposed to happen."

"Then what *is* supposed to happen? Please, enlighten me on the master plan, because I sure as hell would like to know what it is." She pushes herself away from the wall and stands rigid. All the light that she'd carried just a few minutes ago clouds over, and she's crying again.

"This is so like you." He purses his lips and takes a deep breath. In a softer voice, he continues, "I can't do it, Lee."

"Don't call me that."

"Okay, Leda. It can't happen. I've got too much riding on this season for any distractions."

"Distractions? You're worried about football season? Are you serious right now?"

"Yes. This doesn't have to be our life. You have...choices."

"No, Chad. *You* have choices. I have consequences."

"You're impossible. Thinking only of yourself. I don't know why I even bothered." Chad Swanson cocks his chin toward me. "You can have her. I quit." He looks back to her and salutes overdramatically. "Have a nice life." He storms to the houses up the hill.

Leda stands paralyzed, watching him go. I don't know if I should go to her or leave or call for help.

"Chad, wait!" Leda takes off after him. Halfway up the block, she turns toward me, mouths "sorry," and jogs away.

Turns out, she decided for me.

I stand there a few more minutes, my once-pounding heart now in pieces at the bottom of my chest. Like it has any right to break. Like I have any place in this story. In her story. With a sigh, I throw the rest of the candy in the bus stop trash and lumber toward my truck.

When I get there, her bag sits on my floor, mocking our afternoon. Mocking me. I shake my head. What was I even thinking?

She should work things out with Chad Swanson, if that's what she wants. Leda needs all the space and time and whatever else to do what's right for her. Yes, this is for the best. Keep my eyes on my own paper.

Except I can't.

I take the bag with me into the newsroom and drop it in the lost and found. And even though I don't have any film to develop, I close myself in the darkroom, flip on the red light, and fold myself onto the floor.

It's been a week since I've seen Leda. I wasn't there when she came for her bag, and I've avoided both Burger Villa and Elvis Katz since. Not that she'd even be there, just didn't want to take a chance. So imagine the look on my face when I walk into Barry's Bait and Tackle and Post Office to shoot pictures of the Fish Derby winner and she's standing in line.

I mumble a curse on small-town geography and avoid eye contact while setting up my camera.

Leda's voice floats into my corner anyway. "Tristan!"

I close my eyes and exhale through my nose. Turning around, I paste on my best smile. She's holding a large envelope and waving me over.

"Hey, fancy meeting you here," she says.

"Of all the gin joints…"

"In all the world." She waits for me to say something, but I don't. "I would've come to you, but…" She gestures to the line.

"You're mailing something. I see that." I rock back and forth on the balls of my feet and nod to the envelope. The words "adoption agency" are written in the center. My eyes dart to hers, but she's watching the line move. I have no idea what to say without sounding judgy, so I smile and nod like a total loser, hating myself for the stupid expression that's probably fixed to my face.

"Sorry about the other day. Didn't mean to leave you with all that fancy candy jewelry. Hopefully you were able to fetch a fair price on the sugar black market. And thanks for leaving my bag where I could find it. Brings a whole new level to the term 'baggage,' right? I mean, who brings a literal bag with them on a—"

"Leda." I stop her before she can say what I think she's going to say. Because it wasn't that. At all. It couldn't have been.

"But seriously, right?" Her eyes ask a different question, the one I choose to answer.

"Look, I'm doing my best here, but all the emotional whip-lash is confusing." I swipe my hand through my hair. "I get that I'm a mere blip on the screen with everything you've got going on—and rightfully so." I want to say I can't help the way I feel when I'm around her, but I can't. Won't. Shouldn't. "I know you need space, and I'm trying to give it to you. Besides, I'm just trying to figure out how things work around here and get ready for senior year."

"Next," a voice beckons from behind the counter. The crin-kle between Leda's eyes makes an encore as she considers my words. Then, she slowly nods.

"Cool. You'll figure out senior year. I have to go." She side-steps around me and sidles up to the counter. "I need to mail this." Her voice is shaky and too loud.

"Leda."

"Love's a bitch, Duck. Love's a bitch."

"Did you just Andrew Dice Clay me? You know what? Never mind. This, right here, is exactly what I mean." Turning my back to her, I prep my camera and ask Barry what time the winner will be here.

"No. You don't get to be mad." She slams some money on the counter and marches across the room until she's inches away.

"Why? Because I met a girl and thought she was pretty? Maybe even liked her? Then found out she was in the middle of a crisis and wanted to be supportive? Even be a friend? Be-cause I don't see very many around." I gesture to the three older fishermen waiting for the ceremony near the window and oth-erwise empty store. Barry and the other guy behind the counter become super interested in the floor.

"Oh, so your friendship is a *pity* friendship? Screw you!" She flies out the door, slamming it shut behind her. The bells over the top clang wildly.

I rub my forehead over and over, like I could press the memory of my stupid words out of my brain. This is exactly why I prefer being behind the camera. I take a few pictures, jot a few notes. No one asks me questions. I don't make stupid comments. Because what I mean is hardly ever what comes out.

"Hey kid, don't sweat it. There's plenty of fish in the sea." Bernie laughs at his own pun. I return a weak smile and get on with business.

But here's the thing. I don't want any other fish. I'm already hooked on her.

After the shoot, I make my way outside. Leda's sitting on the curb picking at her nail.

San Francisco is technically an incredibly small space. 47.355 square miles. But there are so many people crammed into every nook and cranny, you don't notice.

But here... I don't think it would matter how many square miles this town is because Leda takes up every inch. I take a steadying breath and plod over.

"I was waiting for you," she says.

"Oh."

"I did the thing again, didn't I? Panicked. Was a bit too... much."

"No, this time you reacted pretty much right on." I sit next to her. "I sounded like a jackass in there."

"Maybe a little." She bites down on a smile.

"I like you, Leda. Not because I want to save you or fix you or whatever Dr. Phil might accuse me of." I face her. "I liked you from the first moment you screamed at me in front of Pizza Magic. I like the little crease you get in your forehead when you're mad. I like that you wear a Cranberries shirt and can quote lines from *Casablanca* and *Pretty in Pink*."

"Tristan."

"Let me finish. But I also know this isn't the time for all that. And you're dealing with things I have no clue about." In a quieter voice, I add, "Plus, there's Chad Swanson."

"No, there isn't," she says. I must look confused because she goes on. "That was never going to work. Not long term."

"Do you want to talk about it?" Both dread and enthusiasm boil inside me.

"I thought maybe, if I could explain it right... maybe he'd be open to something other than abortion." She bites her bottom lip and inhales through her nose. When she exhales, her eyebrows arch and her expression resigns itself to a melancholy stare. "He has other priorities." She laughs, but in the way where you know what comes next isn't going to be funny. "Who knew I'd get a life sentence for a summer fling?"

We're quiet a minute as the breeze picks up. She shivers. I can't help but feel relieved about the lack of Chad Swanson in her life. Only a douchebag could say, "Have a nice life" to the mother of his child. Guys like him think their plans are so important, they can't be bothered with accountability. Why should he get all the freedom while her life is forever changed?

"I saw a little of the address on your envelope." I risk peeking at her. She's back to picking at her nail. "Is that what you decided to do?

"Thinking about it. I told my parents I went through with the abortion to buy some time. But I'm going to start showing soon, so I need to have a plan." She bumps me with her shoulder. "Some smart guy told me to figure out what I wanted out of this whole mess, and that's what I'm doing."

"Smart guy, huh?"

"He's all right."

"Hey, is it safe to sit on the curb like this? Should we maybe go somewhere less roady?" I stand and offer a hand to help her up, which, of course, she doesn't take. "I've heard a tale or two that curb sitting can be hazardous to a person's health."

"As long as you aren't behind the wheel, I think it's safe." She smiles her sweet starlight smile, and my heart swells. "Hey, Tristan?"

"Yeah?"

"Never stop offering me your arm. I might take it one day."

THE END

Other Published Works

READ MORE BY DEBORAH MAROULIS

Within and Without – Lakewater Press – 2019

FOR MORE, VISIT
www.deborahmaroulis.com

The Valentine's Eve Not-a-Date Photo Scavenger Hunt

Number One: Wash a stranger's windshield at a gas station

It may be the first thing on the list, but the town gas station is a ten-minute drive in the wrong direction. As the only one in the car born and raised in Devil Springs, Paige Bellamy could easily order their scavenger hunt list for efficiency, but no one has asked her. And Paige still isn't sure she wants to be here.

"I guess we're going to the gas station?" Justin asks. "Unless anyone has a better idea?"

Adriana shrugs, and the brother, seated beside Paige in the back seat, ignores them all to do something on his phone.

"Can I see the list?" Paige says the words without meaning to. Old Paige would have thought this could be fun. Maybe that Paige can be nudged awake for the afternoon.

She's only known Adriana for a few months now, but Paige likes her. As for her other two teammates, she met Adriana's husband, Justin, and his brother (whose name she still hasn't caught) only moments before at the church.

Justin drops the sheet of paper over his shoulder, and Paige catches it and scans. This is so much easier to read than the angled, partially-cut-off picture on her phone that she'd managed to snap inside. When the list was first handed out, Justin grabbed it for their group before she could get a better look.

"So, is that the plan?" Justin asks and looks into the rearview mirror, brown eyes questioning Paige.

His brother (Chris?) emits an impatient groan. "Can you turn the car on while we decide? It's hot."

Paige shifts, suddenly mindful of the heat from the black leather car seats beneath her jeans. February in this part of Florida often means highs in the low seventies, but today is bumping closer to eighty, and the car has been sitting in the sun. Justin tosses the keys into the center console and pushes the Start button.

"We'll need stores for some of these, so we may as well drive to Gainesville and we can go to a gas station there," Paige says.

The brother takes the list from her hand. "I'm not doing number six," he announces.

For this task, a male from the group is supposed to try on a dress and heels in a store. Paige can't picture Justin, a church staff person, doing that either. Maybe they'll have to skip it. "But," the brother points in the middle of the paper, "if we're going to Gainesville, we should do this pyramid thing in The Swamp. I can have some friends meet us there since we need extra people."

"The Swamp" means their sports field for number four will be Ben Hill Griffin Stadium at the University of Florida, and Paige absolutely does not want to go there.

She changes the subject. "We'll pass by the mayor's house on our way, and she has a red truck. We need that for number nine."

"Great!" Justin begins backing up the car. "Tell me where to go."

They ride in almost silence. Adriana selects a radio station, but it plays so low Paige can only hear an occasional chirp or chord. Paige tells Justin when and where to turn, but otherwise looks out the window. She considers asking the brother his name, what he does, how he knows Gainesville people who will show up to be in a human pyramid. But she doesn't.

As the title of the scavenger hunt indicates, it's not a date, and she won't pretend like it could or should be. It doesn't matter that the bearded guy next to her looks like an up-and-coming country music star, magazine cover-ready in a tightly fitted black tee and denim khakis. Almost two years since her divorce, Paige notices attractive men, but she doesn't care. She has her mother to take care of. That, and Jackson had been her one and only love—she has no idea what she's doing when it comes to men.

"That's the house. The mossy green two-story," Paige says.

The brother sets his phone down and looks up. "Gloomy."

Adriana nods. "And she just repainted. Why go with those colors?"

Justin pulls into the driveway, but there's no red truck. "Should we knock?" he asks. "Maybe it's in the garage."

Adriana and Justin agree to go to the door to do the knocking, explaining, and asking. When they get a few feet away, Paige's seatmate turns and says, "I didn't catch your name at the church."

"Paige." The silence between them lingers again, and just as it occurs to Paige she should ask his name, he offers the information.

"I'm Cole. Nicholas officially, but I prefer Cole."

"I like Nicholas." Paige likes Cole too, so she's not sure why she says this.

"My grandfather is Nicholas, my father is Nick, and I had no intention of being called Nicky."

"Or Junior."

He winces. "I'm definitely not a Junior."

More silence and Cole glances at his phone before shifting so that he can slide it into his back pocket. It's a nice, you-have-my-attention, gesture, but Paige doesn't know what to do with his attention. She leans her head against the window and closes her eyes. Coming out and joining this hunt was a stupid idea. Her group is nice, but she doesn't have the energy for nice. She'd rather be in bed binging a new show.

The front car doors open, "The granddaughter's home, but she's not sure when Mayor Kneller will be back," Adriana says.

Paige has known the mayor her whole life, and the woman freaks her out. She feels sorry for the granddaughter who came to live here last fall. The girl arrived wrapped in a sadness Paige understands all too well. Different reasons, same darkness.

"Let's pick a store that has couches and head to Gainesville. We'll find a gas station and another red truck on the way," Justin says while starting the car.

Cole picks up the scavenger hunt list. "And we need a flamingo and something that starts with everyone's name. And there's a fountain right by the stadium, so we can get that when we do the pyramid."

Paige tries to think of a school or park along their route, so they can avoid the university. She'll have to keep her eyes open.

If she decides to care, Paige can help her group win. The Christmas lights on her house are still up (number eight), a fact she hopes the other groups don't remember, and she has a plastic flamingo (number seven) stabbed into a fake, dusty ficus that stands in the corner of her bedroom. Paige guesses a real flamingo would garner more points than the plastic one living in her plant, but she can't think of where they'd find the live version of the bird. What she should be concentrating on is a non-University of Florida-affiliated sports field and fountain.

She's still not sure how Adriana talked her into this. Paige met Adriana at the town grocery store at the end of summer. Adriana, the dutiful young bride of the new youth pastor-slash-minister-to-single-adults at the biggest (albeit still small) church within the town limits, had been aggressively friendly to Paige, one of the few single young adults in Devil Springs. Paige, content with her lapsed Catholicism, had been dubious when she found herself agreeing to give her number to Adriana that day, but the two women had gotten into the habit of texting each other. Paige had also taken Adriana shopping when Adriana needed throw pillows and wall art for her new house. They'd chatted easily, Paige answering Adriana's questions about the area for the entire drive.

Paige had already turned down a lot of offers for dinner and something called a "small group." This time, she wasn't scheduled to work, her dad would be home with her mom, and she didn't have anything else to do. Small towns were inconvenient like that.

Ten picture tasks. Three hours. Four groups of four competing. Extra points would be awarded for coming in under the time limit. Pastor Shepherd and his wife, Lynn, would be the judges and the hosts of the after-scavenger-hunt dinner. Paige doesn't intend to stay for that. She'll use her mother as an excuse somehow.

Number Two: Find something beginning with the first letter of everyone's name

It's another twenty minutes before they are able to cross off two items. There's a gas station in the same plaza as the furniture store. Justin cleans a car's windshield, and Adriana snaps the picture. They go inside the convenience store and each finds a snack food that begins with their name.

Cole chooses cashews. "This is doing double duty." He waves the bag. "Nut for Nicholas. Cashew for Cole."

The young clerk takes their picture, then makes them shake their food for a Boomerang version. After she hands back the phone, Coles grabs everything from the groups' hands and sets the food on the counter to buy it all.

The clerk wishes them luck. Adriana shows Paige the screen. "Look at you! So cute with your pouty face."

Paige is surprised to see that in the back-and-forth video she is indeed making a slight pouty face and adding a shoulder shimmy. She slides over to the static picture and sees the frown she's used to. Cole looks over her shoulder.

"I know it's not PC to tell girls to smile, but we *are* taking pictures," he says, handing Paige her Pringles.

She rolls her eyes but takes the chips.

"Yeah, nope. That's not the expression I was thinking of. You need a lot more practice."

"Two down in thirty-eight minutes," Justin interrupts. "We've got to speed this up."

Number Three: Every member sitting on a store couch

Paige sits sandwiched between Cole and Justin on a light brown leather couch as Adriana hands off her phone to a customer who came in at the same time. Before Adriana can take the spot next to Justin, he draws her onto his lap. In the picture, Adriana's head is thrown back in laughter while Justin leans forward and grins. A wide, white-toothed smile takes over half of Cole's face as he sits, back straight, hands on his knees, but Paige remains expressionless like a confused stranger in their midst. When she sees herself in this picture, she wonders if she should leave. She could feign feeling sick, insist the others keep on, and Uber home.

Her group is too caught up in their streak to notice how out of sync Paige looks.

"That's three," cheers Adriana.

"To campus!" Cole says.

Justin and Adriana echo, "To campus!"

Number Four: Human pyramid made with six⋆ people taken on a sports field

(⋆At least three of your team and other people you can get to participate)

Paige crunches her shoe on a discarded soda can in the parking lot. She doesn't want to be here anymore.

"You guys, I'm not feeling so great. I was thinking..."

Adriana and Justin are far enough behind that they don't hear her, but Cole shakes his head "no" before she finishes.

"Stay," he says. "What else do you have to do?"

"But..."

"And we're your ride. Besides," he nudges her, "we aren't so terrible."

Paige takes a step away and tries a new tactic. "Could we at least start driving back? Campus is always so crowded, and we don't need to go in that direction. We can do the human pyramid at Spring High, or any park really."

But Cole has a response ready for this too. "Saturdays in February are not busy campus days, and I already have three friends coming out to meet us."

Paige reaches the car and waits for Justin to unlock the door. "Spring High is right by my house and our Christmas lights are up, so we can do that one too."

"But we have people meeting us, and there's a fountain there." Cole's tone is laced with impatience, but he catches himself and softens it before adding, "But Christmas lights can be next—that's perfect."

Paige can't keep arguing. The knot in her stomach has clenched too tightly. She knew this day would come eventually. She can picture her dad grabbing her by the shoulders, looking her in the eyes, and saying, "Courage is being scared and saddling up anyway." He'd said it to her on her first day at UF before saying goodbye and leaving her alone in her campus apartment, still waiting on her roommate to show.

As they continue up 34th Street in the direction of campus, Paige's stomach has turned to lead. She used to love this place. Her mom and dad met as freshmen and graduated together. Class of 1983! Since she was a little girl, their family had tailgated and attended every home game. Her sister, Penny, met her husband here; he was class of 2009, she was class of 2010. Paige and Jackson, meanwhile, had been friends at Spring High and gone to UF the same year. They started dating their sophomore year, graduated together, and married three weeks later at the chapel on campus.

Paige has so many memories at this school, but she hasn't been back since her wedding day. At first, she'd been intentionally avoiding it; then she'd gotten too busy because of her mom. Now, so much time had passed that it felt weird. Avoiding is easier than facing, but here she is with strangers who may know some version of the town gossip but have no idea the extent of her history with this place and its impact on her rising anxiety.

"Let's play Two Truths and a Lie while we drive," Justin suggests as he pulls up to a red light.

"Leave it to the youth pastor to organize a game within the game," laughs Cole. "We're not in your youth group, you know."

"What's Two Truths and a Lie?" Paige asks before Justin can defend himself.

"It's a get-to-know-each-other game. You tell two true things about yourself and one lie, and everyone else has to guess the lie," Adriana explains.

"But you all know each other so well, how could you even play?"

"Good point," Cole laughs again, "so you go first."

Since they are heading to campus, Paige can't help blurting, "I married my college boyfriend, and we got divorced five months later."

"Is that two or one?" asks Adriana.

"One." Paige blushes and looks down, but quickly adds, "I help my dad take care of my mom because she had a stroke about a year ago and is on disability, and I'm a manager at a drug store."

"Is that one or two?" Cole asks this time.

Paige had meant for it to be two, but they are both true. She sucks at this game. "One, so two things in all so far, and my third is... I have a sister named Penny and she lives in..." Paige stalls, needing to turn this into a lie. "...Tampa." Penny and her husband live in Orlando.

"I don't believe the first one," says Justin.

"Me neither," says Adriana. "You'd have already told me that, right?"

Cole watches Paige's face and scratches his dark beard. He studies her for so long she turns away, embarrassed.

"Your tone changed when you said the third one. You slowed down like you had to think about it." She glances back and he's still studying her. "Maybe you have a brother and not a sister? Or maybe that's not her name? I think the third one is the lie."

"My sister Penny lives in Orlando." Paige is surprised Justin and Adriana didn't know about her divorce.

Cole slaps his leg. "I knew it!"

"Seriously? You guys haven't heard about... all the other stuff?" Paige figures Justin and Adriana had been in town long enough to be caught up on the town scandals. Because what a good story for the town gossips: *Little Paige Bellamy went off to UF just like her big sister, got a degree in accounting so she could be a CPA just like her big sister, got married right after college just like her big sister. But now, Penny is still on her path of Happily Ever After with her first baby on the way, and poor Paige Bellamy. At least when her mama had that stroke, Paige was home because of the divorce and all. Sure is nice she's able to help her daddy, but too bad the only place hiring in the area was the Walgreens in Williston.*

"Five months, huh?" asks Cole, "But good to get that figured out before kids, right?"

"Who says I don't have a kid?" And Paige wouldn't say she has anything figured out. She'd been left behind when Jackson took a job in Portland and asked her not to move out right away, and then... not at all. She loved him completely, and he wanted space *after* they'd gotten married. She'd never figure that out.

"Oh shit, sorry." Cole's eyes grow wide. They're a lighter, more golden brown than his brother's.

"I don't have a kid."

He exhales. "That's just mean."

Paige's face quirks with the start of a smile.

"Where'd you go to school?" Cole asks.

And just like that—smile gone. Paige looks out the window again. Somehow, she'd missed when they'd turned onto campus. Justin's chosen the tree-shaded route past the golf course. She waves her arms and motions all around her. "Where else?"

"Ouch. Shit. Is it hard to come back?"

"This is the first time since..." She can't finish the sentence.

"Holy crap. I didn't realize. That's why... shit. Let me..."

Justin interrupts, "Will you please stop saying sh—cussing?"

Adriana giggles.

"Yes, Pastor Justin, I will work on cleaning up my language," Cole says, then mouths to Paige, "So fucking annoying."

Paige smiles fully this time, and the knot in her stomach loosens a little.

"I'll change the plan. My friends can meet us at a park off-campus with baseball fields or something." He pulls out his phone.

"No, we're so close." Another family favorite saying runs through Paige's mind: *Suck it up, Buttercup.* They'll be on campus twenty minutes max. She can do this.

"Who's meeting us?" Justin asks.

"Jim, Hunter, and Rusty."

"Like you didn't already know that," Adriana says to her husband, then turns to Paige. "They're all Ag guys. Study partners since undergrad. Roommates now."

"Ag guys?"

"Agriculture—soil and water guys, every one of us," Cole explains.

"Sounds... exciting."

"It's not, so please don't get him started." Adriana laughs again. It's a light, bubbly sound. Paige envies how it comes so easily.

Justin parks across the street from the stadium, and she sees that Cole was right. Campus is empty. A few people are out jogging and walking dogs. A leaf blower buzzes from somewhere. It's warm, but the usual humidity has eased, leaving a crispness in the air. Paige inhales. *I can do this.*

Three guys, all in jeans and solid tees, stand at Gate 18.

Cole introduces them, but it's clear he's only talking to Paige. These guys have met Justin and Adriana plenty of times. Then they make their way into the stadium together. Once they exit the concrete ramps to the bleachers, they have to descend to get to the field. Out of season, it isn't painted.

"I don't think, technically, we're supposed to go on the grass," says Cole, "but we'll be fast."

"I don't want to break any rules," says Justin.

Cole motions around. "Do you see anyone enforcing rules?"

Paige glances to each side; the dozen or so people here are all exercising by jogging up and down the steps.

First, the guys discuss where to go and decide they want to be able to see the "This is... The Swamp" sign behind everyone. The conversation turns to who should be where in their pyramid. Cole suggests he, Justin, and Jim, the tallest of his friends, kneel on the bottom. He thinks Rusty, the shortest of his friends, and Paige should be the two in the middle, and Adriana, the smallest of them all, be on top. That leaves Hunter taking the picture.

"I was thinking Adriana could take the picture. Hunter and Rusty can be the middle row, and Paige can go on top," Justin says.

"That makes no sense. Adriana's so light," Cole argues. He's right. Adriana is maybe five-foot-two and tiny, while Paige is five-foot-six with more curves. She easily outweighs Adriana by 30 pounds. Adriana is the obvious choice for the top of the pyramid.

"It'll be fine," Adriana says.

"No, no way. You can't," Justin says.

"Bro, I get being protective of your woman, but it's a six-person pyramid. She'll be fine," Cole says, then gets into position next to Jim who is already waiting on all fours.

Justin won't budge. "You don't understand."

"It. Will. Be. Fine," Adriana insists. She hands her phone to Hunter and nudges Justin to get in place. "I won't fall. I promise."

Paige thinks this a weird argument but is glad for the distraction to get her mind off her last time in the space, a home game that she'd come to with Jackson and their group of mutual friends. She shakes away the memories and climbs onto the guys' backs.

"Are my knees too bony?" Paige asks as she puts her hand on Cole's shoulder.

"Not at all," says Cole, but Justin doesn't respond, so maybe they are.

"How about mine?" Rusty climbs up and grinds down the knee that's on Cole's back.

"You are dead. Sleep with one eye open." Cole says but doesn't turn. Paige stares down at his neck; it's dusted lightly with a few brown freckles at his neatly trimmed hairline.

Hunter helps Adriana get securely positioned on top before taking the picture. He has to kneel low to get the part of the stadium wall they want in the shot. When he stands back up, he offers his hand to Adriana and Paige as they disassemble. Paige turns to offer her hand to Cole who takes it firmly as he stands. His hand is warm, and instead of letting go he pulls her closer to him.

"Is being back in all the old places weird or are you okay?" He says it low, so no one else can hear him. They are close enough that they could start slow dancing and that proximity feels very okay to Paige in this moment, but Adriana's voice rings out before she can answer.

"See? Cole's friend is a gentleman, and I'm fine."

Justin hugs Adriana and looks her over like an old woman inspecting produce for bruises. Only when he's satisfied that she's truly okay does he take her hand and announce they need to hurry up and get to the fountain.

Paige steps away from Cole and over to her friend. "What's the protectiveness about?"

Adriana glances down at her stomach and whispers, "Ten weeks, but we haven't announced it yet."

Number Five: All Group Members in a Fountain

Cole's friends stay with them since another person is needed to take the next picture—a selfie might not show where they actually are. Paige walks ahead but overhears one of the guys ask if this is a double date. She slows a little, curious how Cole will answer, but Justin drowns him out by urging everyone to pick up the pace.

At the fountain, Justin wants to sit around the edge with only their feet in, but Cole wades into the middle, not bothering to roll up his pants. Paige kicks off her sandals and hops in too. Adriana follows suit.

"Okay, fine." Justin stands up in the water. "We'll probably get more points if we're wet." And just as Hunter takes the picture, Justin bends down to send a splash of water across all of them.

"It's on," Cole says, retaliating with a splash of his own. The boys go at it, so Paige scoots out of the way. Adriana follows, but slips and lands on her butt. The water is only about two feet deep, but Justin is immediately at her side.

"I'm fine. I promise. I'm fine," Adriana says.

"I can't believe I started that. I don't know what I was thinking."

Cole stares down on them, a bewildered look on his face. "Why are we treating Adriana like she's made of porcelain?"

"She's pregnant!" says Justin then closes his eyes and takes a breath. "And that's not how we were going to announce it."

"I'm going to be an uncle. Holy shit."

Paige lets out the loudest peel of laughter, surprising everyone, most of all herself. "The bad uncle who teaches the kid all the words he's not supposed to know."

Cole grins and sends a small splash in Paige's direction. "Count on it."

Number Six: A guy in the group trying on dress and heels in store

Cole has changed his mind about number six. He wants to go to a Walmart, put on a pink dress and shoes, and hold an "It's a Girl" sign for the picture.

"We can text it to Mom and Dad and confuse the… crap out of them."

"Mom and Dad are used to you doing stupid things. They'll roll their eyes and won't think twice about it."

"And we don't know if it's a girl. We won't know the gender for another two months," says Adriana.

"But it might be a girl, and now that *I* know, you have to tell them. This can be the conversation starter."

Justin shakes his head. "Wear the dress for the points, not to show Mom and Dad."

They're almost back to the car. Cole's roommates say goodbye and walk off to a very large (not red) truck a few rows away.

Cole sidles up to Paige. "I feel like I owe you number six since I put you through being back here. I should do something uncomfortable too."

The more time Paige spends with Cole, the more she doubts if anything would make him uncomfortable. When they'd first been in the car together, she thought he was just some aloof guy who would ignore her and be on his phone the whole time, but she'd misread him.

"And I want to get you to laugh again. Paige—" He frowns. "What's your last name?"

"Bellamy."

"Did you change it back after the divorce or is that *his* name?" Somehow Cole manages to take the three little letters in "his" and make them sound as though he's disgusted by them, and Paige laughs.

"I changed it back." Paige also likes how casually Cole can say divorce. Like, it happens. Even at twenty-two. And she's not damaged.

"I'm getting good at this whole making you laugh thing." He bumps his shoulder lightly into hers. "Which is good, because I like hearing you laugh."

In Walmart, Adriana and Justin split away from Paige and Cole to find women's heels that might actually fit a man.

Paige scans the dresses. The only pink dress she finds is knee-length, so she pulls the three largest sizes. Cole has broad shoulders, but they might still fit into something smaller. She's just trying to get something that will cover the butt on a six-foot-ish frame.

Cole looks at the dresses, grabs all three, and goes to a dressing room. He steps out just as Adriana and Justin rush up with a pair of very large nude women's pumps.

"How do I look?" Cole twirls. Whatever size he chose, the dress is still short enough to show off that he's a boxer briefs wearer. He has pale legs covered in dark hair and he looks really, really terrible in this dress.

"You're gorgeous. Now put these on. They're ten-and-a-half and wide. That's got to work." Adriana drops the shoes at his feet and pulls out her phone.

"So pushy. Where's my 'It's a Girl' sign?"

"No time for the sign. Hurry up with the shoes," Justin says while Adriana stands ready to snap the picture.

Cole manages to squeeze his feet into the shoes. "Do they have wigs here? I think a wig would complete this look."

"Wigs don't go with beards," Paige says, and Adriana clicks a picture without waiting for Cole to pose.

"Good point." Cole steps back into the dressing room and emerges in almost no time—dress off, pants on, his shirt and shoes clutched to his chest.

"I'll finish dressing in the car. Let's go see the Bellamy Christmas-turned-Valentine lights."

Number Seven: Entire Team with a flamingo
Number Eight: Group at a house with Christmas lights still up

"When we get to Paige's, we'll have twenty minutes to take our picture and get over to the Shepherd's house. We won't have the flamingo or the last two, but the sheet says we get extra points for being early, so I say that's what we do," Justin says as they pull out of the parking lot.

Cole has chosen to put on his socks and shoes before his shirt, and Paige is trying to look without being caught looking. If this guy devotes as much time to his studies as he does to working out, he will be amazing at whatever job an Ag guy with a Masters in soil and water can do.

Adriana and Justin slip into a conversation about telling the grandparents-to-be sooner than planned now that Cole knows about the baby. Paige pulls her phone out to text her dad and let him know they're coming.

No one's been to the house since her mom's stroke, aside from family, her mom's closest friends, and nurses. Mom gets too agitated too easily—with herself for not being able to speak clearly and her body for being sluggish on one side even after a year of physical therapy. And sometimes, she just gets confused. Paige figures it's best if everyone stays outside.

"You said your mom had a stroke and that you still have to help with her? Does that mean she didn't fully recover?" All of Cole's clothes have been successfully returned to his body, and his attention is back to Paige. She wonders if he's always this good at making the person he's talking to feel like the most interesting person he could be with. In a world where everyone seems to only be half listening because one eye is on a screen, Cole knows how to be focused. Paige finds this both unnerving and exciting.

"It was a severe stroke, but she was young enough that they were slow to realize what was happening. At first, they thought it was anxiety, and then vertigo. She's not ever going to fully recover."

"I'm so sorry," Cole says.

Paige heard this a lot shortly after the stroke, but words of sympathy have long since subsided. Hearing it again brings a sting to her eyes.

"It's hardest on my dad. He's aged a lot since it happened."

"And you. You're home and a caretaker. That's got to be a lot when you're probably eager to do something else."

Paige's eyes sting again, and tears fully form this time. She wipes her sleeve against her face and turns away.

Family and friends only talk about how nice it was that Paige had been living at home when it happened. After the stroke, people kept bringing casseroles and baked goods, and the implied consensus Paige took away from their visits was how convenient her divorce had been for the family. One of her mom's friends had said, "See how God worked that for good," and slowly, Paige had internalized all their words to the point that she also believed it was all meant to be, and this was her life now, never mind her pre-marriage, pre-stroke goals.

She manages to say, "I'm not really thinking about the future right now." At least not her own. She thinks about her mom and dad's future all the time.

When Justin turns on her street, Paige texts her dad to get her flamingo and turn the Christmas lights on. As they pull up the driveway, he comes out the front door, pink bird tucked under his arm like a football. The sky, nearing 6 p.m., glows a bright orange along the horizon, pink above that, and vibrant indigo higher above. It's the most impressive backdrop for one of their photos by far.

Paige's dad hugs her as he hands off the flamingo and kisses her head. "It's good to see you out with friends again," he says quietly to Paige.

Paige introduces him and Adriana hands off her phone for him to take the picture. Paige holds the flamingo, and everyone points up to the lights; then they're back in the car in ten seconds, discussing if they have time for one more shot.

Number Ten: Beatles Abby Road Style Crossing Shot

"We have to drive on Main Street to go back to the Shepherd's house. Right by the diner, it has one of those wide crosswalks we need. It's not like there's a lot of traffic. We'll just pull over, hop out, and take the picture," Paige says.

Cole agrees that they should attempt-the-shot. Justin says they should play it safe. Adriana doesn't care either way.

"We need all four of us in the picture, and it will take too long to find someone to take it," Justin insists as he pulls out of Paige's driveway.

"We have fifteen minutes. It's a seven-minute drive. We can find someone. We'll just holler at a person going into Gloria's," Paige counters.

Cole smiles. "Three hours ago, I was sure you were only part of this game as some sort of blackmail or hostage situation, and now look at you, working out all the details to help us win." He turns to his brother. "Is there even a prize?"

Justin shrugs. "Bragging rights? Maybe some gift cards?"

"How do you not know? Isn't this your job to plan?" Cole asks.

"Mrs. Shepherd did it all so Adriana and I could play fairly."

"Who cares if we're late and miss out on a few gift cards? Main Street, here we come."

"We were going there anyway," Justin mumbles under his breath, but Paige still catches it. She'd be the same way if her sister were here acting like she knew best, and once again Paige finds herself smiling. Cole snaps a picture with his phone.

"I'm Photoshopping this face onto the couch picture where you look like someone just ran over your dog."

"I don't have a dog."

"Then your flamingo."

"That *would* be sad," Paige agrees.

"You looked dead flamingo sad."

"There's not going to be time for Photoshopping. You realize that, right?"

"You don't know to whom you are speaking." Cole holds up his phone. On it there's a picture of The Beatles' famous Abbey Road album cover, and he's already Photoshopped their group's faces onto the bodies. Somehow, throughout the course of the day, he'd stealthily taken a shot of each of them. He holds his finger up to his lips. "Don't tell, or he won't let us try for the Devil Springs Main Street version."

Justin pulls over just ahead of the Main Street crosswalk. Adriana hops out and catches Ms. Agnes, the town librarian, coming out of Gloria's diner. Cole and Paige wait in the road. He grabs her hand.

"This was not a date."

"No, it was not."

"What are you doing tomorrow?"

"I have to open, and I work till two."

"That leaves a free afternoon and evening."

"Unless I have a date."

"Do you have a date?"

"Not yet."

"There's still time." He lets go of her hand and gets into position as Ms. Agnes walks into the road. She stands astride the plants in the center median and directs them until they're spaced to her satisfaction. From behind her, Paige hears Justin complain that they don't have time for this.

As Ms. Agnes hands back Adriana's camera, a red truck pulls in behind Justin's car.

Number Nine: Every member in the back of a red truck

The mayor rolls down her window. "Is there a problem with your car?"

"No, ma'am, we were taking a picture," Justin says. "We'll be on our way now."

Paige grabs Coles hand. "Ten for ten. Let's do it."

She marches them right up to the window. "Mayor Kneller, we're doing the church young adult scavenger hunt thing. We only have one item left to get, to take a picture of our group in the back of a red truck. Can we climb into your truck bed and have Ms. Agnes snap one more picture?"

The granddaughter, Paige thinks her name is Mesa, leans around her grandmother and stares at Paige wide-eyed as though she can't believe someone would ask this. Paige smiles and waves.

"It won't take but a second, ma'am," Cole says and hops into the back of the truck before the mayor can answer.

"Okay?" Paige asks. Cole doesn't live in town. He doesn't understand what it means to get on the mayor's bad side. If you need anything granted, it's not going to happen. Rent a pavilion in the park? No. Noise ordinance extension for a family event? No. Building permit? Indefinite delay.

The mayor sighs impatiently. "If it's for church, fine. Be quick," she barks, and Paige waves for Justin and Adriana to hurry up. Both brothers have their hands near Adriana as she climbs into the truck ready to catch her should she slip.

They all stand in the truck bed, and Cole grabs Paige's hand again. With her other hand, Paige takes Adriana's and pulls their arms into the air, a final pose of victory. Adriana yanks up Justin's hand too as Ms. Agnes takes the photo.

But they don't have time to celebrate. They scramble out of the truck and thank the mayor, who just shakes her head before backing up a little and pulling into the diner parking lot.

"We're already eight minutes late," Justin says.

"But now we have everything on the list," Cole says. Paige agrees that this feels like the better accomplishment.

"Maybe the other teams will be late, too," Adriana says, rubbing Justin's back.

On the way to the Shepherd's house, Adriana shares all of the photos from the day, and Cole starts to Photoshop the couch picture.

He hands her the phone to show off his work, and Paige nods her approval. It's a silly Photoshop. Cole didn't resize her head, so it's four times larger than everyone else's.

"I look like a Bobblehead," she says.

"Bobblehead Paige has the biggest smile, and that's how I'd like to remember it."

The sky glows red like a Valentine all around them as the car continues on Main Street.

"If I pick you up at 5, that'll give us time to go somewhere I promise will be new."

Paige needs new.

She tries to return the phone, but Cole doesn't let go of her hand.

"So it's a date?" he asks.

"Absolutely," she says. "A Valentine's, not-a-photo-scavenger-hunt, date."

Other Published Works

READ MORE BY FAYDRA STRATTON

Devil Springs – Filles Vertes Publishing – 2020

FOR MORE, VISIT

www.faydrastratton.com

Sunflowers and Lavender

Chapter 1

"We've only got two days left before judging begins." Ms. Flynn's eyes find mine over the heads of the other employees at Main Street Deli. "Summer Fun might not be the most original theme, but we've got a lot to work with." She pauses again. "As long as it's done on time."

"It'll be done," I assure them, as five pairs of eyes swivel to where I'm standing in the back corner. New employees don't usually get picked to lead the competition, but my skills with a paintbrush boosted me to the top of the list. Something that didn't escape Marissa and her bestie's notice.

"I hear Downtown Deli's mural is already finished." Marissa's voice is innocent enough, but I break out in a sweat. She gives me another glance. "And it's really good."

There's a beat where no one breathes, then she elbows Mackenzie, and their simultaneous eye rolls have enough gravitational pull to knock the rows of pickles and tomatoes to the floor. Marissa submitted a sketch for consideration, but when the in-store votes were tallied, my picture of kids jumping off the pier won ten to three. The same as when we were kids at summer camp. We don't go to the same school, but our

towns are small enough that the artists find their way together—
I just never expected to be working with her the summer before
my senior year.

"If you need help, just say the word." Ms. Flynn's voice
comes across as compassionate, but it carries a warning: Don't
screw this up.

And maybe let someone else help you.

Problem is, Marissa is the only other employee with the artistic ability to help paint my mural, but there's no way she'd
take direction from me. She's made that clear since our first day.

"As you probably know, the winning business gets a month
of free advertising with the local media, and the winning artist
gets five hundred dollars."

Five hundred dollars is almost as much as I make in a month.
My brain is running through how many art supplies I could buy
when Ms. Flynn claps her hands—her usual ending to the
morning huddle.

"Let's make it a great day!"

We scatter to our positions. Today, I'm stationed at the prep
counter, which means I assemble sandwiches then slide them to
Alonzo, or Lonz as he told us to call him, where he grills them
to perfection. He's worked here for years and jokes that he's the
second mate to Captain Flynn.

The lunch rush passes quickly, and when Ms. Flynn gives
me the nod, I hang my apron on a hook near the back door and
step into the alley. Into my world. The supplies for the mural
are in a plastic bin near the back door, and when I open it, the
smell of paint and brush cleaner washes over me, erasing the past
few hours. This is where I'm truly me.

I pull a smock over my head and step back to evaluate the
mural. Instead of the usual perspective from the pier, I've drawn
the kids so they're jumping straight at the viewer—hands
clasped, faces cracked in smiles too big for their heads. I've
somehow captured what it feels like when you're flying through
the air. My best friend Raina took a picture like this with her
dad's waterproof camera earlier this summer, and I've never
been able to forget the feeling of being inside the moment—
even if I am too chicken to jump myself. I've watched Raina
jump more times than I can count and I crave that feeling of
being free, of flying over the water, but every time I work up

the nerve, something holds me back and I'm left watching the moment from the outside.

The sketching and color blocking are already finished, so now I just have to bring the kids to life. My hands mix paints on autopilot while my mind wanders a block down Main Street to Downtown Deli, to the amazing mural people can't stop talking about, to Lucas and his deep blue eyes and annoyingly perfect wavy hair and a smile that used to do crazy things to my insides.

But I can't think about him right now.

I've got less than forty-eight hours to make this perfect, and daydreaming about five hundred dollars or the boy who makes me so angry I could spit won't help matters. My brush moves as if on its own and everything else drifts away. Painting is like breathing for me, a reflexive movement that comes from somewhere deep inside myself. A sense of calm settles through me as the kids' faces slowly come to life and—

A loud bang startles me out of my trance.

"Emmy! Flynn says you gotta take over the last lunch deliveries." Lonz has a spatula in one hand and an apologetic look on his face. He knows how important this mural is to me. To all of us. "Sorry," he adds, almost as an afterthought.

My grip on my paintbrush tightens. Ms. Flynn knows I can't spare any time. "Why me?"

"We're slammed inside. No one else can leave." He swings the door wider. "Sorry, kid."

I quickly wrap my brushes and seal off the paint, then head inside to wash my hands. Several heads turn my way as I stomp through the kitchen to the delivery counter, and I force a smile—which quickly drops when I see where the food has to go.

The brewery a block away. The one that doesn't serve food and encourages its patrons to order from nearby restaurants. Even though it's a bar, it's super family-friendly, with board games and brewed root beer, and it's not uncommon for families to spend an afternoon there, especially if the weather's bad. Normally, lunch isn't very busy, but this week—festival week—means thousands of extra people are in town, and at least ten percent of them are in the brewery. And I have to find—I read the instructions on the receipt—the Benson family near the front windows and Tommy "somewhere in the middle near the bar."

"Perfect," I mutter.

"Thanks, Emmy!" Ms. Flynn calls from the register with a nod at the line winding past the tables toward the front door. "We'll have more ready for you when you get back."

The scene outside is nothing like the quiet from the alley. Families with strollers and groups of teens swarm the carnival games set up in the middle of Main Street, while flashing lights and ear-piercing bells echo from the rides on the next block. Our town doesn't joke around when it comes to the festival, and based on the sticky smiles and overpriced plush prizes surrounding me, the tourists have found their nirvana.

I weave through the slow-moving crowd and pause to take a breath in front of the entrance to the brewery. Some people love nothing more than to stand in the middle of a crowd, all eyes on them, but others, like me, prefer to sit on the sidelines and observe. Stepping into a packed bar and searching for strangers is very low on my list of things I'd like to do before I graduate high school.

A group of guys in tank tops and shorts stumble out of the door. One bumps my shoulder, then grabs the other as he laughs. "Sorry. Sorry!" His beer breath turns my stomach, and I quickly pull away as they meander into the street.

I yank the door open and want to run back to the alley. Music pumps from speakers on the ceiling, but it's no match for the volume from the people. There have to be five hundred people in here. And I'm supposed to find a random guy near the bar?

A man my dad's age waves from near the window, and a grateful sigh seeps out of me. He's with a woman his age and two sunburned kids who look as miserable as me to be in here. An unopened box of Jenga sits in the center of the table. They must be the Benson family. I use the delivery bags to push my way through people and give the family my biggest smile. "Benson?"

The woman takes the bags. "Yes, thank goodness." She smiles at me as she picks through the bag. "We had no idea it'd be this busy!"

If you've never been to our town for the annual festival, the influx of tourists can be a shock, but the three-story Ferris wheel in the parking lot out front should have been a clue.

"Mom, this has cheese on it." The boy's whine sets my teeth on edge. I normally check the orders before I leave but was so irritated at having to stop painting that I skipped that crucial step.

Mr. Benson scribbles on the credit card receipt and scowls. "You can pick it off."

"These are the wrong chips," the girl says. Her glare could rival Marissa's, and I take a step back, even though she's several years younger than me.

I wait a beat for one of the parents to scold her for her tone, but eight eyes stare at me, frustration clear on their faces. I feel you, people.

Her mom sighs and takes the offending chips. "Just eat mine."

"But I wanted barbecue." Her tone makes it clear she's used to getting her way.

"I can bring them in a few minutes. I just need to—" I glance over my shoulder at the bar. The crowd has multiplied since I arrived, and the volume keeps increasing. "I have one more delivery before I can go back."

"No, she can eat these," the mom says.

I take the receipt and force a smile. "Is the rest of your order correct?"

While they pick through their paper-wrapped sandwiches, I scan the bar for anyone who seems to be waiting for a food delivery. But beer has a funny way of making people forget about things.

Mr. Benson huffs. "The rest is fine."

"Thanks! Enjoy!"

When I turn away, my eyes roll so far back in my head I bump into a toddler running loops around a high-top table. One of the adults grabs her arm and offers a smile, but doesn't pause her story.

I can do this.

The bar stretches the length of the brewery, so "near the bar" really isn't as helpful as it sounds. After a quick pass with my bag held high and no one stopping me, I take a deep breath and ignore the flush creeping up my face.

"Tommy?" My voice barely registers over the laughter and music. I clear my throat and shout louder. "Tommy!"

A few heads turn, but they dismiss me with barely a glance. "Great."

I keep moving, and when I reach the end of the bar, let out an ear-piecing shout. "TOMMY!" A hundred heads swivel as one and I turn twenty shades redder. Despite how loud it is, a chuckle behind me drowns out everything else. A small part of me clings to the hope that the chuckle belongs to Tommy, but I'd know that laugh anywhere.

Lucas.

Reflexively touching my wavy blond hair, which is tied in a messy bun, I slowly turn, hoping the move appears more casual than I feel. Despite having art classes together for the past five years—and being in the same elementary classes before that—Lucas and I haven't spoken in months. His light brown hair hangs in his face in a way that makes him look sweet and innocent, and his blue logoed T-shirt from Downtown Deli makes his eyes pop against his summer tan. Maybe the rest of him looks good too.

There was a time when seeing him from across the studio—paintbrush in hand, eyes focused on his canvas, lower lip caught between his teeth—made my heart gallop out of my chest. Sometimes I'd imagine he saw at me as more than just a friend, and that maybe our casual banter could turn into something more. But he ruined it when he sabotaged my spring project. Discovering black paint splattered across the canvas was worse than failing a class, and when Sarita told me it was Lucas, I didn't want to believe it. Mrs. Atkins accepted my painting as an abstract instead of the landscape I'd been going for, but I've been unable to forgive him.

Apparently my body didn't get the memo.

He shifts his empty delivery bag over his shoulder. "Need help?" For a moment, the painting never happened. His brows crease in a way that seems genuine, and his blue eyes lock on mine as if we're standing in an empty studio, not surrounded by hundreds of drunk tourists.

My body leans toward his, but I regain my senses before doing anything stupid. "Not from you."

His smile fades and his lower lip catches between his teeth.

Does he do that on purpose? To think I used to fantasize about being this close to him. Although he somehow smells amazing, despite the August heat. A combination of citrus and pine and, I don't know, Lucas.

He opens his mouth, but a shout from a few tables over makes us both turn.

"Sandwich lady! Over here!"

"I'm guessing that's Tommy," Lucas says, his eyes still on mine. He seems like he wants to say something else—perhaps the apology I never got in class?—but I turn away.

A college-aged guy waves his arms, and when I hold up their bag of food, the table full of guys cheers.

"Tommy?" I ask as I set the bags on their table.

He gives me a slow once over and steps a little too close, his wide eyes settling near my chest. "The one and only."

I shove the receipt and a pen at his chest. "There's a tip line there too so…" I'm not usually pushy about tips, but the past three minutes have fried the politeness from me. Besides, it's the least he can do for being a creep.

"Got it." He scribbles on the receipt and as he hands it back, his finger trails down my wrist.

A shudder of disgust passes through me, but I force a smile. "Enjoy." I whirl around to leave before they can inspect the order. The last thing I want is to have to talk to them again, but I stop after taking a step.

Lucas is standing where I left him, but he's not looking at me. He's glaring at Tommy and his friends.

"What are you—why are you still here?"

He moves next to me and places a hand on my lower back, and before I realize what's happening, he's guiding me through the crowd and onto the street. "I didn't trust that guy."

The heat from his hand is almost distracting enough to make me forget how mad I am. Almost. Even though I miss talking to him, miss how much I felt like myself when he was around, I twist away and take a step back. "I don't need your help."

"You keep saying that."

"Maybe you should listen."

Before he can say another word, I round the corner. But my anger instantly deflates. Across the street in front of the toy store, my best friend Raina—and the extra- to my introvertedness— is in the middle of a crowd on the sidewalk, hula hooping like her life depends on it. Her long brown braids swing with the movement, and kids inch closer, reaching their hands to touch the hoop as it swivels by.

I cross the street and wiggle through the crowd until she sees me.

"Emmy!" She laughs and the hoop drops to the ground.

"Four minutes, fifty-eight seconds!" a woman with a little girl on her hip exclaims.

"Almost broke my record," Raina says. She picks up the hoop and waves it over her head as the crowd starts to disperse. "Hula hoops are on sale inside! Head in and give them a try!"

"They don't pay you enough for this," I say.

She wipes sweat from her forehead. "This was my idea." She studies me for a moment and her smile drops. "What's wrong?"

"Ugh."

"You had to deliver again?"

"Worse."

She taps a finger on her chin. "Worse than drunk tourists in the middle of a weekday. Hmm…" Her gaze focuses over my shoulder and a smirk dances on her lips. "Lucas."

"Yup."

"What did he do now?"

When she puts it that way, he didn't do anything. It's his existence that pisses me off. "He offered to help me find a customer. Then he got me away from the sleazy customers. And he smelled really good."

"The bastard!"

"I know I'm being stupid, but I can't get over what he did."

"Are you sure it was him?"

This is the hundredth time she's asked me, and as much as I wish it would, my answer doesn't change. "He's the only one who was in there."

"When you found it. But the paint was already dry."

That one detail has given me pause over the past few months, but— "If it wasn't him, why hasn't he said anything?"

"Have you given him a chance?"

My harsh tone from inside the brewery plays back in my head. "Not exactly."

She glances over my shoulder inside the store and gives me a sympathetic smile. "I gotta go. We're still meeting at Gary's after work?"

Our touristy town's ice-cream-shop-to-resident ratio is obscenely high, but local teens avoid the bright shiny places along the water, instead opting for Gary's, the cash-only, family-run place at the far end of Main Street.

"I've been craving their Mackinaw Island Fudge since I woke up."

She laughs. "You and me both. And hey," she reaches for the door of the toy shop. "Maybe he-who-shall-not-be-named will be there too."

My stomach flips and I tell myself that it's because I'm hungry for ice cream.

Not Lucas.

Chapter 2

Half the downtown businesses are represented by the T-shirts at Gary's. The building doesn't have air conditioning, which is brutal on hot days like today, so teens cram onto the picnic tables alongside the building and onto the hoods of cars parked in the street, relaxing after another shift during festival week. We only have a few high schools in our area, and most of us have lived here forever, so I recognize most of the faces, including one shaggy-haired boy who's eating his mint chocolate chip cone like it's the only thing in the world that matters.

"You're staring," Raina whispers.

"I am not."

We inch forward in line, lifting our chins to catch the weak breeze from the fan oscillating in the corner.

"Boy sure knows how to eat chocolate ice cream," she says.

"It's mint chocolate chip," I correct, then immediately close my eyes.

"But you're not staring."

A smile inches across my face. "Nope."

When we step outside with our cones, I lead us to an empty spot at the end of a bench, far away from Lucas and his mesmerizing mouth. The late afternoon sun bakes everything around us—the benches, the asphalt, the customers—slowing the usual energy level out here to a crawl.

"How's the mural coming?" Raina asks. She knows that asking if I'm done will make me short-circuit this close to the deadline, and I appreciate her tact.

"It needs a couple more hours. I was just getting into my groove when I was sent on the deliveries."

She leans her shoulder into mine. "You and your groove."

"What can I say? Painting soothes me." I do my best impersonation of an artist gazing into the distance and accidentally lock eyes with Lucas. But instead of immediately looking away, I hold the eye contact until my entire body is humming.

"Seriously. Just talk to him," she says.

I shake my head, breaking whatever connection we had. "Did you sell any hula hoops?"

She rolls her eyes at the change of subject but humors me. "A family from out of state bought one for each of their kids. Each of their *five* kids. My best day yet!"

"Can you imagine five hula hoops in a hotel room going at once?"

"They're probably renting a house."

"Can't you let me have this visual?" I laugh, but it fades when Marissa saunters out with a chocolate-dipped cone. Her gaze lands on us long enough to dismiss us, then she heads the other direction. Toward Lucas. He nods a hello, but his attention quickly returns to his ice cream.

"Has it gotten any better with her?"

I let out a long sigh. "No. I swear the M&Ms were sent here to ruin my summer." Marissa and Mackenzie pretended to be irritated when Lonz dubbed them M&M in May, but now you'd think they made it up themselves. As if on cue, Mackenzie comes outside and joins her. "It'd be fine if I could ignore them, but she's always finding ways to get under my skin."

Like now. Sure, I'm probably the last thing on her mind, but I can't help wondering if she's trying a little too hard. The way she flips her hair and presses her hand to her chest when she laughs feels practiced.

"Only a month until Labor Day, then you won't have to see her anymore."

Raina's right, but the self-doubt that Marissa has sparked in me feels too strong to go away just because we head back to school.

More teens trickle outside, filling the sidewalk and blocking my view of her, and for a few minutes, the world is beautiful. Until I'm popping the last bite into my mouth, casually licking traces of ice cream off my fingers, when bodies part like the Red Sea, clearing a direct path to Marissa. She's moved closer to Lucas and her hands wave as she talks.

I shift so I'm facing the building, determined not to let her annoy me any longer. Raina waves at a group of kids from our school, and soon I'm peppered with questions about the mural.

"I heard yours is really good."

"You're definitely getting my vote."

"Could you imagine winning five hundred dollars?"

"The perspective is amazing." That one is Raina, my unceasing supporter, and the reason the image exists.

"Have you seen the one at Downtown Deli? Lucas killed it."

Raina kicks him, and his mouth falls open.

"What? I didn't say Emmy's was bad, just that his is good too."

"Well, you're not helping."

"It's okay," I say, willing my eyes to stay focused on them and not on the other end of the sidewalk. "Lucas is really talented. Of course his mural is amazing."

"You haven't seen it?" he asks.

"Not yet." One of my rules as an artist is to not compare myself to others—at least while I'm working—and part of that means not looking at others' work until it's finished. It's too easy to fall into a spiral of despair and self-doubt, and while the tortured artist cliché is a cliché for a reason, I don't want it to define me.

They wander off to an empty picnic table and Raina leans against me. "It's okay to want to see it."

"But I don't." My gaze drifts to him again, and he catches me looking. He has an expression on his face like he's trying to figure me out or is sending telepathic signals that get tripped up on all the other people. Too bad being the second coming of Michelangelo doesn't excuse what he did.

"Well, I do." Raina laughs, and the frustration creeping through me settles down. "Can we walk by when we're done here?"

Before I can respond, Sarita, a girl from my art class, steps into the sun with a double scoop. She shields her eyes, scanning the crowd for a familiar face, and before I can wave her over, she smiles and heads in the opposite direction.

To Marissa.

And Lucas.

Which wouldn't be a big deal, except Sarita is the one who told me Lucas trashed my painting. And now she's talking with both of them like they're best friends.

"Since when do they know each other?" Raina asks.

"Good question."

When Sarita found me gaping at my ruined painting, she was so quick to accuse Lucas that I figured she must have known what she was talking about—even though everything inside me didn't want to believe her. Now I'm wondering if she had ulterior motives.

"Do you think she lied about Lucas?" Raina asks. Then she twists on the bench, her eyes wide, and smacks my arm. "What if she's the one who did it?"

Pieces of the story that never made sense click into place with a hollow thud. Marissa hates me. Sarita and Marissa are friends. Sarita had just as much access to my painting as Lucas, and a heck of a lot more motive since she's apparently cozy with Marissa.

Lucas didn't do anything wrong.

And I've treated him horribly ever since.

"Did I make a huge mistake?"

Raina jumps off the bench and grabs my arm, pulling me to my feet. "Nothing that can't be fixed." She gives a tug, and I plant my feet on the ground.

"No. I'm not going over there."

"Egads, woman. Not now. Let's go see his mural. Then you can decide what to do next."

We toss our napkins in the trash and move through the crowd to cross the street, but I can't help one last look at Lucas. He's nodding to whatever Marissa and Sarita are laughing about, but his eyes are locked on me. My belly does a slow somersault, and I can't stop the smile that spreads over my face.

"Woah, that's intense," Raina says as he smiles back. "Does this mean all is forgiven?"

"I've spent so long hating him. Can I switch back to liking him just like that?"

"Based on the look he just gave you, I say yes."

And based on my body's reaction, also yes. I resist turning around a second time and follow Raina up the block toward Downtown Deli. Since the murals are on the backside of the buildings, we cut through a clothing store—I can't be seen in Downtown Deli wearing my work shirt—and Raina stops so suddenly I run into her back.

"What's up?"

"This is amazing," she says, pointing at the wall.

I've been so focused on me and Lucas that I kind of forgot other businesses have artwork as well. This wall features a landscape filled with lavender and sunflowers, two of my favorite flowers.

"But you'd never see those in the same field," she says.

"That's the beauty of art. You can bend the rules of the world however you want." I step closer to the painting and trail my hand over the brushstrokes. Most people prefer to view paintings from farther away because the strokes blur together, creating the complete picture, but I like to see how the artist made it happen.

"Let's check out the others!"

We stroll down the alley, which is really more of a small drive that runs alongside the downtown parking lot. Wooden structures conceal the dumpsters, and flowers brighten the area so it feels more like an extension of Main Street. Tourists and businesspeople dot the sidewalks, their leisurely pace indicative of the warm afternoon. No one's in a hurry to get anywhere. The other murals are a variety of scenes from around town, and while there are other paintings of the pier, I'm relieved no one else has anything close to mine.

When we reach Lucas's mural, my breath catches. "It's so good. Like heart-stopping good." A sandcastle anchors the center of the mural, its crumbly spires and lopsided walls an exact representation of what we see every time we walk on the beach. But he didn't stop there. Several kids in bathing suits dribble sand and water onto different parts of the castle, while in the background, a young boy runs from the lake toward the viewer carrying an orange pail overflowing with water. The low perspective creates a similar effect as mine, like you're in the middle of the action instead of observing it from afar.

"Yours can beat this."

"I'm not sure." Lucas's talent is no surprise—I've watched him develop as an artist for years—but seeing it on this scale is more intimidating than I expected. I move closer to inspect the brushstrokes. A flush spreads over my face at the thought of his hands creating this, his lower lip permanently stuck between his teeth and his hair falling in his face.

Raina loops her arm through mine and squeezes. "Seriously. Stop worrying about what Lucas or anyone else has created and just focus on you."

I let out a long sigh. "Thank you."

We turn back toward Main Street Deli, toward my mural, and don't speak until we're face to face with my kids. A yearning to be there with them, laughing as I jump into the cool water of the lake, fills me with sadness.

"Emmy, this is really good."

"Yeah, but his is—"

"Finished?" She ducks her head to hide the sheepish expression, but she's right. "It'll be finished on time, right?" Her voice is low, almost a whisper, and I hate everything it implies.

Tomorrow's deadline looms over me larger than Lucas's sandcastle. "Do you mind if I stay to work on this? I really need to put in a few more hours."

"Want me to help?"

Raina's wide eyes nearly undo me. She doesn't have an artistic bone in her body, but she's so caring she'd do anything to help. "No, you go on home. I'll be able to finish if I stay focused."

Because it's useless to even fantasize about winning if my mural isn't done.

Chapter 3

Last night, I painted until Ms. Flynn came out to lock up for the night. Today, my fingers ache and paint streaks my arms, but it was worth it. The mural is ninety-eight percent finished, and once I finish the highlights on the kids' faces, it'll look exactly how I imagined. When I arrived for work, I caught Marissa checking it out, and she even gave me a half-hearted "nice work" when we were prepping for the first customers.

And not a minute too soon. Voting starts today at five.

When the lunch rush finally dies down, Ms. Flynn gives me the nod to go out back and finish. The mid-day light casts different shadows on the wall, and the places that need highlights practically jump out at me. Those details are the difference between an okay painting and one that feels alive, like the subjects are breathing, and if you reached out you could feel the warmth of their skin.

The time passes quickly, and I'm reaching toward the top of the mural, to the closest kid's face, when a voice behind me sends a shiver down my back.

"Emmy, this is fantastic."

I lower my brush and take a deep breath before turning around. Lucas and his younger brother are standing at the edge of the Main Street Deli's property, far enough away that he can't hear my heart pounding in my chest, but close enough that I can see the twinkle in those blue eyes.

A compliment from anyone else usually gets a polite smile and a dismissal that it's okay. But I respect his opinion, and therefore I am now blushing. "Thanks."

He moves closer, leaving his brother at the edge of the parking lot. "Look, I don't know what I did to piss you off, but I'm sorry."

"I'm sorry too." The words are out of my mouth before I can think about them, but it's true. I am sorry.

He cocks his head in surprise.

"Let's just say I was led to believe you did something, and…" I drop my gaze to my sneakers. A splatter of blue paint covers the toe. "I should have known it was a lie."

"Is this about your spring project?"

"Yeah," I tell the ground.

"Did you honestly think I would destroy another artist's work?"

Dread creeps through me at the frustration in his voice. All this time I've been worried about how I feel, but I never considered how he'd feel being accused of something he didn't do. I shake my head, but he's not done.

"And not just another artist. *Your* work."

This time I look up, and he's got to hear my heartbeat now because it's ricocheting off my chest so hard that I can't catch my breath. His hair hangs in his face in a way that makes me want to run my fingers through it, and his eyes lock on mine, daring me to look away.

Which I can't. Because his looks aren't why I haven't been able to stop thinking about him. It's his heart, and the kind of person he is. And right now, he looks like *I* ruined *his* painting. My accusation hurt him as much as I was hurt when I thought he trashed my project.

"Did you really think I'd do that?" he repeats. A breeze swirls the air around us, almost carrying his voice away. A piece of my hair catches in the wind, and his hand lifts like he's going to touch it, but he stops and lets it fall back to his side. His eyes darken for a moment, like he's thinking of something other than paintings and lies and months of missed opportunities.

"I don't know why I listened to her. I should have talked to you."

"Yeah, you should have."

"Saying I'm sorry probably isn't enough, huh?"

The corner of his mouth lifts in a smile that gives me hope. "It's a start."

"I'm sorry. I really am." This time, my hand reaches for him, and I make contact before I can stop myself. My fingers graze his forearm, and for a moment we both stop breathing. The white paint on my fingers contrasts with the red on his arm, and I wonder what it'd be like to paint something with him.

He runs his hand through his hair, breaking contact, and gazes at me in a way I've only dreamed about. "I accept."

Accept what? Oh, my apology! "Thank you."

He gestures over his shoulder at his brother. "I gotta run. But I'll see you later?"

"Yeah, definitely."

He slowly backs up, his eyes never leaving mine until he's side by side with his brother. "May the best artist win."

"I *told* you, he likes you!" Raina slaps the steering wheel as she maneuvers into a parking spot not far from Main Street Deli. It's been four days since my encounter with Lucas, and despite saying he'd see me later, it's like the boy's vanished. We're re-hashing everything he said to figure out if I missed something.

"So, where is he?" I ask. "Later means like, later that day, not a month from now when school starts."

"Patience, grasshopper." Raina cuts the engine and we both flip down our sun visors to check our reflections. I'm not usually super into my appearance, but now that there's a possibility that something might happen with Lucas, I want to at least look pre-sentable. "And for the hundredth time, you're adorable."

I poke her in the side. "So why are you primping?"

She shrugs. "You never know who might be here."

Neither one of us are known for our dating experience, but that doesn't mean we don't like to play the game. The Saturday night during festival week is *the* night to see and be seen. Teen-agers from three counties pack the streets, which close on the final day of the festival, and not being there would leave a hol-lowness in one's soul that's unrecoverable. Or at least really depressing.

We follow the squeals from the carnival rides and stop in our tracks at the mob blocking the intersection. "Do we really have to go in there?" I ask. No cute boy is worth navigating that madness.

Raina shakes her head. "I don't see anyone from our school in there. Let's check out Gary's instead."

The crowd is smaller at the ice cream shop, and filled with more locals than tourists, who tend to prefer the shops closer to the water that have air conditioning. The line snakes out the door, and when I spot Lucas through the window, the turmoil I've tried to ignore for the past four days comes rushing through me.

"I don't know if I can do this."

Raina grabs my arm and pulls me into line. "It's simple. You tell the poor kid who's stuck working on festival Saturday what you want, they'll scoop it, and then we'll inhale it before it melts."

A snort escapes me. "Ha, ha. But seriously. What if he doesn't want to talk to me?"

"He said he'd see you later. Now is later. When he sees you, smile and maybe lick your lips or something."

"Omigod!" I smack her arm, and several heads turn our way. "The art of seduction is the one class I've missed, and I'm not scaring him off by looking like a creeper trying to lick ice cream off my face."

"Well, when you put it that way." We shuffle forward as people step outside. Lucas is paying, and so far, hasn't noticed us. But once he's outside, all he'll have to do is lift his head and he'll see us.

Panic thrums in my chest. "Maybe this was all in my head."

"It's not."

We take another step forward and we're next to the door that's propped open to let the breeze inside. The glass door makes a terrible shield, but I'll take it.

Then Lucas exits the shop and Raina shouts, "Hey, Lucas!" and he definitely sees us.

"What are you doing?" I whisper shout.

"Speeding along the inevitable."

Lucas raises his cone at us and points at a picnic table with a couple other art kids. I send a silent thank you to the stars above that Marissa is nowhere to be seen.

"You can thank me later."

"I can't believe you did that."

"Somebody had to. At the rate you two are going, we'll be graduated before either of you makes a move."

"How do you suddenly know so much about this?"

She waggles her brows as we step up to the counter, and the kid with the scooper blushes. Then Raina blushes. "Sorry, that was for my friend."

He smiles awkwardly and nods at the buckets of ice cream. "What'll it be?"

We place our orders and shuffle down the counter to pay, my nerves worsening the closer we get to the exit. After months of pretending I don't like Lucas, I'm finally free to talk to him like I used to. But what if he's still mad at me?

Raina leans close when we step outside. "What's your opening line?"

"Um, hi?"

"Yes, that's brilliant. Go with that."

I kick the side of her foot. "Do you have a better idea?"

She takes a bite of ice cream and shrugs. "This is the closest to a love life that I've had in years. Just be your charming self and don't say anything stupid."

I laugh. "Thanks. I think."

She leads the way to Lucas's table, and he brightens when he sees us. Shawna and Alex from our art class slide over to make room on the bench, and after a moment of awkward maneuvering and an accidental knee to Lucas's thigh, I'm sitting next to him.

And I can't think of a single thing to say.

Fortunately, Raina's here, and she's never let an uncomfortable silence stop her. "Sooooo, who did everyone vote for?"

"Raina!" My mouth falls open, and I can feel the blush creeping up my neck before Lucas even looks at me. "Sorry," I whisper.

He laughs and gestures at the other people at the table. "We were just talking about that. Since it's poor taste to vote for yourself," he leans closer and his knee bumps mine. "Who are you voting for?"

"Oh. I... Oh, whoops!" I make a big show of licking the side of my ice cream cone, stalling until the proper words find their way into my head.

"She voted for you," Raina says to Lucas, and I'm tempted to shove my ice cream cone onto her nose.

"Then we cancel each other out."

"You voted for me?"

The corner of his mouth lifts in that adorable smile that does crazy things to my insides, and everyone else laughs.

"Him and everyone else," says Wes, a soccer player from school who I don't think I've ever spoken to. He smiles, and I feel like I'm the butt of a joke.

"What does that mean?" My eyes drop to the table. If they've been making fun of me, I don't want to know.

"Nothing," Lucas says, waving a hand to the side and shaking his head. It's hardly subtle, and it makes me feel even worse.

Wes clears his throat and has the courtesy to look embarrassed. "Just that it sounds like a lot of people have voted for you. Your mural is really good."

"Did you hear they closed the pier earlier today?" Shawna asks. She leans forward, excitement brightening her green eyes. "Apparently there were like a hundred kids out there and a fight broke out." She takes a sip of her shake and looks over her shoulder in the direction of the lake. "Sucks, 'cause we were heading out there to swim after work."

"Oh, that would've been perfect," Raina says. "Ice cream is great, but nothing beats jumping off the pier."

Suddenly I feel really small. Even smaller than when I thought they were making fun of me. Because Raina's never made an issue out of pier-jumping, but as her best friend, I should have known she wanted to. "I didn't realize you wanted to do that."

She touches my arm. "I didn't want to pressure you."

"Wait," Lucas says. "You've never done it?"

Five pairs of eyes lock on me. Jumping off the pier is a rite of passage in our town, and I've been able to avoid this conversation for seventeen years. My head shakes, sending my wavy hair in front of my face.

"Why not?!" The disbelief in Shawna's voice is exactly why I've avoided talking about it.

"I don't know, it's stupid."

Lucas's hand touches my arm, and the heat from his skin works its way through my body. "I'm sure it's not."

"It's just..." I wave my hand in front of me. "There's giant rocks under the water, and the waves, and what if I slip on the edge and hit my head or something?"

"You don't have to do flips or anything," Wes says. "And you seem perfectly capable of running in a straight line on slightly damp concrete."

I watch for a sign that he's being sarcastic, but his eyes are nothing but kind.

"And everyone jumps at the spot where there aren't rocks," Alex says.

"And I'll hold your hand," Raina says.

"When you put it that way, I guess it doesn't sound so bad," I say at the same time Lucas says, "Me too." Butterflies swarm in my belly, and I hold his gaze.

"We should totally go," Lucas says, and a huge smile swallows Raina's face.

"Oh yeah?" Just talking about jumping makes me feel bold, and I move my leg so our knees touch.

"Assuming you're not still mad at me?"

My smile fades. "I'm really sorry about that."

"I just wish you would have said something." He looks like he wants to say more, but his eyes drop to my cone and he smirks. "You've got some serious drippage going on over here."

Ice cream runs down the back of my hand, and I lean to lick it, incredibly aware of his eyes on me. Raina kicks me under the table, and I burst out laughing, the tension dissolving with my laughter.

"Let's go walk around," Shawna says. "I want to ride the Ferris wheel."

We finish our ice cream and head to Main Street and the heart of the festival. The next couple hours are a blur of carnival food and laughing and uncertainty, which slams to a stop when Lucas's fingers slide between mine.

And stay there.

I peek at him from the corner of my eye. He's nodding to whatever Wes is saying like he holds my hand every day, but he must notice me looking because he squeezes my hand, sending a jolt of electricity up my arm and straight to my belly. I squeeze back, and his smile nearly melts me where I'm standing.

Things have definitely changed between us, and while the others have to have noticed, no one's said anything—and no one's making a move to part ways so we can be alone.

"The fireworks are starting soon," Riana says with a casual glance at our hands. A smile dances on her lips. "Should we find a spot closer to the water?"

"Sure," Lucas says before looking at me. "Is that okay?"

I nod dumbly. What universe have I stumbled into where Lucas is treating me like his girlfriend? "Yeah, that's cool."

We make our way past the carnival games and food vendors until we reach the waterfront. The fireworks are shot off from across the river and are the finale to the festival. Every square inch of grass is covered with blankets and chairs, but there's still plenty of room in the street. We find an open curb and settle in, Lucas on one side of me and Raina on the other, and when his arm slides around my waist, I can't remember ever feeling this happy.

An explosion rips through the sky, making me jump, and Raina cracks up. "They get you every time!"

"I wasn't ready for it."

"Every. Time."

"Oooh! Ahhhhh!" I shout, not caring that people look at me. It doesn't matter how cool you think you are; when fireworks go off, you ooh and ah.

People walking through the closed streets stop to watch the show, and we settle into a comfortable routine of me oohing, Raina ahhing, and Lucas laughing at both of us. A couple times, I catch Lucas watching me, but I have no idea if he's as surprised as I am at how things have shifted, or if he's thinking about kissing me. Which would make this night perfect.

When the show finally comes to an end, he helps us both to our feet. Shawna, Alex, and Wes wave their goodbyes, leaving me, Lucas, and Raina to follow the crowd toward our cars. I can tell Raina wishes she were anywhere else, but we rode together, and I would never leave her to fend for herself with all these people.

When we reach her car, Lucas shifts from one foot to the other. "What are you doing tomorrow?"

"Besides working?" I ask. "Nothing."

He smiles at Raina and she nods, and the same sense of dread from Gary's sweeps through me.

"What?"

"Lucas had a great idea."

I look between the two of them, and they seem to be debating who's going to spill.

"We thought it'd be fun—" Lucas says.

"To go to the beach—" Raina says.

"And maybe do a little swimming—" he says.

"By way of the pier," she finishes.

I yank my hand from Lucas and take a step back. "When the heck did you plan this?"

Raina's eyes twinkle in the light from the streetlamps. "When you were peeing."

"Awesome."

"What do you say?" Lucas asks.

There are worse ways to spend an afternoon than at the beach with your best friend and the boy you like. I hold up a finger. "On one condition."

Now Lucas's eyes are twinkling. "Name it."

"No one is allowed to laugh if I scream."

"Deal," they say in unison.

"Oh, god, what did I agree to?"

Raina jumps up and down. "You'll love it, I promise."

I raise an eyebrow at Lucas. "Any promises from you?"

He gives me that adorable half-smile, and I nearly swoon when he says, "Maybe later." He steps closer and the next thing I know, he's pulling me against his warm chest in a hug that I never want to end. My arms wrap around his waist, and his heart thuds against my ear. Raina's fanning herself and pretending to swoon too, then he moves away. "Until tomorrow."

"Bye," we both say, then double over laughing.

"Damn, girl," she says, unlocking the car. "Looks like you've got yourself a boyfriend."

Every ounce of me feels like I could float away, but the uncertainty from Gary's wiggles back in. They were definitely talking about me before we arrived, and Lucas didn't want me to know what it was about.

So how can I know if I should trust him?

Chapter 4

The high from last night still carries me when Ms. Flynn gathers us for our morning huddle, despite having stayed up way too late rehashing the night with Raina. She thinks Lucas must have been telling them that he likes me, even though I kept insisting guys don't talk like that. We finally agreed that if it's still bothering me the next time I see him, I'll just be a big girl and ask him to tell me the truth.

"We have exciting news!" Ms. Flynn claps her hands together, and several people wince. Looks like I'm not the only one who had a late night. "As you all know, voting for the Summer Fun mural ended yesterday. While all the entries were wonderful, two were the clear favorites." Several heads turn my way, then quickly back to Ms. Flynn, who looks like she might combust right here in the middle of the kitchen. "I'm thrilled to tell you that *Pier Jumpers* won!"

The room erupts in cheers and applause, and Lonz is hugging me, and Ms. Flynn's smile looks like it might break her face.

"We're so proud of you, Emmy!"

"Great job!"

"What are you gonna do with the money?"

"I have no idea."

"We knew you could do it!" That last comment is from Marissa. Her smile is a little too big to be genuine, but I don't care.

I won!

But Lucas...

This means Lucas didn't win.

And we're supposed to jump off the pier today.

Is he even going to want to see me?

If I were him, I'd want to throw me off the pier. His mural was so much better.

"You okay?" Lonz asks.

I'm standing at my prep station, but I haven't moved in several minutes. "Yeah, just in shock."

"You deserved to win." His smile is so real, so genuine, that I try to stop second-guessing myself.

"Thanks."

By the time lunch ends, word has gotten around, and people come in just to congratulate Main Street Deli and to meet me.

Emmy.

So when Ms. Flynn calls me to the front saying I have a visitor, I'm not prepared for Lucas to be on the other side of the counter. And definitely not Lucas in his Downtown Deli T-shirt and holding flowers. More specifically, a bouquet of sunflowers and lavender.

The warmth in his eyes nearly undoes me. "Congratulations."

"How did you know?"

"Emmy, everyone knows. You're kind of a big deal."

I shake my head. "Not about the contest. The flowers."

His cheeks color and he dips his head, making his hair fall in his face. "I may have had help there."

"Raina. I can't believe she didn't warn me!"

He leans against the counter and hands me the flowers. "Since when do I require a warning?"

Ms. Flynn clears her throat. "Emmy, why don't you take your break now?"

My face flames, but I smile at Lucas. "Want to go out back?"

"Scene of the crime. You got it."

I avoid making eye contact with anyone as I walk through the kitchen, the flowers clutched to my chest. Lucas uses the door for the public, and we step into the afternoon sunshine at the same time.

"Thank you for the flowers."

"I'm glad you like them."

"There's something I wanted to ask you." I take a deep breath, ready to ask him for the truth about yesterday, but he cuts me off.

"Can I ask you something first?" My determination deflates, but he doesn't notice. He scuffs his shoe on the pavement and shoves his hands in his pockets before taking them out and running one through his hair.

Is he nervous?

"Sure."

He takes a step closer, then still closer, until barely a breath separates us. His lower lip catches between his teeth and he inhales through his nose. "Would it be okay—I mean, can I kiss you?"

I must nod, because his eyes close and his head lowers and then the sweetest boy in the universe touches his lips to mine. His lips are softer than I could have imagined. They move slowly, cautiously, until I reach a hand behind his neck and pull him closer. He's everything I hoped for, and I can't believe this is finally happening.

When we break apart, I'm mortified by the scent of grilled sandwiches that lingers on me. "I'm sorry I smell like a sandwich."

He laughs into my hair. "I figured it was me." Then his lips find mine again, and I forget about sandwiches and murals and uncertainty.

This time, I end the kiss. "I really did want to ask you something," I say. He rests his hands on my hips and meets my eyes. My nerve wavers, but I push forward. "Yesterday when we got to Gary's, what were you talking about with the voting?"

His eyes harden so fast I almost miss it. "I was hoping you didn't remember that."

Alarm twists my insides. Was this too good to be true?

He takes a step back and pushes his hair off his forehead. "I may have asked people to vote for your mural."

Everything inside me stills and my pulse roars in my head. "Why would you do that?"

"I felt bad about your spring project getting ruined." He holds up his hands. "Even though I had nothing to do with it. I don't know, I guess I thought this was a way to make it up to you."

My thoughts tumble over themselves. I didn't win on my own. Lucas rigged it for me. "I don't know what to say."

"I swear, it was supposed to be a good thing." He reaches for my hand, but I pull away. "You deserved to win. Don't let this make you think any differently."

"Too late," I say. How can something so wonderful be ruined just like that? "I need to get back to work. Thanks for the flowers."

"Emmy, wait."

I stop with my hand on the door.

"Can I still see you later? At the pier?"

"I don't know."

Then I walk away, not sure about anything anymore.

"Emmy, you have to go. For me." Raina's sitting on my bedroom floor wearing a cotton dress over her bathing suit and the most pathetic sad face possible.

"How can I go with him after what he did?"

She holds up her hands. "Yes, it sucks that Lucas asked people to vote for you, but his intentions were pure."

I raise an eyebrow. "Pure?"

She waves a hand. "Whatever. Innocent. Not malicious." She checks her phone and tosses it back on the floor. "He was trying to be nice."

"Do you know how it makes me feel, knowing I didn't deserve to win? I'm a fraud."

"Do you know how many votes were cast? Thousands. Lucas may be amazing, but there's no way he influenced that many people." She gets to her feet and grabs my hands. "You won because your mural was the best."

Deep down I believe her, but I'll never feel like I deserved to win. Even if Lucas only got a hundred people to vote for me, those hundred votes should have gone to someone else. Like the sunflowers and lavender mural. The owner of the shoe store came in third and could have won with my fraudulent votes.

Her phone buzzes on the floor and we both look at it.

"Also, way to sell me out with the flowers."

She points at the flowers, which are arranged in a vase on my dresser. "Those flowers? You're welcome. Now, put your suit on and let's go."

I let out a sigh and roll my eyes. "Fine, but I'm only doing this for you."

"Sure. Yep. Fine. I'll take it."

Twenty minutes later, we're walking through the sand to the pier. Dozens of kids our age stand in groups midway down the concrete structure, watching as people run and flip and jump into the water. Several girls line up, hands held, and rush to the edge, but one yanks her hands free at the last minute while her friends fly through the air.

"That will be me."

"We won't let you."

"We?"

"Oh, come on. You knew he'd be here."

Despite my disappointment, my belly stirs at the thought of seeing Lucas. Especially in a bathing suit. A smile works its way over my lips, and Raina laughs.

"There's my girl. Now, let's hurry before you change your mind."

Lucas finds us right away, and I do my best not to stare at his chest. He's not chiseled or flawless or whatever they always say about boys in novels, but he's perfect to me. We drop our bags by his shoes, and he runs a finger down my arm.

"I'm really sorry."

Raina waves a hand between us. "Not now. I've got her here, which means she forgives you, but she's bound to change her mind at any moment."

"I can't believe I let you talk me into this."

"It's a rite of passage. You can't grow up here and never jump off the pier."

Lucas grabs my hand and gives me a warm smile. "I'm glad you came."

Raina grabs my other hand. "Ready?"

"No."

"On the count of three," Lucas says.

"Are you sure there aren't rocks here?"

"One," Raina says.

"What if I slip?"

"Two," Lucas says.

"I don't think I can do this!"

"Three!" They both shout, then they tug me forward and we're running and my stomach leaps into my throat and we jump and we're flying—we're really flying!—and we hit the water together.

They let go of my hands while we're underwater, and I kick until my head breaks the surface. I did it! And I didn't die!

Lucas is right next to me, concern etched on his face.

"Well?" Raina asks.

"You were right. You both were."

They smile and I laugh as a wave pushes us toward the steel wall. A flutter of panic makes me swim faster to the ladder built into the side of the pier, and it's not until I'm back on semi-dry land that my heart rate slows.

"I'm so proud of you," Raina says pulling me into a hug. Lucas wraps his arms around both of us, and I finally relax. When I open my eyes, they're both smiling at me.

I finally know what it feels like to live inside the moment.

THE END

Other Published Works
READ MORE BY MELANIE HOOYENGA

The Flicker Effect trilogy – Left-Handed Mitten Publications
Flicker – 2012
Fracture – 2014
Faded – 2015

The Rules Series – Left-Handed Mitten Publications
The Slope Rules – 2017
The Trail Rules – 2018
The Edge Rules – 2018

The Book of Good:
A journal to help you find the good in each day – 2019

FOR MORE, VISIT
www.melaniehoo.com

Jane & Austen's

I never expected my life to change. So when it did, I was kind of let down that it wasn't way more dramatic than a trip to the mailbox. But that's how it had happened. All it took was a tidy manila envelope to contain all the ways in which my life would now be different.

I was a store clerk, and I had been one since I started working for Ms. Jane ten years ago, when I was sixteen. But now, this handful of legal-looking documents claimed I was an owner. Ms. Jane's, Dolldom-N-Bookshop was to be mine, along with $200K to be used for upgrades.

I scanned the papers and then reread them, painstakingly concentrating on each detail. My hands shook when I held the check, and as I tipped the envelope, the keys jangled out onto my kitchen table. I set all of it aside in a neat pile and stepped to the counter to refill my coffee cup. Lord knew how long I'd been sitting there—reading and rereading the legalese—but the mug was cool, and I needed something hot and scalding on my tongue to burn me back to reality, back to the time before I had opened that package. But the coffee pot had turned off hours ago and only the dredges were left. I spilled it down the sink and refilled the carafe to make fresh.

From my kitchen window, I watched the three kids from next door gather their beach towels and inner tubes and set off toward Main Street and then, invariably, on to the creek's cool water. It was that time of year, right before school let out for the summer, when the seasonal creek that curved around town ran quick with mountain snowmelt. Their flip flops slapped across the pavement as they jumped and skipped and sang their way to another Rockwellian afternoon. Because that's the way it was around here, the thing tourists always used to describe our home: "It's like being in a Norman Rockwell painting." And for the most part, they were right, except that it was dying. Dolldom-N-Bookshop wasn't really an *attraction,* and neither were the other ten antique stores lining the historic little gold-mining Main Street of Goldbug Creek, California.

But there was potential for Main Street to change. It could be a bustling center for the town again. The surrounding wineries saw it. A few of the Old West false-front buildings had been bought up and renovated recently, making for great tasting rooms.

The coffee pot beeped. I refilled my cup. I shouldn't be thinking about the town dying. One: locals never admit that. And two: I'd literally walked away from Ms. Jane's funeral plot up on the hill a week ago. She'd been in my grandmother's class, so well into her eighties when she had passed. I considered myself lucky not to find her. When I got to the store that morning, the door was still locked. And that was that. I had called 9-1-1 and they confirmed what we already knew; she was gone. She'd opened that store every day for over thirty-eight years, and always joked that the day she didn't would be the day she died. And lo' that's how it had gone down.

The little balcony off my kitchen had enough room for a side table and one chair, which creaked as I sat down. I'd been renting the efficiency apartment above my neighbor's garage for years now. After college—I barely lasted two semesters—staying with my parents had to be temporary. Ms. Jane was the one that set me up here. She knew the owner had fixed it up, and it was walking distance from Main Street and, therefore, my work-place. I still needed my car, a beat-up Pontiac that spewed a burned oil smell all over town, to get my groceries. But other than that, I walked to work, to the diner, and occasionally to the bar. That was it. That was my quiet little life here, back in the same county I'd grown up in. Until last year, I was one of the few from my high school class that still lived here, but that's starting to change too. Old friends have paired up with new partners and started bringing their young families home.

I sipped the hot, creamy coffee and reconsidered Main Street, the town's main artery. I always thought it would wither—dry up like the mines—with the likes of Ms. Jane and her generation's persistent mistrust of anything new. But maybe I was wrong, and maybe that stack of papers on my kitchen table was proof.

The jingle bells on the door settled into a quiet jangle as I closed it. I kept the sign flipped to Closed. Someone, probably one of the other shop managers on the street, had posted a note on the front window explaining Dolldum-N-Bookshop would be closed indefinitely due to a family emergency. It was little things like this that always made my heart swell for this community. Tourists saw the historical charm of preserved buildings and wine—they loved the wine—but I saw all the ways people helped each other.

But while Dolldum's had been well-preserved on the outside, with its classic brick façade and hand-painted display window, the inside needed some work. A lot of work. For the first time, I surveyed the space with a different eye. Before, I'd just come in, dust and stock the shelves, shoot the shit with Ms. Jane—she had a lot of dirty little songs and limericks she used to sing and dance to—and go home. Gradually, Ms. Jane trusted me with some of the bookkeeping, but it was nothing I went home and stressed about. It was her shop. Now it was mine, and the place was a mess.

The tan and maroon linoleum tiles were uneven and cracked, so much so that in some places I kicked up a bit of gravel. There was no discernable pattern for the metal shelving units that held the books, never once creating an aisle, more like a maze. Hand-written signs, that were just slips of paper affixed with packing tape, adorned each unit, notifying customers of which genre they were looking at. But they were written in fading marker, and the tape was peeling away. The backroom was piled high with boxes and boxes filled with either books or dolls.

Ms. Jane had managed to keep an old desk in a side room office, and it was well organized, along with her filing cabinet in the corner. She was meticulous about paperwork, at least. I flicked on the light switches and went back into the main room.

The dull fluorescent glow highlighted the creepy contours of all those chubby baby doll cheeks lining the shelves. I hated the porcelain dolls. I had told Ms. Jane I hated them, and that everyone else did too. But she was adamant about keeping them as part of the store's kitsch, even though I could count on my fingers how many we'd sold over the years. They had to go.

"Bye-bye, girls." I smoothed the velvety green dress of one of the prettier ones between my fingers. "Time to find you a real home."

"Already plotting how to change things, then?"

"Jesus!" I jumped at the intrusion of this very male voice before realizing it was familiar. "You scared the crap out of me."

"Sorry 'bout that." Austen leaned against the doorframe that led to the backroom and Ms. Jane's—I mean, my—office. I hadn't seen him since the funeral, but before that, I hadn't seen him since graduation. He was one of the kids that high-tailed it out of the county, choosing a more anonymous life closer to the capital. I shook his hand at his grandmother's funeral, but he didn't seem to recognize me. But to be fair, he didn't seem to recognize any of what was going on. "You should try to sell them."

"What?"

"The dolls. I'm sure Grandma saved their boxes; she saved everything. They should bring in a good amount of cash online."

"You think?"

"She always said there was a market for them."

"Just not here."

"Well, right. It's a little niche for Goldbug." He took in a deep breath. As his gaze panned the rest of the store, seemingly nostalgia softened his features.

A ball of nerves formed in the pit of my stomach. An apology felt like the kneejerk reaction upon seeing him in his grandmother's shop, but it was also something I'd been working on. I didn't need to be sorry for what I wasn't responsible for, but the way his shoulders sagged and that sad half-smile did me in.

"I'm sorry—"

"Are you now?" He snapped out of whatever reverie he'd been in, and there was a little bite to his tone.

"About your grandma's passing," I finished, because that was truer.

Austen shifted his stance and he walked farther into the showroom. His hands stayed in his jean pockets, and I couldn't have even guessed at what he was thinking. He wore gray Chuck Taylors, his signature shoe, but everything else about him seemed more mature. We'd been part of the same crew in high school. He'd always been the party guy, and he had a great laugh, the kind that filled up a whole room. From time to time—until it totally became *a thing*—the two of us would stay up drinking and talk till the sun turned the sky gray and then pink. Nothing ever happened. The timing was always wrong. He was in love with someone more punk than me. Or I was dating one of his best friends. But now, seeing him again brought on a spark of feeling I hadn't really been prepared for.

"What have you been up to?" I asked, shoving the feelings back to the depths from whence they came.

"Typical stuff. Graduation. Work. That kind of thing, you know?" He knocked a knuckle on the countertop.

"Not really."

"That's right. You came back, didn't you?"

"I did." I wasn't necessarily ashamed of coming back to Goldbug after only a couple of semesters of college, but everyone made it seem like it *was* something I should be embarrassed about. I waited for him to ask why, but when he didn't, I supplied the answer anyway. "College just wasn't my thing."

People always stopped asking questions once I said that. They would nod with a condescending twinkle in their eye, but they never kept probing.

"What do you mean?" Austen asked. He was crouched behind the counter now. I could only see the top of his head as he lifted stacks of files and old phone books onto the shelf.

"Um…" I faltered and picked up the doll whose dress I'd been straightening when he came in. I twirled a ringlet of her baby doll hair around my finger. It felt glossy and plastic and as unreal as her grainy porcelain skin. That's what being at college had felt like to me: as if I was trapped in a skin that wasn't my own, and no matter how I tried to make it fit, it just kept cracking. But I couldn't really say all of that in a casual conversation with a boy—man—I hadn't seen in nearly ten years. "Just missed home, I guess."

"Hmmph," he harrumphed. He actually harrumphed.

People had no idea how much they were giving away with that arrogant little puff of air. Or maybe they did, and they just didn't care because they thought so little of those around them. Well, dealing with rich tourists that found me and my town so quaint and so adorable and so consumable for the last decade had taught me that it didn't really matter what I said or did. People that harrumphed already thought I was beneath them and their attention.

I wasn't about to let some guy I'd known practically my whole life do that to me too. I set the doll down and marched over to the counter.

"What are you looking for?"

"Nothing that concerns you." A cobweb had caught the edge of his silver-rimmed glasses and he wiped it away.

"Excuse me?"

"It's nothing, Freddie. Really." He pulled another stack of books from the shelf and blew the dust in my direction.

I waved it away. "This is my store now, Austen."

He stopped rifling under the counter and his shoulders slumped with a sigh. "I'm aware."

"Then tell me what you're looking for."

He stood, wiping his hands on his jeans. He was taller than me, but not by much. And I'd totally forgotten how blue his eyes were. He hadn't shaved in what seemed like a few days, and sporadic glimmers of silver shined along his jaw. He cleared his throat. "I'm aware of what the will says, but I think you should know, I will fight this."

The words hit like a thunderclap.

"What? Why?"

"This was supposed to be mine. You know it. I know it. Every family in Goldbug knows it."

"Since when do you care about Goldbug, Austen?"

"Since now."

"You mean, since there's money involved." I shouldn't have said that. I knew I shouldn't have said that the minute the words flew out of my mouth.

He stepped back as if I'd slapped him. "Is that what you think of me?" His brow creased.

"What am I supposed to think? You left and never looked back, until now, when the store and the money that comes with it have been bequeathed to some country hick."

"I think I better go."

"I think so too."

He turned and walked toward the backroom, carrying a small stack of photo albums under his arm. I cleared my throat and held out my hand.

"What?" He asked.

"Keys."

He could barely mask the anger that my asking for the keys had caused. But that's what always happened with tourists when you took away something they thought they were entitled to.

"Honestly, I can see where he's coming from." My best friend, Kendall, took her pretty pink cosmo from the bar and surveyed the crowded room.

"How can you say that?" I counted out cash for our drinks and thanked Gene, the bartender. "I've put my whole life into working at Dolldum." But Kendall was already across the room, settling herself on a high bar stool. No small feat, as she was incredibly short. I grabbed my glass of barbera and joined her.

"I know you don't want to hear it, sis, but put yourself in his shoes for, like, one minute."

"Austen never cared about the store or Goldbug."

"That's not putting yourself in his shoes." Kendall scanned the faces around us, but it was a Tuesday night, so the bar was full of locals—guys we already knew too much about. Her shoulders dropped and she took another drink, her lips rolling in with each sip. "His grandma just died and a good portion of something that was hers went to someone else. I get why he'd be pissed."

"I didn't ask for it."

"Nobody said you did. And I don't think you should give it back or that you don't deserve it. It's just, I get…" Her voice trailed off as her gaze trailed something or someone behind me.

"What? Who is it?" I asked, twisting in my seat.

"Girl, why didn't you tell me Austen got cute?"

And there he was, standing in the doorway wearing an old punk band T-shirt and faded jeans. He kept his hair short, really short, practically buzzed. And he'd traded his earlier silver frames for tortoiseshell ones. His jaw was still unshaved. He looked scruffy, probably a stark contrast to how he looked in the city. But Kendall was right; he was cute, had always been cute. Dang it.

"He's not that cute."

"Liar." Kendall was already patting creamy beige powder over the freckles on her nose. She reapplied a lipstick the same color as her drink and fluffed her hair. "Oooh, it's like a new guy's in town. Only I've known him and his family forever. This is gonna be fun!"

She hopped down from her seat and joined Austen at the bar. The two hugged and shared a laugh. I felt like getting drunk. I gulped the rest of my wine and snagged a handful of stale Goldfish crackers that the bar manager kept on each table. If Kendall wanted him, she could have him. Austen wasn't interested in me anyway; he was pissed, felt like I'd stolen from him. Getting drunk over it was a stupid idea though. I had plans to make, ideas to research about how to turn Dolldum around. If anything was for sure, it was that the store couldn't stay in its current condition for much longer. It would go under and take me with it.

Sweat was pouring off me, and the black uniform wasn't helping. I steadied the tray of the winery's newest sparkling wine on a platter and tried to blow droplets of sweat away from my eyes, unsuccessfully. My mascara was probably washing down my cheeks as if I were crying, which was *totally approachable*. Guests ignored me or looked away as they mingled about the grounds, so I took myself and the tray to the air conditioning. Bless-ed, bless-ed air conditioning.

"How is it out there?" Carlos owned one of the catering companies that the winery often hired for these events. We'd known of each other since elementary school; we became friends when he played my husband in a spring play our sophomore year. There was this moment where, as my acting husband, he had to sweep me off my feet and twirl me around in some melodramatic moment. Every time, it literally took everything in me to remember my next lines. Finally, he ended up writing my next line on his palm in permanent marker to help me out. Basically, he was hella handsome.

"Look at her face, Carlos." His wife, Fay, swatted his arm playfully. "It's as hot as the devil's asshole, right Freddie?" Fay ran a towel under the sink faucet and tossed it to me.

"She's right. It's hell out there." I patted my face and then wrapped the towel around the back of my neck. It felt heavenly. "I don't know why all these events have to be in the dead heat of the day."

Carlos snorted. "Maybe it's cheaper."

"Please, there's more money out there than any of us could ever dream of." Fay stood on her tiptoes, looking out the window. "Look at this one, with her jewelry all on display."

I didn't have to look; it was Austen's older cousin, Sissy, who'd always worn gems, even when we were in high school. The jewels in question were a matching set of diamond-encrusted sapphire baubles that sparkled in the sun: a large one on a ring, another one as a pendant that thumped against Sissy's chest, and two more as dangly earrings. Who even has such things? Or lets a kid wear them? Austen's family, apparently.

Sissy had pretended she didn't know who I was when she'd taken a drink from my tray, but the little huff she'd given had betrayed her. I had wanted to scream, "You think I can live off working at your grandma's store?!" But that would have lost me this second job, and while I worked to get Dolldom making money again, I still needed it.

My phone vibrated in my back pocket.

Where'd you go last night? It was a text from Kendall.

Uh... home

You should've stayed. Things got interesting

Gross. That's what I wanted to type. *Had to work at the winery today. Charity event*

When are you off?

3, I think. Depends on who shows up for the evening shift.
I hit send.

Coffee? She asked.

I loved Kendall, but listening to her gossip about hooking up with Austen after working this event sounded tedious. At least there'd by caffeine, and I needed some because I had plans to clean out some of Ms. Jane's old stuff later today.

Sure, I texted back.

"Freddie, you better get back out there. Mr. Raymond's on the prowl." Fay turned back to the rows of tiny hors d'oeuvres and picked up a tray. "Take these, they're ready."

My stomach growled as the rich smell of tomato over fried polenta cakes wafted around my head. "These smell amazing."

"That's because they are," Carlos said. "Towel."

"What?" I asked.

He gestured toward the back of his neck. "Towel."

"Oh, right." Sadly, I wrenched the wet cloth from around my neck and slapped it on the nearest prep table.

Outside, waves of heat radiated off everything: the cars parked along Main Street, the dry earth, Sissy's necklace. *Shit.* She sauntered my way, this time making direct eye contact. *This is sure to be awkward.* I wondered if that pendant was hot against her skin. It certainly captured the sun's rays.

"Freddie, correct?" Her speech had a clip to it that I associated with wealth, if only because that's how they all talked on my soap opera.

"Hi, Sissy." I wasn't going to let her pretend as if she didn't know who I was. "Polenta cake?"

She looked at the tray with disdain, but hunger lurked behind her eyes. She licked her front teeth and seemed to have a difficult time saying no. In response, I took one from the tray and popped it in my mouth.

"You sure? They're pretty darn good. You remember Carlos? He's the chef."

The only thing that registered on her face was longing. For Carlos? For food? I couldn't be sure which.

"Well…" She paused and smoothed her blouse over her flat stomach. "I think you should know my family plans on fighting

Grandma Jane's last will and testament. That shop should stay in the fam—"

"Austen's already made me aware."

"He has?" Her surprise lasted just long enough for me to put a pin in it. Maybe there had been some disagreement about the store and what should happen to it in the end. Maybe Austen was just following through with his family's wishes. But what about his grandma's wishes?

"Of course he has. We ran into each other and he told me as much."

"Well then, you can expect to hear from our family's lawyer."

"Great. Now, if you'll excuse me."

She looked confused, as if she'd forgotten that I was still the one with a job to do. I held up the tray, and she finally took an hors d'oeuvre. When it hit her tongue, her head tilted back and she mumbled, "Mmm. Oh, that's good." She took a couple more, and I left to meander through the rest of the crowd.

I should've known after that little exchange that Austen was at the party. But it still came as a surprise to see him leaning against the oak tree, mingling with a grown-ass gaggle of groupies. Some things never changed. People were always drawn to him, especially women. Even I had to admit the gentle confidence he exuded paired well with his fun-loving sense of humor. When Ms. Jane talked about him—and she did often—the story always ended with praise for Austen's creativity or his intelligence or his charm. Because of her, I knew more about him than anyone here: how he'd struggled with deciding on a major, how he didn't call enough, how he'd always tried harder to impress his dad, and when his dad died a few years ago, how a little of Austen's spark had gone out and hadn't come back.

A party-goer helped themselves to some of the food on my tray. I didn't hear what they said, as I was too lost in my thoughts about Austen, but I nodded and smiled and noticed they had something stuck between their teeth. With my tray almost empty, I decided to head toward the oak tree. I wanted to eavesdrop, and my uniform basically made me invisible to most of this crowd.

As I got closer, the women surrounding Austen laughed hysterically. There was a manic, desperate pull to their engagement with him. Each one was dressed beautifully in short-short dresses with stiletto-heeled sandals that sunk into the ground, but still highlighted their tanned and toned and somehow shiny legs. They competed for attention: one talking louder than the others, one arching her back so that her breasts stuck out, one rolling and licking her lips. It was a sight.

Austen divided his attention among them, laughing at the right time, asking questions when appropriate. He wore a simple pair of tan slacks and a baby-blue button-down shirt with the sleeves rolled up, exposing strong and freckled forearms. Watching him, I thought of Prince Harry. Prince Harry with a buzz-cut, but still.

One of the women in front of him lost her footing and started to fall. He caught her, and it could have been a romantic moment between the two of them—that was probably what she'd been hoping for—but as he helped her stabilize, instead of making eye contact with her, his gaze met mine. A wave of heat and embarrassment washed through me. I'd been watching them for too long; had he noticed earlier? His eyes searched mine, then narrowed. I turned and walked the other way. After our last encounter, I couldn't afford a showdown at this job, but I also couldn't drain the well of feeling that sprang up the moment his eyes met mine. For the first time in a long time, I'd suddenly felt seen, but that had quickly been crushed by guilt for the circumstances that now stood between us. His grandmother and parents were gone, and now I'd taken his legacy. I guess that's what Kendall had meant when she'd urged me to see his perspective.

"Freddie! Wait up!"

Great. I managed to get myself into the building and away from guests before he caught up to me. I stopped at the bar and nabbed a glass of sparkling wine from a tray before it went out.

"Hey," he panted from the heat. "I wasn't expecting to see you here."

"Well, Dolldom only pays about half the bills." I slid the champagne flute across the bar top and he took it.

"Really?" He asked before gulping the chilled wine.

"Uh… yeah." Jesus.

"Listen"—he cleared his throat—"I'm sorry about… the other day. I was upset." He stared at his hands, then straightened his glasses before looking at me. And there it was again, behind the grief, a look that made me feel like I was the only person alive.

"I get it."

"We were friends once." He leaned on the bar but didn't take his eyes off me. "Remember?"

"I thought you'd forgotten."

"I don't forget." He laughed, and it was raspy and took me right back to all those nights we sat on rooftops, finishing out the night drinking cheap booze and smoking too many cigarettes while everyone else snored in the rooms below. We'd talked about music and the future and leaving. I didn't know then that I wouldn't get all that far. "Anyway, Kendall told me that you were upset about how we'd parted in the store, so I wanted to apologize."

Kendall. They totally hooked up. And just like that, all the air escaped from my lungs and I couldn't breathe. "Right. Okay, thanks."

"Sissy wasn't too hard on you, was she?"

"I can handle your cousin." I started gathering items on my tray, stray napkins and empty glasses. "And none of this is going to stop me."

He considered my words and smiled. "Right then."

"I'm moving forward." I said it as much for myself as for him. "Whether you bring in all your fancy family lawyers or not."

"Hopefully, it won't come to all that." He touched my arm and a flush of warmth spread over me, and all of a sudden, I hoped he would kiss me. It was stupid and childish. Something, I realized then, that I'd wanted since we were teenagers. It hadn't happened back then—there were close calls, moments where his gaze met mine or our hands grazed as we settled onto the roof—but it never progressed, and it certainly wouldn't happen now that I held his family's business in my two hands.

"I have to get back to work."

He took his hand away and all that hope went with it.

I changed at the house and was making my way to Two Ships Café on Main Street when Kendall texted me a picture of her fancy latte.

Be there in a sec, I texted back. My plan for the rest of the day was to power up with Kendall and then start tackling the trash heap that was Dolldom. The first step to making that place mine was to clean it out, which meant getting those ugly-ass dolls off the shelves.

It was a beautiful day, now that I wasn't serving. As I turned onto Main Street, I was struck by its loveliness. All the buildings were boxy, and the architecture was out of a different time, particularly the 1800s. It was the type of street where history and the present kind of coexisted, where, if I listened carefully, I could still hear horses' hooves striking the ground and mighty wagon wheels churning. A flock of pigeons took off from their perch on top of the old mercantile building and swooped down toward the creek. Their calls and flapping wings were a backdrop to the meandering window shoppers and wine enthusiasts weaving from one tasting room to the next.

Caddy-corner to Dolldom was the café. Kendall had nabbed one of the tables outside that lined the walkway. She waved enthusiastically and her messy bun flopped with the motion.

"Hey girl. How was work?" Kendall asked. She scrolled through her notifications, not making eye contact.

"Fine." I wasn't sure I wanted to mention Austen being there. I wasn't sure I was ready to hear how their night went. "I'm gonna order."

"Freddie!" Katie, the barista, greeted me. She had been a year behind me in high school, maybe two. "What can I get for you?"

"Iced coffee with a shot of caramel."

"The usual. You got it." She scanned my card, and I signed. "Hey…" She got to work on my drink, scooping ice and pumping flavor. "I heard the old lady left *you* the doll shop."

Of course she had. All of Goldbug would know by now that I was the new owner. "Yep."

"What are you gonna do with it?"

"I'm not sure." Lie. But if I told just one person, there was no chance it would remain a secret. Plus, who knew what would happen with Austen's family ready to sic their lawyers on me? One thing was sure: the money that came with the store needed to be used to save it, not pay a bunch in legal fees.

"I heard the family wasn't too happy about it."

"That seems to be the consensus."

Katie handed me my drink. I said thanks and joined Kendall outside, who was still scrolling her Instagram feed when I sat down.

"Do you follow Austen on here?"

"No. I didn't know he was on there."

She turned her phone toward me and showed me a picture of the two of them from last night. They were still at the bar, drinks in hand. Their faces were pressed together, and their easy way of being around each other practically oozed from the phone. My heart fell all the way past my lungs; thankfully my rib cage was there to catch it.

"Cute," I said, which was true.

"Ohhhh"—Kendall's eyes got all big, the prickly points of her mascara-laden lashes touching her eyelids—"my God. You like him."

"Shut up." I snorted. It was absurd. Maybe I liked him in high school, but that didn't matter now.

"Why didn't you say anything last night?"

"I don't like him. And even if I did, you shot out of your seat the second he walked in. It's not like you gave me the chance to say anything. Plus, he hates me. And now you two have hooked up. So, it's never gonna happen." I was rambling, grasping at every possible circumstance that proved there was no hope for Austen and me.

"We didn't hook up." Kendall took a sip of her latte.

"You didn't?" I was shocked. Very few men escaped Kendall's charm once she set her sights on them.

"Nope. Had a couple drinks. Joked about old times. That was it." Kendall put her phone away. Her long fingernails clacked against the plastic. "He and I were always good at being friends. But you..." She paused, probably for dramatic effect. "You two were much closer back in the day, weren't you?"

"I guess." I shrugged. "I don't know."

"Spill it, Freddie."

"We just… it was kind of like an unspoken agreement. Like, I always knew that once people started settling down, he'd find me, and we'd go someplace quiet to watch the sunrise."

"And?"

"And that was it. Nothing ever happened."

"Ugh. That sounds frustrating as hell."

I laughed. "It was. But it was exciting, too. Kinda romantic in a way. There was always a chance something might happen. At least, I felt that way."

"Well, now's your chance to make something happen."

I shook my head. "Not with Dolldom between us." I looked over at the dilapidated building and was struck with a sudden panic that the $200K might not be enough.

"Girl, I've watched you turn down every guy in this county. Here's one you like. You gotta go for it."

"Yeah, maybe."

"Freddie, seriously. Stop being such a sad sack. You just got everything you want handed to you; all you have to do is take it. You know how many people don't get that shot?"

She was right, and that's what I loved most about Kendall. She wasn't the kind of friend that stood around and handed out butt pats for every little thing. She always told the truth, even when it stung a little.

"Go on now. Get." She shooed me away from the table.

"Now?" This seemed abrupt, even for her. "I have to go get the guy now?"

"No time like the present." Another notification dinged on Kendall's phone. "Plus, I've got a date."

"With who?"

"You don't know him." That was impossible, and I said as much.

"No, really. I met him after Austen left the bar last night. New guy, moved out here from the Midwest. I got myself a bonafide corn cob, Freddie."

I couldn't help but laugh. "All right, you wanna come buy the shop after? I could use the help."

"If I can walk."

"Ew. Stop."

"What? I plan to get some. Don't slut-shame me."

"Bye, Kendall." My chair scraped against the sidewalk, making an awful noise. "Text me later."

"You know I will." Kendall cradled her latte in her hands. "And Freddie, I really do think you should make a move."

"Maybe, if I see him again."

"It's a small town."

Right. Yes. How could anyone forget. I walked away thinking about Kendall's advice. I was making a move, just not a romantic one. The dusty windows of Dolldom-N-Books were my future now. It was unfortunate that nothing had ever happened with Austen, but I wasn't even sure he felt any of the same sparks I felt when we touched. No. It was so much better to throw myself into turning this place into a thriving business, because I needed to survive way more than I needed a man.

Sifting through back stock inventory was a nightmare. Ms. Jane—God bless her—with this hodge-podge of crap, made Dolldums seem more like a yard sale or a thrift store. I brought a big box containing lots of doll-sized coffin-like boxes to the front of the store and started packing away the girls. Maybe I could turn this whole experience, the store's transformation, into something on social media. I could get Kendall to take good pictures of the dolls and start from there. Beyond the porcelain girls with their round, off-time blinking eyes, were the Kewpie dolls—cherubic glass baby angels—that were equally as creepy. They all looked the same, replications of some odd standard. Boxing them all up and dusting the empty shelves gave me a weightless feeling, as if just starting the process equaled success.

I lugged the boxes to the back room and labeled them For Sale. Then I went into Ms. Jane's old office, took a beer from the mini-fridge, and opened my Instagram app for a quick online creeper session. I found Austen in Kendall's list of followers and clicked on his account. Luckily, it was public.

His pictures were typical—beers, meals, friends, selfies. Farther down the page, there were a lot of photos of a puppy. It was a cute little Jack Russel Terrier named Foggy. Adorable. I clicked Follow and almost immediately got a request back to follow my private page. I hit Accept and set my phone down.

The beer was shit beer. I would've liked to head over to the bar and pick out something better, but I needed to start a business plan. Which was what, exactly? I wanted to just streamline the store's inventory and only sell books. No more kitsch, just books. And I felt like that was gonna be the store's new name: Just Books. Some shelves would be dedicated to best-sellers, but the rest of the space would be dedicated to indie press books, because I couldn't help but root for the underdogs. Hell, I was one. There'd be a stage for readings and signings, and that was it. Simple. Except that everything in the current market said it would fail. Everything I looked up online said that people didn't go to bookstores anymore. It was a huge risk to stake a career on such an unstable market, and a burning weight of anxiety anchored itself in my chest.

My phone buzzed with successive notifications. I swiped and saw that Austen had liked a bunch of my pictures and commented on one. *Bold move.* I hardly ever posted selfies. Instead, my feed usually focused on what I was reading and flowers and found things. But last week, Kendall had snapped a picture of me after we finished a five-mile hike to the next town. My smile was huge; I'm sure I was laughing at one of her disgusting jokes. When I had first seen the picture, I recognized a part of myself that somewhere along the line, I'd lost. It was a rare moment when time had peeled back and there was a younger, more open version of myself. And Austen commented as much: "There she is."

I commented back. "I've always been here." Because that was true. Even though the weight of the world crushes parts of me sometimes, I've always been me, and I've always been a part of Goldbug. He's the one that left.

My direct messages dinged. It was from Austen. *What are you doing right now?*

My shoulders slumped. Of course, I was at the one place that caused tension between us. I wasn't about to lie about it though. *At the store.*

Can I come over?

I bit my lip. Well, this could go a bunch of different ways, but the longer I hesitated to answer, the more he'd suspect I was weighing the options. So I typed, *Sure.*

A rush of excitement flooded through me, and that's when I noticed my chipped nail polish and dusty clothes. Shit. I looked a hot mess. In the bathroom, I splashed some water on my face and found an old lip gloss at the bottom of my backpack. I took my hair out of the bun and zhushed it as best I could, hoping it might pass for beach-blown. When I realized it wouldn't, I wound it back up again and pulled a few tendrils free. I wasn't sure what was making me even care about any of this; it wasn't like Austen and I had made up or anything. There was still 1,600 square feet of his grandma's store between us. He could be coming over right now to serve me with papers demanding his property back, or maybe he wouldn't even be alone. Instead, his whole posse of a family might come barreling through those doors to take what was theirs.

"Hello!" he called from the front. I must've forgotten to lock the door.

"Back here!" I answered, not even poking my head out to greet him. I had just enough time to take in a couple deep breaths before he joined me in the office.

"I see you're getting rid of some stuff."

"I am…"

"Good. It probably needs an update."

"Ya think?" I gestured at the cracked linoleum and the stained walls.

"Right." He ran his hand along the edge of the desk. "I guess I've got a bit of a blind spot when it comes to this place."

"I think that's natural. You wanna drink?"

"What do you have?"

"Shitty beer."

"I brought this. If you want to crack it open."

I recognized the label from the winery where I work. "Is that the barbera?"

"Yes. Do you have an opener here?"

Ms. Jane always had wine while she did the finances. So, yes, there was a corkscrew in her top left-hand drawer. She kept a set of four glasses on top of the filing cabinet. I grabbed two and went to rinse them out in the bathroom. When I came back, Austen had the wine open and waiting. I held out the glasses and he poured.

I always liked to let my wine sit a minute before taking a drink; Austen had no such hang-ups. He gulped nearly half of it down immediately.

"This is special," he said. He sat on the desk's edge.

"What's that?" I had no idea what he was talking about but sincerely hoped this wasn't about to get weird.

"The wine."

Barbera was common here, so I checked the bottle. The date put this particular bottle at nearly thirty years old.

"I hate to break it to you, but these are only supposed to age four-to-six years. Tops. Most wine is ready the day it's bottled."

He didn't seem to care, or to be listening for that matter. He stared at an embroidery near the door quoting Sylvia Plath. He took big sip after big sip and then poured himself another.

I wasn't really in the mood for... whatever this was turning into. I set my glass on the closest shelf, the glass clanking on the wood. "You mind telling me what this is about?"

"It's my parents' anniversary wine, Freddie." He pro-nounced Freddie sarcastically. "I found it going through some old things for the estate sale."

"Okay, but why are you here, Austen?" I pronounced his name as harshly, and he flinched.

He wiped the corners of his mouth and finally—finally—his gaze met mine and everything else melted away. The store, the old wine, the years of not seeing each other: all were gone in that instant. It was if we were on a roof again, surrounded by sparkling stars. He stepped toward me and his hand touched my face. A jolt passed through my body at the unexpected rush of contact.

"I always thought we'd end up together."

I huffed, even though his thumb drew a line over my cheek-bone. "You left."

"So did you."

"I came back."

"So did I." He licked his lips, and I forced myself not to kiss him. I'd wanted him for so long that I needed him to make the first move here and now. It couldn't be the other way around, not for me anyway.

The pace of my heart quickened. He was here. I was here. He was touching my face, my neck, tucking a loose strand of hair behind my ear. Whatever the reasons were that nothing had happened when we were kids, they didn't matter now. Whatever the reasons were that kept us apart right now, well, they mattered, but I shoved them aside and let my fingertips graze his forearm. And then we were kissing. I could taste the too-old wine on his tongue as it met mine. The smell of him—piney and sweet—surrounded me, then everything became hot and drastic and needy as he lifted me onto the desk, and I unbuttoned his shirt.

I heard myself sigh as his kisses trailed down my neck, but when I opened my eyes, the office came crashing down around me.

"This will never work, will it?" I don't know why I said it. If I could have glued my mouth shut, I might've, because he stopped kissing me and his shoulders slumped, still in my embrace.

"Freddie, don't."

"I'm right though."

He inched backward to look at me, but I couldn't meet his gaze. Instead, I looked at his chest and let my fingers run over the ridges. I wanted him, actually *yearned* for him. Every inch of my body buzzed with the possibility of having him. But with him and his family possibly coming for me and my livelihood, well, reality really does bite sometimes.

He took my hand in his and kissed it, then put it back in my own lap. I could've cried when he started buttoning his shirt.

"I better go." His voice wasn't much more than a whisper.

"You don't have to, Austen." I was grasping at straws. "We can talk about it, figure this whole thing out."

"Maybe another time." Austen grabbed for his parents' anniversary wine. It slipped from his grip and the bottle shattered when it hit the floor. "Great," he said with a heavy sadness.

"I got it." After what he'd drank, and my glass still on the counter, there'd only been about one glassful left in the bottle. It had splattered everywhere, but the glass shards would be harder to clean up.

"I can't let you do that."

"You can and you will. I've got a shop-vac. It's not a huge deal."

He laughed a bit.

"What's so funny?"

"Nothing." He laughed some more. Annoyance, like bile, rose in my throat as I opened the closet door for the vacuum. "It's just... that bottle should have been a keepsake, right? But I lost it, in the store that you now own. It's just kind of... apropos, I guess."

"Well, it was shit wine."

He laughed again and pointed at me before sauntering from the room.

For weeks, I expected to hear from him. While painting the shelving units a mustard-yellow, I thought he might call. When I ordered the light fixtures, I checked my email obsessively. And finally, when I moved into the upstairs apartment, I waited for a letter from his family's lawyer to appear under my brand-new door. But there was nothing, not a word. No clues on his social either.

"He's probably just gone back to his life in Sac, Freddie." Kendall had come over. We were pre-celebrating tomorrow's grand opening by drinking too much and taking pictures of all the dolls for me to post for sale online. She posed one of the cuter ones—mostly because its eyes didn't roll around and blink like some of the others—in front of a white backdrop and sprinkled flower petals around its stiff little body. "Open the curtains. You get good light in here at this time."

I did as she instructed, and a shaft of bright light shined through the space. Kendall snapped a few pictures, her phone clicking as if there were an actual shutter, before she changed out dolls.

"Are you excited for tomorrow?" she asked.

"You call it excitement; I call it cause for anxiety-shits." I packed the cute doll back in her box.

Kendall snorted. "You're such an Eeyore."

"What?"

"An Eeyore. From *Winnie the Pooh*."

"The depressing donkey?"

"Yeah, that's you."

For whatever reason, that comment hurt a little, even if she might be right. "I'm not an Eeyore. I'm just realistic, logical."

"A downer."

"Fine. Not all of us can be a Tigger."

"Fair enough. But for the record, I didn't say it was a bad thing." She snapped a few photos of a doll with brunette ringlets surrounding a cherubic face. "Did you invite him?"

"Who?"

"Stop playin'. You know who."

"I did." I took a long sip of wine. "I DM'd him the invite. All I know is he saw it."

"He didn't respond?"

"Nope."

Kendall made a "tsk" noise. "Are you worried they're gonna pull the rug out from under you?"

"How could I not be? Threats were made about bringing lawyers into this whole thing and then... nothing? Seems like I got off too easy."

Kendall put her phone down and took me by the shoulders. "Freddie, it's okay for you to have all of this. And actually, it's what Ms. Jane wanted. If she'd wanted the store to stay in the family, that's exactly what she would've done, and their lawyers probably advised them accordingly." She brought her face closer to mine. Her eyes were an intense russet brown, made more striking by her black mascara and thick eyeliner. "They can't take this away from you."

"I know, you're right. I'm just waiting for a shoe to drop, I guess."

"God, girl. When are you going to be happy?" She shook me a little before letting go.

"I can't."

"It's been years now. You're home; you're safe."

"You don't get it."

"Because you don't ever talk about it. Make me 'get it.'" Kendall fluffed a doll's dress.

"I'm not a victim."

"Well, you sure suck the air out of the room like one."

"One: that's offensive to actual victims of crime. And two: screw you, I do not."

"Freddie, you came back to town nearly four years ago and I still don't know exactly what happened while you were at college. You tiptoe around it like it was huge, and there are a whole lot of rumors. But I've yet to hear from you what brought you back to Goldbug."

"Mama was sick."

"Yes, we all know that. It's a small town. But I also know my friend, and she never used to be this scared to be happy. Spill. It." She snapped a few pictures of the doll in front of her.

"Fine. I flunked out, Kendall. Nearly every class, I failed. I just couldn't keep up with the pace, or something was wrong with me. I don't know. I felt overwhelmed and panicky *all the time.* I was lonely. I could barely breathe. And then Mama got sick, and I was honestly relieved to have a reason to just give up."

"That's it?" Kendall bent over, laughing. "Lord, I thought you were gonna tell me some God-awful story 'bout being raped or nearly shot or something. So you think because you failed once—"

"Multiple times. It was like five or six classes, total."

"Okay, so you think because you failed six times, you can't ever succeed?"

"When you say it, it sounds stupid."

"Freddie, that's because it is. You have anxiety or you're depressed; we'll get you to a doctor."

"That's easy to say. Everyone thinks it's like a switch. It's not; it's a whole process."

"I'm sure it is. In your head, this is all much bigger than it can ever be in my head. But as your friend, I'll take you there until you can take yourself." Kendall paused, then took a few more pictures. "Don't let a past freak-out hold you back. You've done amazing with the store, and it's going to be a huge success. Especially with that sassy new clerk you just hired."

"Is that your way of telling me you want a job?"

"I'd like one, yes."

"Fine. Right now, all I can do is minimum wage."

"That's okay." She swooped me up in a hug. "I'll get you my other work schedule so you can work around my availability. We're gonna have so much fun!"

"And you don't need to take me to the doctor, Kendall. I've been seeing one since Mama died."

"Well, that's good."

"It is." With someone else knowing that my brain worked differently, the room took on this kind of anti-gravity feel. My therapist said that could happen, and I'd laughed at her. How could it? Everything in the world was heavy. But maybe that's what friends really do—lighten the load.

It was here. The night. My nerves formed a tight little heavy-weight in my stomach, and I kept going to the bathroom. Kendall had been with me all day, putting last-minute touches on everything. But for now, she was back at her place getting changed for the party. Tonight was sure to be a success, if only for the locals being curious about the changes I'd made.

The sign and the name were still under wraps. I realized Just Books was very lame. The new—absolutely, ridiculously per-fect—name for the store came to me in the middle of a sleepless night. The actual sign that would hang over the sidewalk had gotten here just yesterday morning, and Kendall and I had de-cided it would be perfect for me to unveil it during the party, after the thank-you speech. A part of me wished Austen would be here to see it; another part of me pushed that wish away in order to make room for myself in this space of ownership.

At six o'clock, people started arriving. Fay and Carlos had volunteered their cooking skills and time, as well as most of the wait staff at the winery. The winery owners donated the wine for tonight's event. I had a lot of support, and knowing that loosened the anxiety tentacling around my lungs. People wanted me to succeed.

I wove my way through the crowd, giving hugs and thank-ing people for coming, when I noticed a group of Ms. Jane's friends huddled near the display window.

"Go get'um." Kendall slapped my ass and sent me forward.

I didn't argue with her approach. I knew myself; it would've absolutely taken a slap on my ass to get me over there.

"Welcome, ladies." I held my arms out. "What do you think of the new Dolldum?"

The ladies exchanged loaded glances, and Clairice—I took her to be the leader—cleared her throat. "Freddie, dear. You've done wonders with the place!"

I could breathe. "You like it?"

"Honey, it's so beautiful." Clairice placed her lace-gloved hand on my forearm. "Your mama would be so proud."

I took a moment to see what they saw: hand-blown glass orbs in orange and red hues purchased from the artist's studio at the end of the street hung from the ceiling. They cast a delicate illumination over the newly painted shelves and marble counters. I'd gone with a light stain on the immaculate hardwood flooring found underneath all the cracked linoleum tiles. When I pulled some of the drywall away, I had found exposed brick and decided to work with the natural beauty of the old building. It was a lovely space, now that the clutter had been cleared and books were the main event. One wall contained titles from the New York Times bestseller list; the rest of the shelves were filled with books from local independent authors and small press books. In my heart, these were the artists that would help keep a place like this alive, and so I featured them and would continue to do so, since I'd had a stage space built for author talks and writing workshops. My goal was to create a hub around creating and writing. Hopefully, I wouldn't fail this time.

"You did an awesome job." The deep crackle of Austen's voice brought me out of my reverie.

"What are you doing here?"

"I wasn't going to miss this. Even if it's not in the family anymore, it's a part of me, a part of my hometown and Main Street." Austen nabbed two glasses of wine from a tray being carried past us. "Shall we do this correctly this time?"

I took a glass from him. "What do you mean?"

"I mean, let me make a toast. To you and all you've done to keep my grandma's place here. It's more than I've done, and I'm thankful for it."

I clinked my glass against his. "I wasn't expecting that."

"I've had some time to think. It was all quite sudden."

"And your family's law team?"

"Advised us that while we could contest, it would likely not hold up in court. I realized then that if we fought for it that would likely be the end of this place."

"You've got that right. I wouldn't have been able to afford a fight in court and—"

"Keep Dolldum's alive. Although, I doubt it's called Dolldum's anymore, is it?" He sipped his wine. "This *is* better than that anniversary swill."

My cheeks got warm remembering what had happened after he'd opened the swill. Could there be an actual shot at romance? Had the stars finally aligned and allowed for the right timing for us to be a thing? "I have something to show you."

"More than all this?" His blue eyes twinkled over his glasses. He seemed amused; maybe he'd remembered that night too. "Back in your office, maybe?" Oh, he definitely remembered.

"No, not that."

He deflated a bit.

"Follow me." I grabbed his hand and dragged him toward the door.

"You're making me leave? I basically apologized."

"Shut up." I stopped and turned toward him. "You're ruining this moment and that's usually my job."

Outside, the evening air was cooler, nearly brisk compared to the heat of day. The old-fashioned streetlamps clicked on as we stood on the sidewalk. A few cars buzzed by, and farther down the old street, voices and laughter carried. Most of the other businesses were already closed for the day. Their storefront windows were darkened, but mine shone bright.

"What is it?" Austen asked.

"This." A large package wrapped in brown paper leaned against the wall. "I want you to see it first." I tipped the package forward and slid my finger underneath the masking tape, then unfolded the wrapping to reveal the store's new sign and name: "Jane & Austen's" was written in a cursive font over an open book and quill. It was everything I'd hoped.

He literally gasped and crouched, running his hand over his grandma's name. "You named it after her."

"And you. And Jane Austen, obviously. Do you like it?" I kneeled next to him and nudged him, playfully.

"I love it." He kissed me then. Slow, at first, then more urgently. But I still had a party to attend to, so I put my hand on his chest to stop him.

"Help me with this." We rewrapped the sign and stood up. I dusted the bottom of my skirt and picked up my wine glass. "I better go inside."

It was his turn to grab my hand, pulling me toward him. His chest felt firm against mine, and his arms wrapped around my waist. Our foreheads nearly touched.

"You know I've loved you since high school, right?" he asked.

The words took my breath away. Had I known? No, I decidedly had not known. This whole thing between us had played out as something unrequited for me, but now... it wasn't?

"Why didn't you say anything?"

"I don't know. I was a kid. It was a crush, and I had lots of them. Only this thing with you... it's stayed with me."

I bit my lower lip. Ever the realist, I added, "But you live in Sacramento."

"Actually, that's the other piece of news. I moved home, working remotely at the house while the estate is settled, and then I'll go from there."

"So you would, like, be here. In Goldbug. Full time."

"That's my plan."

I wrapped my arms around his neck, being careful not to spill my wine down his back, and let my lips graze his. "Welcome home, Austen."

Other Published Works

READ MORE BY JESS MOORE

The Evolution of Jeremy Walsh
— SunFire Press, YA Imprint of NineStar Press — 2018

FOR MORE, VISIT
itwasjess.wordpress.com

Love-Locked on the Roberto Clemente Bridge

The alarm sounded in Sienna's room. She slammed the snooze button.

Jeez.

Her new year's resolve to get up early and fulfill her resolutions had vanished, as it had the day before. And the day before that. She *should* be taking the Nike running shoes out of the box. She *should* be putting green food in a blender and whirling up a day's worth of nutrients in one delicious (okay, tolerable) drink. She *should* be listing five things she was grateful for in the untouched yellow journal that sat on her nightstand.

Sienna opened her eyes, tiny blue slits in the darkness. She could make out colored Christmas lights on the window of the apartment across the alley. They blinked in a steady pattern around a silver, store-bought "Happy 2028" sign. In December, the sign and lights served as a festive reminder of upcoming holiday cheer. Now, in January, they symbolized a fleeting effort to hang on to the fun a bit longer, to stave off the dreary Pittsburgh winter that lay ahead.

The alarm sounded again; Sienna hit snooze and shut her eyes. She heard the faint sounds of Nate getting ready for the gym.

Please don't knock on my door. Please don't knock on my door. Please don't—

The sound of Nate's fist on wood invaded her small room. Sienna pulled the covers over her head just as he opened the door. His deep voice sounded. "No-go again, I see."

Sienna pulled down the covers and peeked out so she could see him. "Shut up, Nate."

"Just saying, you make a New Year's resolution with a friend—"

"You're not my friend."

"Okay. You make a New Year's resolution with your roommate—"

Sienna sat up and adjusted her T-shirt. "You're not my roommate, Nate. Remember? Three weeks until this arrangement is up." She pointed to her wrist. "Tick-tock, Nate."

Nate smiled as he edged out the door. "Well. Someone woke up on the wrong side of her cauldron."

"Tick-tock," she called after him. Sienna watched him retreat. His calves flexed as he walked, his sweatshirt pulled over muscular arms and broad shoulders. He ran a hand through light-brown tousled locks that framed his face differently every day.

Not that she noticed. Or cared. After Grant, she would not fall for someone else, especially not her little brother's friend.

As a favor to Ryan, Sienna said Nate could stay in her apartment for three months so he could "build up a reserve." As far as Sienna could tell by Nate's comings and goings, there was no reserve being built nor, did it seem, a concerted effort to find an alternate arrangement. Not her problem. Time was up in three weeks. That would be that.

The alarm sounded for the third time. 8:07. Shit. She was meeting the Fosters at Starbucks at 10:00 and still needed to think through the questions. Sienna pulled out pen and pad from her nightstand and made notes in swirly black ink. Once satisfied, she planted her feet on the cold floor, forced herself up, and made her way to the bathroom. She started the shower, then moved to the sink and splashed water on her face. She lifted her head and peeked in the mirror. Blue eyes and an angular face started back at her. "Spectacularly blue," Grant had called them on their first date.

Did Grant's new girlfriend have "spectacularly" blue eyes?

Sienna shook the memory of Grant and his girlfriend from her mind and stepped into the tub. Her foot touched something soft and slimy. She jerked it back with a start.

What the...?

Sienna looked down. A giant, puffy spider stared back at her. She reached down, picked up the toy, and turned it over in her hand. The corners of her mouth turned up in a smile before she forced them downward. This was not funny; it was infuriating. "Nate!"

No answer.

"Oh right," she said under her breath. "Mr. Perfect's at the gym."

Sienna wrapped herself in a towel and moved into the kitchen, spider in hand. She spied the blender, pre-filled with Nate's green smoothie ingredients, lifted the lid, and plunged the spider into the green slop. She moved back toward the bathroom and stepped into the shower. When she stepped outside the door a few minutes later, Nate stood there, holding the blender.

"Really, Sienna?"

She pulled the towel tight around herself. "There was a toy spider in my tub, Nate. Do you know anything about that?"

"It's for work." Nate walked into the kitchen and put the blender on the counter. Sienna followed behind.

"Yes, and as I've asked before, what grown man plays with toys for work?"

Nate pulled off his sweaty T-shirt. Sienna stood back. She didn't care about—didn't even see—the six-pack. Nate continued talking, unaware, apparently, of his partial nudity in the kitchen. "You know this already, Sienna. I don't play with the toys. I market them. I need to use them to sell them." He picked the spider out of green goop and washed it off in the sink. He held the dripping spider out to her. "So. Tell me. Did it scare you?"

Sienna opened her eyes wide. "Do you mean I was part of some marketing test?"

Nate put the spider on the counter and put the blender on its base. "Well? Scary or no?"

Sienna grabbed the spider from the counter. "The only thing scary about this,"—she held the spider close to Nate's face—"is what I am going to do for revenge."

Nate lifted an eyebrow. "You do look quite threatening in that pink towel." His eyes swept downward. Sienna willed herself not to blush.

"Consider yourself warned," she said and turned on her heel. She heard the blender whir.

Twenty minutes later, Sienna was dressed in a black shirtdress with high boots. She pulled a coat on, then arranged her long, dark hair evenly over a red scarf. A pop of color on a cold gray, day. She walked out of the apartment building and gave a glance up to the window across the alley. The window was open. The man who lived there was balling up the previously blinking colored lights like yarn. Sienna stepped forward and the Main Street sign came into view on the corner, part of it obscured by bits of sticky snow. Most of the time, the sign didn't bother her. She passed it dozens of times every week. But it had been almost a year to the day. Sienna stood still as crowds pushed passed her, visualizing that night. She and Grant had stood under the Main Street sign at midnight, falling snow illuminated by the streetlamps overhead. He'd bent down on one knee, pulled a box from his pocket and slowly lifted the lid.

A man ran into Sienna; the vision of Grant's proposal vanished with the interruption. "Sorry ma'am," he said without stopping.

Sienna held up her hand to signal it was okay. She observed her naked finger then glanced back at the sign. She put Grant out of her mind and made her way down busy streets lined with gravel-encrusted snow. She crossed the Roberto Clemente Bridge, her breath smoky puffs in the cold. She fingered a few of the hundreds of locks on the bridge through gloved hands and shook her head.

Sienna had been given the assignment about the locks months ago from the editor for *The Pittsburgher*, a small fledgling magazine featuring unique stories about the city. "Find couples who locked their love on one of the bridges," Roy had said. "We'll run an article for Valentine's Day."

Sienna had done the background research immediately. The practice of couples placing a lock on a bridge as a symbol of their love allegedly originated in Serbia during World War I. Locks on the Pont des Arts over the Seine in Paris, the most famous of the locks' bridges, were cut off in 2015 due to excess weight. Over 700,000 locks were removed. But the practice was still popular in Pittsburgh, where thousands of locks covered three bridges.

Thousands of locks would make the story easy.

Or, so Sienna had thought.

She interviewed four couples and returned to Roy. He glanced at her sample article and pointed a gnarly finger at her description of each of the twosomes. "Boring. Boring. Boring. Boring. We have to do better than this, Sienna, if we are going to compete. Find something unique." He thrust the pad at her and turned his back. Sienna had stood wordlessly in the cluttered hallway.

It was less than a month to the deadline, and the Fosters had been her first real lead. Their love lock was the start of a million-dollar business, they had told her on the phone.

Sienna pulled open the door to Starbucks and checked the crowded space. A woman with pink highlights waved in her direction. She smiled absentmindedly and continued to scan the room. "Ms. Sienna Dewey?" the pink-haired woman said. "We're over here. We're the Fosters."

Sienna adjusted her gaze on the woman and the thin, blond man sitting next to her. They couldn't have been more than twenty-five, about her age. She'd expected an older couple with fitted suits and coiffed hairstyles. She looked again at the Fosters, both of whom wore baggy black sweatshirts with a white lightning bolt insignia on the front. She smiled at them, stepped toward the table, and sat down. The man, Lester she recalled, slid a cup of coffee to her. "Cream and sugar okay?"

She smiled. "Perfect." Sienna took a sip of the steaming drink, then pulled a notepad and pen out of her oversized bag. "So. I'm interested in your story."

Lester fingered a barely visible blond goatee and looked at the woman next to him. "Jewel?" he prompted.

Jewel leaned forward. "So, our business," she started, pointing to the lightning bolt logo on her shirt, "is Laser Llamas."

She said the name in a whisper as though another patron might hear and steal the idea. "We train llamas to perform at county fairs."

Sienna nodded and wrote "Laser Llamas" on the pad.

Lester took over. "The llamas race through different obstacles. Tires, bridges, tunnels."

"We're training them to jump through hoops," Jewel added.

Sienna's radar flared. She sat up straight. "And this is a million-dollar business?"

Lester and Jewel looked at each other. After a moment of silence, Lester tapped his finger on the table. "It will be."

"Wait—" Sienna started.

Lester held up his hand. "It's not just llamas we're training," he continued. "We're going to train all sorts of unusual animals."

"Like snakes," Jewel added.

"Just imagine," Lester said, "a snake jumping through a hoop."

Sienna pushed her chair back. "That's ridiculous. Snakes can't jump."

"Yet," Lester corrected. "Yet."

The beginnings of anger snaked through Sienna's body. What a waste of time! She was about to bring up the physics of snakes then remembered Grant's criticism about her realism.

Sienna took a deep breath and assumed the optimistic persona of the woman she imagined Grant dating now. "Of course. With a bit of training, anything is possible!"

Lester nodded, encouraged.

"Right?!" Jewel added.

"But what does all this have to do with the locks on the bridge?"

"We came up with the idea as we locked our love on the Roberto Clemente Bridge," Jewel said. She looked into the distance as she spoke, as though she were viewing the beautiful scene in her memory. After a moment, her expression turned serious and she refocused her gaze on Sienna. "And we want you to tell the story of our love."

"And how it spawned our business," Lester added.

Sienna looked at Lester, then at Jewel. No way was this legitimate. She picked up her pen and held it as if poised to take a note. "And your lock on the bridge?" Sienna asked. "Where did you put it?"

Lester and Jewel answered at once, each giving a different location.

Sienna nodded and put her pad in the bag. She stood and slung it over her shoulder. "I think we're done here."

"Wait—" Lester started.

Sienna shook her head and pulled out a business card. She handed it to Lester. "If you teach a snake to jump through a hoop, call me."

Sienna turned her back on the Fosters. She pushed through the crowd of patrons waiting for coffee and out onto the street, barely feeling the cold as her internal mantra whirled. What a waste of time! And the Fosters were her last lead. She would miss her deadline. Or have to use the other boring story. And if the magazine made cuts? How would she stack up if she couldn't even report on fluff?

Sienna reached the door of *The Pittsburgher* and shoved it open. She stepped through the dim space, heaved her belongings onto her desk, and slumped in the tiny office chair with the broken wheel. She hated that wheel. It made her feel off balance.

"Rough morning?" a fellow rookie reporter asked from his adjacent space.

Sienna held up a hand. "Don't ask."

She moved her bag and turned on her computer. When the screen illuminated, she searched Laser Llamas. "Coming soon," the site said. Next to the lightning bolt insignia, there was a picture of a black llama with the nameplate "AJ." Sienna visualized the animal jumping through a hoop. Crazy.

She spent part of the day on other projects and part of the day trying to punch up her original locks story. Roy was right. It was boring. Maybe she should try to find people who regretted putting a lock on the bridge? Bad stories? She tapped her pen on the desk. No. It was supposed to be a romantic story for Valentine's Day.

Her foot was out the door at five. She forced herself to put the story out of her mind even as she walked over the Roberto Clemente Bridge. When she arrived at her apartment, Nate was opening a box in the kitchen. "Marley Spoon," he said without explanation.

Sienna dumped her coat and bag on the kitchen chair and rubbed her hands together for warmth. "Nice."

The first three boxes of Marley Spoon, a weekly food service which sent recipes and ingredients, had been a gift from her father's new wife, Jenny—a woman Sienna had tried, and failed, to hate. After the first three boxes, Sienna was hooked. Nate had been too. They perused the website weekly to choose upcoming meals. Nate's favorite, and hers, were the Mexican Chipotle Meatballs.

Nate pulled the recipe card out of the box. "Yes!" He punched his fist in the air. "Caramelized Onion Burgers."

Sienna grabbed the card from Nate. "Wait a minute. We didn't order these. I explicitly remember ordering Asian Lettuce Wraps." She put the card on the counter and stepped toward Nate. She poked his chest with her index finger. "Nate Watson. Did you change our order?" She crossed her arms and tried to suppress a smile.

Nate put his hand on his chest. "Sienna! I'm insulted. These Marley Spoon orders are sacred. To think you'd accuse me of changing one? What next? Will you charge me with theft?"

"I don't know. Did you take something?"

"Mmm. Mmm. Mmm. So incredibly rude. Good thing I found an apartment today."

Sienna's small smile vanished. She felt her heart dive in her chest. Nate was leaving?

But wasn't that what she wanted? Wasn't that the deal? The silence lengthened; Sienna struggled to find her voice. "Well, it's about time," she said finally.

"Two weeks," Nate said and handed her a potato to chop for the homemade fries. "I'll be out one week before the deadline." He started his "cooking playlist" on his iPhone. Sienna closed her eyes. She'd miss cooking to these songs. She visualized herself cooking alone in silence, then opened her eyes abruptly. Stupid. She could make her own dumb cooking playlist with the same dumb songs. She didn't need Nate for that. She didn't need Nate period. She moved to the counter began to chop.

They finished cooking in companionable silence. Over dinner, Sienna told Nate about the Fosters and her fear of missing the deadline for the locks story.

"What if you stalked the bridge?" Nate asked as he cleared her empty plate.

Sienna followed him into the kitchen with their glasses. "You mean like a stake-out?"

"Yeah. See if anyone comes by to put locks on. Catch them in the act." Nate rinsed a dish and handed it to her.

She dried it. "What are the chances of me being there at that exact moment?"

Nate handed her another dish. "None, if you're not there."

"It's a ridiculous idea."

"Well, you've had weeks to do it your way."

Sienna slammed a foot down and looked at Nate. "Wow. Harsh much?"

"Just saying."

She reached over him to put the clean plates in the cabinet. She thought about Nate's idea. What did she have to lose? "Okay. I'll do it."

Nate smiled. "Awesome." He shut the dishwasher, started it, then turned and looked at her with a small smile. "So," he said as he walked to the front hall, "now that I've helped you with your job, you need to help me with mine." Nate returned to the kitchen with a large rectangular bag. "There's something we need to try out in here."

Sienna pointed to the bag. "Oh no. Is there another massive toy spider in there?"

"Nope." Nate reached in and pulled out a box. He spoke in a dramatic game-show-host voice. "We're going to play 'Mind Your Manners!'" He flipped it so she could see the cover of the box. Four children were depicted laughing around a game-board.

"You can't be serious."

"Oh, but I am." Nate began to read from the box. "Rude is rampant. 'Mind Your Manners' will teach your child the lost art of polite society essential for tomorrow's success. They'll learn manners AND have fun." He looked at her. "So? Are you ready?"

Sienna took the box and scanned it. "I'm not sure I'll ever be ready for this." She shook her head and handed the game back to Nate. "We're going to need some beers."

When Sienna returned with two Rolling Rocks, Nate had the board set up. It looked similar to a Candyland board, but instead of pit stops like 'Licorice Castle' and 'Peppermint Forest,' there were areas with names like 'Compliment Corner' and 'Please and Thank You Park.'

Sienna sat on the couch next to Nate and took a sip of her beer. "I'll be red." She grabbed the token.

Nate turned to face her and raised an eyebrow.

She stared at him. "What?"

"Can I be red, PLEASE? This is a manners game, Sienna. And apparently just in time."

Sienna hit her forehead with her hand and spoke in a formal tone. "Why of course, Mr. Watson. May I be red, PLEASE?"

"Why certainly, Miss Dewey. Be my guest."

Sienna observed him as he read the directions on the box. A plaid flannel shirt fit tight across his shoulders. He had on black-rimmed glasses, which Sienna knew by now he wore only at night. The glasses suited him. Not that she noticed.

Nate looked up at her and explained the directions. "First one to Manner Mountain wins!"

They took turns picking cards and advancing their tokens. Three turns in, Nate was sent to Compliment Corner. "I'm supposed to compliment another player," he said, pointing to the directions. "I guess that's you."

"I guess it is." Sienna put her arms behind her head and sat back.

Nate averted his eyes a moment, then looked at her. "I think you look very pretty in that dress."

Sienna sat up. *Don't blush. Don't blush.* "Well, thank you."

"I mean it," Nate continued, moving back on the couch with what seemed like an intent to take her all in. "You are really beautiful."

Sienna felt her heart beat so hard she was sure Nate could hear it. She felt her cheeks redden. The moment stretched out in endless silence until, finally, Nate broke it. "You're supposed to compliment me back, you know." He waved the rule sheet. "It's rule number three."

Compliments for Nate jammed in Sienna's mind.

I like that your cowlicks fall differently every day.

I like that you're goofy when you Facetime with your two-year-old nephew.

I like that you sing off-key in the shower.

I like how I feel when I'm around you.

Sienna opened her mouth with the intent to say something real, something meaningful, but as she did so, a vision of Grant flashed in her head. She rubbed the empty space on her ring finger and recalled the feeling of sliding the ring off, of handing it back to Grant. She had actually been so dense that she hadn't known what Grant was getting at until he directly asked: "Can I have the engagement ring back?"

Nate's voice broke her thoughts. "Well?"

"You make a mean caramelized onion burger."

Nate's face fell momentarily. "Right," he said, nodding. "I do make a mean burger."

They continued to take turns in rote succession, conversation now stilted and false. When Sienna landed on 'High-Five Highway', she made a joke, but it fell flat, the prior camaraderie gone. The game ended. Sienna didn't remember who won.

The next morning, Sienna heard Nate getting ready for the gym. He didn't knock on her door. She left before he returned and made her way to the bridge.

You make a mean caramelized onion burger?

God.

She assumed a position in a coffeehouse with a good view of the bridge and thought again about Nate. Maybe she wasn't dumb. Maybe he hadn't meant it the way she thought. "You look pretty." Like his mother might look pretty. Or his sister. Or a dog, for God's sake. It's not like he said he loved her or something.

An hour passed. Foot traffic continued in a steady stream across the Roberto Clemente Street Bridge as nine-to-five workers hurried to high rises. Owners crossed with dogs of varied sizes. One man walked two tabby cats on leashes. But no one stopped at a lock. Sienna didn't expect them to, really. It was before ten in the morning, hardly a prime time for a loving exchange. She should come back at night.

Sienna gathered her belongings and walked back across the bridge, observing the locks more closely. They were a mix: standard gray, colored, engraved. Some were locker-locks, some hearts. Sienna stopped at a gold one with the word 'remember' hand-painted in blue. She fingered the lock. Remember what? A person? A place?

A voice sounded behind her. "You know Margot?"

Sienna turned. A petite woman with gray hair and a heart-shaped face stood staring at her.

"Margot?"

"Margot. That's her lock. I'm Helen, a friend." Helen held out her hand. Sienna ungripped her fingers from the lock and took the extended hand; a sliver of excitement bubbled in her chest.

"I don't know Margot, but I would like to learn more about this lock."

"Well," Helen said. "That's a Margot story. But, if you wait, she'll come by. She does almost every day. Usually after lunch."

"Really?" It was happening. Sienna couldn't wait to tell Nate. He would totally gloat that the stake-out had been his idea. Her lips creased upward at the thought.

"You can't miss her," Helen continued. "She's tall, seventy-two years young, and her eyes are crazy blue. Like the sky. Blue like yours." Helen stood back and stared at Sienna. "Maybe you're a long-lost relative?"

Sienna laughed. Ten minutes later, she was back in position in the coffeehouse, buoyed by the potential story. At ten after twelve, a tall woman with bright white hair in perfect curls walked onto the bridge. Sienna held her breath as she approached the lock. *Stop. Stop. Stop.* The woman passed it without so much as a glance. Sienna exhaled.

Maybe she should be standing on the bridge? The door opened and a gust of cold air blew in. It would be cold, but worth it. Sienna bundled herself in her coat, grabbed her bag, and made her way to the bridge. As she walked, she formed questions in her mind. What did 'remember' mean? Why did Margot visit the lock? And how could she introduce herself without scaring the woman? Sienna was so engrossed in her thoughts as she approached the lock that she rammed into a speed-walker.

"Sorry," Sienna said, sidestepping her.

"No problem." The woman waved and looked at Sienna. Her eyes were crystal blue.

Worth a shot. "Margot?"

The woman stopped. "I'm Margot. And you are?"

"I'm Sienna!" she gushed with uncharacteristic enthusiasm. "I'm a reporter! I'm doing a story on these locks." She touched the 'remember' lock. "Is this one yours? A woman told me it was yours." Sienna took a breath and focused on Margot.

Margot stepped back. She gave Sienna a guarded look.

Shit. She was scaring her!

Sienna inhaled. "I'm sorry. Can I start again?" She explained about the assignment for *The Pittsburgher* and her failed attempts to put together an interesting story. Margot stood with her hands on her hips. She was athletic looking with stylishly cropped gray hair and the sky-blue eyes Helen had referenced. She had wrinkles, but they framed her face in a way that made her look knowledgeable, not old, not seventy-two.

Sienna finished her explanation. Margot looked out at the Allegheny River. Had she lost this lead already? In desperation, she shared her experience with the Fosters the day before. "Don't make me write about those crazy llamas," she joked.

Margot looked at her, eyes penetrating. "Laser Llamas?" Then she started to laugh.

Sienna joined in. "So? Would you be willing to share your story?"

Margot stopped laughing and touched the lock. Her expression grew serious. "I will."

"So, yes," Sienna confirmed.

"Yes," Margot said with more confidence. Sienna forced herself not to cheer.

Margot had an appointment after lunch, so they agreed to walk together the next morning. Sienna watched her power-walk back down the bridge, excitement building in her chest. She had to tell Nate! With long, brisk steps, Sienna descended the bridge in the opposite direction of Margot, then weaved through crowds until she reached Castle Toys. She burst through the door and strode to the reception desk. "Nate Watson?"

A stocky man in an Avengers T-shirt tipped his head to a conference room with glass windows. "Right there, doll."

Sienna turned and saw Nate through the window, pointing to a document. She waved in his direction; he looked up. A moment later, he stood before her. "Sienna? Is everything okay?"

"Yes! You won't believe it!" She began to tell Nate about Margot and the 'remember' lock. Midway through the story, a young woman in a short blue dress with a swingy, blonde bob materialized by Nate's side. She shot Sienna a look then touched Nate's shoulder.

Sienna shut her mouth, realizing with a start how inappropriate it was for her to be here. Had she just burst into Nate's office prattling on about locks? She fingered her ponytail and remembered that, in her effort to avoid Nate this morning, she'd rushed out without make-up or doing her hair. She eyed the adorable woman, who was looking at Nate with an expression all too familiar to Sienna.

She looked at Nate the way Sienna wanted to.

Sienna took a step back from Nate and his tiny cohort. "Sorry. Just got excited there. I–I can tell you later."

"You can tell me now. It's fine. We were just talking about the launch we have starting next week."

"It's for spinny tops," the woman explained. "I'm Katy," she said, extending her hand. "And you are?"

Sienna took Katy's hand. She had long, bubble-gum pink nails and a slew of bangle bracelets that jingled as they shook. "I'm Sienna. Nate's roommate."

"For another two weeks," Nate said in a joking manner. Sienna couldn't tell if it was for Katy's benefit.

Sienna felt her face begin to redden. She had to get out of there. "Really. There's not that much more to tell. I can catch you up later. Get back to that launch now." She waved, made her way to the door, then pushed on it when she should have pulled. Twice. When the door finally swung open, she glanced back. Nate and Katy stood staring at her. "Go spinny tops," she said with an air punch, then spilled out on to the street.

As she made her way back to the office, Sienna couldn't shake the image of Katy and Nate. Katy clearly liked him. Did Nate feel the same way? He looked like he did. And why not? She was young and attractive. Nate was a single guy. Of course he liked her!

She was visualizing Nate picking Katy up for a date when she felt her foot plunge into a puddle. Damn it. Sienna pulled it out and shook off the excess water. The one day she wore canvas sneakers instead of boots. Cold, wet water seeped into her sock; she decided to work from home. She took the left on to Main Street, glancing at the sign. A vision of Grant popped in her head; she shook it off. First Grant and now this obviously one-sided crush on Nate. There would be no love on Main for her, that was for sure. She needed to focus on work.

Once home, Sienna spread out her notes on the kitchen table and set to work with renewed intensity. Time passed quickly and she was surprised when she heard Nate coming through the door.

Nate held up a take-out bag as he entered the kitchen. "I know it's not a Marley Spoon night," he said, handing her the bag. "But I thought we should celebrate your lead."

Sienna peeked in the bag then looked at Nate. "Mexican Chipotle Meatballs! Where did you find them?"

"You think I'm going to reveal my sources to you?"

Sienna took the bag and put it on the counter. "Mmm. I guess that's fair."

They prepared plates of meatballs and salad, then talked as they ate, the awkwardness of the prior evening gone. Nate guffawed when she told him she was power walking with Margot the next morning. "Good thing you broke in those new running shoes," he said with an eye roll.

"She's in her seventies. I can keep up." Sienna pointed to the last meatball with her fork. "Split it?"

Without answering, Nate sliced the meatball in half. They finished the meal and watched a rerun of *Schitt's Creek*.

"Good luck tomorrow." Nate rapped her on the shoulder as they got up from the couch.

"Thanks, Nate." She watched as he made his way down to the hall into this room.

Thirteen days until he moved out.

Margot was already at the base of the bridge stretching when Sienna arrived.

"So sorry."

"Don't apologize," Margot said with authority. "You're not late. I'm early."

"Well, I'm usually late," Sienna admitted. She bent down to touch her toes.

"That's a habit you should break." Margot's tone was matter of fact.

Sienna stood and observed her more carefully. She was stretching her calves, apparently oblivious to her cryptic comment. Sienna shrugged. Some people were direct like that. "My mother's been telling me that for years," she joked.

"Wise woman. I usually walk three miles. Does that suit you?"

"Sure," Sienna lied. She'd walked a week ago with Nate and quit after less than a mile.

Margot set the speed. She started down the Three Rivers Heritage trail that followed the Allegheny River. Sienna followed, tried to mirror Margot's movements. Long strides, arms pumping. She concentrated on the rhythm, unable to recall the list of questions she had made as she did so. They passed the Pirates stadium, passed yellow-seated Heinz Field. Smoky clouds from their breath puffed in front of them. Sienna opened her mouth to finally speak, but Margot beat her to it. "So, you want to know about the lock."

"Yes. Please." Sienna pulled a small tape-recorder from her pocket. "Can I tape you? Is that okay?"

"Yes," Margot said without hesitation. Sienna pressed the play button with a thickly gloved hand.

Margot spoke in a formal tone, almost as if she were reciting a rehearsed speech. "Sam and I met in the Peace Corps. In Honduras. We worked on hillside agriculture extension—basically, educating people who lived in the hills on strategies for farming. We hit it off right away." She paused as they passed the Carnegie Science Center. "It was the closest I've ever felt to love at first sight." The trail turned woodsy. Sienna quickened her pace to keep up as Margot continued. "When our time in Honduras was over, Sam wanted to date. I—I said no. I wasn't ready, couldn't, didn't want to admit my feelings. We said goodbye at the airport. I immediately applied to grad school, became a hydrologist."

Sienna stepped around a brown snow mound. "Sorry. Hydrologist?"

"I studied how water moves across and through the Earth's crust. I became a specialist, traveled the world bringing clean water to remote areas. It was fantastic. And rewarding. A dream life. But do you know what?" Margot paused; Sienna waited. "Everywhere I went, something would remind me of Sam. A sunrise. A cool species of birds—Sam loved birds. Or a kind of food. I never stopped caring, never stopped wanting to be part of Sam's world."

Margot stopped talking. Sienna waited, riveted, wanting to know more about Sam, more about the lock. The silence stretched on; Sienna couldn't wait. "What happened?" she asked in a blurt.

Margot's pace slowed. "Sam tracked me down here about twenty years ago. Felt the same way, apparently. Wanted to spend the second half of our lives together."

"And you're together!" Sienna rushed to the conclusion.

"No."

"No?"

"No." Margot didn't elaborate. They turned and began to walk back down the trail. When they reached Heinz Field on the way back, she spoke again. "There's a piece to the story you don't know."

"Is he married?" Sienna asked.

"No."

"A drug addict?"

"No."

"A criminal?"

"No!" Margot laughed then became serious again. "Sam is a woman."

Sienna's response was immediate. "So."

Margot took in a deep breath. "'So' in 2028. No 'so' in the 1970s when we met. It wasn't accepted back then, not like it is now. Do you know that, until 1973, homosexuality was listed by the American Psychiatric Association as a mental disorder?

Police regularly raided gay bars. Gay wasn't something you wanted to be associated with, let alone BE. And my family wouldn't have approved. I'm not sure they wouldn't have disowned me, to tell you the truth."

They reached the end of the three miles. Margot stopped and pulled a water bottle out of a fanny pack. Seeing Sienna empty-handed, she reached behind and pulled out a spare. Sienna nodded and took the bottle. "So, I understand your thoughts in the 1970s. But why did you turn her away when she came again?"

Margot looked out at the river a moment, then back at Sienna. "I was fifty-two then. I'd spent a lifetime hiding; it's all I knew. I wasn't ready to 'come out' as they say." Margot made quotations with her hands as she said the phrase 'come out.' "On the last night she was here, Samantha took me to the bridge. She said she respected my decision but wanted me to remember she still loved me. That she would wait until I was ready. And then she put the lock on." Margot directed her gaze toward the lock. "I pass that lock every day and regret my decision."

A cyclist zoomed by; a woman pushed a crying toddler in a stroller. Margot stood still, shoulders hunched. She no longer looked like the formidable woman who'd traveled the world bringing clean water to remote areas. She looked like a broken-hearted teenager.

"Margot," Sienna said gently. "You should try to find her."

"I have. She either can't be found..." Margot turned her gaze from the lock to look at Sienna. "Or doesn't want to be." She stood straighter, regaining the composure of the woman Sienna had met the day before. "Which is why I want to do the article. It's not that I think I'll find Sam. I just want to admit how I felt about her." She paused, chugged the end of her water, then stood with resolve. "I won't be ashamed of who I love anymore."

Instinctively, Sienna grabbed Margot's hand and squeezed. "And you don't have to be, Margot. Let me help you with this."

Margot nodded, and they agreed to walk again the next morning.

When Sienna returned to the office, she worked up an outline, then showed it to Roy. He read through her notes and then held the yellow pad over his head. "Now this," he said to the three employees in the cluttered office, "this is a story." He thrust the pad back in Sienna's direction. "Good work, Dewey. Now write it up."

Sienna spent the next several days engrossed in the story. She met Margot several more times and, out of respect, showed her the article before handing it in. Margot nodded as she read. "Good. Good." She made a few notes in the margin, then handed it back. "Just some details about the agricultural work." She appeared to swallow a lump in her throat, then looked directly at Sienna. "Thank you."

The February edition of *The Pittsburgher* sold out for the first time in the history of the magazine. Roy was ecstatic, his praise of Sienna almost maniacal. "We have something *The Gazette* doesn't," he yelled out from his office the day after the sell-out. "And she's sitting right there." He pointed at Sienna, then announced: "Cake in the conference room!"

Sienna, two reporters, and an office assistant followed Roy to the small room. An icing-laden cake with the caption "Congratulations Sienna" sat in the center of a round table. Sienna's peers stood politely on the outskirts. Sienna could almost see speech bubbles over their heads: "When can we get out of here?" or "I have shit to do."

Notwithstanding the clear body language of everyone in the room, Roy passed out tiny plastic cups of sparkling cranberry juice with unbridled enthusiasm. Once everyone had a glass, he held his in the air. "A toast to Sienna!"

"To Sienna." The response was dull and rote; Sienna wanted to crawl into a hole. She forced down a piece of cake then made an excuse to leave.

"Of course. Of course," Roy said, rapping her on the shoulder. "Take all the time you need."

Sienna walked to her apartment. When she entered, she saw a dozen of Nate's boxes in the foyer. The first box had materialized a week ago; Sienna had successfully ignored it. But now, the boxes had multiplied, and Sienna could no longer avoid the obvious: Nate was moving out in a few days.

She'd been busy with the article; Nate hadn't been around much. When she hadn't seen him in nearly two days, she'd sent a text: *Are you still alive or can I have your stuff?*

Nate's response was immediate: *Still alive. Sorry to disappoint, Dewey.*

And where have you been Mr. Watson?

Katy and I have been working on a project.

Sienna had stared at the response; Katy's name jumped out as though Nate had typed it in all caps and bold. She thought about Katy in her cute dress and perfect, blonde bob. Was she the new roommate? A girlfriend? Nate could do worse.

Sienna bent down to look more carefully at the labels on the boxes, all in Nate's perfect handwriting. Books. Pants. Toys. She smiled at that one. Toys. Only Nate. She shook her head and fingered the box. Just as she did so, she heard Nate's voice. "Planning to break into my toy box, Dewey?"

She stood straight and turned. Nate grinned at her. "No need," he continued. "I saved you one." He walked to his room and returned with the spider. "Here. Catch."

Sienna caught the airborne spider and laughed. "How generous of you." She put the spider on a side table.

Nate approached her with his phone. "Hey. Have you seen these Facebook posts about Margot?"

Sienna's heart dipped. "Margot?" She hadn't seen anything. Sienna took Nate's phone with trepidation. Had Margot's news not been well-received? She began to scroll. Post after post. All supportive. All wanted Margot to find Sam. Someone had even started a group: 'Find Sam xoxo.' Did Margot know? Would she be okay with this? Sienna handed the phone back. "I have to tell Margot."

"I think she knows." Nate took a moment then handed the phone back to Sienna. It was a Facebook post from Margot: "Sam. I love you. If you see this message, if you want to be found, I'll be at the lock at 8:00 p.m. on Valentine's Day. XOXO. Margot." The post had been shared fifty-two times; it had only been up an hour.

Sienna looked at Nate. "Wow."

Nate nodded. "I know."

Valentine's Day was in three days.

Sienna met Margot for dinner the day before Valentine's Day. She'd assured Sienna that she would be okay if Sam didn't show up. Sienna warned of potential protesters; Margot was ready for them too. "I need to do this," she told Sienna. "For me."

When Sienna returned to the apartment after dinner, she literally bumped into Nate in the hallway. He turned, surprised, then smiled when he saw her. "Hey Dewey. You're just the person I wanted to see."

"Is that so?"

"I'm about to feed Velma's gecko—she's away for the night. Want to join?"

Sienna put her hand on her chin as though pondering a very serious question. "Do I want to feed a gecko? Hmmm... Okay."

Nate gestured for her to go ahead of him. When they reached the door, he put the key in the lock.

"And her name isn't Velma," Sienna teased. "It's Theresa."

"She'll always be Velma to me." The first time Nate had seen Sienna's neighbor, he'd insisted she was the embodiment of the Velma character on Scooby Doo. Sienna had insisted that wasn't true. "Come on," he'd encouraged. "Picture her in an orange turtleneck." Sienna had smiled at the image and, from then on, could never see Theresa without thinking how she'd look in thick, round glasses.

Nate hummed the Scooby Doo theme song as he turned the key to the door. He glanced back at her as he pushed it open. The apartment was identical in layout to Sienna's but furnished all in blue and gray.

"Velma's got nice taste," Nate opined as he lifted the note of instructions off the front table. "So, apparently, Sunshine is in her bedroom."

"Sunshine? It's not named Sunshine."

"Yes, SHE is." Nate turned the paper so Sienna could see the name.

Sienna nodded. "Okay, then. Sunshine it is."

Nate read through the paper. "Wait. It looks like she takes medicine. There's supposed to be a dropper in the fridge."

Sienna walked to the fridge. A dropper with a Post-It note with the word "Sunshine" on it stood front and center. Sienna grabbed it and turned to Nate. "Got it."

"And she eats crickets. But that's after the medicine."

"Okay," Sienna said. "Medicine first."

She followed Nate to the bedroom. Sunshine's cage sat on the dresser, illuminated by a heat lamp. Sienna stepped forward and peeked in. The bottom of the cage was covered in sand; a decal of a desert scene lined the back. There was a hammock in one corner, water in the other. Sunshine was hiding under a tunnel of fake wood, her black and yellow striped tail visible from the opening.

"Okay," Sienna said again, handing Nate the dropper. "Get to it."

Nate took the dropper and opened the top of the cage. He reached down and touched the top of the tunnel. Sunshine moved suddenly. Nate jerked his hand back.

"What? Is it hot or something?" Nate didn't answer. Sienna looked at him. He stood, frozen, staring at the cage. "She's still under the tunnel." Sienna reached down and lifted the wood structure. "See."

"Right." Nate reached down again. When his hand got within an inch of the gecko, he yanked it back.

Sienna looked at Nate's face more carefully. A bead of sweat had formed on his forehead. She smiled. "Nate Watson. You're not afraid of this little gecko, are you?"

He looked at her, smiled, then covered his mouth. "I don't like reptiles alright?"

Sienna suppressed a smile. "Didn't you used to play ice hockey? Don't you lift weights every day? Are you telling me that a big, tough ice hockey player is afraid of a little Sunshine?"

Nate stood back and crossed his arms in what appeared to be an attempt to look outraged. "Sienna Dewey. Are you suggesting that there is a link between being strong and a love of reptiles? I heartily dispute that."

"Do you now." Sienna grabbed the dropper, reached down, and lifted the gecko out of the cage. She held her hand toward Nate. "Isn't she cute?"

"No, she is not." Nate stepped back.

Sienna slowly inserted the dropper into Sunshine's mouth and pushed. Small bits of medicine dribbled out as she put her back in the cage. "See," she said, clapping her hands together. "Easy peasy."

Nate picked up the instructions off the table. "It says you're supposed to massage her stomach to make sure she digests the medicine."

"It does not say that."

Nate turned the sheet around, laughing. "It does."

Sienna took the paper and read instruction number three out loud. "Massage Sunshine's belly for at least one minute to ensure full digestion of medicine."

Sienna put the paper down and looked at Nate. "I'll do it, but I'm not doing it alone. You're going to get over your fear of reptiles. Come on now." Sienna reached into the cage, turned Sunshine on her back, then grabbed Nate's hand. She looked at him. "We'll do this together." She put her hand over his then guided it down toward the gecko.

Nate shook his head. "I can't believe you're making me do this."

"Well, I can't believe you're afraid of reptiles."

Sienna guided Nate's index finger in gentle circles around Sunshine's belly. The gecko looked surprisingly relaxed, even happy, with the interaction. "See," Sienna said, "she likes it." When they'd completed the massage as instructed, Sienna let go of Nate's hand. He closed the cage and turned to her, his face an inch away.

In the next moment, Nate's lips were on hers, hands encircling her body. She felt herself acquiesce.

She shouldn't do this.

She would get hurt again.

She pulled back.

Nate stepped away from her, his eyes wide. "Sorry. I didn't mean to—"

Sienna opened her mouth; no words came out.

"I should go." Nate stepped out of the room. A moment later, Sienna heard the door shut. She slumped down on the bed.

She liked Nate. Why couldn't she just tell him? Why couldn't she just let things happen?

Grant.

That was why.

College sweethearts, Sienna had always believed Grant to be her soulmate. They'd met freshman year at Pitt and Grant became all at once her boyfriend and best friend. They were the stereotypical 24/7 couple, always together. Sienna had expected to get married; she hadn't expected Grant to fall in love with someone else. She hadn't expected Grant to call it off. Nate moved into the apartment two months after Grant moved out.

If her relationship with Grant had failed, what hope did any relationship have?

Then again, the thought of Nate leaving brought a visceral pain to her gut. Sienna wanted to see his tousled hair in the morning, make dinner together at night. She wanted a life where there might be a silly spider in her shower or a ridiculous board game set up on the coffee table.

Sienna ruminated and watched as Sunshine crawled into her hammock. Being without Nate would hurt.

Sienna stood. She either had to go for Nate or let him go. She couldn't manage the uncertainty anymore. She fed Sunshine the crickets and turned off the heat lamp per instruction seven. She locked up, resolved to tell Nate the truth. She marched to the apartment, courage intact. She opened the door and strode in.

The apartment was empty.

The next day, Sienna checked her phone excessively for messages from Nate. She jumped at every notification:

Ping! Was it Nate? No. It was her sister.

Ping! Was it Nate? No. It was Roy.

Ping! Nate? No. A telemarketer.

Twice, she almost called Nate herself, her index finger hovering over his contact, but kept still by an invisible, emotional forcefield. What would she say if she called him anyway?

Sorry I spurned your overture.

I actually DO like you.

Wanna go out tonight?

No, no, and no. All cheesy. All corny.

And what if Nate said no? What if the kiss had been an impulse he had been glad she'd thwarted? What if he didn't like her after all?

By 1:00 p.m., Sienna had become so distracted by thoughts of contacting Nate that she turned off the sound on her phone. She forced herself to focus on work. It was a big day, the day Margot planned to wait for Sam on the Roberto Clemente Bridge. Valentine's Day.

Of course, Sienna planned to be at the bridge; she'd promised Margot. Plus, Roy had asked her to cover it as a follow-up story. Sienna finished work early, then went home to prepare. The week's box of Marley Spoon greeted her in front of the empty apartment. She squeezed her eyes shut when she saw it. She really hoped it wasn't Mexican Chipotle Meatballs. Velma (aka Theresa) had left a note on the door: "Thanks for caring for my Sunshine!!!!" There were three happy faces underneath the words. The existence of the Marley Spoon box and the multiple smiley faces irritated Sienna. Couldn't a girl move on in peace already?

Of course, when she entered the apartment, Nate's stupid toy spider stared at her from the kitchen table. Sienna picked it up, put it in the trash, then sat down. She drummed her fingers on the table and, after a moment, extricated the spider from the top of an empty spaghetti box. It wasn't like she hated Nate. And the spider was a funny memory.

She ate cereal instead of making Marley Spoon, then put on her warmest clothes for the wait with Margot on the bridge. It was supposed be only twenty degrees at 8:00 p.m. Sienna got to the bridge early; Margot was already there in front of the lock, dressed in a tan parka with a fur-lined hood. The fur framed her face; her cheeks were ruddy from the cold. She looked like a sophisticated Eskimo.

A small crowd had gathered on the bridge, a few reporters in their mix. Sienna scanned the surroundings for protesters. None. She breathed a sigh of relief and looked at Margot. "Are you ready?"

Margot nodded and rubbed her gloved hands together. "I'm ready."

Sienna looked more carefully at Margot; she seemed happy and relaxed. Would she be okay if Sam didn't show? Sienna peeked at her watch. 8:52. She scanned the growing crowd for an older woman. No one. But it was hard to see in the dark. And she might be caught behind someone on her way. Sienna craned her neck to see if she could get a better look at the crowd. When she turned back, a newswoman stood behind Margot holding a cordless microphone hooked up to a speaker. The reporter touched Margot's shoulder. "I'm Carly Kennedy for PWC news. Would you like to make a statement?"

Margot turned toward the woman; Sienna couldn't see her face, didn't hear her response. Then Margot was holding the microphone. Sienna drew in a breath and reflexively put her hand to her mouth. Oh, Margot. She seemed so vulnerable, so exposed. Sienna almost regretted her part in the story.

Then Margot's voice... It was not the voice of a weak or apologetic woman. It was the voice of someone taking a stand. "Hello!" Margot said.

"Hello!" the crowd echoed.

"I'm Margot Morgan, and I've loved Samantha Gray for more than fifty years."

There were cheers; one man blew into a noisemaker. A few in the crowd waved supportive signs.

"I don't know if Sam is here tonight, and I don't blame her if she's not. I've spent a lifetime hiding from who I am, from who I love. But no more."

More cheers. The sign wavers became wilder in their efforts; a poster depicting a hand-drawn heart with "Sam + Margot" inside blew into the water. Sienna watched the written senti-ment float away just as Margot put her hand on the lock. "Sam put this lock on the bridge so I would remember her love for me. And I do remember. And I invite all of you all to remember those you love. Don't forget to tell them. Don't ignore your feelings. Don't be like me and spend your life alone because you're afraid. Be honest. Be bold." She paused. Sienna could feel her heart beat in her chest. Margot spoke again. "Samantha, if you're here, please join me."

The crowd silenced; posters lowered. Everyone looked about their immediate surroundings, all bound by the shared hope that Sam would appear. A minute stretched out; no one came forward.

Sienna took a step toward Margot. She seemed frozen in place, a plastered smile on her lips.

Oh God.

Could she say something that would help? Something that would deflect the agonizing attention?

Another minute passed. The crowd began to disperse. Sienna grabbed the microphone. "I think we've all had that someone special we've been too scared to acknowledge. Anyone? Anyone?" There was a moment of silence before a woman in a purple pom-pom hat a few feet away raised her hand. Sienna stepped forward and handed her the microphone. "Jimmy Ruchio." The pom-pom woman handed the microphone to the man next to her. "Marion Adams." A teenaged girl behind them waved her hand; the microphone was passed back. "Ryan McAllister."

A dozen or so in the crowd took the microphone, acknowledged unspoken loves. As each of them stated a name, Sienna became braver. She wanted to heed Margot's advice. Don't wait. Be bold. The microphone started back toward her; Sienna would take it and say his name: Nate Watson. Nate Watson. Nate Watson. She heard it in her head, felt it on her lips. Her silent admission soon to be made public.

In the next instant, the microphone was in Sienna's hand. She stared at it a moment, then lifted it to her lips. "N—"

"Margot!" A voice interrupted. "Margot!" A woman pushed through the crowd on the bridge, her features obscured by heavy winter gear. "Margot. It's me."

"Sam!" Margot began to walk toward the woman; the woman walked faster toward Margot. Margot reached the woman, stopped, and looked at her face. "Sam." They fell into an embrace, then turned and lifted joined hands to the crowd. Pandemonium broke out. Signs waved. People cheered. The lone noisemaker blew over and over as the crowd encircled the women. One man on a boat let off a firework.

The crowd pushed Sienna away from Margot and Sam, but she could still see their faces. Margot was crying. Sam, too. Then they lowered their hands, then embraced again, joined heads illuminated by the moonlight. They pulled back and Margot looked through the crowd, eyes resting on Sienna. "Thank you," she mouthed. Then she turned to Sam and grabbed her hand. "If you'll excuse us," she called to the crowd, "we have a lifetime to catch up on!" The crowd cheered. The man on the boat released another firework. A news van appeared at the base of the bridge.

Sienna watched Margot and Sam descend the bridge, fingers entwined, heads close together. And a new resolve formed in her gut. She would not lose Nate over fear. Maybe Nate didn't like her. Maybe he would hurt her. Maybe it wouldn't work out. But knowing one way or another would be better than regret. Sienna was sure of that now.

Sienna started toward her apartment. The crowds, heavy at the center of the bridge, were sparse toward the bottom. As she crossed over toward Main Street, a lone figure hovered under the street sign. As Sienna drew closer, the man under the sign came into focus. She smiled.

Nate.

"Sienna," he called to her as she approached. "How did it go? Sorry I missed it."

Sienna reached Nate, still smiling. "It was amazing. When Sam showed up, Margot's face lit up. And the crowd was so supportive. It was a beautiful moment." Sienna visualized Sam and Margot hand in hand as they walked down the bridge. "Truly beautiful." She shut her eyes, then looked at Nate. "But I think I know how to make the night even better." She stepped toward him, cradled his face in her hands, and kissed him. "Nate Watson," she said, stepping back. "I have been wanting to do that for a long time."

Nate appeared stunned. Then he grinned at her. "Well it's about time, Dewey." He pulled Sienna closer and gave her the most tender kiss she had ever experienced.

When the kiss was over, Nate didn't let go. They stood on the corner, limbs locked, Sienna's head resting on Nate's shoulder. A man bumped into them as he passed; they stayed in position, an immovable fortress of new love. Light snow fell softly around them. Finally, Nate stood back and looked at her. "Do you have any idea how happy you just made me?"

Sienna took his hands in hers. She glanced at the Main Street sign then looked at Nate. "Yeah," she said, squeezing his hands. "I think I do."

One year later

As they passed by Main Street, Nate stopped and turned to her. "Do you know what day it is?"

"Friday," Sienna said with a smile as she adjusted her hair over her coat.

"And?" Nate asked.

"Valentine's Day?" Sienna put her hand on her hip in mock frustration. "Isn't that why we're going to dinner?"

Nate leaned against the signpost. "Very funny."

Sienna grabbed Nate's scarf and pulled him toward her. "Okay, fine. It's the anniversary of our first kiss."

Nate put his arms around her. "I think it's an event worth remembering," he whispered.

Sienna looked up at him. "Me too."

"So—" Nate stood back and pulled a lock out of his pocket.

"So, you want us to lock our love up there on the Roberto Clemente Bridge?" Sienna pointed to the bridge.

"That's right," Nate said, dangling the lock.

"Isn't that terribly serious? The locks can never come off, you know."

"That," Nate said, taking her hand, "is a risk I am willing to take."

They walked toward the bridge, Sienna's hand protected in Nate's large one. When they reached the locks, Nate pointed to a spot near the bottom. "Good?"

Sienna nodded. "That's a perfect spot."

As they bent down to place the lock, Sienna saw the Main Street sign out of the corner of her eye.

Main Street: the place of her first kiss with the man of her dreams.

Sienna had her love on Main after all.

THE END

Other Published Works

READ MORE BY LEANNE TREESE

The Language of Divorce – Filles Vertes Publishing – 2019

FOR MORE, VISIT

www.leannetreese.com

About the Authors

Intertextual
Relations
Brandy Woods Snow
www.brandywsnow.com

Brandy Woods Snow is a Young Adult author, journalist, wife, mama of three, Christian, and proud Southerner. Born and raised in the area of Greenville, South Carolina, she still resides in the rolling foothills of the Upstate region, though she plans to one day retire to the state's famous Grand Strand. Brandy has a Bachelor of Arts in English and Writing from Clemson University. While creative writing pursuits have always held her heart, she's built a career as a journalist and editor. Brandy has more than 19 years' experience and a strong platform that includes articles and columns published in *Delta Sky Magazine*, *Greenville Business Magazine*, *Columbia Business Monthly* and *Home Design & Décor Magazine* (Charlotte and Raleigh).

When Brandy's not writing, reading or driving carpool for her kids, she enjoys kayaking, family hikes, yelling "Go Tigers!" as loud as she can, playing the piano and taking "naked" Jeep Wrangler cruises on twisty, country roads.

Brandy's debut novel, *Meant To Be Broken*, is a YA Contemporary Romance exploring the blurred lines between truth and lies within the confines of the modern-day Deep South. Her second YA Contemporary Romance, *As Much as I Ever Could,* will be released in May, 2020 with Filles Vertes.

Chasing the Story
The Adventures of
Victoria Miller

C. Vonzale Lewis

www.cvonzalelewis.com

My name is Carla Vonzale Lewis and I like my martini's shaken…never stirred. I was born in Georgia but please don't mistaken me for a Georgia peach. I'm more like a prickly pear. Speaking of being born, someone asked me recently if I remember my birth. And I have to say, yes, I do remember that handsy doctor pulling me out into the cold. Right Bastard!!!

Despite being born in the South, I grew up in the North. California to be exact. Every once in a great while we get to experience all four seasons. But mostly, it's just heat.

My debut novel, LINEAGE, was released July 16, 2019 and I will ride that joy for the rest of my life.

When I'm not concocting my next contemporary fantasy story, I enjoy reading, binge watching shows on Netflix, and trying to convince my husband that getting a dog is a wonderful idea.

Culture Clash on Main
Shaila Patel

www.shailapatelauthor.com

As an unabashed lover of all things happily-ever-after, Shaila Patel's younger self would finish reading her copy of Cinderella and chuck it across the room because it didn't mention what happened next. Now she writes from her home in the Carolinas and dreams up all sorts of stories with epilogues and Indian-American characters who look like her.

Shaila is a pharmacist by training, a medical office manager by day, and a writer by night. She is a member of the Romance Writers of America and the author of the multiple award-winning, #ownvoices, young adult paranormal romance trilogy called the Joining of Souls. She loves craft beer, tea, and reading in cozy window seats—but she'll read anywhere. You might find her sneaking in a few paragraphs at a red light or gushing about her favorite books online.

The Storm of the Decade
Prerna Pickett

https://prernapickett.com/

Prerna Pickett was born in India, grew up in Northern Virginia just outside of Washington DC, lived in Idaho for a while, then in paradise AKA Hawaii, before moving back to the mainland. If You Only Knew is her debut and set to release winter 2020 with Macmillan/ Swoon Reads

Silver and Gold

Patty Blount

http://www.pattyblount.com/

Patty Blount grew up quiet and somewhat invisible in Queens, NY, but found her superpower writing smart and strong characters willing to fight for what's right. Today, she's the award-winning author of edgy, realistic, gut-wrenching contemporary and young adult romance. Still a bit introverted, she gets lost often, eats way too much chocolate, and tends to develop mad, passionate crushes on fictional characters…and Gilles Marini….and Sam Heughan. Let's be real; Patty's not nearly as cool as her characters, but she is a solid supporter of women's rights and loves delivering school presentations.

Patty is best known for her tough issues novels. The Internet Issues duo includes SEND and TMI. The #MeToo duo includes SOME BOYS, a 2015 CLMP Firecracker winner, and SOMEONE I USED TO KNOW, a 2018 Junior Library Guild Fall Pick, as well as a double winner of the 2019 Athena Award (Best YA Contemporary and Best of the Best). Visit her Social Media at pattyblount.com, where you can sign up for her newsletter. She blogs at YA Outside the Lines and is also active on Twitter and Facebook. When she's not writing, Patty loves to watch bad sci-fi movies, live tweeting the hilarity, and scour Pinterest for ideas on awesome bookcases. Patty lives on Long Island with her family in a house that, sadly, lacks bookcases. She loves hearing from readers, especially when they tell her she's cool (even though she knows it's not true), and is easily bribed with chocolate. *Read…roar!…revel.*

Star-Crossed Lovers and Other Strangers
Deborah Maroulis

www.deborahmaroulis.com

Born and raised in a small town in Northern California, Deborah Maroulis is lucky enough to surround herself with the things and people she loves. She teaches English and mythology at her local community college, studies myth and depth psychology in her Ph.D. program, and writes contemporary Young Adult novels. She lives in a slightly bigger town than the one she grew up in with her husband, newly-adult children, and her daughter's very spoiled, semi-retired service dog.

The Valentine's Eve Not-a-Date Photo Scavenger Hunt
Faydra Stratton

www.faydrastratton.com

Faydra Stratton is a writer, high school English teacher, wife, and mom to three boys. Her youngest son has Fragile X Syndrome, a spectrum disorder similar to autism but with a known genetic cause. Faydra attended the University of Florida (Go, Gators!) for undergrad and UNC Wilmington where she received an MFA in creative writing. Faydra was born and raised in West Palm Beach, FL and now resides with her family a little further up the coast in Port St Lucie. When not teaching, reading, or writing she loves all things beach life from laying out to kayaking, paddle boarding, boating, and snorkeling. But not scuba diving. She just can't clear her ears.

Faydra's debut novel,Devil Springs, is a YA Contemporary set in the southern grit of a modern Flannery O'Connor landscape and shows the effects of the small-town religious on local teens.

Sunflowers and Lavender

Melanie Hooyenga

www.melaniehoo.com

Multi-award-winning young adult author Melanie Hooyenga writes books about strong girls who learn to navigate life despite its challenges. She first started writing as a teenager and finds she still relates best to that age group.

Her award-winning a YA sports romance series, the Rules Series, is about girls from Colorado falling in love and learning to stand up on their own. Her YA trilogy, The Flicker Effect, is about a teen who uses sunlight to travel back to yesterday. The first book, FLICKER, won first place for Middle Grade/Young Adult in the Writer's Digest 2015 Self-Published eBook awards.

When not at her day job as Communications Director at a local nonprofit, you can find her wrangling her Miniature Schnauzer Owen and playing every sport imaginable with her husband Jeremy.

Jane and Austen's
Jess Moore

www.itwasjess.wordpress.com

Originally hailing from the Midwest, you can always expect an "ope" from Jess or one of her characters. She moved to historic gold-country California ages ago and only looks back east when the leaves are wild with color. (Well, and also, for Cincinnati chili. Let's keep it real.) She spent years building careers in both teaching and social work, but now, she writes in the very early morning while her family sometimes sleeps.

Love-Locked on the Roberto Clemente Bridge
Leanne Treese

www.leannetreese.com

Leanne lives in New Jersey with her husband of twenty-five years and their three wonderful children. When Leanne is not cheering her kids on in their activities, she can be found running, watching Philadelphia 76ers basketball games, or spoiling her two beloved dogs. Favorite locations include the Jersey shore, Martha's Vineyard, and any place that sells books or coffee, preferably both. A passionate student, Leanne's dream life would include going back to college and majoring in everything.

Leanne is a graduate of Lafayette College and The Dickinson School of Law. A former attorney, she is now lucky enough to write full-time!

IF YOU ENJOY…

EMOTIONAL JOURNEYS ✓
ROMANTIC THEMES ✓
IMMERSIVE SETTINGS ✓

CHECK OUT ONE OF THESE OTHER FVP TITLES!

WWW.FILLESVERTESPUBLISHING.COM

 @fillesvertespub @fillesvertespub @FVpublishing